LAND OF THE
JONAH FISH FRY

—A NOVEL—

OLIVIA KESSINGER

Printed in the United States of America

First Printing, 2018

ISBN-13:
978-0692176603
ISBN-10:
0692176608

Library of Congress Control Number: 2018911124

Cover Image and Design by Linsey Bailey

For information contact: Kessinger Publishing
P.O. Box 201
Marshall IN 47859

kessingerpublishing@gmail.com

Visit olivia.kessinger.wordpress.com

For my Grandmothers and Mothers:
the ones I got by birth and by marriage,
with love

Acknowledgements

A special thanks to the following:

Kateland Vernon—a friend and fellow writing major from IWU who read not one, but two drafts of this manuscript and edited, encouraged, questioned, and gently corrected. If this novel is enjoyable to read, it is because of her powerful English nerd skills. Her encouragement kept me from hiding this story away in the attic.

Karen Zach—my junior high English teacher who was a little too eager to pull out her red ink and take me to task for starting roughly one thousand sentences with "And." I've left a few "And" sentences to give her something to mutter about. Again, if this novel is enjoyable to read, it's thanks to Mrs. Z.

Lindsey Bailey—the freelance artist who read my manuscript and worked with me to create the cover. I think the image speaks for itself. This novel is really two works of art: hers and mine, and it was a joy to collaborate with her. If you'd like to see more of her artwork, you can find her at www.lindseyswop.com

This novel is a work of fiction. Though set in my home town (or rather, home county) it is not to be read as a Parke County history, nor is it meant to imply anything about real life people or places.

That being said, I am indebted to the people and places I come from. They have shaped me into the woman and writer I am, and I wrote this story as an offering of gratitude.

One
Wilma (Willie)
2016 Remembering 2003

My husband doesn't even remember the first time we met. It's probably a good thing that he didn't notice me then. I was thirteen; he was eighteen. Five years is a big deal at that age.

His grandmother and my granny worked together at the Turkey Run Inn; his grandma was the head cook and mine was the head auditor. They were also lifelong friends: a pair of sixty-something, no nonsense, 'tough ole birds.'

Back then—a whole thirteen years ago now—one of the perks of being an Inn employee was free access to the indoor pool. My mom was a teacher just down the highway at Turkey Run Elementary, and often times in the summer she'd need to go into her classroom to prep for the upcoming fall. She'd drop my siblings and me off at the Inn if Granny was working and we'd get to go swimming.

This particular June afternoon—the day I fell into puppy love with my would-be husband, and he first barely acknowledged and then forgot about my existence—my brothers were at an all-day baseball tournament. My sister was enjoying the privilege of having both her license and a summer job.

I hated the thought of sitting through one more kid baseball game, getting sunburnt with a side of boredom, and I begged my mom to drop me at the Inn with Granny. At thirteen, I could be trusted to swim by myself without drowning or destroying State property.

Granny met me in the lobby with the key in hand, and a stern look that reminded me that no grandchild of hers would raise havoc and besmirch her good standing as a trusted employee.

Her eyes said, 'Don't run on the deck; only use one towel; keep all noise at a respectful level; and for the Love of God Himself, don't pee in the pool like you did that one time."

"Granny, I was six!" my eyes said back.

"Well, still. You'd better go ahead and visit the restroom," this she said aloud. I trudged off to the restroom. When I returned, she handed me the key.

"I'm off in two hours, so you need to be out and dried off by then."

"Ok!" I grabbed the key and ran off.

"Walk!" she yelled after me, causing me to slow mid-stride.

For an hour and a half, I swam laps and floated on my back with my eyes closed, daydreaming about the latest paperback novel I probably shouldn't have been reading.

I got out of the pool, toweled off my skinny, little, flat-chested body and threw my shorts and tank top back over my aqua-marine one-piece. Next summer, I vowed to myself, I'd have a bikini and the boobs to fill it out. Although, the annoying part of my brain reminded me, boobs and a bikini wouldn't do me much good when I was still swimming under Granny's supervision.

As you've probably gathered by now, that summer I was on the brink of puberty, the hormones in my body cranked up to the "OH MY GOD, BOYSSS!!!!" level.

In two months, I would get brand new five subject notebooks and scribble hearts, various boys' last names, and "inspirational" quotes and sayings like "a moment on the lips, forever on the hips." (My mom had a conniption fit when she saw that one, and she lectured me about body image for weeks.)

I was thirteen, body conscious, and boy crazy, so please, please, judge me kindly, because what happened next is not pretty.

I walked back into the lobby and over to the glass door that led to the offices behind the front desk. Granny was sitting at her desk, a stack of envelopes in one hand. She was talking to her friend, Cheryl, the head cook who always made me chocolate milkshakes. In fact, there was that large Styrofoam cup perched on the edge of Granny's desk; I could see the mountain of whipped cream pushing against the plastic lid.

Cheryl noticed me eye-balling my milkshake. She stopped her conversation mid-sentence to pick it up and hand it to me.

"Here you go, honey. No cherry, extra whipped cream."

"Thanks, Cheryl!" I said, taking the milkshake and plopping down in another office chair.

"Don't get Martha's desk sticky!" Granny warned me. I waved her off with my spoon, dripping chocolate shake onto my shorts.

"Whoops."

Granny gave me another look that said clearly, "See? What did I just tell you." I grabbed a Kleenex out of the box on Martha's desk, and dapped at my shorts while Granny and Cheryl resumed their conversation.

It was in that exact moment, as I was smearing chocolate deeper into the denim of my shorts, that the bell on the glass door tinkled. I looked up and, to this day, I still see this scene in slow motion.

The most beautiful boy—no, man, not boy—was walking through that glass door. He had green eyes, wavy brown hair grazing his shoulders, toned muscles underneath a tye-dye t-shirt and tanned, muscular legs under his cargo shorts. He was wearing leather flip-flops and a cologne that even now I can smell and get jelly-legged. (Luckily for me he still wears that same scent.)

I hate myself for describing it to you this way: but I became very aware of all of my body parts just looking at him. It was like the heavens opened, the angels sang, and a rainbow ended over the top of his sandy curls.

In contrast, he didn't so much as spare me a second glance.

"I'm gonna' marry this man." My thirteen-year-old, hormone riddled brain thought as my hand involuntarily clenched my Styrofoam cup so hard that I put five finger-shaped holes into it and milkshake started oozing out.

"Willie!" Granny yelled at me, "What did I just tell you! Look at the mess you are making child! Wilma Louise, I swear, just when I think I can start trusting you more, you make a mess like you're six years old still."

There I was, convinced I was becoming a woman, sure I'd just laid eyes on the man I'd love for the rest of my days, and my Grandmother was so helpfully pointing out that I was barely out of diapers.

For thirteen years, Granny had been my favorite person on the planet, but in that moment, I hated her. In that moment, I would have sold her to invading aliens at a discounted price.

As if the oozing chocolate mess and my

Granny's reprimand weren't enough to shame me, I made it worse by instantly tearing up.

"Don't cry, don't cry, don't cry!" I screamed in my mind, willing all the moisture in my body to dry up. But the harder I tried not to cry, the more distraught I became. Before I could so much as say, "Hi, I'm Wilma, but you can call me Willie for the rest of your life," I was blubbering like the six-year-old I'd just been accused of being.

"Hey kid, it's OK. It sucks when you spill your ice cream, doesn't it?" The most beautiful man in the world, who would wear a black tuxedo with a navy blue tie on our wedding day, was calling me "kid" in that sing-songy voice you use to calm devastated small children.

I was a devastated small child to him which made me cry all the harder.

My Granny huffed and went in search of paper towel. The most beautiful man patted my shoulder, looking both uncomfortable and bored that he had to comfort a kid mourning the loss of her milkshake. His shoulder-pats did nothing to help my frayed nerves especially because now my shoulder felt tingly from his touch.

I don't overstate this when I say I asked God to kill me right then. Let it be over. Milkshakes are ruined by this embarrassment; I'll never be old enough for this man; he'll find some gorgeous college girl before I even get boobs. What is there to live for???

Cheryl took pity on me. She grabbed the waste basket, took the dripping, punctured Styrofoam cup and tossed it in, then grabbed fistfuls of Kleenexes and shoved them into my hands.

"There you go, honey. Wipe the worst off and

then go to the bathroom. I'll clean this up." Her twinkling eyes met mine, and I could see that she knew. She knew how this most beautiful man was affecting me, and she found it incredibly humorous.

My face flamed with embarrassment and anger as I bumbled my way out of the office to the restroom. I washed my hands and arms of the sticky ice cream, splashed handfuls of cold water on my face, and used wet paper towel to blot at the stains on my shirt and shorts.

The absolute last thing I wanted to do was return to that office, but I knew I'd never hear the end of it if I didn't make an effort to clean up my mess. So I sucked in a soul-deep breath, braced myself and walked back toward my humiliation.

The mess was cleaned up when I walked in, not a trace of chocolate ice cream anywhere, and everyone was tactfully avoiding eye contact with my swollen, red gaze.

The most handsome man was lounging in the chair I'd vacated, rocking it back and forth. I'd walked into laughter, but missed the joke, and assumed it had been about me. Whatever it had been, his humor had softened Granny back out, and she was chuckling as she swatted at his head.

Then Cheryl pulled me into a hug as she said, "Willie, let me introduce you to my grandson Morgan. He's getting ready to go to his first year at Purdue; he's working on the grounds crew and staying with us at the farm. Morgan this is Wilma Louise, Jane's doll of a granddaughter."

"Nice to meet you." I mumbled at my feet. "Granny, can we go?"

"Alright, alright. Hold your horses. Sure you don't want another milkshake since you barely got two drinks before that fiasco—"

At my violent head shake, she said, "Suit yourself. Keys, purse, yes, we're ready then. Oh my, it's twenty after already? Well you know they don't pay overtime for chit-chat! Cheryl, I'll see you tomorrow. Morgan, you stay out of trouble."

"No promises," he told her, grinning, as we left the office.

Granny chuckled almost all the way to the car, and said, half to herself, half to me as she buckled her seat beat, "That Morgan. He's a good one. Too handsome for his own good though. But then, I don't have to tell you that, do I?"

She looked at me, all earlier frustration replaced with that same knowing look Cheryl had given me. I teared up again, and she gathered me into her arms. She smelled like her perfume, the Inn's fried chicken, and printer ink.

"Oh, honey. It's alright. You've got a solid three years of not knowing if you're coming or going, getting tongue tied and flustered every time you see a handsome man. But before you know it, this stage will pass. You'll grow into yourself, and you'll look back on this day and laugh."

"I'll never ever laugh about this!" I wailed into her smock, my forehead pressed uncomfortably into her nametag.

"Yes, you will. You just wait and see. Then the next thing you'll know, you'll be having this talk with your granddaughter, trying to convince her there's life after puberty."

--

Two
Carolyn
Excerpt from *Nymph of the Oak Tree: A Tale of Coming Home*
Sunday June 14th, 1959

Three weeks ago, Colleen had gone forward at church during the closing hymn. She'd knelt at the altar, crying, while the congregation swayed to "Come Thou Fount of Every Blessing." The matriarchs of the church—women who had changed Colleen and Carolyn's diapers, scolded them about climbing the oak tree in their Sunday dresses, and taught them the proper way to line up pot-luck dishes at a church picnic—swarmed Colleen, praising the Lord on their way.

Pastor Simon knelt in front of Colleen, put his hands on top of her head, praying quietly and privately at first, then growing louder. "Praise Jesus! OOOh Praise the Lord Jesus! His child has come home! She has repented and come home!"

Carolyn just barely contained a snort. What in the hell could Colleen possibly have to repent for? And when, exactly, had her baby sister, the girl who could quote half the Bible from memory, strayed from God's fold and needed to return home? If ever there was a heaven-bound homebody, it was Colleen.

This was just like Colleen. She was practically addicted to altar calls. The slightest invitation, the slightest call to repent, and there was Colleen, on her knees, confessing some minor sin. It was embarrassing. Carolyn sighed and shifted in the pew. Her back ached; a trickle of sweat was running down her spine.

The cardboard fan clutched in her hand was only stirring around hot air; she stopped fanning her face and plunked the fan back into the hymn holder.

Dammit Colleen, she thought. We were almost out of here. Now it was going to be another twenty minutes, at least. Everyone was going to have to take a turn hugging Colleen, welcoming her to the fold. They'd have to sing at least four more, high pitched hymns. All four verses. Stand at the end. Then Pastor would spend an agonizing five minutes, inviting the Holy Spirit to come, and badgering everyone else to listen to the Spirit's prompting. Get right with the Lord today!

He would try to make eye contact with Carolyn. It had been Pastor Simon's goal to prompt repentance in Carolyn ever since his second Sunday as pastor, over a year ago now, when he heard her say "God dammit to hell" when she tripped on the front steps while running and smashed her shin.

Young ladies who say "God dammit to hell" on the church steps, were special cases, in needed of a larger dose of Jesus than the average sinner.

That's what everyone thought about Carolyn: that Christ had his work cut out with her.

Carolyn didn't know what she believed. But she'd be damned if she was going to get saved just to give these people the satisfaction of feeling like they'd finally molded her into an acceptable version of herself. Molded her to be more like Colleen. The soft-spoken, sweet, spiritual hypochondriac.

Colleen was standing up now, turning to face the congregation.

Pastor Simon and his wife, Cheryl, who held their sleeping baby, Patsy, were flanked on either side

9

of their favorite student.

Colleen's face was tear stained, her expression ethereal. It annoyed Carolyn to no end.

"Colleen has come to Jesus." Pastor was saying.

Carolyn struggled not to roll her eyes. Colleen had been coming to Jesus since she was a small child. She'd showed up to get saved so often, that Jesus was probably trying to wiggle his way out of their next meeting. For God's sake, didn't she know he had *other* people to save?

"She would like to be baptized! Halleluiah! Will you join her? We are having a baptism on June 14th, three Sundays from now. All are welcome!"

Now, here they were, on Sunday June 14th. Carolyn had been awake for over an hour, staring at her ceiling. The spider web crack was getting bigger, branching out. All of her life, Carolyn had been watching this crack grow, more and more plaster chipping off. Every morning, she traced the lines over and over with her eyes; it soothed her. But it wasn't working this morning.

For three weeks now, everyone had nagged and nettled her about her salvation. Or rather, her lack of salvation. Her parents, Pastor Simon, Cheryl, Belinda (her Sunday school teacher), and Colleen had encouraged, lectured, and guilt tripped her to come to the Lord. There was no better time. No one knew how much time they had before God called them home. No not tarry; do not take the eternal destination of your soul lightly.

Was there some kind of Christian cliché book out there, containing all the insane phrases saved-people said to non-saved people?

At first, Carolyn could ignore it or quip back

something to shut them up. But after three weeks, they'd worn her down.

Maybe she should just give them what they wanted. It went against the grain. Against her whole personality, really, to fake who she was to make people happy. How many times had Mother and Dad actually wished aloud that she be more like Colleen? Too many for her to remember. It stung, every time.

Yet, it was only a few hours on a Sunday. A few hours of acting, of feigning a conviction and conversion that she didn't feel. The trade-off was that maybe then they'd all leave her alone about it, satisfied that she was God's problem now. They'd done their part to drag her to the Lord.

She'd do it, she decided. She'd get baptized with her sister, maybe even muster up a few tears and a brief testimony. She'd let them dunk her under, say the words, pronounce her saved. After today, after this religious ritual was checked off the list, her life could be her own.

--

She'd gone swimming in this creek more times than she could remember, swallowed mouthfuls of this water by accident, unaware that she was swimming in holy water. It was just an ordinary country creek, except for twice a year when suddenly it was pronounced holy, capable of washing away the dirtiest of sins.

They were a party of five sinners: Colleen and herself, Roland, the sixty-year-old Judson drunk, Martha, a young mother and Timothy, her six year old son.

They were surrounded by the congregation, fifty people parading from the church to the creek, wearing their Sunday best. Women in hats and gloves, and carefully ironed, knee length dresses. Men in their best suits. Children in outfits that came with a severe scolding, lest they be tempted by a mud puddle.

"Stay out of the water!" All of the mothers hissed at their offspring. "If you so much as put a toe in, you better be going to Jesus because you're gonna' need Him."

The to-be-baptized were dressed in white. Why in God's name they were supposed to wear white to get baptized in a mineral rich creek was beyond Carolyn, but she didn't make the rules. Her cotton dress was going to be ruined, just ruined, after this.

Carolyn was fourth in line, behind Colleen, Timothy, and Martha, and trailed by Rolly. Carolyn couldn't help but suspect that they'd been lined up by level of sin. At least she'd been stationed before Rolly; she looked back and gave him a wink. She was fairly certain that he was getting saved because he too had been badgered into it. Or maybe the church ladies just promised him fried chicken legs in exchange for his repentance.

Finally, it was her turn; she waded into the water and stood before Pastor. She'd heard his question three times now, so she knew what to expect. "And do you, Carolyn Calvert, profess faith in the Lord Jesus Christ and from this day forward vow to follow Him?"

"I do," she mumbled, feeling a twinge of guilt at the lie.

But then she was being pulled back and swished under, catching the first part of "In the Name of the Father—" before water filled her ears. She came up, sputtering, to the sound of applause. Her mother was crying on the creek bank, her father smiling. I've finally made them proud, and it's a lie, Carolyn thought as Cheryl ushered her out of the water toward Colleen, who was waiting with a towel.

She walked into Colleen's arms, let her envelop her in the worn towel, noticing, out of the corner of her eye, Sanders, a boy from school, casting glances at her. If ever there was someone who needed the sin washed off of him, there he stood. She tightening the towel around her, feeling exposed in the clinging, wet cotton of her dress. Was this over, yet?

It wasn't. Baptism Sundays lasted all day. The church service in the morning, followed by the baptisms in the creek. After that, the men and children milled about the church yard while the women hustled to uncover and set out pot-luck dishes. The afternoon was spent eating, visiting, and playing yard games: sack and wheelbarrow races, croquet, ring toss.

The church picnic didn't end until late afternoon, and even then, it was only the adults and young children who got to leave. Sunday evenings were youth meetings. Attending youth meeting was nonnegotiable when she was a sinner, and even more expected now that she was born again. Carolyn couldn't exactly skip going when she was supposed to be playing the role of the newly-redeemed. She was supposed to be excited about Bible study.

There was only about ten of them, a group of teenagers and two adult leaders. The first hour was spent in "fellowship" followed by a light supper, then Bible study. After Bible study, they had another half hour for socializing before it was time to leave.

This was Colleen's social life, where she

thrived, where she led. Carolyn, in contrast, counted the minutes until it was over.

Tonight was even harder. She was exhausted from a day spent in the sun; a day spent dealing with other people's excitement over her fake conversion; a day spent trying to live up to the part. She really just wanted to go home, take and bath, and go to bed.

So far, she'd made it through the meal and Bible study, only another half hour of small talk to go. Then she would be free.

Carolyn remembered, suddenly, that she'd left her white dress hanging in kitchen down in the basement. Perhaps she could bleach the mineral stains out of it, and be able to wear it again.

She excused herself and headed for the basement stairs, not bothering to pull the chain on the overhead light. Carolyn could navigate this church in her sleep.

She had just grabbed her still-damp dress when she heard the door click shut behind her. She could barely see, but she knew who was there.

--

Three
Willie
2010

A lot happened in the next several years (high school, for one thing), but for brevity's sake, let's skip ahead to the Christmas break of my sophomore year of college. That made me twenty and the most handsome man in the world twenty-five. Only I'd sort of forgotten all about him. I'd pined for him, dreamed of him nearly every night, until I was fourteen. Then I'd put his tye-dye t-shirt out of my mind and moved on to other boys. I'd had a few junior high boyfriends; one serious high school boyfriend who broke my heart, and one college guy I dated on and off depending on our schedules and movie budget.

But I was a young woman, raised from a line of "tough ole birds." I had plans that included a bachelor's degree in journalism, followed by a decade of travel writing and living out of hotel rooms, before I moved home, settled down and cranked out novels and babies. Two babies; twelve novels. And a series of short stories.

Thankfully, I'd outgrown my boy-crazed phase. I'd given my virginity to the high school boyfriend, an experience that had left me feeling cheated and wondering if that was it about sex. The casual boyfriend was fun to kiss, but I could accurately describe my feelings toward him with a shoulder shrug and "ehh, he's fun." So I probably wasn't going to let it go much further than making out on his futon.

Love was optional to my ten-year plan, a take it or leave it detail; and if I did fall in love early on, he better be ready to go with me. Like hell, I'd be his shadow, put my dreams on hold.

I went home for Christmas and spent a lot of time at Granny's house because she was recovering from knee-replacement surgery and threatening to kill Grandpa for hovering one second and disappearing on her the next second.

When I came to visit, she put me to work, sorting out and "organizing" her sewing room. It was a bedroom with my mom's old bed, dresser, night stand, and sewing table. The rest of the room, except for a two-foot-wide path from the door to the sewing table, was stacked nearly floor to ceiling with boxes of fabric, quilt batting, stuffing, scissors, thread, needles, buttons, patterns, and half-finished quilt tops.

I don't know what the hell she expected me to do: she literally about stroked out on me when I passed her bedroom, headed to the sewing room carrying a box of Hefty trash bags.

"Willie! Wilma Louise! What are you doing with those trash bags?!" She yelled, scrambling to push herself up on her elbows, a wild-eyed look of terror on her face.

I turned back and popped my head into her room, trying to appear innocent. She was propped up on pillows in her bed, her right leg elevated and iced, glasses sliding down her nose, newspaper open to the obituaries.

"Oh, I just thought I'd start by throwing away some of that trash."

"What trash? There's no trash back there. You mean the waste basket? You'll only need one bag for that little bit of lint and fabric scraps.

Actually, save those fabric scraps, I might be able to use them."

"Granny, how, exactly, do you expect me to organize that room when there's not so much as a foot of open space to move anything?

"Can't you put things on the shelf in the closet?"

"Oh, you mean that death-trap of haphazard boxes ready to fall and kill someone? Yeah, it's stuffed so full you can't even slide the door an inch either way."

"Well, put some under the bed then."

"Also full. It's all full. The whole room's a fire hazard, and honestly Granny, it isn't safe for you to try to navigate that squirrel path with one bum leg. Do you have warranty on that new knee?"

"Wilma, I did not ask you to come over here just to sass me!"

"Well, what did you ask me here to do, then?"

"I asked you to get that room up to your mother's standards so I can go back in there and sew in peace!"

"Well, then we're going to have to get rid of some of that junk if you want to get Mom off your back."

"It's not junk!"

"You've got boxes of moth-eaten fabric from 1970!"

"Don't you dare throw that out! I know what all is there, young lady!"

"You are unbelievable. Why did you ask me to come do a job when you had no intention of letting me do it?"

"You're just as bad as your Mom. What do you think, that I like being confided to this bed, helpless and dependent on the good-humor of my smart-ass descendants?"

"No, but you could try being a little less of a pain about it. I'm beginning to see why it takes Grandpa thirty minutes just to walk to the mail box."

"You leave your grandfather out of this. He has been a saint taking care of me! A saint! And he needs a break! God forbid the rest of you help out!"

"Help out?!? Maybe if you didn't nit-pick everyone into a constant state of agitation, we'd all visit more! Uncle Randy is missing half an eyebrow because he's developed a nervous tick from the stress of trying to keep you happy! And Mom is drinking wine like its water. You know she's one ISTEP test away from alcoholism as it is!"

Granny snatched up the newspaper and brandished it at me. "You see these! This is what you're all doing to me! You're going to put me right here on this page, two measly paragraphs, to sum up my life, and then you're going to throw out all my stuff! Don't think I don't know!" She tossed the newspaper at me in disgust.

At this moment, we both heard Grandpa cough suspiciously from the living room and then turn up the volume on the news. Awkward silence descended upon us, because what do you say when your grandmother accuses you of a pre-mediated murder plan by way of tossing out fabric scraps, thus causing her to have heart palpitations?

For lack of something else to do, I bent over and picked up the newspaper. That's when I saw her.

Staring up at me, in black and white, was Cheryl. Cheryl Lewis: May 31st 1944 to December 15th 2010. Five paragraphs summing up her life story, ending with a list of survivors, the most handsome boy's name tucked in the middle of a list of grandkids. Morgan. Morgan Lewis. Tye-dye shirt, sandy-brown curls, teasing glint in his eyes as he bantered back and forth with his grandma and mine.

And Cheryl. Oh Cheryl. The woman who always remembered I hated cherries; who put extra whipped cream on my extra chocolate milkshake because I needed fattening up. The woman who didn't believe in sugar highs in children, so long as they didn't go home with her.

She had always been one of those peripheral people in my life. Someone I wasn't close to exactly, didn't really know much about: say, for instance, that she went to a beauty academy to learn how to do hair. Or that she buried her fourth child, a son, aged six weeks. And then somehow found the courage to have two more babies after that for a total of six.

But the thing about peripheral people, or "extras" in the drama of my own life, is that I just assumed they'd always be there. Cheryl: Granny's friend, maker of milk-shakes, matriarch of Morgan, always and forever aged mid-60s.

But then one day, she was 75 years old, having a fatal heart attack, and the next, I was reading about her funeral arrangements in the *Sentinel*.

I sat down on the foot of Granny's bed, pulled the navy and gray afghan over my lap.

I let my fingers trace the zig-zag pattern Granny had crocheted; acknowledging, perhaps for the first time, that her art would outlive her; that one day all that would be left of her were hints of her existence, countless spools of yarn crocheted into afghans, and blocks of fabric sewn into quilts.

"Oh Granny," I whispered. "I'm sorry."

"She was my friend since before I can even

remember. I don't know how to be me without her."

    When she said that sentence, she didn't sound like my grandmother with decades of life behind her. She sounded like a seven-year old, faced with the prospect of going to school after her best friend had moved away.

--

Four
Jane and Cheryl
An Adapted Excerpt from Cheryl's personal journals
1961

"Hello!" Jane yelled cheerily as she walked toward her friend. She stopped to kiss Jack, who was sitting on a blanket on the grass, gumming away at the blocks left to entertain him. Jane swiped at the dirt smudge on his mouth. "Hi, Darling boy. Does that mud taste good?"

A gurgle-laugh was her response.

"It's good for him, you know. Eating dirt," Cheryl said as she walked up to them and plopped down on the blanket, panting and holding her side. Patsy was right behind her, a fresh strawberry clutched in her hand. "Whew. I shoulda got out here this morning to pull these weeds." Cheryl tugged off her straw hat and wiped the sweat from her forehead. "And don't you look nice, sitting next to grubby ole me. Come here, honey pot." She opened her arms and Patsy snuggled in.

Jane shrugged. "I'm dressing for the part."

"Did you get it, then?"

"Yes."

Cheryl squealed and lunged across the blanket, pulling Jane into a hug. "Oh, congratulations! I am just *that* tickled for you! And a bit jealous! A working woman!"

"Mmm. I'd rather have one of these though." Jane said, pulling Jack back onto the blanket as he crawled away.

"They're more trouble than you think." Cheryl said, brushing a leaf out of Patsy's hair.

She continued, "at least at a job, you can clock out and go home. This lovey has me up all hours of the night; and this one is running me ragged with all the things she gets into when I'm feeding Jack. What was I thinking having two back to back like this, I'll never know." Cheryl said carelessly, then seeing the look on her friend's face, was immediately contrite. "Oh, honey. I'm sorry. I shouldn't be so flippant. I know you do. It'll happen."

"Will it?"

"Of course!" Cheryl said, but she glanced away. Then she looked back, grasped Jane's hands, and said, "Yes, it will. I believe that you'll be a mother. And our babies will play together, and go to school together, and who knows? Maybe even two of them will marry each other, and we can share grandbabies in our old age and drive them all mad."

Jane smiled while shaking her head. "I can't even imagine being a mother, let alone a grandmother. But here you are, with my life all planned out for me, start to end. Believing when I can't."

"What are friends for?" Cheryl said, then, gesturing at Jack, "Grab that stick from him, will you? Before he shoves it down his throat or stabs himself in the eye."

After rescuing Jack, Jane said, "So are you going to ask me about the interview or make me talk about myself shamelessly?"

"How was the interview, dear?"

"Rather boring, actually." Jane waved the question off. "But you won't believe who else was there, interviewing for another job."

"Are you trying to tempt this pastor's wife into gossip?"

"Possibly."

"Well, keep your voice down. Trees and toddlers have ears, you know. We might be heard."

"Carolyn Calvert."

"Oh," Cheryl said, looking away. Then she said in an overly cheerful voice, "Well, good on her then. Carolyn is a hard worker."

"Yes, but why does she need the job? Last I heard, Cain had proposed."

"Jane, stop fishing. I don't want to talk about it."

"Oh, you're such a fuddy-duddy! Did she really reject his proposal publicly like everyone is saying?"

Cheryl sighed. "It was awful. Though I'm not sure which of them I felt more sorry for. Carolyn has always talked quite bluntly about how she doesn't want to get married. For the life of me, I can't figure out why Cain thought it would be a good idea to propose in front of all their family and friends at their graduation party. What was she supposed to do?"

"Perhaps not slap him across the face."

Cheryl shrugged. "She panicked. I could see it written on her face. He shouldn't have put her on the spot like that."

"And his mother really called her a stuck-up snob and slapped her back?"

"Stuck-up snob, yes. Slapped her, no. But she looked like she wanted to."

"All in your church yard." Jane shook her head. "I've got to quit the Quakers; you Baptists have much more fun."

Cheryl snorted. "Hardly. That's the most

drama I think that church has ever seen. Thank goodness. It's quite upsetting, actually. Cain and his family are now driving over to Marshall for church. And Carolyn won't come back either. Her parents are in Simon's study, every few days, hounding him on what is to be done. Like it's up to him to solve this; like they think Simon's the kind of pastor and man who will help orchestrate a marriage the bride doesn't want." Cheryl was getting worked up now, anger creeping into her voice.

"I didn't mean to upset you."

"You didn't. They did. It's hard to be a pastor's wife, to watch your husband carry the weight of so many other people's problems. And to witness those same people make so many demands of him, make him feel responsible for their every pain. They expect too much."

"What can they possibly expect? Carolyn is an adult. If she doesn't want to get married, that's her business. Young heartache is not a new thing; Cain will recover and they'll both have full lives."

"Umm. I suppose it sounds simple. But the whole church has chosen sides over this. Most of the church ladies had their wedding planned. And now, our church has lost a family who's been there for years and years. No one is happy about that. No one is really in Carolyn's corner either. Not even her parents."

"Poor girl."

"You've changed your tune. I thought you came here to gossip about her?" Cheryl asked.

"So I was curious. I'm not a saint like you, Oh Pastor's Wife. Maker of babies and homemade bread. I like a good story of Parke County gossip. But that doesn't mean I wish Carolyn anything but good."

"Perhaps wish a little harder for her; she needs it."

--

\

Five
Willie
2010

I went to Cheryl's funeral because Granny couldn't because of her knee. She tried, but her doctor, physical therapist, Grandpa, all of her children, and a few church ladies stood their ground and threatened to barricade the door if need be.

The viewing and funeral were pushed into one day, December 23rd. An extra crappy time of year to die. Granny was thinking and vocalizing the same thoughts.

"I just know Cheryl. She always bought Christmas presents in July, stashed them away for months, and had them wrapped and under the tree the day after Thanksgiving. You know how I know this? Because one year I tried to get her to go Black Friday shopping with me, and not only did she treat me to a lecture about the greed of Americans trampling each other for a deal the day after we all give thanks, but she informed me of her tradition of wrapping presents and putting up decorations.

"So I just keep picturing all those presents under her tree. And her poor family, opening what she got them, two days after putting her in the ground!"

"I suppose it's nice though, in a way." My cousin Leanna said as she curled Granny's hair. "Right? I mean, at least they'll all know how much she loved them."

"I don't know," I said. "It sounds emotionally exhausting. The paper said she had six—well, five living kids and ten grandkids, that's a lot of presents, and a lot of crying every time someone opens a gift."

"That's true." Leanna nodded. "Plus, what if she was a terrible gift giver? And you're trying to be all sentimental about your gift from beyond the grave, but you really can't imagine where she got polyester pajamas and why in the world she thought you should have them?"

"Or worse: what if she forgot someone?" I said. "Everyone's there, opening their perfect gifts, feeling all loved, and they get to Tommy's turn, and there's nothing. Tell me that doesn't mess with you. I mean, if she were alive she could play it off that it's on its way. But now, poor Tommy's going to spend the rest of his life wondering why his grandma hated him."

"I'm not sure there's a therapist who would touch that," Leanna said.

"Are you two really joking about my best friend's death?" Granny demanded.

"Sorry, Gran," Leanna said, appropriately chastised.

"Yes, I wonder who we learned gallows humor from?" I teased.

"Fine. But at least get your facts straight," Granny said. "If she was going to forget any of her grandkids it would have been Carter. She had a hard time liking him."

Leanna and I gaped at her. "I thought grandmas just automatically loved all their grandkids equally," Leanna said.

Granny arched her eyebrows, and said, "Do they?"

"Well, now I'm not sure of anything," Leanna muttered under her breath.

"Calm down. If Granny has any least favorites, it's me," I told her.

"You are the one who tries me the most, Wilma Louise. No doubt about that," she said, but she winked at me.

--

If you're going to wear three-inch, peep-toe, black heels to a funeral, you want to know how popular that person was, to give you an approximate idea of how long the viewing line will be.

Cheryl was two hours worth of funeral-line-standing popular. Two hours! Standing in line outside, in Indiana December, in heels that gave me blisters just looking at them, and a dress that might have been this side of inappropriate for a funeral. Or this side of inappropriate for anything.

I realized this when I felt a couple Indiana icy wind gusts in areas you don't want exposed to the elements.

Then I spent the next sixty minutes with foot cramps, chilly nether regions, and serious doubts about what I was doing there and what I was wearing.

Why didn't I wear pants and boots? I asked myself.

You know very well why, I responded.

Does it make me a terrible person if I'm trying to attract a grieving man at his Grandma's funeral?

You don't want the answer to that question.

An hour in (and approximately 15 minutes from the door and sweet, sweet warmth), I had no interest in seeing the most beautiful man again if it meant standing there one more minute.

My feet were a bright, angry red, and staring at them, I decided this was the color right before frost bite blue set in. At least maybe they'd stop throbbing if they went numb.

I could go wait in the car, I thought. But the line trailed out behind me and cars were still pouring into the parking lot.

I am throwing these shoes in the dumpster immediately, I thought. And the dress too. Finally, I couldn't stand it any longer.

Ten minutes from the door, with a line of people trailing before me and behind me, I turned my screaming feet and hobbled out of the line and across the parking lot. "Excuse me, excuse me." I kept muttering to people dressed in winter appropriate clothing; ignoring the rude, but dead on comments of a few women, and the half-hidden glances of a few men.

I was a moron. It's one thing to believe in the freedom of self-expression through fashion, to lecture about how women shouldn't have to dress to protect ourselves from men's lusts. It's another thing to do it in 28 degree weather.

My nearly frozen fingers fumbled in my purse, digging around for my keys. Finally, I found them and hit the unlock bottom on the key fob. I couldn't get my car started fast enough, and I threw the heater knob over to full blast, begging it to hurry and heat up.

I found three sweatshirts and a blanket on the floorboard and grabbed them. I kicked off my destined-for-Goodwill-or-the-dumpster heels, and pulled my legs up and underneath me, sitting on them.

I layered the sweatshirts and blanket over my body, shivering so hard my teeth actually clattered together. It was twenty minutes before I could drive, the heat still on full blast.

I really, really just wanted a hot bath. I didn't feel like driving all the way home, and Gran's was closer so I went to her house.

Now listen, dear reader. You really don't want to show up at your grandparents' house dressed in a dress that wouldn't have fit you at age two. Apparently, my brain was also suffering from frostbite, and had frozen into the Really Dumb Ideas Department. I went anyway.

"Gran!" I called out as I walked in the front door, sighing as the warm air hit my body.

"Back here!" I heard her call out from her bedroom. I passed my snoozing Grandpa in his recliner, the TV muted on CNN. I pulled an afghan off the couch and wrapped it around my shoulders as I padded back to her room in bare feet.

"Was there a lot of people at the funeral, honey?"

"Yeah. The line was two hours long." I hollered back.

My mind was on the tub and the sweats I remembered I had left from the last time I'd spent the night. "Gran, I think I'm going to grab a quick bath if you don't mind. It's freezing out there!"

"Come here, just a second, honey. I can't reach my reading glasses."

I hesitated. My brain was beginning to thaw, and I knew enough to know Gran did not need to see me dressed like this. Especially since I'd been at her best friend's funeral.

"Umm, can it wait? I really want that bath." I said from the hall.

"Willie, are you telling me you can't spare your laid-up grandmother two seconds to get her glasses?"

Damn Grandmother guilt. I twisted the blanket tighter around me and went into the room, quickly grabbing her glasses. Maybe she wouldn't be able to see good enough without them.

As she fumbled to put them on, I turned and made a hasty exit to the door. But as I turned, my foot caught in the trailing afghan and I started to fall. In an effort to save myself, I let go of the afghan and threw my hands out.

I steadied myself in the descending awkward silence.

"Wilma Louise," she said.

I grimaced and turned to face her. "Yes?" I asked in the most innocent voice I could muster.

"What. Are. You. Wearing?"

"A black dress."

"A dress? Are you sure it's not a shirt? Perhaps it was labeled wrong."

"It's not that short."

"Your underwear is pink. And a thong."

I yanked on the hem of my dress.

"That isn't going to help," she told me. Then, "You actually went to my best friend's funeral dressed like this? You paraded in front of her grieving family looking like a walking lingerie ad?"

"Well, I didn't actually make it inside."

"Oh? Security escorted you out, did they?"

"Gran! No. It's just—well, it was sort of cold. And the line was like two hours long. And I just, well, I didn't make it. . ."

"So, let me get this straight. My best friend dies at the same time I'm laid up with a knee replacement, and the granddaughter I send in my place, to represent me, and extend my grief, can't hack the cold, because she's dressed, like—like—this!" She gestured at me.

"Well, I admit it wasn't the best choice given the weather!"

"It wasn't the best choice given moral decency!"

"A woman shouldn't have to be ashamed of her body or sexuality." I told her, warming up to my lecture on women's lib.

"Who said anything about being ashamed? But she shouldn't flaunt it either."

"I'm not flaunting anything!"

"I just don't understand how you don't have any damn sense. Or respect for me. Or just the desire to avoid frostbite. Especially frostbite in certain *areas*." She gave me a pointed look.

"OK, so I probably should have worn leggings. . ."

"Pants. You should have worn pants."

"Well, it's too late now. What's done is done." I said, throwing one of her favorite sayings back at her.

"What time is it?"

"Two."

"The funeral starts at three."

"So?"

"So? So you didn't actually pay my respects. So you're going back."

"I'll freeze! I'm just now thawing out."

"Well, obviously you can't go back out in that dress! Get in my closet," she said, pointing.

I groaned, not liking where this was going. "Gran, I don't think—"

"You're right. You don't think which is why you're going back out dressed like a seventy year old woman instead of a nineteen year old bimbo."

I started pushing hangers around, looking for something presentable.

"You can wear my funeral suit," she told me.

I groaned again, then reached to the back of the closet and withdrew a black pant suit from the early 90's. The pants had stirrups; the jacket had shoulder pads. I was going to be forced back out to the funeral in stirrup pants and shoulder pads.

So there I was thirty minutes later, walking into the funeral home, dressed like a bad 90's flashback. The line had all but fizzled out. There was only five people in front of me. Everyone who had stayed for the funeral was seated, waiting for the viewing to end and the service to begin.

There he was again. The most beautiful man in the world, shaking my hand, accepting my mumbled condolences, completely not noticing me.

I stared a few moments too long, lingered in front of him long enough to make it awkward. He'd lost his college boy looks and settled into adulthood. I did the quick math in my head: twenty-five. His hair was shorter, but not crew-cut short. He was clean-shaven, wearing glasses, and dressed in a suit that was a perfect fit. I don't want this description to get bad-romance novel cliché, so I'll end it with just saying he looked good. Good enough to fluster me all over again.

I was supposed to grow out of this awkward and flustered around a handsome man crap.

Yet, here I was, locked kneed and tongue tied in front of a man I've never even had a real conversation with.

"Well," I finally said to him, "It was good to see you again. I mean, not at your Grandma's funeral, of course, but just in general, I've been wanting to see you again—" OMG; my brain screamed, STOP TALKING! Morgan gave me a brief puzzled look before gently squeezing my still-extended hand, and then dismissing me with a polite smile. Walk away, I told myself. Get out of here. NOW.

Even after I removed myself from the receiving line, I continued to hover, unsure of what to do with myself. I was pretty sure a lady in the family line was glaring at me too. At that moment, my stomach growled, reminding me that I hadn't eaten lunch. At the back of the room I saw a table laden with finger foods: veggie and fruit trays, cheese and crackers, meatballs on toothpicks, pastries.

Was that just for the family? Or anyone? Maybe I could just nab a cookie on my way to a seat in the back.

I was reaching for a napkin and cookie when I saw a flash of movement out of the corner of my eye. I looked down to see a little curly, blonde-haired girl grabbing carrot sticks. She lifted one to her mouth and took a loud, snapping crunch of a bite.

"You know," I told her, "those taste a lot better with Ranch dressing." I heaped a spoonful on a plate for her and offered it to her. She gave me a suspicious look, then dipped a carrot in Ranch and took another bite.

Her eyes lit up. This time she dipped her carrot again, but instead of eating the carrot she just licked the Ranch off, again and again. I needed to get out of here before her parents caught me teaching their child unhealthy Ranch addictions.

But for some reason, I was drawn to her and struck up a conversation. "Have you ever tried peanut butter and celery? That's good too."

She shook her head, as a voice snapped behind me, "She can't have peanut butter. She's severely allergic. Please don't feed my daughter."

I turned around to find myself staring at him. And he looked seriously perturbed. I opened my mouth to apologize, but no words came out.

"Tara, mommy's here. Are you ready to go home? The funeral is getting ready to start." He crouched down in front of his little girl, hooking a wild curl behind her ear. She shoved the carrot she'd been licking ranch off of into his mouth. Then she spotted her mom, yelled, "MOMMY!" and shot off across the room.

He has a child. A child who has severe peanut allergies and a mommy.

I'd always thought my first encounter with him would be the most embarrassing experience. This day was surpassing that, lapping my spilt milkshake memory again and again, replacing it with a new level of humiliation.

I needed to get out of there. But I also needed to stay for the funeral.

"Sorry," I told him. "I shouldn't feed other people's kids. Lesson learned." I tapped my head, like I was physically locking that lesson into my brain.

"Look, I didn't mean to snap at you. It's just very scary taking her out around food. She knows her restrictions, but she forgets. And if she eats even a little peanut product, her airway constricts to the point where she can't breathe."

"No, no. Don't apologize. I really should have thought. I definitely don't want to be responsible for restricted airways in a child. Or in anyone for that matter. Yup. . .So. . . anyway, again, sorry about your grandma. And almost killing your child. Now I'm gonna' go sit down."

And then, without waiting for a response, I plunked myself into a seat. As soon as the service ended, I discreetly slipped out.

--

We had Christmas dinner at my grandparents' house. Gran usually did the bulk of the cooking and bossing, and it was killing her to be confined to her recliner, watching everyone else muck it up. She yelled instructions from the living room, but we only humored her for the first hour. Then everyone got selective hearing and did things however the hell they wanted.

My Aunt Rhonda (Uncle Randy's wife) darted a glance toward the sitting room where we were holding Gran hostage, I mean where Gran was sitting. Confident Gran was safely out of eye and earshot, Aunt Rhonda slowly and guiltily withdrew a box of Pillsbury pie crust from her bag.

My mom, who was wrist deep in questionable looking pie dough, gasped. "You didn't!"

"I did."

"We can't."

"You know you want to," Aunt Rhonda whispered.

"She'll find out."

"I won't tell if you don't."

"Are you two talking about pie crust or pot?" My dad asked, coming up and slipping his arms around Mom's waist.

"Shh!" Mom and Aunt Rhonda said in unison.

The middle generation also kept avoiding the living room and sending in the third generation to visit with Gran and "keep her company."

It was my turn. "Hey, Gran, how ya' feeling?" I asked, plopping down on the couch.

"Your mother made the mashed potatoes with milk didn't she? I told her to use cream."

"Umm, I'm not sure."

"Oh, of course, that's the catch phrase today. 'I'm not sure.' Or 'I don't know'."

"Sooo, what's new with you? Know any news?"

"And how would I know any news? I've been stuck in this house for weeks. Nobody comes to visit and when they do, nobody tells me anything. They just ask if I need anything. You know what I need? I need your mother to make the damn potatoes how I tell her. And I need your uncle to stop fluffing my pillows and then hustling out of the room."

"OK, no more pillow fluffing. Got it."

She harrumphed and crossed her arms, then sighed and uncrossed them. "I'm unbearable, aren't I?"

"Like a menopausal woman, at the county fair, in 90 degree weather, chasing a runaway cow." I told her. (It was an inside joke from a true family story.)

A better granddaughter would have told a little white lie. I wasn't that kind of granddaughter, plus I was still mad at her about not telling me that Morgan was married. I knew that she knew. And I knew that she knew I would want to know.

She raised her eyebrow at me. "Leanna told me it was understandable that I was irritable and nobody minded."

"We both know Leanna is a liar." I said.

Gran chuckled. "So, I'm that bad, huh?"

"There's talk of serving you Christmas dinner on a TV tray instead of bringing you to the table. The vote is tied because Grandpa refuses to say either way."

"I'm being shunned?"

"Well—we weren't going to call it that. We were going to give you a line about your comfort being important to us. But yes, basically shunned."

"My family is despicable."

"I would use the adjective browbeaten."

"So you're saying I should back off?"

I shrugged. "What are your feelings toward a nursing home?"

"Not good." She sighed. "All right, I'll rein it in slightly."

A moment later she said, "You never did tell me how Cheryl's funeral was."

"It was a beautiful service," I told her.

"And?"

"What?"

"Did you see him?" She gave me a look.

"You know good and well that I saw him. You also know good and well that he's married with a child! Why didn't you tell me?" I snapped at her.

"I didn't tell you that he's married because he's not. I didn't tell you about Tara because sometimes I like people to figure things out on their own. It's one of the few perks of getting old: you get to sit back and watch your grandkids be surprised by life."

"That's a total crap answer," I told her.

She shrugged.

"He is to married though," I said. "I saw her. She's unfortunately gorgeous."

Gran was shaking her head. "No. He isn't married. She is—what are you kids calling it these days? Ahh, yes. A baby momma. But they aren't married. They weren't even really a couple. They had one of those one night stands. His last semester at Purdue. Tara will be three in January. They decided not to try to make a go of being a couple, but they're co-parenting."

"How do you know all this?" I asked, then added, "I'm impressed by your up to date terminology."

"Thank you. I try to stay current on all the phrases. I was thinking about getting one of those Facebooks. What do you think?"

I shrugged. "I'll be your friend, but then I only post boring, Grandma appropriate things. Don't add Toby though. You don't want to know about the things he posts."

"He's still smoking the pot, isn't he?" Granny asked.

"It's just 'pot' not 'the pot'. But yes. And you didn't hear it from me. Aunt Gina is trying to pretend he isn't; even though he reeks of it today."

Gran snorted. "I'm going to count my pain pills later."

"I think you're fine. He's not popping pills, as far as I know. Anyway, you never told me how you know all of this about Morgan."

"Oh, Cheryl and I talked it to death. She was just devastated at first. And then again when she found out they weren't even going to give marriage a go. In our generation, if you got in the family way, you hurried up and got married whether you liked it or not. But they're making it work. And once Cheryl held Tara, she got over it. A year ago, Trish—that's Tara's momma—got married, and I think she's expecting again. Anyway, Cheryl always said she figured you would end up with Morgan."

"She said that?" I asked.

"Since that day with the milkshake. She said one day Morgan would look up and there you would be, and this time it'd be him all tongue-tied."

"I doubt that. He didn't seem too impressed with me last night either."

"Oh? Why do you say that?"

"Nothing major. I only almost fed Tara peanut butter."

"Dear God," Gran whispered. "She would have had a reaction. Child, you don't have the sense God gave a gnat! Whatever possessed you to feed a child you don't even know?"

"I don't know! We were both standing there at the food table, and she was munching away on carrots, no problem. How was I to know she had food allergies?"

"You weren't. That's the point. You just don't feed kids these days without their parents' permission. Everyone knows that."

"Well, I didn't! I'm humiliated enough, you don't have to lecture me. Anyway, there wasn't actually peanut butter there; I just suggested that she try it sometime later."

"Hmm. That's not so bad then. She knows she can't have peanut butter. What did you think of her? She's a spunky little thing, isn't she?"

"She looks like pure adorable mischief. And her hair!"

"Yes, that hair. She gives them fits if they try to tame it or pull it back at all. It's easier just to leave it as it is."

"I think I'd like to know her," I said.

Gran gave me a look. "Would you?"

"What's that supposed to mean?"

She was silent for a long moment, as if she were choosing her words carefully. Then, "Do you still want to be a travel writer?"

"Yes," I said.

"And you've no plans of settling down. Anytime soon?"

"Well, no. I guess not."

"Then you have no business getting involved in a child's life. Breaking it off with a man is one thing; breaking it off with a child is another."

"So you think that once a person becomes a parent they're off limit to anyone who doesn't have immediate wedding plans?" I asked, unable to keep the slightly whining tone out of my voice.

"I think they're off limits to anyone who doesn't at least have serious intentions. I'm sure single parents date all the time and things don't work out. But if you *know* this isn't the life you want for yourself—at least not for several years—then you shouldn't get involved."

"So what, I'm just not allowed to date anyone until I'm ready to get married?"

"You're not allowed to date Morgan," she said, sounding protective. I wanted to say, hey, aren't you my Gran? Aren't you supposed to be looking out for me, not him? But I didn't.

Instead I said, "It's not like he's interested in me anyway. I didn't exactly leave a stunning impression."

"Oh well, perhaps it's for the best. Nothing distracts a girl more from her dreams than falling in love with a handsome man. I would know."

"So, you really don't think women can have it all?" I asked, genuinely curious.

"Having it all makes for tired women," she said in her oh-wise-one voice, and then she closed her eyes and shooed me out of the room. On my way to the door, she cracked one eye open, and called out, "Tell them I know about the Doughboy. I'll let it slide this time."

"Smart move," I told her. "They really don't serve homemade in the Home."

"You with the jokes about putting me away. I'm going to die one day, you know, and then you'll regret all the sassy things you've said to me."

"I doubt that. Everyone knows you're going to outlive us all just so you can get that last word."

"Now there's a thought."

--

Six
Carolyn
Excerpt from *Nymph of the Oak Tree: A Tale of Coming Home*
1961

That summer, after deciding she would not marry Cain, she realized she would need a job then. If she wanted to be alone, be in control of her own life, then she needed to be able to support herself.

She got a job as secretary at the court house. Spending her days filing papers, running errands, and answering the phone, she found a sort of peace in the monotony. Wake up, go to work, come home. Out of each paycheck, she gave her parents a portion and saved the rest. Carolyn had plans of saving enough to rent her own place and buy a car too.

And then, she met him.

--

He was a lawyer, with plans to be the county judge. Averagely handsome, charming, and self-possessed, he was a man of great confidence; he knew what he wanted and then worked until he got it.

At thirty, he was married with two young children, active in every aspect of public life.

Perhaps Carolyn wouldn't even have noticed him the day he came into the auditor's office (she was in the habit of ignoring men), but her co-worker, Mindy, said something to him that caused Carolyn's head to snap up.

"I just think what you're doing for that poor girl is just wonderful, Gerald. Poor thing—to live through what that man did to her." Mindy shook her head. "What would she do without you to fight for her? I hope they put him away for life."

"Thank you, Ma'am. I can't talk about the trial, or my client, of course. But thank you for your encouragement."

He finished his business, smiled at Mindy, and then caught Carolyn's eye and smiled at her. "Ma'am. Miss. You all have a nice day."

"Who was that?" Carolyn asked Mindy once he'd gone.

"You don't know Gerald? I thought everyone did! He's a lawyer. And a baseball coach. Deacon at church."

"Oh. Who's he defending in court?"

"My goodness, honey! Are you sure you're from around here? Have you really not heard about the Mackey girl?"

"Who?"

"The fourteen-year-old girl," Mindy lowered her voice and edged closer to Carolyn. "who was raped and nearly beaten to death this spring? They searched for two days for her; found her in the woods, somehow alive. She was able to tell them who did it. One of her father's farm hands." Mindy shook her head. "I tell you, young girls just aren't safe anywhere anymore."

Have we ever been? Carolyn wanted to say but didn't.

"Anyway," Mindy was saying, "Gerald's the lawyer defending her. And she couldn't have a better defense. He'll put that bastard—whoops," Mindy grimaced, clapped her hand over her mouth, and looked around. Thankfully, no one was in the office to hear her cursing, and she went on. "he'll get him put away for years. I just know he will."

That was all Carolyn heard; not that Gerald was married with children; not that he was much older. Just that he was a defender of women, a man who fought monsters. She loved the idea of him before she knew him.

--

Seven
Willie
2013

I went back to college after that Christmas break, and five semesters later, in the spring of 2013, I graduated with a double major in creative writing and journalism. I spent all of my senior year writing and rewriting my resume and applying to forty-seven jobs at various newspapers and magazines.

By the time I graduated, I had absolutely no offers. No interviews. No internships. No money.

At every stage of my life, there had been a next step, mapped out the whole way for me, with rest-stops and free time penciled in. And now, suddenly, there was no next step: just a violent plummet into my parent's basement.

As it wasn't even a finished basement, and often had garden snakes take up residence, I opted out of moving back home. My parents also informed me that should I move back, I would be paying rent.

I moved in with Gran instead, for two weeks, after which I seriously contemplated becoming the snakes' roommate. Then I thought: sweet mother of all the holy things, what have I become? I went out and got two part-time local jobs: one at the IGA and the other at the library. Then I drove around Parke County looking for a cheap little house to rent.

I found one in the little town of Judson. It was a white, two-story house with ginger bread trim and a front porch with a swing. It had been in the same family for going on four generations, but no one had lived in it for years.

They'd kept the house up though. In 2005, the Grandmother had passed away, leaving her son and granddaughter in charge of her property. Rather than sell it, which seemed like another blow to their grief, they decided to rent it out. You know, put some life back into it. They finally posted it on social media and the local newspaper as a house for rent. I found the ad.

For $400 a month rent, I couldn't pass it up, even if there was literally nothing in that town except a closed post office and a church.

I met the owners there one June morning; it was 9:30 and already 85 degrees. I was wearing a yellow tank top with cut off jean shorts and white sneakers. My hair was pulled back into a pony-tail, with a ball cap on top, and the hair at the nape of my neck was curling with sweat. When I parked in the drive they weren't there yet. I adjusted my sunglasses in the mirror and decided to go sit on the porch swing.

Despite the heat, it was a peaceful morning with a hint of a breeze. I pushed off against the concrete with the toe of my sneaker to rock the swing back and forth. Five minutes later, a Ford truck pulled in behind my car and a man in his fifties and a woman in her thirties got out.

I got off of the swing and walked over to them as they walked up the steps. "Hi," I said, holding out my hand, "I'm Wilma, but everyone calls me Willie."

"Hi, Willie. You probably don't remember me, but I know your parents. We went to school together. I'm Rob Beal and this is my daughter, Erin Nicholas."

Erin stepped forward and shook my hand. "Hi, I was several years older than you in school, but we both went to TR."

"Yeah, I kind of remember you," I said, even though I really didn't.

"Well, why don't you come on in, and take a look around," Rob said. "Figure out what you think; if you can see yourself living here. I tell ya', I have quite the memories in this house. It's where my mom grew up. . .anyway, I told you that already. Here we go; key sticks a bit." With a bump of his hip as he turned the key, he got the door to unlock and give. He held his arm out, gesturing inside and let me walk in first.

The musty smell of an un-lived in house smacked me in the nose, making me think of friendly ghosts, moth balls, and a layer of dusty memories.

Everything was outdated; the most recent remodel was done in the 1970s, Rob told me. But the lights finally came on after a few moments of flickers. Erin started throwing windows open, mumbling something about how she should have come over earlier to air it out.

Besides being dated and dusty, it was in good shape and clean. All the appliances needed patience and understanding, but they did work with enough coaxing.

"I'll take it," I said.

--

I told Gran the next morning, over breakfast, that I had found a place to live and was moving out. Despite our two weeks of constant snipping at each other, I was worried she would be upset and try to talk me out of it.

The words were barely out of my mouth before she sighed deeply (like with relief) and said, "Oh, thank God! I was worried I was making you too comfortable here and you'd stay!"

"You wanted me gone?! And what do you mean too comfortable? You've been nitpicking my every move!"

"See—you finally took the hint. I was trying to figure out what to do next! Your Grandpa and I need our privacy." She actually raised her eyebrows at me.

"Eewww! Granny!! I can't un-think that! I'll be gone in a week," I said, trying to guilt-trip her.

"OK, dear. That's wonderful news," She told me cheerily as she carried her oatmeal bowl to the sink. "I'm sure I could badger your cousins into helping you move. When should I tell them to be here? Tuesday?"

"That's tomorrow!" I protested.

"Too soon?" she asked, already halfway through dialing my cousin's number. "Because your Grandpa and I have plans."

"Ahhh! Stop it! I'll move today!"

--

I'd been living in the Judson house for a couple of weeks when I began having dreams about her. Only when they started, I didn't know they were about *her*. In the beginning, I thought it was just my over-active writer's imagination, bored from long days slicing lunch meat and shelving books.

I had the same dream three times before I started paying attention. When I had it the fourth time, I got spooked. It was pretty much the same every time, not even a full dream, more of just this snapshot image.

It was a young woman, not much more than a teenager really. She was standing in a creek at dawn on a spring morning, the mist just beginning to give way to the first rays of sunlight. She was wearing a white cotton dress, water dripping off the hem, and her hair was wet and loose around her shoulders. I wasn't really a character in the dream; I knew instinctively that I was dreaming about the past, long before my birth. And yet, she was just standing in the creek, staring right at me. I wasn't there, but I was there.

Like I said, the first few times I just woke up and forgot about it. Then the day before the fourth dream, I was driving the back country road out of Judson and looking at the scenery out of my peripheral vision, and realized all at once, that's the creek! I got chills.

But being the logical person I am, I shook myself out of it. Of course, it was normal to take real life settings and dream about them. No big deal.

But that night, the dream morphed just slightly. It started out with the same image, the same girl, the same knowing that she saw me. But then, after staring at me for a long moment, she turned and pointed at an old oak tree that grew on the bank and stretch its branches low over the creek. I had this somber knowing overtake me; I knew *something*, some truth, some revelation to my bones, but it was a knowing without words, without explanation.

By then I couldn't shake the image of the girl. She began to haunt my imagination, but not really in a sinister way. I didn't fear her; I didn't feel cursed or threatened. I didn't even believe that she was a real ghost; I never saw her anywhere but in my dreams.

What I did feel was annoyed.

I can't really explain it. The closest I can get is it was like I knew she had a story she wanted me to tell, but I couldn't hear her, couldn't figure out what the story was.

If it was not exactly frightening, it was at least frustrating.

Four years of studying writing, forty grand in student debt, and for what? For two-part time gigs at minimum wage jobs and a depressing case of writer's block.

Then here was this image, this story eddying at the edge of my mind; a story without words.

In one of my writing classes, I think it was nonfiction, we were taught that writer's block is really just fear or laziness. An excuse; a cop-out. Just keep writing, write nonsense, write mediocre crap you'll destroy later in the dark morning hours when no one will witness you slaughtering your embarrassing prose.

The Muse, God, the fairies, whoever it is who passes out stories, is paying attention. They only give stories to the diligent, the writer willing to face the blank screen and taunting curser.

So pick up random images, stolen scenes from real life and write them until you're blessed with the real story you're supposed to tell.

What crap.

Whoever says that writing is a gift hasn't been doing it very long.

Whoever says writer's block isn't a real thing is just currently a writer in the throes of prose. Ask that same writer about writer's block when she's currently in between novels and she'll tell you she's fine, but she's late for AA.

There is nothing more frustrating than knowing you used to have the gift, but it's left you now, left you for someone else.

That is why so many writers are also addicts or mentally ill or estranged from their families. Because the thing that fills them up, also sucks them dry.

The "in between novels" is a big black hole where you wish you'd been called to literally any other profession. Like farming. Or selling water softeners.

I didn't even want to read; I put books away at the library, but I refused to let myself see them. Not the classics, not my favorites, and definitely not the new best-selling author who came out of nowhere!

The only storylines I was interested in were sitcoms and Netflix documentaries.

I'd resigned myself that maybe everyone was right: writing was a risky major. I should have studied something more practical, like business or nursing. Never mind that I didn't know what I feared more: numbers or blood.

So there I was, trying to acclimate myself to my life, convinced I'd been fooled all along. I wasn't a writer; the talent had left me. But at least it had left when I didn't have a story to tell anyway.

And then, thanks to my subconscious, here comes this story. I know, really know, it's a good one too. But it comes without words.

Just an image of a girl standing in a creek, pointing at an old oak tree.

What the hell am I supposed to do with that?

--

Eight
Willie
2013

Then God or the universe or the writing fairies or whoever did me a favor and my stove crapped out.

I called Rob about it, and he said he'd come look at it; not to worry, he'd coaxed that stove back to life more than once! When he came over to do that, we got to talking about the house and his mom growing up there.

At first, I was just asking questions to make polite small-talk and cover the sound of his muttered curses as he tried to speak life back into the stove. He seemed like the kind of guy who preferred to pretend he never cursed, and preferred if you pretended too.

"Did your mom have any siblings?" I asked, knowing immediately I'd become too nosy.

He got instantly awkward, and hesitated before mumbling, "Uhh, yeah. A sister."

A more polite person would take the hint from his body language and change the subject. At this point, of course, you have to know I'm not that person.

"Oh, what is her name?" I asked, blatantly ignoring his obvious discomfort.

"Her name was Carolyn," he muttered, not looking at me. His usual larger than life, tell you anything chattiness had vanished. I hadn't missed the past tense either.

"Oh, I'm sorry. Has she passed too? I didn't mean to be insensitive," I said, as I continued to be insensitive.

"She died a long time ago, before I was even born." He was silent, then seemed to rouse himself out of whatever bad memories had surfaced and slapped the side of the stove in an almost affectionate way. "Well! I think you're right! No bringing her back this time; she was a faithful old girl, but her cooking days are done. I'll just head down to Menard's and get you a new stove. Think you can survive another day or two without cooking?"

I shrugged. "I don't really cook anyway."

Rob shook his head and wagged his finger at me. "Every girl should know how to cook, young lady. Way to a man's heart, and all that." His teasing eyes and the fact that I'd just been nosy about his dead aunt saved him from a lecture on gender stereotypes. Plus, he was the kind of landlord who bought new appliances without hinting that I pay for it.

He left and came back the next day with a new stove in the back of his truck and his son-in-law to help him unload and install it. I asked if I could help, but Rob just waved me off, so I tried to stay out of the way.

As they were getting ready to leave, the son-in-law turned to me and said, "Oh, Erin wanted me to ask if you'd care if she came over to get some things out of the attic?"

"Sure. I don't work this coming Tuesday if that would work. Just have her call me when she wants to stop by."

"Thanks!" They both waved as they left.

That Tuesday Erin sent me a text in the morning asking if she could stop by in a couple of hours. I told her to come on over. She got there around 11:00 and after we made small talk for awhile, she went to the attic, and spent the next half hour making trips up and down with various boxes.

She'd been up there for another fifteen minutes, without coming back down, and I was beginning to wonder if she'd had a heat stroke. Then she hollered down the stairs, "Hey Willie, can you come up here a sec?"

Halfway up the stairs, a heat wave hit me, and I hoped this would be quick. I couldn't figure out how she could stand to be up here so long. She was sitting on the floor in the middle of the attic, sweat literally rolling off her forehead, a couple small trunks open in front of her. I walked over and peered in: the trunks were filled with old journals and photo albums.

"You're a writer, right?"

"Umm," I hesitated. "Yeah."

"Here. Flip through one of these." She thrust a photo album in my hands.

While it looked interesting, I couldn't understand why we had to risk heatstroke to flip through old photos. Then I flipped it open at random and there she was, in black and white: creek girl. In the photo, she was standing on the porch, *my* porch, her arms wrapped around a white post, her head tilted back slightly as she laughed. It was her, beyond a doubt. I searched for a notation and found it in the margin: 1959, Carolyn.

I could hear my heartbeat throbbing in my eardrum and had to sit down.

How had I dreamed of a real-life person who had lived in the same house as me nearly sixty years earlier?

To be clear, this was the first picture I'd seen of her. The first mention I'd heard of Carolyn was that awkward conversation with Rob a few days earlier.

I had started dreaming about Carolyn weeks before I knew anything about her. Why?

One thing was clear to me: I wasn't going to solve the mystery sitting in the attic.

"Hey Erin? Mind if we continue this downstairs?" I asked.

"Good idea!" She said, swiping sweat off of her forehead. "I'm roasting alive up here."

A few minutes later, we were both sitting at the kitchen table, trying to cool down and catch our breath from lugging those chests down the stairs. I got us both a glass of ice tea which we guzzled quickly. Once we could easily breathe again, we started sorting through the notebooks, journals, and photo albums.

It took about an hour before we had them in some semblance of order: it looked like the first journal began in 1953. Carolyn had written out, in childish cursive, her full name: Carolyn Eleanor Calvert, age ten.

That journal, and the next couple after it, were the recollection of ten to thirteen-year-old girl: her falling-outs with her girlfriends, her first crushes, her struggles with math, her promises of vengeance against her sister for stealing her clothes.

As she got older, her penmanship progressed from sloppy to controlled; her spelling got better; her sentences more descriptive. I laughed so many times at her random burst of passion. I could feel the energy radiating from decades-old penciled cursive.

I could picture her hunched over her journal, scribbling furiously, biting on the nub of the eraser as she recorded her latest argument with her mother who wouldn't let her watch the birth of a litter of kittens because it was "unsuitable for a young lady to witness."

Right there, on page twenty-six of journal three, Carolyn, aged fifteen wrote, "Mother thinks witnessing a cat giving birth will give me impure thoughts about sex. Well, she just said 'an early introduction into the ways of nature.' She didn't say sex. She doesn't know that I know about how cats—and women—come to have babies. Not that I care about that part. The sex part. But I'm fascinated with the birth part! That's why I wanted to watch Lizzy have her kittens! I think I want to help women have babies, but how can I know for sure if I'm not allowed to witness any creatures give birth?"

Erin and I barely spoke as the next two hours passed, except to point out passages we thought the other should read. We didn't even talk about what we were doing, why Erin felt comfortable sharing her unknown aunt's journals with a stranger. We both just stated reading and couldn't stop.

Through the years, Carolyn's writing style developed and changed. She grew into her voice. She wrote honestly—perhaps too honestly—and spared no one, least of all herself. She was both childish and wise, immature and insightful. She had us rolling our eyes and then sighing in turn.

When deciphering faded pencil became too much work, we switched to photo albums, turning black pages slowly and carefully because they were already starting to crumble in spots.

There was Carolyn and her sister Colleen in every stage, from babies to girls to teenagers, together, separately, with their parents. They looked happy, loving, whole.

Yet, I'd spent my whole life observing people, and I knew from Erin's body language, her wistful sighs, her wet sounding chuckles, her eyes tearing up, that something had happened to this family. Something that time hadn't healed; something painful enough to have trickled down two generations.

We probably would have kept reading, but we got hungry and stopped for lunch. Over lunch meat sandwiches and chips on the front porch, Erin started talking without me asking.

"I never even knew her," she said.

"She died before your dad was born right?" I asked.

She gave me a questioning look and I shrugged. "Your dad mentioned it."

"Mentioned what?"

"Not much. Just that his mom had a sister named Carolyn and she died before he was even born."

"Well, that's more than he's ever said to me about her. I mean I knew that, but it's like pulling teeth in my family to get anyone to talk about Aunt Carolyn."

"Yeah, I picked up on that. Your dad was super uncomfortable. I was probably too pushy though."

"Good!" Erin said forcefully. I must have given her a strange look at her exclamation because she sheepishly apologized.

"Sorry. It's just I'm so sick of the secrecy. It's weird. If anyone ever mentioned Carolyn's name in front of my Grandma Colleen she practically shut down for three days. It was standard family policy to just act like Grandma was an only child and Carolyn never existed."

"So you don't have any idea what happened to her?"

Erin shook her head. "None."

"But the attic? You came over today for the journals right?"

She got a vaguely guilty look on her face. "Well, OK. I knew about those. When I was a kid, in '95—I remember because I had a cast on my arm and '95 was the year I broke it—anyway, Grandma brought me over here one time to get stuff out of the attic, old china dishes and lamps, that kind of stuff. When we were up there, I started going through boxes and found those journals and pictures. I asked Grandma about them—who this Carolyn was—and she freaked out on me! It was the first time I remember my Grandma being really angry at me, so I started crying. Then she was crying, while still yelling. We never talked about those boxes after that. I just kind of assumed she'd gotten rid of them. Then ever since Grandma's funeral, I started wondering if they were still up here."

"Uhh, are you sure we should be going through them?" I asked. "Won't it make your dad upset? And your Grandma? I mean, dead or not, you don't piss off your Grandma."

"I don't care! I'm over it! My dad was an only child; I'm an only child; my grandma is gone now. I'm literally running out of family and family history on this side. My husband comes from this huge family, where everybody knows everything about everyone else. And it's overbearing and annoying and perfect. I don't have that. My Mom died a few years ago. And I don't care if it makes anyone uncomfortable anymore! I want to know what happened to my great aunt and if I have any other relative out there!"

"I'm not sure her teenage journals are going to tell you that," I mentioned.

"I've got to start somewhere." She paused. Then, "I need help though."

"Nuu-uhh. I know where you're going with this. It's one thing for you to upset your dad, but I've got to live here you know! And that's the first rule of cheap renting, don't piss off your landlord."

"Come on, Willie. I know this is your thing! I know you are just itching to dig into those journals! I found your blog, by the way, that blog you wrote your junior year as you went around ghost writing for people in the nursing home. Tell me you're not interested in chasing a new story."

"I've given up that bit of myself. Chasing a story only leads massive student debt and potential homelessness."

"It also might lead to giving a family a bit of peace."

"So now I'm a writer and a therapist?"

"Alright. Mind if I just leave those journals here for a bit anyway?" She said far too casually.

"I know what you're up to," I said.

"I'm not up to anything! My car's just full. I'll stop by in a couple days to pick them up, OK?" She stood up and walked to the edge of the porch.

"Whatever. They'll be here. Unread."

"Sure they will. See you later, Willie. And, hey, thanks!"

"Don't thank me!" I yelled after her as she got into her car and shut the door. "I'm not doing anything that requires gratitude!"

--

Of course, I read them. But you know this.

Nine
Carolyn
Excerpt from *Nymph of the Oak Tree: A Tale of Coming Home*
Late October 1961

Carolyn had spent every morning of the last two weeks sneaking outside to puke up her breakfast behind the house, hiding in her mother's hedges. She could no longer trick herself into believing it was a stomach bug.

The horror of it washed over her again, prompting her to gag and continue vomiting. When she finished, she wiped her mouth with the napkin she'd snatched from the breakfast table.

She couldn't even throw up in the bathroom like a respectable woman. She had to do it in secret, so her parents or Colleen wouldn't hear.

Whatever was she going to do?

Her parents were just now coming around to her after she'd rejected Cain. She couldn't very well go inside, sit down next to her father reading the newspaper, and say, "Mother, Dad. I've some news. I'm expecting the child of a married man. Pass me some dry toast will you, it's all I can keep down?"

Telling Gerald didn't sound much more appealing either. Although he had to know it was possible. He'd taken precautions, but there'd been a few times. . .

She'd have to tell him though. Would he leave her? Would he leave his wife? Perhaps they could go away, start over somewhere new, just the three of them.

He'd never leave his other children though. She knew that.

But she couldn't stay here in this town. Not with this secret that would quickly become visible.

The back door slammed shut, and Carolyn stiffened.

Colleen was practically skipping down the steps. Off to see her boyfriend then. Good, ole Colleen in love. Doing things the traditional way; the *right* way their mother would say. There would be no puking secretly in the hedges for Colleen.

"What are you doing out here, Car? I thought you'd gone upstairs to get dressed. You'll be late for work if you don't hurry."

Carolyn was trying to think of a response that sounded normal when she noticed Colleen's eyes dart to her feet. The puddle of vomit was not as well hidden as Carolyn had thought.

"Oh Carolyn, you're sick! You poor dear. Go back to bed right away; I'll call in for you and let them know you're taking a sick day."

Before she could think better of it, Carolyn blurted out, "I'm not sick, Colleen. I'm pregnant." She reached out and grasped her sister's hand, clinging on tightly as she watched Colleen's face.
--

Willie
2013

I made the mistake of mentioning to Granny that I was a tad lonely living by myself. The next thing I knew, Mom and Granny got me a cat-lady starter pack. Mom paid the adoption fee and Granny purchased all the cat-rearing supplies.

I've always thought of myself more as a dog person. But perhaps my aversion to cats was really just a legitimate fear that I might become one of those writers who lives with seventeen cats and never leaves her house.

As I don't seem to be in any danger of becoming a recluse author (at least not a successful one), adopting and housing *one* cat seemed acceptable. But Granny must have been concerned that I wouldn't accept their gift because she went ahead and named her for me.

"This is Lolly," she said, talking to me like I was six. "As in Lollypop because you always loved Lollypops as a little girl. Also because you don't leave Lollypops out in the rain, so it will be a good reminder," she said this peering at me over her glasses that were sliding down her nose, and waited for that information to sink in.

"I know the basics of care for an indoor cat, Granny."

"Well, forgive me, if I haven't forgotten the incident of 1996."

"How was I to know that a hamster could overheat outside?! I thought he needed some fresh air. And I was six!"

"My point is, pets should be brought inside in harsh weather," she told me.

Several days later, I was running late for my shift at the IGA when lightning forked through the sky. I remembered that I'd let Lolly out that morning and hadn't let her back inside. She'll be fine, I told myself. Then Granny's voice echoed through my mind; at the same time, the radio interrupted the song with the blast of a weather siren, followed by a severe storm warning, in effect immediately.

I glanced at the clock. Late or not, I'd have to turn around and go let Lolly back in.

Five minutes later, I whipped my car up to the street in front of my house, not even bothering to pull in the drive. I threw it into park, left it running, and hurried out of the car, running across the yard and up the steps.

I rushed through the house and through the back door, into the yard, yelling, "Lolly, here, kitty kitty!" But I didn't even have to look for her; I nearly tripped over her at the corner of the house. She let out an agitated meow and bounded inside.

As I was getting ready to leave, she wound herself around my legs, tripping me up and getting under foot. "I have to go to work, Lolly." She let out a whiney meow and rubbed against me some more.

"Here, I'll top off your food and water. But really, you'll be fine you crazy cat. It's just a storm. Try not the shred all the furniture, OK?"

I was putting down a freshly full water dish when I hear a loud crash and the sick scraping sound of metal against metal. I jumped and dropped the dish, sending water sloshing onto the floor and Lolly. She shrieked and darted off.

"What the--!"

I rushed out onto the front porch and stared, slack-jawed, at my car.

A large Ford truck was pulled up next to and in front of the back of my car. The forty foot hay trailer the truck was pulling was smashed into side of my car.

The farmer who'd side-swiped me was throwing a grown-man tantrum at my bumper, complete with a lot of foul language, stomping, and angry air-punching. He grabbed his baseball cap off of his head and threw it to the ground then gave one of his truck tires a forceful kick.

I was having trouble processing what had just happened; I literally couldn't do anything but stand there, on the porch, listening to this man's creative combination of curse words.

Then he saw me and directed his anger at me!

"YOU!" He yelled. "Is this your car?"

"Yes," I said, my hackles already up.

"Who in the hell leaves their car parked in the middle of the damn street?"

"It's not in the middle of the street! And I was just running in for five seconds—I'm late for work."

"You're parked a solid three feet from the curb! Why didn't you just park in your *driveway*!?"

"I was in a hurry! I told you—"

He made a show of looking from the curb to the front door and then from the drive to the front door, and admittedly, there wasn't much of time-saving distance to justify my parking in the street—but, that wasn't the point! He hit my car with his big stupid trailer.

"Of all the things I needed today," he ranted.

"Oh right, because you're the only one affected by this. Look at my car! I can't drive it like that!"

"Look lady, if you don't have the common sense—"

"No, you look. Maybe you shouldn't be driving a truck and trailer if you don't know how to handle turns and tight spaces."

His eyes blazed and he reached down and snatched his hat off the ground, shoving it forcefully

66

back on to his sandy-brown, wavy hair.

And that's when I realized.

It was him.

Thankfully, I wasn't the least bit attracted to him. No, really. The only physical contact with him I was interested in was a solid sucker punch to his gut. I was so damn sick of seeing this man when I was at my worst; I was sick of him only knowing me as the silly/scatter-brained/irresponsible idiot when I knew that wasn't who I really am.

Then it hit me. Maybe I'm not the problem. Maybe he is the problem!

Morgan Lewis brings out the worst in me! He always gets to walk away looking good. Whereas, I get to walk away with milkshake stains and no self esteem, or the knowledge that I almost killed a child. And now, I get to be known as the stupid girl who couldn't park correctly.

So. There was only one thing left to do. Handle this unfortunate situation with a level of dignity that he wouldn't expect.

"Listen," I said in a forced calm voice. "This sucks for both of us. The only thing to do is call the police, let them file a report, and exchange our insurance information."

A flash of lightning forked through the sky. One Mississippi; two Mississippi; three, I counted in my head, not making it to four before there was a loud CRACK of thunder. The storm was here. The rain let loose a moment later.

He glared at me for another long moment, then sighed and walked up to the porch, pulling out his cell phone. "You're right. I'll call. What's your name and address?"

I stared at him, my brief moment of calm

evaporating. My cheeks flamed. "Are. You. Kidding. Me?"

"What?"

"You really have no clue who I am, do you?"

"Should I?"

"I don't know if I should be relieved or insulted that you don't remember me!"

"Uhhh. . ."

"Willie! Jane's granddaughter! We've met two times before now, and they were both humiliating experiences for me. The first time, I was thirteen and had a crush on you, and made a complete idiot of myself, spilling my milkshake and bursting into tears. Then years later, at your Grandma's funeral, I almost poisoned your daughter by suggesting she eat peanut butter."

"Oh—shoulder pads! Yeah, I really didn't like you that day either."

"Fantastic. Just freakin' fantastic."

"Calm down, it was just a little joke. I'm sure you're a great person."

"Oh, that's nice. Gee, thanks. I only spent all of junior high having dreams about you, and all you can say about me is you're sure I'm a great person."

Did I really just say that? Did I really just tell him I used to fantasize about him? Let me just walk out into the open yard and pray for lightning to strike me.

"Look lady, I didn't mean to insult you— you're very beautiful and all, it's just I've had a shitty day—"

"Oh my God, stop talking! I wasn't trying to ask you out! I don't need you to reassure me that I'm beautiful! And stop calling me LADY!"

"Fine! Fine! Let's just call the police and get

this over with. You're making my head hurt."

"Well, don't expect me to offer you any Tylenol!"

A policeman came and took a statement. We exchanged insurance information as the tow truck was showing up for my car. Morgan and I were both stressed and seething and he stomped off to his truck, getting drenched in two seconds. He climbed in, slammed the door, and drove away.

I was way beyond late for work, and I hadn't even got around to calling in. I was probably going to get fired.

Sure enough, when I checked my voicemail, I had three missed calls from my manager. The first: concerned; the second: annoyed; the third: "you're about to be fired" tone.

--

Ten
Willie
2013

I was in the middle of organizing bills into piles of "pay now" and "ride the grace period" and "candle light's better anyway" when I heard a car door slam. I went and looked out the front window, and then yanked the door open and stepped out onto the porch.

"What are you doing here?" I demanded with my arms crossed.

"I've got a bit of a favor to ask you, Willie," he said.

"Oh? I'm sorry, but I'm fresh out of favors. Turns out, your insurance is disputing the claim. Something about it being my fault for parking in the street."

"Yeah, I heard. But that's for our insurance companies to duke out. Nothing we can do."

"Sure, you can say that because it looks like it's going to settle in your favor! What am I going to do if I have to come up with the deductible? I'm surviving paycheck to paycheck as it is, and now, thanks to your bad driving skills, I don't have a car, and I lost my job!"

"You lost your job?"

"Yup, turns out employers like you to show up. Preferably on time."

"I'm sorry. Seriously. Where did you work?"

"Now you're interested in my life?"

"Look, how many times do I need to apologize? I feel like a jerk! But it was an accident and it was partly your fault!"

I glared at him. "The IGA."

"What?"

"My ex-job. Deli girl at the IGA. Because that's what four years and forty grand in student debt gets you these days: discounted lunch meat."

He chuckled. I didn't want to, but I smiled in response. Just a small smile.

"Do you get discounted cheese too, or just lunch meat?"

"Employee discount on all items. So basically, I was living the dream." I said.

He shrugged. "Gotta take what you can get around here. It's one of the trade-offs of getting to move back home."

"Who said I wanted to move back home?" I replied, unable to keep the sharp note out of my voice.

He looked at me for a long moment before saying, "Ahh, I see. You're one of those leave and don't look back Parke County kids, huh?"

I shrugged. "If so, the joke's on me." An awkward pause. "So, what's this favor?"

Just then, another door slammed and seconds later a curly head came bobbing around the truck, up to her dad.

"Dad! I need to GO NOW!"

"This is the favor: can Tara use your bathroom?"

Tara was jumping from leg to leg. There was no way I could say no; plus I liked *her*. Morgan could pee behind a tree before I'd have pity on him though.

"Sure, come on in." I held the door open, and Tara darted through. "Straight through the kitchen on

71

the right." She took off through the house and a second later, the bathroom door slammed shut.

Morgan and I stood awkwardly by the stove, unsure of what to say.

He finally cleared his voice. "Thanks for this. She insisted on coming with me to bale hay today; tractor has a buddy seat just for her. Anyway, we're at a field just a mile out of Judson, and suddenly she has to go. She freaked out, saying she couldn't make it home, and we were going by your house, so I thought—" He trailed off.

"Sure. No problem," I said.

More awkward silence. He turned and looked at the new stove he was leaning against. "Nice new stove you've got here. Doesn't match the rest of the antique appliances though."

"Thanks. The old one finally died. This one bakes things real nicely. Not that I would know. I don't really cook much."

"What do you do, survive on lunch meat?" He asked.

"Used to. I need a new plan now: No more discount. I'm trying to conserve the three pounds I have left. It's tricky though, because they all expire in three days."

"I am sorry about your job," he repeated.

"So you said," I shrugged. "I'll find something else."

"Will you?" He asked doubtfully.

I stared at him. Honestly, this man—could he be more dense?

"Hey, fun fact: when you contribute to someone losing their job, and they try to let you off the hook by feigning optimism you both know is fake, you don't call them on it. You instead say something equally fake like, 'When God closes a door, sometimes He opens a window.' Or 'Hey, I have an uncle who has his own meat packing plant! With your deli experience, you'd be golden. Want me to pass your info along?'"

"I really do have an uncle who's a butcher."

"No, you don't."

"Yeah, I do. Well—he's not technically my uncle anymore. He was married to my aunt several years ago. But she's a bit hard to handle, so the family just wanted to claim him instead. We all keep in contact on the sly so Aunt Nell doesn't find out."

"Where are you going with this?" I asked.

"Just if you really wanted a butchering job, I could actually hook you up."

"Umm, I'll pass. I'm just this side of becoming a vegetarian. But I'm sure your almost-uncle is a great guy." Then I added,"Tara's been in there for a long time. Shouldn't you check on her?"

He pushed off against the stove and walked back to the bathroom, where he rapped his knuckles on the door. "Tara? Honey, are you OK?" Then, "Tara, is that water I hear running? What are you doing?"

When she responded by giggling, he sighed and eased the door open and peeked his head in. "Tara! What are you doing? You don't come to a near stranger's house and take a bath in her tub!"

"But look how cool her bathtub is Daddy! And look—I found bubbles! Can we light these candles?"

"Get out, right now! Not only are you being rude, but I have work to get done!"

"I don't wanna' bale hay anymore!" I heard her whine.

"You asked to come along."

"But it's hot! I wanna' stay here."

"No. Get out now."

I heard a splash, and then a super dramatic "Whoops! Oh no! I knocked my clothes into the water!"

Morgan let out an exasperated growl. "You have got to be kidding me, Tara Elizabeth. You did that on purpose."

"No, I didn't!" she whined.

Nobody believed her.

"But now I have to stay!" she said with glee.

He turned and looked at me. "Would you mind?" he asked.

I stared at him, eyebrows raised. "You can't be serious."

"Look, I wouldn't ask, but I've got hay on the ground and a very short window to get it put up. Tara's mom is out of town and my Mom usually watches her when I can't. But when Tara said she wanted to farm with me today, Mom made other plans."

"You want me to watch your child? Who barely knows me?"

"Yes?" he said it like a question.

"And what is it *exactly*, in all our lovely encounters, that makes you feel comfortable leaving your child in my charge?"

"You have a cat."

"I've always heard humans are slightly harder to keep alive. Especially the little ones."

"Look, she's five. She's taking a bath by herself and not drowning. She listens pretty good most of the time. She knows the rules. She only has one food allergy, and we've already been through

74

that. And for whatever reason, she likes you."

"Oh gee, thanks. Again, with the flattery.
Anyway, she doesn't like me; she likes my bathtub."

At just that moment, the door opened wider
and Tara poked her wet head out. She'd wrapped
herself in one of my new terry cloth towels (a splurge
from when I was rolling in two paychecks) and it
trailed the ground and pooled at her feet.

"I like you AND your bathtub!" She told me
as her hair drip, dripped water onto the floor. She
grinned at me, a cheek dimple flashing in her right
cheek, but not her left.

How could I say no to her? She looked like a
fairy child who'd just emerged from a swim in an
enchanted lake. I was fairly certain this child had cast
a spell over me.

"Fine. But you should know that I know
zippo about kids. So as long as your standard is
'return alive and mostly unscathed' I can probably
manage that. But don't expect me to be the babysitter
who does educational crafts and makes up my own
songs."

"Alive and mostly unscathed is my parenting
motto," Morgan replied.

Granny had been right. Falling in love with a
man was one thing, but it was another to give your
heart to his child. I knew five minutes into it, that I'd
take Morgan just to get Tara. She was my soul
daughter from the second her Daddy left and she gave
me her classic, sly grin.

"Your house is haunted," she told me, matter
of fact.

I laughed. "Ghosts aren't real."

"Yes, they are."

"OK, whatever you say. Here, let me fix your

towel." I twisted her towel into a toga, and pulling my clip from my hair, fastened the towel shut with that. Then I went and got a smaller towel for her hair.

"Flip your head upside down." She did and I wrapped the towel around her hair, twisted it tight and flipped the tail back over her head.

Tara ran to the mirror. "OOH I love it! Show me how to do that!"

We spent the next few minutes in the bathroom having a hair wrapping tutorial. She insisted on trying to wrap my hair, but it kept slipping out, making her frustrated.

"It's OK," I said. "You'll get the hang of it."

"Is that your makeup? Can you put some on me?"

"Uhh," I hesitated, unsure about the rules. "Well, maybe just a little blush and lipstick."

"My mom lets me wear eye shadow too," she told me in a voice that was a little *too* persuasive. "Especially purple. And glitter. Do you have any glitter? OOOH nail polish! Do my nails, Willie!"

Twenty minutes later, she was perched on the toilet seat, waving her nails in the air, bits of cotton balls squished between her small toes to separate them. I now had the blow dryer out and was combing out her tangles. She chattered at me the whole time, telling me a litany of mismatched things: she had a little brother named Leo who was sort of cute, except he pulled her hair a lot. She could do cart wheels and she was learning how to do somersaults. Her mom and dad weren't married, did I know that?

"Do you like my dad?"

"He's OK."

"He broked your car!"

"Yeah, but it was an accident."

"Yeah. Like the time I wrecked my bike. See, I got stiches right here." She jabbed under her chin. "You ever got stitches?"

"A couple times."

"What for?"

"Oh, I cut my finger cutting potatoes one time. Another time I was barefoot and stepped on a piece of glass."

"Did you have to get a shot?" This she whispered.

"Yeah. A tetanus shot and a shot to numb it."

"I have to get shots before I can go to kindergarten next year."

"Shots aren't too bad. They just hurt for a second."

"A second's a long time."

"I'm sure you'll get a sticker or a sucker afterward."

"Nope. Daddy said he'll take me to the Diamond Store!"

"The DIAMOND store!" I exclaimed, only halfway being dramatic. What kind of over-indulgent parenting was this???

"Yeah! You know, that store by the courthouse, with the horse ride?"

"Oh, you mean the DIME store. Big difference kid." The store was actually called GM Variety, which sold a *variety* of things, including hamsters and pet mice, old-timey toys, candy, cooking ware, cleaning supplies, house décor knick-knacks, beauty products, fabric and craft supplies, and more. A lot of people called it the "Dime Store" because way back when, you could buy things for a dime.

"I got lost in there one time when I was a little

girl," I told Tara.

"Oh no! What did you do?"

"Well, I wandered around all the aisles until I found the hamsters. I knew where I was then, and I could get to the toy section from there. But my Granny had to have them call my name over the intercom because she kept looking for me, going one direction, while I was going another. And by the time they found me, she was so mad she wouldn't let me get any taffy out of the fill-a-brown-bag candy bins."

"No taffy?" Tara whispered.

I shook my head. "I didn't think it was fair either."

"We could go get you some taffy now," she helpfully suggested.

I laughed. "How can we do that, when you don't even have any clothes to wear? Speaking of that, we'd better dry your clothes. Come on."

I scooped up her dripping clothes out of the tub, wrung them out, and carried them out of the bathroom.

"Where's your dryer?" Tara asked me, looking around.

"Oh, it's in the basement."

She took one look down the steep, dark stairs and shook her head adamantly. "Huuh, uhh. I'm not going down there!"

I laughed. "Suit yourself. I'll be back up in a minute."

I flipped on the light, went down, and put her clothes in the dryer, turning it on.

When I came back up, Tara was perched on the top stair, in a battle stance, clutching a broom. Lolly was winding her way around Tara's legs, meowing to get Tara to pet her. But Tara was too focused for kitty-snuggling.

"What are you doing?" I asked her.

"I'm gonna' fight the ghosts back if they come up here!"

I tried really hard not to laugh because she was dead serious.

"Well, how exactly is a broom going to help?"

She gave me a dirty look. "It's all I had."

"Next time, I'd go for the vacuum. Suck 'em right up."

"But then they'll be stuck inside! And when you vacuum, they'll come out again!"

"That's true. Hmm. I suppose I could just hang a sign, asking them politely to leave."

"Ghosts don't read, Willie!"

"Well, I guess I'll just have to live with them then. They're friendly ghosts; haven't bothered me at all."

Tara stared at me for a moment, like she thought I was nuts. Then she nodded solemnly. "You're brave. But you should keep this broom. Just in case."

--

Eleven
Carolyn
Excerpt from *Nymph of the Oak Tree: A Tale of Coming Home*
1961

"You'll have to help me, Colleen." Carolyn said frantically, grasping at her sister's hands. They were in a hotel room in Chicago, on a "Sister's Trip." A last girls' getaway before Carolyn got married.

Things had gone very, very badly. She'd finally told Gerald and he'd seemed to take it well. Told her he'd take care of it, and they could tell her parents together.

But on the evening they'd agreed to tell them, Carolyn opened the front door to find Gerald standing there. He wasn't alone. Next to him was Sanders.

Carolyn recoiled back, backing away from the door. She was out of control, unable to grasp what was happening.

Then her parents were there, in the hallway, confused, but polite. They greeted both gentlemen. Invited them into the kitchen, leading the way. Sanders followed behind them, casting Carolyn a look.

Before going in himself, Gerald grabbed her elbow and jerked her toward him. "If you don't marry him, if you tell the truth," Gerald hissed to her in the moment they were alone, "I will take that child from you and you will never see him again, do you hear me?" In that moment, Caroline realized what was happening. She didn't know how, but she knew that Gerald knew her other secret, and was using it against her.

It spiraled after that. They all sat at the table; Sanders told her parents that he and Carolyn were a couple. They'd done wrong and were expecting a child, but he loved Carolyn and wanted to do right by her.

Her mother wept. Her father stared at Carolyn coldly, and then looked away and refused to look back.

Gerald took over after that. Talking about how he went to church with Sanders, and how Sanders had come to him asking for advice and help. These two were just kids in love. Who hadn't let youthful passion get the best of them at some point, ehh? Arrange a wedding quickly, and who would ever know?

Her parents readily agreed. Her father was getting up to call the pastor and set a date, when Carolyn blurted out: "It isn't true! The baby is Gerald's! Don't make me marry this man, Daddy!"

Her father slapped her so hard across the face that she toppled out of her chair. "First a whore and now a liar. You'll marry him all right and be grateful for it."

From her crumbled spot on the floor, as she cupped her palm against her stinging cheek, she realized things in quick succession. No one was coming to her rescue: not her father, her mother, or her lover. They feared scandal far more than they loved her. The quickest way to protect themselves was to silence her and wed her off.

She would have to rescue herself. Herself and her child.

She would have to run away.

But how?

The date they were planning was only two weeks away; not a day to spare if the baby was to be a "honeymoon baby" born a bit early.

Colleen.

Colleen was her sister. She would help her.

So Carolyn, in the next few days, appeared to come around. She apologized to her parents and begged for their forgiveness; assured them she would, of course, marry Sanders. She just wanted one thing: a trip to Chicago with her sister before she settled down as a wife.

They agreed.

Here she was with Colleen. They'd spent the day in the city, shopping and sightseeing; pretending to each other it was a jolly excursion. It was just after Thanksgiving, the Chicago air was crisp and cold enough to take their breath away. They went into many stores to get warm as much as to browse.

Now, in their hotel room, Carolyn was confessing to Colleen her plans to run away instead of going home.

"You have to help me."

"Carolyn, I don't understand. You told me yourself you were pregnant, but how could you let him touch you? After everything!"

"You know I didn't! Sanders isn't my baby's father."

"Who then?"

Carolyn looked down at her hands, then back into her sister's face, knowing this would crush her. "Gerald."

Colleen gasped and placed her hand over her mouth. Then she got up and walked into the bathroom, where she stayed for quite a while.

When she reemerged, she sat down next to Carolyn, but didn't touch her or look at her.

"How could you?" Colleen whispered. "He's married, with two small children. Oh, Carolyn, is nothing sacred to you?"

Carolyn winced and covered her shame with flippancy, "The sex was great."

Colleen recoiled and Carolyn felt something break between them.

"When will you stop wreaking havoc on people's lives? On your own?"

"I don't need a lecture, Colleen!"

"You're right; we're beyond that point, aren't we? No lecture can undo what you've done!" She gestured at Carolyn still flat abdomen.

"No, it can't! I can't undo the past. MY past. I'm sorry for it now, but it is what it is."

"I just don't understand you. I don't understand how you can do the things you do. You're so selfish. And then you expect everyone to just fix it for you, move on and forget how you've hurt us. You never face the consequences of your choices! Someone else has to clean up your mess!"

"I'm facing this one!" Carolyn yelled.

"No, you're running away!"

"I can't stay and marry him!"

"Why not?"

Now it was Carolyn's turn to flinch away as if she'd been slapped. It would have hurt less if she had been slapped. "Why not?! You know why not! You and no one else." Then a thought occurred to her in horror. "You didn't, did you?"

"What?"

"How did Gerald know about Sanders?" Carolyn demanded.

"I don't know!"

"Don't you?"

"For God's sake, Carolyn! You think I told him!? What kind of person do you think I am to betray you like that?"

The look on Colleen's face convinced Carolyn. "Fine. I believe you. But still. You think I should stay and marry him? After what he did to me? What kind of hell do you think you're assigning me to?"

Colleen started to say something, then stopped herself, looking miserable.

"No, say it! Say whatever damn thing you're thinking! I want to know."

"Just, maybe. Maybe that night wasn't exactly like you thought."

"Excuse me?"

"Never mind."

"No. Go ahead. You were saying, maybe I led him on, maybe I had it coming, maybe I called it something different so I wouldn't have to face the consequences of my choices, right?"

"Well. . ."

"Well, what?"

"Did you?"

"How can you even think that of me!?"

"It never entered my mind before you had an affair with a married man. But now I don't know you at all."

"And I don't know you either."

Carolyn stood up abruptly, walked over to the other bed and crawled in, pulling the covers over her head.

"Carolyn, don't be like that. I didn't mean it."

"On the contrary, I think you did. Goodnight,

Colleen. I won't be troubling you further. From here on, I'll face my consequences myself."

Despite Colleen's further pleading, Carolyn ignored her. Eventually, Colleen gave up and went to sleep.

When she woke in the morning, Carolyn was gone.

--

Twelve
Willie
2013

Around 8:30 that night my cell phone rang. I looked at the screen to see "Morgan Lewis" and ignored the flipflop of my stomach.

"Yes?" I asked, answering his call in what I hoped was a breezy, confident voice.

"Why did you tell my daughter that your house is haunted? Who tells a five-year-old ghost stories?" He demanded in that annoyed tone I was very familiar with by now.

"I told her they were friendly ghosts," I said sheepishly.

"Who tells a five-year-old that her house is haunted at all??"

"She told me!" The words were out before I even knew I was going to say them.

Long pause. "Willie. Ghosts aren't real."

"Sure. Everyone believes that until about 3:15 am in a 100 year old house that set empty for decades. Then you start questioning all kinds of stuff."

A sigh. "Look, I don't care what YOU believe. But Tara has been crying for the last hour and won't sleep."

Now I sighed and said, "Put her on the phone."

There was some mumbling, and then Tara's little voice asking, "Willie?"

"Oh, honey. Listen, ghosts aren't real. I was just playing along because I thought we were being silly. But there are no ghosts in my house, OK?"

"Yes, huh. I saw three."

"You did not."

"Yes, huh! A mom and a dad were sitting at the kitchen table. And a girl was showing them a paper and she was crying."

"Tara, where did you see this in my house."

"Well, I didn't see it in your house. I dreamed it tonight and then I woke up because Daddy was shaking me. But the dream was in your house!"

"That's just a nightmare, Tara. Sometimes nightmares seem very real. But ghosts are not real."

"How do you know?"

"I just do, OK? I've been sleeping here for weeks and not a single ghost has bothered me."

"Maybe they're just waiting."

"There's no reason to be scared."

"I'm not scared for me! I scared for you!"

"Listen, what if I promise to sleep with your broom by my bed?"

"You told me brooms don't work 'gainst ghosts."

I had said that. I was out of ideas. "OK, Tara, what do you suggest?"

"Anti-ghost spray."

"What?"

"Daddy has some; he knows how to make it." And with that, she hung up.

And that's how Tara and Morgan ended up at the Judson house at 9:00, spraying "anti-ghost spray" into every corner, vent, closet, and under all of my furniture while Lolly darted away and hissed at his squirt bottle. Tara sent Morgan down into the basement and instructed him to spray "twenty sprays, Daddy. No, fifty."

I tried not to giggle, but one slipped out.

Morgan gave me a grumpy look, but that only added to the comical effect of his appearance: a grown man, two days' worth of stubble, sleep-weary eyes blinking behind protective goggles, a red Chef-Dad apron tied around his torso and yellow rubbber gloves (for further protection) on his hands. He was carrying around a hairdresser spray bottle, vanquishing my house of ghosts at his daughter's instruction.

By ten o clock, Tara was either satisfied that the ghosts were gone, or too tired to worry about my safety any more.

Morgan, still in his full ghost-fighting regalia, scooped up Tara. She curled into him, nestling her head against his shoulder, and I tried not to literally sigh aloud.

"Would you mind getting the door for me?" Morgan asked, quietly. I nodded and opened it. He walked through.

"Oh, here. Let me get your truck door too!" I said as I jogged down the steps in front of them and went to his truck.

"Thanks," he said, brushing passed me to ease Tara inside. I forced myself to step back.

"Well, thanks," I said lamely. "For umm, getting rid of the ghosts. I'm sure I'll sleep great tonight." And then I blushed because my mind immediately conjured up an image of him in my bed. Luckily, it was dark and he couldn't see my face.

"I hope you do," he was saying, and it took me a moment to reprogram my brain and realize he was responding to what I said, not to what I'd thought. He couldn't read my mind. Thank God.

"Well, good night, Morgan."

"'Night, Willie."

As they drove off, I heard Gran's voice in my

head, telling me not to get involved, and knew it was too late.

--

A few days later, I got a call from the IGA manager telling me I could have my job back if I wanted it. But would I please call Morgan Lewis back and tell him to stop bothering them?

A girl with bills can't afford pride; I told him I'd be on time for the next day's shift.

My first evening back came with a slew of difficult customers. But this lady standing on the other side of my counter was the absolute worst.

"Here you go ma'am." I said, zipping the baggy closed as I pressed the air out. I handed it over the top of the counter.

"What's this?"

"Umm-the honey ham you asked for," I said as I rolled my neck trying to work the kink out, hoping that she'd take the hint and be on her way.

"I said sliced not shaved. I don't like shaved. It's too thin and crumply. I have never ordered it shaved." She was getting good and worked up now. "It falls right out of the sandwich. Do I look like I want to listen to my husband bitch and moan about a messy sandwich?"

Bitch and moan sounded about right, I thought, as I silently held out my hand and took the lunch meat back. I forced myself to mutter an apology even though I was sure she'd said shaved, not sliced.

A few minutes later, I handed her a new package of sliced ham. "Here you go, ma'am," I said as politely as I could.

"You really ought to check your attitude young lady," she told me.

"What?" I asked, genuinely confused.

"I ought to report you to the manager."

"For what?" I asked, my voice ticking up a notch.

"You really didn't need to slap the price sticker on there with such sass."

She had to be kidding. Who stood at the deli, at the local grocery store, near closing time, chewing out the counter girl about sassy stickering?

I opened my mouth, but no words came out. I couldn't think of a response that didn't involve four lettered vocabulary that would surely get me re-fired.

"Is this old biddy giving you a hard time?" a man asked.

The "old biddy" and I both spun our heads to see who was asking the question. She had her mouth open to rip him a new one, but upon seeing him, launched herself against him in an affectionate bear hug.

You've. Got. To. Be. Kidding. Me. I thought for the second time. Only—only in a small town.

"Oh Morgan, you rascal! I was ready to ream you up and down for the biddy comment, but no woman can be mad at you!" she gushed.

"I beg to differ." I thought, then realized I'd spoken aloud when they both turned to look at me: her with an icy glare, and him with a raised eyebrow and a bit of a smirk.

Then they turned back to each other and launched into a ten minute conversation catching each other up on their lives. I dismissed myself after two minutes of awkward eavesdropping. I hadn't asked the "old biddy" if she wanted anything else with her *sliced* ham. But the mood I was in, she could just drive herself the thirty miles to the nearest big box grocery store if she did. They deserved her.

Corporate chains should take all the pain-in-the-ass shoppers. Leave us little guys the sweet elderly couples and the stay-at-home moms wandering the aisles in their hour of allotted "free time." Those moms, out shopping, *without* their kids—they practically begged the checkout boy to bag just a little slower. Oh, no, make it last. Please. I can't go home.

Just earlier today, I'd had one of those stay-at-home moms-without-her-kids almost swoon when I told her I was having trouble with the price sticker printout and it was going to take a minute. "Oh, you just take your time!" She exclaimed.

Moms out shopping with their kids though—that is a different story. You ask them to wait for a computer glitch and they look around at their kids in raw panic. One has to wonder what kind of hell toddlers put their mothers through to turn grocery shopping into a grown woman's worst nightmare.

I was remembering a toddler's epic meltdown in the bread aisle when I heard Morgan clear his throat. I finished wiping the counter down, maybe just a little slower than I usually would have before I walked over to him.

"Yes?"

"Glad to see you've got your employee discounted ham back," he said.

"Yeah. Thanks for that, by the way," I told him.

He shrugged. "It was the least I could do."

"That is actually true."

"Could I get a pound of ham?" he asked.

"Company policy dictates that I say yes and ask how you'd like that sliced."

"Shaved. Mostly. Except for the very last quarter pound: I'd like that thick sliced," he told me. I think he was trying to be funny.

"Ha, ha."

"I'm kidding. I don't actually need anything." he said.

"Oh?"

"I—ah, just came in for some of the basics. You know, milk, eggs, and bread. And I saw you, so I thought I'd say hello."

"Hello," I said.

"Hello." He was staring at me weirdly. It was probably the hair net combined with the stained smock.

It had been a long shift. I really just wanted to finish cleaning up and get out of there, but he was sort of hovering.

"Did you get your car fixed?" He asked.

"It's in the shop. Your insurance covered it by the way."

He nodded. "I know." Then, "So how are you getting back and forth to work?"

I wrinkled my nose. "I'm on the hitch-a-ride-from-various-family-members program. It usually comes with a side of guilt and a lot of pointed gazes at the gas gauge and the clock."

"Who's picking you up tonight?"

"My Grandma."

"Jane?" He asked

"Yeah, Granny."

"I haven't seen her in ages! How's she doing? I used to run into her all the time at Grandma's house when Tara was a baby. Tara had colic; I'd be at my wits end, and Jane and Grandma would take her from me and send me outside to split wood. I'd come back in, calmed down for the first time in hours, and Tara would be cooing at the pair of them as they told her stories of growing up together."

I tried to imagine it: him as a new father with a colicky baby, going over for Grandma therapy. Something maternal kicked into overdrive; my womb practically sighed. Then my mind centered on an image of him sweaty from splitting wood and veered off in a whole different direction.

He's a muscular, wood splitting, calloused-hands-on, single dad who likes to hang out with Grandmas. Don't look him in the eye! Stay strong!

"Hey!" He said pulling me out of my daydream. "Why don't you call Jane and tell her I can take you home?"

"No, that's OK. You really don't have to do that."

"It's not a problem."

"I'm sure you have places to be. I don't want you to have to wait around on me."

"It's a Tuesday night. I'm a single Dad and Tara's at her mom's. I came to the grocery store at 8:30 for social interaction."

"Ahh…"

"I mean, if you want to." he said, suddenly backing off, like he'd thought he was being pushy.

"Yeah, I guess. I'll just shoot her a text and see if she's left yet. Give me a sec."

"Your grandma texts?"

"Yup. She actually refuses to get old."

I dug my cellphone out of my pocket and typed a quick text.

Me: *Hey Gran, have you left yet?*

Gran: *No. You told me to leave at nine. Is it nine?*

93

Me: *Don't get sassy. I just wanted to let you know I don't need a ride now.*

Gran: *Hitchhiking is the quickest way to end up on* Dateline.

Me: *I'm not hitchhiking.*

Gran: *Then how are you getting home?*

Me: *Aren't you nosy?*

Gran: *Well, who is he then?*

Me: *Who said anything about a 'he'*

Gran: *A granddaughter would only stand her Granny up for a gentleman friend*

Me: *I'm just trying to save my dear old Gran some time and gas.*

Me: *I don't have a gentleman friend*

Gran: *If you want to save me some time, stop dragging out this conversation. You know texting hurts my carpal tunnel.*

Me: *It's Morgan.*

Gran: *Morgan?? Why are you still talking to me? Do you want him to find another girl in the frozen food section?*

Me: *Fine. Point Taken. Good night, Gran*

Gran: *I'll be praying for you!*

I couldn't think of a response to "I'll be praying for you" in the context of the situation, so I just slid my phone back into my purse and walked back toward Morgan.

"Alright. I'll finish up and meet you in the parking lot if that's OK?"

"Sure," he started heading toward the front door.

"Morgan!" I yelled; He turned back toward me.

"Aren't you going to get your milk and eggs and bread?"

He looked confused for a moment. "Oh! Right. Yeah."

He was sitting on the tailgate of his truck when I got out to the nearly empty parking lot. He jumped down as I approached him.

We were both equally awkward this time; a nice change of pace since it was usually just me.

"Thanks again for the ride," I said as I clicked my seatbelt. I tried to discreetly look around at his truck: booster seat in the right back seat; goldfish crackers, animal crackers, and what I assumed was, at one time, fruit snacks were smashed into the seats and scattered in crumbs on the floorboard. Also on the floor board was a small library of children's books, enough stickers to detail the entire truck, a hodge-podge of toys, and no less than 50 hair ties and clips and bows.

Mixed into this nest was a large toolbox with tools spilling out, empty coke bottles, crumpled fast food sacks, grease stained work gloves, tow straps, and a large jug of motor oil. And a self-help book on single fatherhood.

"Sorry for the mess," he said catching my eye. "I'd say it's not usually like this, but that'd be a lie."

I smiled. "I particularly like the red sparkly head band that's peeking out of the top shelf of your tool box."

"Oh yeah. The top shelf is Tara's. One day, she just dumped all my sockets out and filled it with her stuff, and then gave me a look, daring me to question it."

"Did you?"

He gave a mock shudder. "Hell no. Found a new place for my sockets."

I laughed. "I think she has you right where

she wants you."

He grinned. "You have no idea. She's my buddy though. I work a lot and she has to go with me, but she's always a good sport about it, so I figured she's earned a little shelf space."

"I was driving a tractor at age nine for my dad. Some of my favorite memories."

He was driving down the highway now, and turned to glance at me, "Ahh, I forgot you were a fellow farm kid. But I thought you couldn't wait to get away?"

"Just because I want to do something else with my life doesn't mean I hate where I come from," I snapped.

"My bad. It's just you always seem a little, I don't know, disdainful about being back in good ole PC."

"Ouch," I said. But it wasn't untrue.

"It's just, I had these plans you know? And I worked really hard; did the whole college thing, took on the massive debt, studied my ass off. But instead of landing any kind of writing job out of college, or even just getting my foot in the door somewhere, I ended up back here with a couple part time jobs. And it's not that I'm a snob about working at the grocery store and the library. I'm really not. I just can't figure out how, after four years of work, I ended up back where I started," I said.

"Come on. You've been out, what two or three months?"

"Two and some change."

"So you've been an alum for a whopping nine weeks? How many grads actually land their dream job right after graduation? Very few. You just take what you can get, go where you have to go at first. Then one thing leads to another. . ."

"Are you really going to give me a pep talk?" I asked.

He shrugged. "I just think you're being overly pessimistic, that's all."

I wanted to say something snippy but decided to change the subject instead.

"So how about you? Was it your plan to end up back here?"

He laughed. "Not exactly. I actually had a teaching job lined up over in China. Teaching English—no seriously. It was a program to work off that student debt you talked about. But then, well, Tara happened."

Most women would probably zone in on the whole "I got another woman pregnant and am now a single father" bit, but all I heard was that he was a fellow English nerd. As if he needed one more thing in his favor.

"You were an English major?" I asked.

"Nope. History and Education."

"So you wanted to be a history teacher?"

"Didn't want to. I am a history teacher. You didn't know that?"

"How would I know, I'm not stalking you!" I said, a little too defensively. Then added, "I thought you were a hay farmer?"

"That too. But it's a side gig. During the school year I teach high school kids to care about the past. Or try to anyway. On my 'off' time I farm. Turns out you really can't pay the bills on either of those jobs alone."

"Where do you teach?"

"Turkey Run."

"Could you do me a favor?" I asked.

"What?"

"Stop saying things that make me like you."

He laughed. "You don't seem like you're in any danger of liking me. I think the majority of our conversations have been arguments."

Ten minutes later, he had pulled into my driveway, and killed the engine, but neither of us made a move to get out. I released my seatbelt and turned to face him.

"You know, the first time we met, we didn't argue, you just barely noticed my existence. Which was worse."

"Ahh, the milkshake day, right?"

"Yup. The milkshake day. Forever seared onto my memory while you have no recollection."

He shrugged. "Sorry. I remember you now."

"Right, because I either leave no impression or bad ones. It's hard to forget someone who almost causes your child to have an allergic reaction and then goes on to cause you to have a wreck."

"So, you do admit it was your fault!"

"Sure, now that the insurance claim is settled in my favor. I will admit to forty percent blame."

"Forty percent! If you hadn't parked in the street, I would have driven by your house just fine."

"Fine. Fifty percent. But that's my highest offer."

"My insurance rate has gone up!"

I shrugged. "Look where you're going next time."

He gave me a look that was part annoyance, part amusement, and shook his head at me.

"Of course, if you hadn't left your car parked in the street, we wouldn't be sitting here now. And I am kind of enjoying being around you."

"Oh, kinda, huh? You really know how to lay on the flattery."

"Well, if you liked that, how about this for flattery: that hairnet is a real turn on."

My hand jumped to my head. "My hairnet— oh crap! I completely forgot!" I yanked it out of my hair, my cheeks burning. I resisted the urge to flip down the visor and check my hair. My braid had tumbled loose when I pulled the hairnet off, so I released the elastic and ran my finger through the worst of the tangles.

The mood in the truck shifted; he was watching me and I was watching him back. And then suddenly it was his hands in my hair instead of my own. My stomach flip-flopped as he pulled me to him and kissed me. I pressed my hands against his chest and kissed him back. And then we were making out, losing track of time and where we were. When we finally broke apart I was sitting on top of him in the driver's seat.

"Would you like to come inside?" I asked, breathless.

He gave me a long look that made me blush and glance away. Then he opened the door and swung us both out and carried me through the yard to the front porch. We kissed the whole way, only stopping so I could fumble for my keys.

He put me down and I turned to unlock the door. I was just about to turn the key when he put his hand on my hip and turned me back toward him.

"I'm sorry, but I can't do this."

"What?" I asked.

Seriously? What was happening? Was I being turned down?

And then: an image popped up in my mind.

My Granny praying for me. I groaned; that's what she'd meant. I'd bet my last paycheck she was praying at that exact moment that her Granddaughter not be able to seduce that wonderful, single father, Morgan. And apparently, Jesus was listening, and leading not into temptation.

"I want to," Morgan was saying. "I wanted to right there in my truck, Willie. Believe me. It's just I've done the whole one night stand thing and it didn't end well. No, I mean, it did—I got Tara out of it, so I can't regret it. But I'm a dad now, not some college idiot, and I can't just go around having sex with women I pick up in the grocery store."

My face was burning in embarrassment and anger. "*What?* A woman you picked up in the grocery store!? Is that all you think of me? That I'm offering you casual sex because I'm bored on a Tuesday night with nothing better to do in a small town? Believe it or not, I don't do one night stands either, asshole. I thought—I don't know—I thought, we could. . . I don't know—start something real or whatever!"

"I'm sorry Willie, that came out badly. That's not what I meant."

"Would you just leave?!" I yelled, then glanced around at my neighbors' houses with the lights on, and lowered my voice. "Every single time I see you, it's more humiliating than the last! I'm sick of it! I'm sick of you!"

He tried to take my hand; I swatted it away. "Come on, Willie. Let's not leave it like this! Sit with me and let me explain!"

"I'm not interested. You need to go. Just go. Message received loud and clear!" I snapped.

"What I want to know is why, if you were the one to shut this down, I'd be a nice guy about it, respect your boundaries and walk away. But I shut it down, and you berate me, and make me out to be some terrible asshole for turning you down."

The words "turning you down" did nothing to improve my mood; neither did him accusing me of having a double standard. He wasn't going to give up the argument though, so I turned, opened the door and stomped inside, slamming the door shut. Then I leaned back against it and listened.

"Oh right, real mature Willie. Real mature." Then I heard him stomp off the porch, slam his truck door, and drive off.

--

Thirteen
Willie
2013

I roamed around the house for a good hour, picking things up and smacking them back down, furiously scrubbing the dirty dishes in my sink, and sweeping the floor with enough vigor that dirt and dust skittered from one end of the kitchen floor to the other. Lolly, who had been sleeping in the window sill, jumped down, gave me the side eye, and darted away from my broom angrily.

"Ass, ass, ass," I muttered under my breath. When I ran out of things to clean, I ran a bath, poured myself a glass of wine, turned on some music, lit the candles, and climbed in. The combination of all that eased some of the anger out of me, leaving embarrassment and sadness in its place.

Nothing makes a woman feel more vulnerable than rejection.

I tried to tell myself it was his issue, not mine, and all that. But I still found myself doing a body inventory and critiquing my looks.

If it wasn't my appearance, then maybe the problem was my personality.

If he had said he didn't want to rush into anything, that would have been different. If he had said he didn't want something casual because he wanted to be sure about us first, I would have been sexually frustrated but not humiliated. I probably would have appreciated his seriousness.

But he hadn't made it sound like he wanted to go slow to set the foundation for a real relationship.

He had made it sound like he didn't want a one-night stand because he didn't want to tangle his life up with mine.

So the real question was what was wrong with me that he didn't want to get involved?

To be fair, I'd pretty much always been overly awkward or angry around him. Or wearing an old woman's funeral suit or a hairnet. I was snarky and snippy and cussed too much. I had a bad attitude about my current living and working situation. In his own words, I was "disdainful" about that whole thing.

It can't be pleasant to be around a disdainful woman.

I should try to be more pleasant, I told myself.

Then there's the whole he has a daughter thing. Maybe he didn't think I was mother material? I didn't think I was mother material.

He let me babysit her though, one side of my brain reasoned.

Yeah, for a few hours. And you told her your house was haunted, the other part of my brain chimed in.

Honestly, this was stupid. I was NOT the kind of girl who cried in the bathtub with a glass of red wine because a guy had rejected her. I was NOT the kind of girl who second guessed everything about herself and seriously considered altering her entire personality and looks for a guy. (Never mind that those were things I was currently doing.)

The problem was obviously him. Hadn't I realized this before, so many times? How many awful encounters did it take for me to get the hint? He is just not for me. Period. Never mind that he's this muscular farmer with grease stained, calloused hands who can repair a tractor *and* use those same hands to put his daughter's hair into a ponytail.

Never mind that he looked reeeally good every. Single. Damn. Time. That I saw him.

Never mind that kissing him made me forget why I was mad about moving back home. Never mind that I would so much rather be doing something with him instead of taking a bubble bath by myself. Never mind about any of that!

I had nothing to be humiliated about.

I'd had a crush on this stupid man for over a decade now, and I'd tried, finally, to do something about it.

So it didn't work out. Maybe this is what I needed to finally get this man out of my system and move on. Tomorrow, I told myself, tomorrow I would dive back into the job application world. I would apply to no less than five jobs a week, all over the country. Anything and everything even remotely related to writing. I'd tweak my resume again; I'd send almost-groveling emails asking for interviews.

Maybe deep down, one of the reasons I'd allowed myself to move back home was because of Morgan. Maybe I'd secretly always been waiting to see where that would go. Maybe I'd always taken Cheryl's belief that we'd end up together as some kind of foreshadowed destiny.

But what it really was, was complete BS. Bull. Shit. Capital B; Capital S.

I was not going to wait around for some guy to be my destiny. I had dreams and goals, and if I'd gotten sidetracked and overwhelmed with all the job rejection in the last six months, that was completely understandable. It made sense that I'd needed a break and some downtime to regroup and figure my life out.

But that was over now. It was time to get

back out there!

Resolved and energized, I pulled the plug. I stepped out of the tub, dried myself off and wrapped the towel around my hair, trying to vanquish the image of Tara with her hair in a turban. I slipped into my robe and knotted the sash, then left the bathroom, in search of my laptop.

--

I was staring at my resume on my laptop, biting my lip and picking at my nails twenty minutes later. Lolly had made up with me, and was meowing in my lap as I stroked her fur absentmindedly.

I kept getting distracted by the stacks of Carolyn's journals in the corner. I'd read through all of them, and then resolved to put her and her mystery out of my mind. I stacked them back into the chests, tucked them into a corner, and texted Erin a half dozen times, reminding her to come pick them up.

Her family. Her drama.

She either texted back a pitiful excuse why she couldn't pick them up yet or ignored me entirely.

So here I was, like a junkie trying to quit writing cold turkey, and being forced to walk past these mysterious, tantalizing journals every day. And now, tonight I had decided to give writing another go. But not *that* kind of writing. I didn't want to get mixed up in my landlord's secretive family past and risk losing my cheap rent.

Yet, now, this story was the only thing I was interested in writing!

As if she sensed my weakening, Erin chose that moment to text me.

Erin: *Hey, look. I'll pay you.*
Me: *What?*
Erin: *I'll pay you. Name your price. Track*

down what happened to my aunt, write this story.

Me: *I can't take your money.*

Erin: *Why not? You want a writing career. I have a writing job for you. I don't see the problem here.*

Me: *Umm, hello? Your dad?*

Erin: *Let me worry about him.*

Me: *Are you going to worry about finding me a new place to rent when he kicks me out?*

Erin: *Yes. If I have to.*

Me: *$400 rent? Or cheaper? Good luck with that.*

Erin: *If it comes to that, let me worry about it. But listen, my dad isn't some heartless jerk. He might be angry and hurt, but I'll take the fall, OK?*

Me: *This is a bad idea.*

Erin: *Is that a yes?*

Me: *3,000.* I texted an outrageous amount, thinking for sure she'd say that was too much and let it go.

Erin: *Done.*

Damn, I thought. I can't turn down three grand.

Me: *Fine.*

Fine—what a word! A word to acknowledge begrudging agreement or mediocre wellbeing. Will you do this for me—fine. How are you feeling—fine. It's a lackluster word, without passion or optimism. Just this side of negative.

It's the word I used to give permission to the Muse to tangle my life up with theirs.

--

Fourteen
Willie

For the next several days, I used every bit of my free time to research Carolyn Calvert. There wasn't a lot on her; just a few mentions in the county newspaper for things like school awards. There was small announcement about her baptism; another about her graduation, that sort of thing.

I spent most of my time combing through newspapers and other public documents from the 1960s, learning a lot of interesting, but unrelated information.

I was lost in Carolyn's journals one afternoon when I heard his truck pull into my drive. I swung the door open for Morgan before he managed to knock. His hand was poised in the air and everything, and he looked shocked when I motioned him inside without an argument.

"Look, Willie—I"

But I held up my hand and cut him off. "Hold up. I can't talk now; I'll lose my train of thought."

I wandered back into the living room where I had my research strewn all over the floor, couch, and coffee table. He followed (I don't want to say "like a lost puppy" but the image does come to mind).

"What is all this?"

"My first paid writing job."

"That's awesome! But umm—what exactly is the project?"

I sighed as I plopped back down on the floor. "Well, remember when I told Tara my house was haunted with a friendly ghost?"

"No, I'd forgotten about that. She sleeps well by the way, thanks for asking."

"Such sarcasm. Well, it turns out this house really does have a ghost: Carolyn Calvert."

He gave me a look.

"No, seriously!"

"How many times do we have to go over this? Ghosts are not real."

"Whatever. Believe what you want. Anyway, not so much ghosts as dreams; never mind. My point is, Carolyn Calvert is—was—a real life person! She was born in 1943 and she grew up in this house! She'd be Rob's—my landlord—aunt. But she's like this hush, hush family scandal because she had an affair with a married man, a lawyer. And she got pregnant. Anyway, the short of it is everyone shunned her, and she left, and no one knows what happened to her, or her baby. Well, no one's who's talking anyway."

"Let me guess: you found her diaries or something? But how is this a paying gig?"

"Well, if you wouldn't interrupt me: I'm getting there. Erin, that's Rob's daughter, so Carolyn's great niece, is fed up with all the family secrecy and wants to know what happened to her. She knew about the journals and sort of bullied, sort of bribed me into taking this job, finding out what happened, and writing it down."

"So you're going to dredge up some Parke County drama for a few bucks?"

I gave him a look.

He threw up his hands. "What? I'm not judging! I'm just wondering if you really want to get involved. You know how this small town is. What was the guy's name by the way?"

"Gerald."

Morgan cut in, "She had an affair with a man named *Gerald*?"

"I'm sorry. What name were you expecting?"

He shrugged. "Gerald just doesn't sound like a cheater's name."

I rolled my eyes. "If you're going to stay would you at least sit down?"

He looked around. "Where?"

I gestured. "Oh, here, there, wherever. Just move a pile! No! Not that pile! Don't shuffle papers! Oh, sweet goodness! Just—move. Let me do it."

I moved a pile off of the couch and pushed him into the seat. "Now, listen. And don't interrupt me."

"What if I have questions?"

"Fine, so long as they aren't smart ass questions."

"No promises."

"Where was I?" I asked.

He stayed silent. "Oh, are you asking me?"

"Yes."

"Well, I believe—very humbly, mind you— that you were telling me about Gerald."

"OK, yeah. Well, I researched this guy's name around 1961 and found out he was a lawyer. He was one of those guys who was super involved in everything; on all sorts of community boards, bank board, church board. Friend to little old ladies, kid's baseball coach, the whole bit. I even turned up pictures of him with his kids and wife in her pearls and white gloves at a church picnic fundraiser."

"Sounds like a great guy."

"Carolyn thought so. Although how women

are ever attracted to men who would cheat on their wives is beyond me. I mean, how could there ever be any trust?"

"Maybe she thought he'd be different with her."

"I guess so. That's what she wrote about anyway. How they couldn't help it and all that because they were meant to be."

"But they didn't end up together."

"No, they didn't," I said.

"What happened?"

"She told him she was pregnant with his third, and this time, illegitimate child."

"He claimed it wasn't his?"

"No, I think he was too arrogant to even imagine she would sleep with anyone else. He knew it was his, but he didn't want to own up to it. Bad for his reputation, you know. She wrote that he promised to make it right, and they set a date to tell her parents together. But when he showed up, he had a guy named Sanders with him. He'd gotten Sanders to lie and say the baby was his; that he and Carolyn had been having a secret affair. Her parents bought the story, especially because this well-known, well-loved Gerald was sitting there, pretending to be concerned about these two young lovebirds.

"So anyway, she was blindsided completely. When she got around to protesting the lie, he dad actually slapped her. He told her she was a whore, and she would marry Sanders and be glad of it."

"Shit," Morgan said.

"I know! There she was, just a kid really. Pregnant with a powerful man's baby, completely alone with no one who believed her. And she was being forced into a creepy marriage by her own parents."

"What did she do?" Morgan asked.

"She played nice. Pretended to go along with the whole thing. Convinced the only person she had left to help her: her sister. The two of them convinced her parents to let them take a trip together, one last pre-marriage, pre-baby sister trip. So they took the train to Chicago. And in Chicago, Carolyn disappeared. Colleen came back alone."

"Hold up, how do you know this? I mean, I'm assuming they didn't write their plan down, if it was supposed to appear that Colleen was tricked," Morgan said.

"Well. OK. You're right; it's just a hunch, I guess. The last sister trip really did happen; that's Carolyn's last journal entry, the planned details of that trip. I guess I don't *technically* know, for sure, that Colleen was in on it. I just really want to believe that she helped her sister."

"So how do you know she disappeared in Chicago?"

"Because there's a train ticket stub in Carolyn's journal—Colleen must have put it there. But that's it. The last record this family has of Carolyn. Colleen came home and built a whole life here, married, had a son. But there's nothing of Carolyn. And according to Erin, no one was even allowed to speak of Carolyn."

"Alright. So what happened to her?"

"I don't know. I can't figure out where she went to from Chicago. But Rob believes she died before he was even born for some reason. So his mom must have told him that, or lead him to believe it. I don't know."

"And that's the last journal she wrote?"

Morgan asked, pointing to the one next to my right foot on the floor.

"Yup."

"Can I see it?"

"Sure. But there's nothing in there; she didn't leave behind a single clue about where she was actually going. That was the whole point."

He ignored my tone, and picked up the journal, flipping through the pages, and pausing to read occasionally. After a few minutes, he sighed and tossed the journal back down onto the floor, a little too forcefully.

The journal landed on its side and flipped over. A piece of paper fell out.

I picked it up. It was a business card, yellowing, the right corner folded over and creased with age. It said, "Grant Brother's Funeral Home: owned and operated by George and Gibson Grant." The phone number and address were printed underneath. Asheville, North Carolina. I had noticed it before when I went through her journals, but I hadn't thought much of it. I went to stuff it back between some pages.

"That could be something," Morgan said hopefully, reading over my shoulder.

"Or it could be absolutely nothing. Why would she leave it in here if it were a hint? More than likely, it's just a scrap piece of paper she used as a bookmark."

"Still. You should ask Erin if the names mean anything to her."

I shrugged and picked up my phone, typing out a quick text. *Do the names George and Gibson Grant mean anything to you??* I hit send.

A few minutes later, she texted back, *Hmm, I*

think my Grandma's Dad had distant cousins, or
maybe it was a war buddy with the last name Grant.
It sounds vaguely familiar, but I'm not sure.

"Distant cousins!" Morgan exclaimed. "See, there's a connection! Wouldn't a young, pregnant girl who's been rejected by both her boyfriend and family look for some kind of distant relative for help?"

"I don't know," I told Morgan. "Maybe."

"You should go there!"

I shook my head. "That's a wild goose chase."

"I thought writers loved wild goose chase."

"Maybe those of us with extra money and running cars do. But I don't even have built up time off of work. Or a vehicle, remember?"

"So call in sick."

"For a week?"

"Terrible stomach flu. Nobody wants near that. Especially a grocery store."

"Alright, so I'll just hitchhike to North Carolina."

"I'll take you."

I stared at him.

"Look, it's not that much of a favor. I take loads of hay to Kentucky fairly often, so you tag along, and we go a little further south after I drop the hay off." Morgan shrugged.

I tried to think of a polite but direct way to say no. But a part of me really wanted to go. But then I could easily imagine the awkwardness of a long road trip with him. Did I really want to subject myself to further humiliation?

Then as if reading my indecision, he said, "Tara's going with me."

"Alright. If I can get the time off of work, let's do it."

--

In the end, the library was flexible. I just told the truth; I was chasing a story across the U.S. Librarians are suckers for that.

The IGA manager was slightly less understanding. So I quit. Or maybe I got fired? The details are fuzzy.

--

Fifteen
Willie

The day we were leaving, I was a mess of nerves. Excited about Carolyn's story. Nervous about traveling with Morgan. Questioning all my life choices basically. But at least Tara was going; she'd chat right through the awkward tension.

He knocked on the screen door. "Come in!" I hollered. Morgan stepped into the kitchen as I wheeled my suitcase to the front door and looked around for my five year old friend.

"Where's Tara? In the truck? Shouldn't we make her come in and use the bathroom one last time before we go?"

"Umm—she's not going. Trish called me last night and said Tara had been up all night throwing up. I've still got to go deliver this hay, but look. If you don't want to go, I completely get it."

I was torn. It was true that Tara was the buffer between us; Morgan and I had never really resolved anything after that time we'd almost slept together.

We'd seen each other a few times since then, but always with the buffers of either Tara's spunky presence or Carolyn's mysterious story between us. We didn't talk about "us" or what had happened. We both just ignored it.

The idea of a long truck ride alone together left us both looking for a way out.

He expects me to say no, I realized.

That annoyed me.

We had an agreement. He knew I still didn't

have a reliable vehicle for long road trips; he knew how important this project was to me; he knew I needed this.

Yet he wanted me to put that all on hold because he couldn't stand the idea of being in my presence? Nuu-uhh. Tough luck, buddy. I'm coming.

"I'm good. Let me just grab my purse. I'll be right there," I told him.

He opened his mouth to say something, then clamped it shut and turned and walked out to the truck. I petted Lolly one more time and told her goodbye (my neighbor had agreed to feed her and check on her while I was gone). Then I made sure the coffee pot was off and followed Morgan.

The first few hours were nothing but awkward silence. The radio played in the background, thankfully. But that was it. We didn't even try to make small talk.

It took about three and half hours to get from my house to a small, organic cattle farm about fifty miles from Lexington, Kentucky. Morgan sold organic hay, and this farmer wanted to try out a load before committing to larger orders.

It took a couple hours to drop off the hay and talk to the farmer. Which means it took about twenty minutes to dump the self-unloading trailer and move the bales with a skid steer into his barn. The rest of the time was farmer chit-chat.

I mostly sat on the truck bed, trying to remember I'd hitched a ride and shouldn't complain. But it was getting hot. I was hungry, and I really just wanted to get to Asheville.

At noon, the farmer's wife came outside. She was probably in her early thirties with small children hanging from her legs and elbows.

We made polite introductions; her name was Valorie, but she rattled off her kids' names in rapid fire, so I didn't catch them all. "Why don't you come inside and have lunch with us?" She asked. "You know our husbands are going to be a while." Without waiting for my response, or disclaimer that Morgan wasn't my husband, she turned back to the house— children, dogs, and a couple chickens following her across the yard.

I didn't want to be rude, so I followed too.

The door was left open for me, so I walked right into the kitchen. Toys and stray socks littered the floor, sippy cups and plastic Disney plates filled up the farmhouse style sink. A blur of kids and a dog ran through the house, shrieking, barking, and knocking into every piece of furniture possible.

"Don't mind the mess. Or the noise," she told me, as I shut the door. "Do you have kids?"

"Umm, no."

"Well, take your time. Just kidding; they're the best thing that's ever happened to me. Although I'm not entirely sure they won't also be the death of me."

"How many do you have?"

She stepped out from the fridge, holding jelly, a bag of carrots, and a box of generic tubes of yogurt. She nodded her chin down to her belly where I noticed a slight bulge. "This is number five."

"Congratulations!" I said.

"Thanks." She smiled. Then she caught a flash of movement out of the corner of her eye, dropped her armload of lunch onto the counter, and in two strides reached the kitchen table where she pulled down a toddler who crouched over the butter dish, shoving chunks of butter into his mouth, eyes darting around. He reminded me of Gollum from *Lord of the Rings*, feverishly devouring raw fish.

"I swear, this one's life goal is to have diabetes before he's three. Stay off the table! Don't make me go get your father!"

She made a half-hearted paper towel swipe at his buttery face before he darted off. She sighed and plopped down in a kitchen chair. Her eyes fluttered shut. "I'm sitting in syrup." She didn't bother changing chairs. "My kids know 'I'll go get your father' is a meaningless threat this time of year. We won't see him until November."

"Uhh," I said, feeling slightly uncomfortable.

"I mean, it's fine. I knew what I was getting into marrying a farmer, right?" She gave me a look implying that I also knew what it was to be married to a farmer.

"Oh, Morgan and I aren't married."

She literally sighed wistfully. "I miss those days, when you're just dating and daydreaming. I pictured all of this—" she gestured around. "But damn. I never imagined there'd be so much *stickiness*. Or curdled milk. My children and I play this game daily: They hide half full sippy cups throughout the house, and then sit back and watch while I frantically search for them before they curdle. Did you know a decent sippy cup costs about eight bucks, and I have two kids still drinking out of them? We have a strict yearly sippy cup budget. But I find one of those suckers tucked down the floor vent all winter, and into the trash it goes. You can't pay a mom enough to wash that out."

She paused to tear open a yogurt tube with her teeth, squirting some onto her shirt. She deftly swiped it off, licking her finger, then held the box out to me, asking "want one?" I grabbed one. "Anyway, what was I saying? Oh, yeah, somebody should just make a list of all that kind of stuff, the curdled sippy cup hide and seek, the fact that you'll spend twenty damn minutes every morning just looking for clean socks, never mind about matching, that kind of stuff. Someone should write it down and give it to pregnant women, so when they're losing their minds, thinking it's just them, they'll have the list to refer to. But then again, maybe none of us would reproduce if we read the list first." She laughed.

"My mom actually wrote a list like that for each of us kids," I said, "she titled it 'You put me through all this and still made it to graduation. Congratulations.' and gave it to each of us when we graduated high school. After she gave it to my sister, who's the oldest, it became like a rite of passage thing. We looked forward to getting Mom's list of the crazy shit we did to her."

"I think I'll steal that," Valorie said.

"I would definitely write the butter thing down," I told her, as her toddler son tried to stealthily creep back to the butter dish. She lassoed him with her arms and pulled him into a hug. He instantly went from butter thief ninja to cuddle monster, snuggling into his momma for kisses.

I smiled. For all the mess, the trade-off of love looked pretty fair. But I made a mental note to research birth control extensively.

By one o clock, Morgan and Tim, Valorie's husband, made it inside, still talking farming as if they'd been lifelong best friends.

His children shot out of their chairs, clamoring to reach their Daddy and be the first swung up into his arms. Morgan moved out of the way, so as to not be trampled, and grinned at me.

"You ready to go?" He asked.

"Sure," I said, wiping my mouth and then carrying my plate to the sink. I made a move to wash it, but Valorie waved me off.

"Don't worry about it. I'll get to it in oh, eighteen years and five months."

We said our goodbyes and thank-you's; Tim promising to be in touch about future hay, and then we left. Tim had told Morgan we could leave the hay trailer and pick it up on our way back, so Morgan unhooked it, and we were on the road.

It took almost six hours to drive from their farm to Asheville, by the time we got there it was late evening. We grabbed some dinner and checked ourselves into our rooms at the hotel.

After a hotel breakfast around nine, we got directions to drove out to the funeral home.

Then we were there: in the parking lot of Grant Brother's Funeral Home. It was just a few miles outside of Asheville, an old, well-kept, two story, red brick home/funeral home. The home set in a valley on five acres, with a small fenced cemetery nestled in the embrace of the mountains. And the trees! Something inside me both stirred and calmed at their sight.

I wasn't really a tree hugging hippie. I was just a regular person who cried watching the *Lorax* and who knew, if I was having a bad day, sitting under a tree would immediately calm me down.

But I was beginning to feel pulled toward trees. Random memories would surface: my junior year of high school when our biology teacher would take us hiking in Turkey Run State Park and teach us how to identify various trees and plants. I vaguely remember rolling my eyes a few times, but secretly loving it. Now, I wish I'd paid more attention.

I would remember in college, studying the imagery of trees in so many works of literature. How the poets in all generations keep coming back, keep using the tree as metaphor after metaphor, finding meaning in its roots and leaves and branches. Using the tree as a symbol for so many abstract ideas.

I'd done a google search on Asheville, and stumbled across an article about the *Asheville Tree Commission.* A group of people whose job was to protect and preserve the trees. The Modern Day Keepers of the forests. A buried word from lit classes popped up in my mind: Druid. Protector and knower of trees. Gateway, secret keepers. I had a vague memory of learning about the Druids believing the Oak tree was a portal between this life and the next.

I didn't know what exactly—if anything—this had to do with Carolyn. But just like the dream, I *felt* it. The knowledge of something. I just couldn't figure out what.

I suppose to the end of my days I'll be a Hoosier girl. I love the beach as much as the next person, but the secret truth is I love rich, dark dirt so much more than sand. Anyone who's never been to the middle and southern end of Indiana assumes it's all flat corn fields.

But Parke County, and further south, looks nothing like the north. Sure, we have plenty of fields of corn and soybeans and wheat. But we also have hills and woods and creeks, and a whole state park with cliffs carved out by water and time.

I suppose it is the combination of being a

farmer's daughter, raised in the backdrop of Turkey Run State Park, that's made me believe that as long as I could always touch the dirt and the trees, I was connected to something more than myself.

To be honest, I love the ocean, but it also terrifies me in its vastness. A country creek, though, puts me at peace.

I spent my childhood playing in the woods on our farm, wading the creek, building tree forts, walking across fallen logs. My cousins, siblings, and I had a whole pretend world in the woods; we could be anyone and everyone. In the warm months, we'd pack picnics and spend the whole day there. In the winter, we'd sled down this one hill in the woods which ended at the creek bed. It was an added challenge and thrill to stop just short of the thin ice. (Don't worry; it was shallow. We'd get wet but not drown if we fell through.) One summer, we cut a maze through the tall weeds and grass, a path that led to our favorite tree fort. We collected a hodge-podge of old dishes, tarps, blankets, and played "the old days." That was probably our favorite, most common game "the old days."

In every season, the woods were different: snow-covered trees in the winter, silent under the crunch of our boots; green and verdant in the spring and summer, a symphony of bird song; deep, rich colors in the fall as the plants and animals settled down to sleep. Always changing; always alive.

It's not so hard, really, for me to believe in forest magic and tree fairies. All you have to do is walk into the woods, take it by surprise, and hear the hush fall over it. The silencing of nature's secrets. But if you stay there long enough, without ax or greed, it starts to whisper again.

So even though I was in a different state, I was home because of the trees. I was listening to their secrets. If I'd had my doubts before, I *knew* as soon as we arrived in Asheville that Carolyn had been here too.

Morgan and I knocked on the front door, and it was answered by a stylish, middle aged woman in a pant suit. She smiled at us, a practiced smile of someone used to greeting and helping complete strangers on a regular basis.

"Come in," she said. "I'm Verona. How can I help you?"

"Hi, Verona," I said, stepping into the foyer, noticing everything: the plush, maroon carpet, the stairs with polished banister, the closed doors down a hallway to our right, the opened concept room to our left and ahead of us.

"I'm Wilma, and this is Morgan. We were wondering if we could speak to the owners, the Grant brothers?" It was a long shot; I had no idea how old George and Gibson were or if they were even still alive.

"I'm sorry dear. George and Gibson haven't owned this funeral home in 40 years."

"Oh."

"My father bought this funeral home off of them in 1973. He kept the name because it was so well known."

"Oh," I said again.

She paused, looking at us. "Is there something you needed from them?"

"Well, I'm not sure. I'm doing some research for a family named Calvert, and I believe they are distant cousins. I just had some questions," I said, not wanting to get into the whole thing.

"For George or Gibson?" She asked, sounding strangely protective.

"Umm, either?"

"They stayed in contact through the years. Dad was fairly good friends with George. I'm afraid to say that George and Claudia—his wife—have both passed on. I think they have a daughter. Gibson is still alive; he lives in an assisted living home with his wife, I believe."

"Any chance you know what that assisted living home is called?" Morgan asked.

She gave us another long, hard look as if trying to judge our intentions and character.

"I might have a phone number."

"You might or you do?" Morgan asked, sounding a bit pushy. I tried to tell him to back off with my eyes.

"I suppose it wouldn't hurt to give him a call," she said. "Wait right here." Then she stepped into one of the side offices and closed the door.

"Sheesh. Last I knew, you couldn't harm someone over the phone. What do we look like exactly?"

I gave him a once over. "Well, I look fine, but you have midwestern, red-neck written all over you."

"Me?? It's probably your thick, Hoosier accent that's got her in there, calling her husband or cousin or local good 'ole boy sheriff to come check us out."

"You have to admit it's strange to just show up asking questions about brothers who owned this place forty years ago. I'd be cautious too."

At that moment, she poked her head out of the office and said, "I have Gibson on the phone. He said he'd talk to you."

We walked into the room, and I picked up the landline phone. On second thought, I put it on speaker. I wondered briefly if I could ask Verona to leave, but that seemed rude. Her body language clearly said she wasn't budging anyway.

"Hi, Mr. Grant. Can you hear me OK?"

"Because I'm old, you assume I'm hard of hearing?" A gruff, gravelly voice demanded.

"Uhh, no. I was just making sure the connection was OK."

"It's 2013; phone connections have never been better! Unless you're using one of those dadgum cell phones, then all bets are off."

"OK. . .well, umm Mr. Grant."

"Gibson. My name is Gibson."

"Alright, Gibson. My name is Willie."

"You don't sound like a man."

"Well, no. I mean—I'm not a man. Willie is short for Wilma."

"Oh, an old-fashioned name. You don't sound old enough for your name."

"I'm twenty-two."

"Dear God, what were your parents thinking? You should be a Jessica or an Ashley. Maybe a Tiffany."

"OK."

"OK, what? OK you'll change your name, or OK, shut up old man?" He asked.

"Uhh."

"Did you call me just to stammer and stutter or is there a purpose to this phone call? I'm missing bingo."

"I'm sorry. I didn't mean to take you away from your activities."

"Activities! Bah! I only play the Bingo

125

because it's the closest I can get to gambling here."

"I'll get right to the point."

"I've been waiting."

"Sir, I think you are related, distantly to a family named Calvert. Is that correct?"

He paused, before saying forcefully. "I don't believe so. You're mistaken."

"Are you sure? I'm specifically trying to track down a woman named Carolyn Calvert? I know her family back in Indiana—"

He cut me off, this time the anger unmistakable. "I've never heard of a woman named Carolyn Calvert! Goodbye!" Click, the line went dead.

Morgan, Verona, and I looked at each other in silence.

Then Morgan said, as he pushed up out of the armchair he'd been sitting in, "Well, I bet the nurses all love that guy."

"He's a bit gruff," Verona admitted.

"Is that the word?" Morgan asked. "I was thinking of another."

We began walking toward the foyer.

At the door, Verona reached out and touched my arm. "You said Carolyn Calvert, yes?"

I nodded.

She sighed. "Come with me. There's something you should see."

She led us outside, across the parking lot and yard, toward the cemetery. She unlatched the old iron gate and led us through. Toward the back of the cemetery, we stopped at a small plot under an oak tree.

As we stared at the weathered stone, Verona said, "When I heard that name, my heart stopped. I don't remember all the names here, but the heartbreaking ones. . . those I have etched on my memory. I'll leave you. Come back inside when you're ready."

Morgan and I stood there in silence as she walked away.

On the simple stone, a simple inscription: infant daughter of Carolyn Calvert March 18th 1962-March 21st 1962.

Three days.

It was just really sad, I told myself. Of course, we turned to each other for comfort. One second, we were standing side by side, reading the gravestone of a three-day old infant, and the next we were in each other's arms. We were both crying: him as a father who's held a three-day old daughter; me as a writer who has spent countless hours poring over Carolyn's journal entries about her scandalous, but wanted pregnancy. Her loss felt like my own.

No wonder she'd disappeared and never come back. Rejected by her lover and family, she flees to protect her child, and then loses that child in a premature birth. If her dates had been right, her child wasn't due until the beginning of May 1962. March 18th would have been seven weeks early; nothing too scary into today's world of NICU and medical advances. But in 1962? What were the survival rates of preemies then? And what if she'd had birth defects or complications during childbirth? Lack of good care?

I had so many questions; and yet, the answers all led to here, the grave of an infant.

I could finally understand why all evidence of her existence dropped off suddenly. But even though I could understand it, I hated it. We had officially hit a dead end to her story; the hopelessness of it all crashed into me like a punch to my gut.

"It's just not fair!" I wailed. "He goes on to live this privileged life where everyone thinks he's this upstanding man, father, husband, and lawyer, and she loses her daughter!"

"God, it's awful. What happened to Carolyn after this? I can't even imagine what would become of me if I lost Tara. I can't stand to even think of it! We have to keep looking for her," Morgan said.

I don't know if it was the emotion in his voice, the desperate hope that made him animated, or the fact that he was referring to my writing project as "ours," but whatever it was caused me to feel a wave of affection. I couldn't help it: I reached up and kissed him.

He was completely still for a moment, then he wrapped his arms tightly around my waist and kissed me back.

We made our way back to the funeral home in silence.

Inside there wasn't much to say to Verona. Her wariness toward us was gone, banished by shared grief over a nameless infant. I was out of questions; out of leads. I just wanted to forget the whole thing. Tell Erin to leave it alone; no healing was coming out of this.

Verona took down my contact information though. I could tell she was curious now; she wanted to know what I knew about this Carolyn Calvert; wanted to know the connection to this funeral home and the Grant brothers. But I wasn't in the mood to give anything away.

--

Sixteen
Willie

In spite of our sadness, or maybe because of it, we spent the rest of the day acting like typical tourists, visiting all the local attractions, namely the Biltmore estate. It was as impressive as everyone always says, and it took hours to walk leisurely through the whole mansion and grounds. Then we toured the shops and ate lunch in one of the restaurants on the estate. While our wanderings served as a welcomed distraction, Carolyn lingered in our minds and on our moods.

We spent the late afternoon and early evening touring the rest of the city, buying trinkets for Tara; listening to the street musicians; browsing countless boutiques and shops.

Dusk had fallen; the city of Asheville switching from daytime to night life; the glow of the city radiating for miles. It felt like the mountains took a step in, wrapping themselves protectively around the city.

Morgan and I got a quick and mostly silent dinner and then drove back to the hotel.

My thoughts were a jumble of half thoughts tumbling into other thoughts.

I couldn't stop feeling Carolyn's grief. I couldn't stop imagining her tiny infant in a coffin; Carolyn standing at the headstone, looking at a mound of fresh dirt.

Then my thoughts would switch to that kiss and I'd glance at Morgan next to me. I tried to tamp down the feelings and what-ifs circulating in my mind.

Part of my brain was denying what I was planning. The other part of my brain was wondering how a lady asks if he'll stop and get condoms.

Then the idea of birth control and unexpected pregnancies had me coming back to Carolyn.

Should I or shouldn't I?

How does a mother survive burying her child? How does she not just climb into the grave herself?

What kind of underwear and pajamas did I pack? Oh shit, I packed that ratty t-shirt and shorts, didn't I?

How can I be thinking about a grieving mother and sex at the same time?!? Shouldn't these thoughts cancel each other out? Shouldn't I be focused on one and forget the other? Am I a special kind of weird-o?

But the truth is, I'd realized, standing in the cemetery, how fragile life is. I know it's cliché to have those "grab life in the now because it ends soon" moments in a cemetery, but it was true.

Was I really just going to give up on a relationship with Morgan because I might be rejected again? Was I really not even going to try? Oh, sure, I'd been telling myself the reason I was letting him go was because I had better things to do: a writing career to focus on.

But the truth was I was afraid. I was afraid of not being good enough for him and Tara. Afraid he knew that. Afraid he'd say no.

But wasn't it better to try for love and be rejected than die with regrets because I was a coward? No, seriously, I'm asking. Someone let me know.

We had adjoining rooms at the hotel. I know,

I know: you're rolling your eyes and saying "of course, you did."

You think you know exactly where I'm going with this, don't you?

Well, listen, dear reader: we did not have sex that night. It wasn't from lack of trying.

We parted ways in the hallway without so much of a "I'll leave my side of the door unlocked." That was sort of unspoken and assumed.

I opened my suitcase and rummaged through it, taking stock of what I'd packed. The options weren't great if the goal was seduction: jeans and shorts, an assortment of tank tops and t-shirts, the kind of underwear and bras a girl wears when she's the only one who sees them. I had packed a bathing suit in the hope that the hotel would have a pool, but it seemed kind of awkward to put on a one-piece *without* the intention of swimming.

What was I going to do, walk into his room wearing my one piece with a modesty skirt and lean against the door, and say, "Hey, there."

How exactly did one go about making a sexy, hotel room entrance?

I'd probably trip.

Heels! That would help, right—I dug through my shoe bag. I'd only packed flip flops, tennis shoes and hiking boots in case we had to do any muddy hiking.

OK, so I could clunk over there in my navy-blue polka dot one piece and my tan hiking boots.

I laughed at myself, just this side of hysterical-sounding, and plopped down on the bed.

Just forget it, I thought, as my stomach gave a nervous leap and roll. I was making myself feel sick with nerves.

The two times we had kissed, I'd wanted nothing more than to find the nearest bed. In-the-moment passion, I could do. Pre-meditated seduction: that was turning out not to be my thing.

Seriously, I was feeling nauseated. That could not be a good sign.

I had just resigned myself to room service and channel surfing when Morgan knocked on my door.

"Hey, Willie, are you decent?"

I rolled my eyes and pushed myself off of the bed with a groan. That settled it; no way I was going to try to be alluring when he asked if I was fully clothed before opening the door.

I opened the door and said, "Yes?"

"I was just thinking," he said, as he stepped into my room, "we should try to get ahold of that Gibson guy again—I know he shut us out pretty quickly today. But it had to be a shock; maybe he's had time to process it and will hear us out. We could probably get the assisted living home address from Verona now. I think she's come around to us."

I ignored the way he looked in his white t-shirt and basketball shorts. His hair was wet from the shower; his face stubbly with two days-worth of beard. And, worst of all, he was wearing the same cologne that had turned my insides to jello all those years ago.

It was seriously annoying how physically attracted to him I was. I wanted to be able to just turn it off, especially because I never seemed to affect him quite as strongly.

Focus on his words, I told myself.

"Umm, I don't know. He was pretty angry on the phone. I can't imagine it would be better if we just dropped in unexpectedly. He strikes me as the kind of old man who lives in a primitive cabin with a basset hound and greets visitors with a sawed-off shot-gun."

"You know he lives in a nursing home! As far as I know, they strictly ban firearms. We'll call ahead and just not take no for an answer. Come on Willie; it's our only lead right now. I just have this feeling that he knows something."

Why, why did he have to be a history buff? Why did he have to throw himself into my project with such passion and energy? It would be so much easier to stop liking him if he'd stop saying things like "*our* only lead."

We weren't an "our."

Ahh, screw it, I thought as I pushed him up against the doorjamb, wrapped my arms around his neck, and kissed him. He lost his balance for just a moment but caught himself and pulled me tight against him.

My stomach gave another nervous roll. Why did passion have to feel like nausea? If I was going to do this, I'd like to enjoy it, I thought.

And the next second, I was breaking away from him, and darting for the bathroom.

I wanted to die of humiliation (again), but ten minutes into throwing up, vomit burning through my nose, I seriously thought I was more likely to die from puking.

Might as well, I thought, because there was no coming back from this. Supposing I eventually stopped retching, there was no way I was going back out there. He could just leave me at the hotel and I'd hitchhike back to Indiana.

Morgan kept trying to check on me, knocking on the door. Thank God, I'd had the sense to lock the door because he'd already tried to come in. No way I was letting him see me like this. Hearing it was bad enough.

Twenty minutes later, I emerged from the bathroom with no dignity or food left in my system.

Thirty minutes after that, he darted into my bathroom, and by the sound of it, upchucked everything he'd eaten in the last decade.

I'm not going to lie: I was kind of relieved. The sound of him vomiting helped me feel less embarrassed.

We spent the rest of that long night taking turns puking. During our vomiting "breaks," we laid next to each other in bed (I'd stripped the nice comforter off), moaning and groaning and channel surfing. Every so often, we'd try to sip water and start all over again.

I'm going to stop describing this scene because I'm running out of verbs for "vomiting." If you've been a human for any time at all, you can already taste it in your throat, so my work here is done.

Around three am, slightly delirious with the beginning of dehydration and lack of rest, I painfully rolled over to face him.

"Are you awake?"

He groaned in response, and I took that as a yes.

"Do you remember the story of Jonah and the whale?"

"What?"

"Do you remember that story?"

"My Grandpa's a pastor. Like there's a Bible story I don't have memorized," he said.

"Don't need the attitude. A simple yes would

suffice."

"Fine—yes."

"Well, you know the part where there's terrible storm and sea, and they try every ritual to get the gods to cool it, and Jonah finally says, hey, my God is the real God and this is my fault. God's punishing me; throw me overboard and the storm will end?"

"Yeah, that's pretty much the plotline."

"Again, with the attitude."

"What's your point, Wilma? I'm kind of trying to concentrate on not pooping my pants over here."

I couldn't help it; I started laughing so hard my sides hurt.

"Glad you find this funny."

"I'm sorry! It's just I've been annoyingly attracted to you for so long, trying to find a way to stop liking you. And you talking about pooping your pants might have got the job done."

"Fantastic. Glad I could be of assistance. Now, would you mind shutting up, please."

"No, I had a point. Hold on. . .I'll think of it again. Oh yeah, the sex."

"Seriously?? We're going to talk about sex? And what does that have to do with Jonah and the whale? Don't take this the wrong way, but you're kind of a weird-o."

"I have a point! Just listen. What if God smited—or is it smote?—us with this terrible stomach virus because we entertained thoughts of premarital sex?"

"I always thought the scariest result of premarital sex was pregnancy. But you're right, this is way, way worse."

"I'm serious! Maybe we're total heathens for wanting to do it, and this is our judgement."

"I'll swear right now never to look at you lustfully again if the diarrhea will just stop."

"Buddy, I'd throw you into the ocean myself if I could just keep down a glass of water."

I'll always remember that as the best and worst night of my life. Around 5:00 am, the worst of it was over, leaving us spent and listless—and not in the way I'd been hoping for. My whole body ached, my abs were sore, my throat raw, and my brain fuzzy.

I wanted an ice cold can of 7-Up more than I'd ever wanted sex with Morgan.

I seemed to be slightly better (a loose term) than Morgan, so I stumbled through a quick shower and then ventured out to the vending machine with a handful of crumpled dollars and quarters.

I came back with bottles of 7-UP and packages of crackers. We sipped and nibbled like we might never trust food again, and after we held that down for a few hours, I ordered room service soup for an early lunch. I gave them Morgan's room number and met the server over there. I wasn't going to subject some poor employee to our sick room. I'd already resolved that we'd be cleaning before we left; there's just some things you don't expect people to do for you.

We'd extended our stay for that day and another night; ate our soup and passed out.

We woke up at four feeling almost human. Morgan got a shower and left to go buy cleaning supplies. When he got back we scrubbed, mopped, and disinfected the bathroom and bedroom and bagged our sheets and towels in three trash bags that I labeled it "For the Love of God, don't open. Vomit-covered. Throw away." It was the only thing I could think to do.

The fumes ran us out of my room, into Morgan's. We ordered room service again: more soup and grilled cheese. We ate them while we watched TV.

Sex was the farthest thing from our minds; he could have laid there naked, holding a Hershey bar and I would have said, "Umm, no thanks." But after a while we cuddled against each other and held hands.

"Want to trade back rubs?" I asked.

"That sounds great."

He was running his fingers through my hair, and I was about to doze off when his phone buzzed with a text message. I grabbed it off the nightstand to hand it to him, glancing (yes, purposefully) at the screen. It was a text from Trish.

They texted regularly; I'd noticed that. Whichever parent had Tara updated the other about her wellbeing several times a day. And they called at least twice a day to exchange what I'd begun to refer to as "Tara stats." What she'd eaten, how she'd slept, how she felt, the funny things she'd said or done, the newest epic tantrum she'd thrown. They texted pictures of her with funny captions.

It was impressive to witness, the way they communicated about their daughter. I'd only seen Trish once, at a distance, and didn't know her at all. But I heard the way Morgan talked to and about her, and he was always respectful. I'd never once heard him complain about her or talk down about her.

The way he treated his ex and mother of his child amazed me; it really did. It spoke volumes about his character. But I'll admit that there was small voice nagging me, questioning if he had feelings for her. How could two people have sex and then a child and not have some feelings involved?

She had married Zack when Tara was a small toddler, and had another child, Tara's brother Leo. So she'd moved on, but why hadn't Morgan? What if Gran had missed something and it had been more than a one-night stand on his end?

I tried to shake these thoughts out of my head, quash my insecurities and jealousy. What would I rather: that he hated Trish, the mother of his child? That he wasn't a dad at all and had never been with another woman?

I loved Tara; I couldn't wish her away. She was what mattered. Tara having both her mom and Dad get along was what mattered.

"How's Tara?" I asked, resolved to be a classy woman, not a cavewoman ruled by primal jealousy.

"Back to herself." Morgan chuckled as he showed me the picture on the screen. It was a shot of Tara hiding in her closet with a chocolate covered face and a cupcake in her hand. The deer-in-the-head-lights look said it all. She'd been busted.

"I'm glad she's feeling better," I said.

"Me too."

"Nice of her to share her germs with us though."

"Isn't it, though?" He snorted. "I've been sick more times in the last five years than I had in the full twenty-two leading up to her birth. One of the perks of being a parent."

"Sounds lovely. Maybe I'll stick with raising cats."

We scrolled through the other photos Trish

had texted, ending on a shot of Tara playing with her brother and step-dad.

Before I could check myself, I blurted out, "is it hard for you?"

"Is what hard?" He asked, but the look he gave me said that he knew exactly what I meant.

"Umm, is it hard watching her have this whole other family, and—" I stopped, wishing I'd kept my mouth shut.

He finished my question, "and not being a part of it? Having to make space for another dad figure? Watch her grow up with a sibling who doesn't belong to me? Hearing about the stories and adventures she has without me, while I sit at home eating frozen pizzas? Yeah, sort of. But you know what? That's my problem. Not hers. And I know it's just as hard on Trish when Tara's with me; we both have to make sacrifices, but it's worth it because our little girl is happy and knows she's loved."

"Did you and Trish ever try to make a go of it; you know, be a family yourselves?"

He looked at me and then took a deep breath. "You don't pull any punches do you, Willie?"

"I'm sorry. I shouldn't have asked. It's just—I've been wondering. Gran said. . ." and then, I physically clamped my hand over my mouth.

"No, go on, Gran said what?"

"Dang it. I'm a moron. Ahh, she just said it was this casual thing between you and Trish, and that you never were a real couple, just ahh, co-parents."

"Do you really want to get into this, Willie?"

"You don't have to tell me."

"I'll tell you if you want to know. Oh, what the hell. It's not like this weekend is going as we planned anyway. What's a little more awkward after you throw up with someone?"

"OK," I said, my voice sounding feeble.

"It was a one-night stand. I'm not exactly proud of that. Trish and I knew each other from a few classes at Purdue, but not very well. And then, about a month before graduation, we ended up at the same party, and drank too much. And then one thing led to another and when I woke up in the morning, she was in my bed, and we were naked. The really bad part is neither of us have very clear memories about that night."

Maybe he couldn't remember, but I could picture it vividly. And I didn't want to.

He kept talking. "When she woke up and saw me, she immediately started crying. It was awful. I remembered enough and know myself enough to know it was consensual if that's what you're worried about. But still, seeing her cry made me feel about two inches tall.

"She started telling me her whole story as she was sobbing and blowing her nose on my sheets. All I could do was sit there and listen and pat her back. A few months earlier she'd broken up with her boyfriend Zack—yeah, that Zack, her husband—but she still loved him and knew she'd made a mistake. But she'd just found out he had a new girlfriend. She went to that party pissed off and depressed and got drunk to forget about him. So basically, I was just rebound sex. It's not like I was in love with her either, but that still sucked to hear.

"Anyway, we both agreed that it was a mistake, and we should try to forget about it and move on with our lives. So we did; we both graduated and left campus. But two months after that, she'd tracked me down through a mutual friend and asked to meet me.

"We met at a coffee shop in Lafayette, and I just knew when she ordered decaf. Before she even opened her mouth, I said, 'you're pregnant, aren't you?' She started crying again. So I'm sitting there, shocked, you know? But trying to be a decent guy and comfort her. But inwardly beginning to freak out myself as it sank in that I was going be a father.

"She pulled herself together and launched into this speech on how she couldn't even consider abortion, so don't ask. She had this real defensive tone, and it pissed me off, so I started yelling, but quiet-like because we were in public. I went off on her about how she shouldn't assume that I was the kind of guy who'd want her to get an abortion. It was my kid too! I told her how she didn't know me at all, but I'd be damned if I'd give up my rights to my child.

"So we sat there, glaring at each other, feeling each other out. But when it dawned on both of us that we were on the same page, that we both wanted this baby, we calmed down a bit and started talking. By then she was almost done with her first trimester, but still not showing. She hadn't told anyone else; she was afraid of how her family would respond.

"I told her I was bat-shit terrified of how my family would respond, and she laughed. That helped. She filled me in on her doctor appointments and her symptoms. She told me she had a feeling it was a girl. And by the end of our meeting, I had her next doctor appointment written down.

"I went to all of her appointments. We started making plans and buying baby stuff. We told our families together when she was five months along; that pretty much sucked because everyone kept assuming we'd just get married, you know?

"The pressure kind of got to us. So we gave dating a shot. It didn't go well; she was still in love with Zack; we weren't really attracted to each other; the only thing we had in common was our baby. I don't know. It felt forced, and we fought a lot when we were trying to be a couple. The weird thing was when we weren't trying to date, we got along pretty well. So we finally gave it up, and told our families to get over it; we weren't going the traditional route to make them happy and ourselves miserable. Those were some fun conversations.

"She had an apartment and a job in Lafayette, so she stayed there, but I got a teaching job and moved back home. Tara was born, and we both fell in love with her. The thing is, I never loved Trish, but seeing her love my daughter, I don't know, it made me care about her, respect her, you know? And vice versa. We both just understood what Tara means to each of us; how it would cripple us if one of us didn't get to be her parent.

"We promised that we'd find a way to raise her together; that neither of us would fight the other for full custody. Trish had Tara the most when she was a baby; she was nursing her, and Tara was so dependent on her mom. I got that and didn't push it. But I'd see her every couple of days, at least. On the weekends, I'd keep her one night so Trish could get some rest. Tara had colic pretty bad for those first few months. That was hard. When she got a little older I started keeping her more and more. Now we have a pretty good routine; we both get pretty equal time. We can fill in for each other when we need to. That's a perk, I guess." He chuckled.

He stopped talking, and I searched for an

appropriate response.

"Wow. That's—just wow. I don't feel like many people can figure out how to co-parent like you two."

He snorted. "I think I might have sugarcoated some of it. Don't get me wrong; we have our fair share of fights and misunderstandings. It was hard when Trish got married because the whole dynamic shifted. And it's not really hard for me to watch Trish with Zack because we weren't ever really romantic. But it is hard for me to watch my daughter have another daddy, not gonna' lie about that. But he's a good guy; he really is, so I just make myself deal with it." He shrugged.

"You're a good guy yourself," I said quietly.

He shrugged again. "I try."

We went home the next day, stopping at Valorie and Tim's to get the trailer. The drive back to Indiana was much more relaxed. We were comfortable around each other. Funny what vomiting and diarrhea will do to bond people.

--

Seventeen
Adley Grant
Excerpt from *Claudia Grant: A Daughter's Perspective*

I swear, the first sound I really remember is the sound of pages turning as my uncle Gibson read to me. He always bragged that he started reading to me the day I was born. He said he wanted me to know the power of words before I knew how to talk. I'd sit in his lap, and he'd read to me. And not children's books. He'd read me works by authors like Twain, Tolstoy, and Emerson.

Of course, I didn't understand any of it. But I loved listening to the rise and fall of his voice which mimicked the rise and fall of his chest. I'd curl up in the crux of his arm, lean my head against his chest, and close my eyes.

Gibson had a radio voice, an old voice, a strong voice. He had a voice that could start or stop a riot. He had a voice that could make women swoon; until they saw the body that voice came from.

Gibson, or Gimpy Gib, was born with physical deformities in his legs. Suffice to say he was not an able-bodied man, nor was he even tolerable looking. But the abnormalities that riddled his body, leaving him unable to walk, and unattractive didn't touch his mind; he was brilliant.

Not obnoxiously brilliant, not the kind of brilliance that won't tolerate other, less than brilliant minds. He saw people. Really saw them, even when they refused to see him.

My father, the one who gets the credit for

coming up with the "Gimpy Gib" nickname, and Gibson were twins. In honor of a story old as time, a knock-off of Cain and Abel, Jacob and Esau, they were complete opposites. For the beginning years of their lives, they hated one another.

My father was handsome, and strong, with almost no book smarts, whereas Gibson was ugly, and weak, and brilliant. For the first twenty-five years, they despised each other. But they were also obligated to each other, and they both had a strong sense of family duty.

Their parents died within two months of each other when Gibson and Dad were eighteen. By then, Dad had married my mother, Claudia, and moved into a small house in town, five miles from home. Together, they inherited joint partnership in the funeral home their parents had started: a business George didn't want and Gibson couldn't run.

As Gibson was physically unable to care for himself, and as there was no other family, Dad and Gibson were forced back into the same house, the red brick, two story funeral home. Claudia loved Gibson (not romantically, mind you, just brotherly/sisterly love). So many people have misunderstood their relationship, and I tired of the rumors years ago.

Dad was her husband; Gibson was her friend. Dad and Gibson couldn't tolerate each other; Mom was caught in the middle of loving them both and trying to keep peace in her house. It was a triangle that didn't bode well. Dad would leave for work—he had a second job at a saw mill--pecking his wife on the lips on his way out the door, and then it would just be Gib and Claudie, as they called each other. He made her laugh, made her think. In turn, it was Claudia who cleaned his room, who cooked his favorite meals, who took time to sit with him and listen as he discussed his ideas.

Claudia, who had married Dad out of high school, started flipping through Gibson's collection of books. Then she started reading. Then she started thinking. Then she formed opinions; the worst of which was this: before she started bearing babies, she wanted to take some courses at the local college.

This did not settle well. While Gibson encouraged, Dad belittled. He fumed. He raged. He demanded that his wife stay in the home and put away these crazy notions.

She did not listen. For a while, she tried to persuade Dad to see the value of an educated woman. For a year, she tried.

And then, throwing off all the sermons pounded into her head, all the submissive wife doctrine knitted into the fibers of her aprons, she just left.

She went to the city. Lived first with an old spinster aunt, then in a rented room; got a job; enrolled in college; saved all her money; didn't answer any of Dad's letters. She entirely ignored the minister from back home who came to her aunt's, drank coffee, and told her how displeasing she was being to the Lord. When he opened his Bible to Proverbs 31, and began reading, she simply stood up, and left the room.

They didn't get divorced. But for five years, they were separated entirely. No communication of any kind. The spinster aunt wrote Daddy when Mom moved out and gave him her new address. Just in case, and because a husband should at least know where his wife was living. Then the aunt occasionally wrote him letters to update him about

Claudia's life. He read the letters; I know this because I found them, years later, in a box, their envelopes slit open. But he never responded.

Then Gibson got sick with a cold that turned into pneumonia. The state of his already weak body only complicated the illness. He spent weeks in the hospital; almost died, yet somehow, pulled through. Then he was sent home, still weak, with no one but a bitter brother to take care of him.

The strangest thing happened to Daddy and Gibson during that first week at home together: maybe they realized that they were the only family they had left; maybe it's just impossible to help someone go to the bathroom, or let someone help you go to the bathroom, without some measure of affection. Maybe they finally expressed the twenty-five years of repressed emotions, and then decided to let it go.

They never said what happened that week. But somehow, they began to care for one another. And then even like each other.

Daddy had people to bury and trees to cut down; he couldn't afford to miss work. They had no money to hire a nurse. At first, Gibson insisted he could survive eight hours alone, thank you very much. He told his brother just to leave a sandwich, a bedpan, and a book, and he'd manage.

They even tried this for one day. But mid-morning, Gib went to transfer himself from the armchair to the wheelchair and fell. He broke two of his fingers and badly bruised a hip trying to catch himself, and then lay on the cold floor for two hours until Daddy came home for lunch.

Something had to be done. Claudia, who by then had graduated with a degree in elementary education, and who was applying at schools for open teaching positions, was the only solution.

Daddy did for Gibson what he wouldn't do for himself: he went after his wife.

Later in life, she would admit that, had he shown up and asked her to come back for his sake, or the sake of their marriage, she would have laughed in his face. But he talked of Gib, and only Gib. He stood in her kitchen, twisting his hat in his hands, staring down at the floor, and told her the state of things.

He didn't apologize for their broken marriage; neither did she.

She invited him to sit down. He did. She offered him a cup of coffee, black, just like he always drank it, and a piece of pineapple upside down cake. He never liked pineapples; she knew that. He ate the cake and told her it was delicious.

Maybe it was that obvious lie, that putting off of his own desires to respect her that made her soften, just a bit. Maybe it was the fact that he got up and washed off his own plate, something he'd never done in years of marriage.

More likely, it was that after he sat that clean china plate gently back in the cabinet, he turned around and looked at her, sitting at the table, coffee cup halfway to her lips, and said, "I hear you're a teacher now."

She took a slow sip. Sat the cup down. Said, "Not yet. I finished my degree. But I haven't been given a position."

Then my father gave my mother the first sincere compliment in their entire relationship. He said, with real confidence, "You will. Any school would be a fool to turn you down. These fancy city kids are lucky to get you."

They made some more polite small talk for an hour. He didn't ask her to come home like he'd planned. He would say later that he just couldn't ask her. He saw her there, in her own kitchen, her own apartment, her own life. He said for the first time, he really saw her; not as his wife, not as the woman who cooked and cleaned and crawled into bed next to him.

He saw her as a woman who was capable of thinking her own thoughts and building her own life. He couldn't ask her to give it up.

So instead he told her he had to get going. He told her thanks for the pineapple upside down cake. He leaned in and awkwardly kissed his wife on the cheek. At the smell of her perfume (which was still the same), he retreated and hustled toward the door.

She followed him, holding the door open. He was almost across the threshold, when she reached out, and placed her hand on his arm. He stopped but didn't turn around to look at her.

"I suppose even country kids need good teachers," she said. "I can't start until next fall anyway. One school's as good as another to start at."

He took a moment to clear his throat, then said, "Thank you." He left.

Two weeks later, she moved back into their home.

Now, I don't want you to go assuming things just picked back up with my parents after a five-year intermission. For one thing, Claudia settled in the guest bedroom. Gibson and Claudia, however, fell quickly back into their old camaraderie. They had much to talk about, and much in common.

Claudia applied at the local school, but they didn't have any openings at the time. She was given the top spot on the substitute list, and told they would keep her in mind when a position opened up. She began subbing often the next fall, and subbed throughout her life, but she never became a full-time teacher.

Instead she discovered her true vocation: authorship, while waiting for what she thought was her dream career. She filled her days with writing a novel and caring for Gibson. He gradually grew stronger and needed less help. She wrote more and more, finishing her first novel within a year of being home. (She would go on to publish fifty novels, several collections of short stories, and a handful of poems throughout her life, becoming the famous Claudia Grant.)

She resumed some of the household duties, but both Gibson and Daddy had become fairly competent at cooking and cleaning in her absence. Out of fear she might leave or gratitude that she'd returned, or maybe just a genuine interest in those "feminine" chores, they each contributed to the running of the house.

They were like three polite roommates.

But underneath the pleasantries, there lurked a broken marriage, made worse by the gossips in their small town. Few could understand their arrangement, even fewer could be kind and keep their opinions to themselves.

My mother refused to return to the church they'd formerly attended; she wouldn't forgive the minister for quoting Proverbs 31 to her all those years ago (it's a grudge she died with). Women who had been friends with her in school suddenly whispered about her behind their hands studded with glinting golden wedding bands.

My father would get strange looks at the grocery because what man does the shopping? What wife lets her husband do the shopping? What exactly was going on in that home?

The rumors were complicated by the presence of Gibson. I don't suppose I need to explain what people assumed about the crippled twin brother and the estranged wife who were home alone all day.

The truth I will say only one time: my mother and Gibson were never lovers.

But for the first year of her return, neither were my parents. And in many ways, my father was jealous of the relationship between his wife and brother.

When my mother returned, she and my father were kind to each other, but little more. Things were awkward. Their love for each other was stale, layered in years of silence, and before that, years of conflict. To keep a fragile peace, neither of them were willing to bring up past hurts.

So they were polite. They spoke only of casual occurrences, mere flippancies.

For a year, they didn't have a single disagreement. Nor did they have a single real conversation. And then my mother got a letter in the mail.

Her manuscript had been accepted for publication. My father hadn't even known she was writing.

He came home from work that day and walked into the house to find my mother jumping up and down, screaming with glee, and clutching a letter in her hand. Gibson was sitting in his wheelchair, face beaming as he clapped for her.

"What's going on?" My father asked in an

amused voice.

She stopped jumping, pushed the letter into his hands, and smiled. As he read, she explained. "My novel—" she gasped to catch her breath, clutching at a cramp in her side, "they want to publish my novel! George, they want to publish my story! I'm going to be an author!"

He had come to that point in the letter, but instead of smiling, he stared dumbly at my mother. "You wrote a book? When did you write a book?"

"She finished it months ago, George. It's really quite good," Gibson said, not catching the tension between my parents, and saying the very worst thing.

George jerked his thumb toward Gibson and demanded, "He's read your book, and you didn't even tell me about it?"

Her smile fell from her face. "George, it's just. . . I didn't mean. . .I thought. . ."

George held up a hand, turned away, and left the house, slamming the door.

He was gone for hours. When he came in at 10 pm, Gibson had shut himself up in his room, and Claudia was sitting at the kitchen table, an empty coffee cup and her manuscript sitting on the tabletop.

He didn't see her sitting there at first. He kicked off his boots, looked up and saw her. "Oh. You're still up."

She nodded, then asked, "Did you eat?"

"Wasn't hungry."

"How about now?"

He shrugged.

"I left the soup on the stove. I'll get you a bowl."

He sat down at the table; a moment later, she

put the bowl and a spoon in front of him, then sat down with him.

She slid her manuscript across the table. He glared at it.

"Would you like to read my novel?"

"Oh, I'm allowed now?"

"I didn't know you would want to read it."

"You didn't offer," he said.

"I'm offering now."

"And what if my opinion falls short of Gibson's?"

"Is that what this is really about? Gibson read it and you didn't? Isn't this what it's always about? I was a fool to think things had changed."

"No, no! It's not about Gibson. Not really. It's about the fact that you'd rather talk to my brother about something important than talk to me. Your husband!"

Their voices were rising, quickly escalating toward a fight that had been brewing for years.

"He shows interest in my life! You think I don't want a *husband*" she sneered at the word, "who shows interest in my life? I've wanted that since we got married. And since we got married you've given me no hints that you care about anything that's important to me!"

"No interest? What about this past year? I've tried, but you don't let me in! Gibson gets all your conversations, all your thoughts! I get polite small talk over dinner!"

"Gibson, Gibson, Gibson! You know why Gibson and I talk? Because he loves me—" At the hard look he gave her, she protested, "No, not like that! It's never been like that, and you know it!"

There was a silence for half a moment, and

then my father asked, "Do I?"

Claudia opened her mouth but couldn't form words. She stared at him for a long moment, then threw out her arm, and overturned his warm soup right into his lap. Then she jumped up and rushed out of the room.

He got up to go after her, splattering soup off his lap and onto the floor. Then sat down. Then got up again; and sat back down.

He sat for a while; remembered he was sitting in a mess of soup. Pulling off his stained trousers and shirt, he tossed them into the dirty laundry hamper. He got a bucket of warm soapy water and a rag and cleaned up the mess.

After that was finished, he got a new bowl of soup (by now, his stomach was growling). He sat down in his underwear and undershirt and ate. All the while, he stared at her manuscript. Finally, he pulled it toward him and began reading.

It was 1:00 am when he stopped reading. He picked it up and carried it down the hall to his wife's bedroom. He knocked on her door; she didn't answer. He knocked again, a little louder. Still nothing.

The thought of going in and rousing her occurred to him. He even put his hand on the knob but before turning it decided it against it. He went to his own bed.

Her story swirled in his head though, and he couldn't sleep. George wasn't an avid reader, just the newspaper or occasional magazine. He hadn't read a novel since school; didn't see the need.

His wife had done what no other author had ever achieved: she'd made her husband enjoy fiction. He'd started reading her novel to prove a point; to prove that he was interested in his wife's work. One chapter in and he discovered he was actually interested in her story. Then he forgot it was *her* story; he forgot the author altogether.

As he laid in bed, unable to sleep, his thoughts jumbled together. One moment he'd be thinking about how to fix his marriage, how to pursue his wife all over again. Then his thoughts would drift back toward her story.

The truth was it was just plain good. He hadn't expected that. How horrible was it that he knew so little about his wife that he hadn't expected her to actually be talented? He wanted to tell her it was good. He wanted to ask how she'd thought it all up. He wanted to share in her excitement that it was to be published.

Just before daybreak, he got out of bed, went to her door, and knocked.

He heard a mumbled, sleepy, "Come in."

He went in and hovered at the end of her bed. She sat up, pulling the covers up to her chin. "What do you want?" She demanded.

"I was just wondering—are you really going to kill off the doctor?"

She stared at him for several moments, hovering on the brink of reconciliation, just before jumping in. "If I tell you, it'll spoil the ending." She paused, then said quietly, "Do you like it? Tell me honestly."

It was the genuine grin that split across my father's face that saved their marriage. "It's the best damn thing I've ever read," he told her; and she always said that was the only book review she ever really needed.

--

155

I am Adley Grant. I married once, but I kept my maiden name. That was how much pride I had in it. Convenient also, when I divorced later.

Undoubtedly, you recognized my name not for its own sake, but for my mother's. It is of course, the reason I kept my maiden name: pride in being her daughter, and the shameless advantage that name and relation gave me in the world of storytelling.

I am a decent storyteller myself—although I tend to ramble. But compared to her, I am a minor writer who will be forgotten or maybe mentioned as a tag-along thought when my mother's name is mentioned. As in, "Oh, yeah, didn't Claudia Grant have a daughter who dabbled in fiction as well? I believe I read one of her short stories. . .not bad."

Make no mistake, I am not jealous. I am still in awe of my mother. To be in her shadow is an honor.

My best piece of writing is actually the biography I wrote about my parents a decade after their deaths, *Claudia Grant: A Daughter's Perspective*. I think that is my job, not to write fiction or try to imitate my mother's gift, but instead to tell the real story of *them*. The story of the adults who shaped me and Bud: Mom and Dad and Uncle Gib. And her—the fourth one, my Aunt Lynn, the woman who can talk to trees.

--

Eighteen
Willie
2013

After we got back from Asheville, Morgan dropped me off at home, and we both seemed reluctant to let our trip come to an end. But I had to get to work, so I made myself tell him goodbye and watched from the porch as he left. He had to go pick up Tara; I could tell how much he was missing her.

During the next week, I picked up the phone so many times to call, but always put it down. I didn't want to intrude on his time with Tara after he'd been away from her for four days. Plus, he was busy. I'd see him drive by with his tractor and baler or a load of bales and we'd wave at each other, but he never stopped.

I was busy myself. When I wasn't at my shifts at the library, I was writing, or searching for another second job. I was at a dead-end with Carolyn's story; I would have to tell Erin that at some point. But I wanted to record what I had discovered leading up to and ending in the cemetery. She should get at least that much of Carolyn's history, even if it ended in pain and grief.

Then at the end of the week, Morgan stopped by.

"Hey," he said when I opened the door. "Do you want to help me out?"

"Depends." I told him.

"Think you could heft some bales around and help me stack them in the barn?"

"I knew you were just keeping me around for

my muscles!" I joked.

He gave me a look that made me blush. "Yeah, that's it," he said. "So, you in or out?"

"Why not? I need a break from the computer screen. Give me a second to change my clothes."

"Want some help with that?" he asked.

My face got redder. "Such a cheeky fellow you are." I said, shaking my head at him. He shrugged.

"Never know, if you don't ask."

I shooed him out the door and sprinted back to my bedroom to put on jeans and boots.

We spent the next hour unloading bales and stacking them. I was a fairly strong woman, but he still outpaced me three to one. By the time the last bale was stacked, I was gasping for breath and he was barely winded.

I smelled like sweat and had pit-stains on my t-shirt and a glean of moisture on my face. My arms were itchy from the hay. I needed a shower, but I was happy to stay in that barn with him and the smell of fresh cut hay.

I sat down on a bale as he handed me a bottle of water. "Thanks." I took several long gulps. He sat down next to me with his own bottle.

"Tara back at Trish's?"

"Yup. All weekend."

"I miss her."

"Me too. Well, mostly. She's had a lot of attitude this week, argued with me about every damn thing. So I'm also kind of glad for a break."

"Oh, she likes to argue? I really can't imagine that."

"Hmm, yeah. It's got to be from Trish. I'm a real easy going, mellow guy."

"Sure, you are."

"Hey, we haven't had a fight in like a solid week!"

"Umm, that's not true. We argued about the route we took home after we missed our exit for the third time."

"You think it's easy to drive a truck and trailer on the interstate?"

"If I say it's a piece of cake, will you have a mellow rebuttal?"

"Try me."

"OK—I'm a better driver than you. You whine an awful lot about that trailer. Don't own it if you can't drive it."

"I'll let you try sometime," he said.

"I can't imagine that I'd run into anyone's car."

He tackled me and pinned me flat on the bale. "Take it back?"

"Or what?"

And then he was kissing me and I was kissing him back. After several long moments, he eased off me and said, "Come inside?"

I leaned up, wrapped my arms around him, and pulled him back down to kiss him again.

"OK."

He got up, grabbed my hand, and pulled me up.

In his bedroom, he picked me up and sat me down on the edge of his bed. He pulled my shirt over my head and unbuckled my jeans. I took his shirt off and unfastened his belt. As I slid his zipper down, I thought this is really finally happening.

And it did.

We finished undressing in haste, and he

pushed me gently back on his bed, giving me one long look up and down, before joining me under the covers.

I won't describe it. Some details should stay between two people.

Afterward we took a shower together, washing each other's hair, and laughing about stupid things.

I felt new around him, vulnerable, but in a good way. My only other experience with sex had been awkward and left me with a feeling of shame. There was none of that this time.

I vaguely felt like I *should* feel guilty. We weren't married; we hadn't even talked about what we were to each other. But I couldn't regret it. Unmarried or not, what we shared was the real thing. I couldn't imagine ever wanting or finding that with someone else, and I knew that to the end of my days, I'd treasure this memory.

We made a chicken, spinach, and cheesy white sauce pasta dish while we listened to Tom Petty and Dave Matthews and told each other stories from our childhoods.

After the last dish was placed in the dishwasher, he came up behind me, put his hands on my hips and started kissing my neck. We went back to his bed and stayed there all night.

It was only when I woke up at two am, with a film over my unbrushed teeth, that I thought two words: birth control. We'd made love three times without any birth control. I tried to get my groggy brain to call up information about ovulation and start counting days from my last period. But I couldn't remember. Then I looked at Morgan, snuggled my body back into his and drifted off to sleep, thinking

"oh, well. What are the odds anyway?"
--

Nineteen
Cheryl and Jane
An Adapted Excerpt from Cheryl's personal
Journals
1962

"I don't know. Don't you think it makes me look fat?" Jane asked, twirling in front of the mirror in Cheryl's bedroom.

"Hardly. You fill it out far better than I ever did."

"And that's a great irony of life, isn't it? How you've had two children already, and are probably working on the third, and somehow you've stayed skinnier than me through it all."

"I'd give my eye teeth for your curves."

"No thanks, I don't need more eye teeth. What are eye teeth anyway?"

"I don't know. They sound like something I could give away and not miss. Are you going to take it or not?"

Jane put her hands on her hips and scrutinized herself in the black cocktail dress one more time: cleavage plumped up tastefully in the heart shaped neckline, bell skirt curved gracefully over her hips.

"What exactly is a Baptist preacher's wife doing with this dress, anyway?"

"Nothing. Absolutely nothing. That's why it's in perfect condition. I love this dress. But I'm willing to give it to you in hopes that it will inspire your husband and we can put this nonsense behind us."

"What if. . ." Jane began but then trailed off.

"What if what, dear?"

"What if there's someone else?"

"Then he's a fool," Cheryl said harshly and quickly, causing Jane to flinch. "And he's no fool," she added.

"Perhaps I'm the fool then."

"What are you talking about?"

"I'm thinking about leaving, Cheryl."

"What? Why?!"

"Because this is not a marriage! This is not what I signed on for! A husband who doesn't show affection."

"You two used to barely be able to keep your hands off each other."

"I'm not talking about that, Cheryl. And you know there's a difference. Sex is one thing; affection is another."

"That's hardly grounds to leave a man, Jane."

"Isn't it? Isn't the whole point of marriage to know and be known? Or is it just to live together, do his laundry, cook his meals, and bear his children? And we see now I can't even do the last one." Jane bit her lip as she began to cry.

"Is that what this is about? I told you, honey, the babies will come."

"No, they won't! Damn it, but we are too good of friends for you to continue lying to me! We both know motherhood is not coming to me!" Jane yelled.

They stared at each other in silence for a moment, Cheryl trying and failing to find the right words.

"It's alright, though. In some ways, it makes it easier. There's no children between us, so it'll be just two broken hearts. And probably just one." Jane dashed at the tears on her cheeks.

"You can't do this," Cheryl whispered.

"I can't or I shouldn't?"

"Both. It will crush him. It will crush your families. It will crush you!"

"That might be. But I can't stay in a cold marriage for a day longer. It's done Cheryl. I'm only telling you so you wouldn't hear it from someone else."

Cheryl was crying now. "Where will you go?"

"Chicago."

"That'll make two of you then. Two small town girls disappearing in the big city."

"What are you talking about?"

"Carolyn, of course."

"I'd heard whispers. So, it's true then? She's disappeared?"

"It's hardly as mysterious as that. She left a note for her family so that they'd know she left on her own free will. Small comfort, though."

"Why'd she do it?"

"They were trying to force her to marry again. Although I suspect there's more to it than that. They're being quite tight-lipped about the whole thing."

"Good for her."

"Umm," Cheryl said, noncommittedly. Just then, Jack cried out and Cheryl left the room to go get him. She came back as Jane was slipping out of the dress and smoothing it out on the bed.

"I don't think I'll borrow this, after all," Jane said, watching her friend pat her son's back as she held him against her shoulder.

"Two weeks. Give it two more weeks. Don't

make this decision rashly."

"Rashly? Cheryl, this has been months coming. You think I haven't been trying?"

"I'm sure you have. I'm just asking for a couple weeks. If nothing else, let Carolyn's disappearance settle in before you give my church ladies something else to gossip about? You owe me that. You have no idea how they can be to the pastor's wife. Coming to me *in confidence with prayer requests* when what they really mean is gossip. And they know you are my dearest friend. There will be no end to the questions. Simon and I have our anniversary trip coming up; let us go away for that in peace? Please?"

"Fine. Two weeks. But only because it's you who's asking."

--

"You want us to do what?" Simon demanded at supper that evening.

"Please, Simon! She's going to leave him! We have to do something!"

"But give up our vacation? Cheryl, we've been saving for this trip for a year. Your mother is set to take the kids! Both kids! For two nights! You bought that lingerie; that's right, I saw it hanging in the back of our closet. I've been thinking thoughts people think pastors don't think, Cheryl. I want to take my wife away and have you to myself for a weekend, is that so much to ask?"

"No, of course not, dear. And believe me, I'm just sick over the idea of not going. But they're our dearest friends, and they're this close to calling it quits!"

Simon pulled Cheryl onto his lap and whispered something in her ear. She swatted at him but grinned.

"See, that's what you'll be giving up," Simon teased her.

"My mom can still take the kids, honey. We'll have a romantic get-away right here in our own home. Picture it, picnic on the living room floor, complete with candle light and fancy cheese."

"You know as well as I do that if we don't leave, people will come around needing just a moment of our time. And just imagine how awkward it will be when you open the door wearing that lingerie. Or nothing at all."

"Obviously, I would put a robe on first."

"Obviously, I do not wish for us to be disturbed."

"I don't want my best friend to lose her husband."

"That's between them, honey."

"But they just need a nudge! A chance to get away from reality and remember how to be a husband and wife. Remember when it was us who needed the nudge? Sometimes a couple needs their friends to believe in their marriage when they can't."

Simon sighed. "Fine. But your mom still takes the kids; and we hide the car, lock the doors, and keep the lights out!"

Cheryl squealed and kissed him on the lips. "I do love you. Thank you, honey."

She got up and began walking out of the kitchen to go check on the kids. She paused in the doorway and looked back at her husband. "That was a dirty trick, what you whispered in my ear. Reminding me of all the sleeping we could do on a weekend away."

Simon laughed as he watched his wife leave.

Twenty
Willie
2013

After that night, Morgan and I couldn't be alone together without making love. We learned all kinds of things about each other in those coming weeks; I said things to him I'd never imagined I'd be able to utter with a straight face. And yet, with Morgan, I felt no embarrassment; we didn't hold back. No secrets; no shame; just intimacy and fun.

We did use condoms after that first night, and I called to schedule an appointment to get on the pill. Pregnancy wasn't really on my radar though. The only child I wanted in my life was Tara.

When I wasn't working or writing, I was hanging out with Morgan and Tara, putting up hay, going to the park, drawing on the sidewalk with chalk, learning all kinds of theme songs to kid cartoons.

When Tara was at her mom's, well, we didn't waste our alone time. His place; my place; on the floor; in the shower; at 3:30 am when we woke up to a thunderstorm.

I was happy. Happier than I'd ever been. I was having amazing sex with the man I'd loved for a long time; I was writing scene after scene of a new novel, images and dialogue coming to me easily; and I was becoming part of a family. I'd found my people. I'd found my purpose. I'd found my place.

And then—the fourth P.

The thing about going to get on birth control: doctors take all the fun out of sex by asking awkward questions while meeting your gaze without blinking.

My doctor asked me matter-of-factly if I was already sexually active or just planning to be.

"Umm, already."

"Alright; and have you been using other forms of birth control?"

"Condoms."

"Every time?"

"Yes. Well, umm, not the first time. Well, actually the first three times." My face was red from my forehead to my chin.

"How long ago was this?"

"Six weeks, I think."

He met my eyes with a long gaze, not judgingly, but bluntly.

"Have you missed a period?"

"Uhh. Well, yeah. Maybe. I haven't had a period in these six weeks, but that's not uncommon for me. I've never been exactly regular."

"You'll need to take a pregnancy test then. I won't prescribe you birth control until we're sure you're not pregnant. I'm a bit overly cautious about this compared to other doctors. My rule is complete abstinence for two weeks, followed by a pregnancy test to be sure. And I'm going to have you take a test today since you had unprotected sex six weeks ago. And especially since you haven't menstruated in six weeks."

"I really don't think I'm pregnant. I haven't felt any different," I told him, trying to convince myself more than him. But now doubts were surfacing: how I'd been smelling things more strongly, feeling slight queasiness in the mornings, how I could pass out into a deep sleep almost instantly.

I can't be pregnant; I can't be pregnant; I can't be pregnant.

But the look in my doctor's eyes confirmed what I knew deep down: I very well (and very easily) could be pregnant.

He gave me the simple, "pee in the cup" instructions and left me. I went across the hall to the bathroom.

Even though I'd gone to the bathroom when I'd first got there, my bladder was full again (another sign I'd ignored). The combination of my shaky hands and the task of aiming for a small plastic cup resulted in a bit of a mess. I wondered how many other women had dribbled their urine on the toilet seat which grossed me out. I did my best to clean up, labeled my sample, and put it in the collection cabinet.

Then I went back to the examination room and waited.

But truthfully, I already knew.

All I could think about was that night in the hotel and Morgan talking about how he'd never really wanted Trish; he'd only wanted his child.

I tried to tell myself we were different. We weren't some casual, drunk one-night stand. Even if we hadn't said it or made plans, we loved each other. Didn't we? We were building some kind of future. Weren't we?

When the doctor came in he gave me one compassionate look, and I burst into tears.

"It's positive, isn't it?" I blubbered through my tears.

"Yes, you're pregnant. And my guess is, based off of what you've told me, you're six weeks along. Of course, you could have gotten pregnant later, even with condoms, but I'd say the six weeks is a pretty good bet."

"What am I going to do?" I whispered.

"May I ask if you are in a relationship with the father?" He asked kindly.

"Yes. At least I think so. But it's not like we were planning our wedding, you know."

"In my experience, the best thing to do is talk to him. Figure out where you both stand. I know this is a great shock. What you need to do now is go home, take some time and let it sink in. I would advise you to seek out a few close people you can trust—your mom, a friend? But before you leave, let's schedule you for two weeks from now, OK, for your first ultrasound? Good, here is some literature and two months' worth of prenatal vitamins. Here is a list of things to avoid." He handed me a plastic hospital bag of pregnancy goodies, and then patted my hand. "Take you time; Marna will schedule you at the front desk. Take care Wilma; I'll see you soon."

I cried all the way home, my vision blurring and my nose running.

I was going to be a mom? How could I have let this happen? How could Morgan have let this happen? I mean, the guy knew he had super mobile sperm, intent on knocking up unsuspecting, unmarried ovaries! You'd think after one unplanned pregnancy the guy would carry around a twelve pack of condoms.

But then again, how stupid, how cliché was I? It's not as if that first night happened out of nowhere! I'd been circling around the idea of having sex with him for weeks leading up to that! Why didn't I plan ahead? Why didn't I go get on birth control at the first "I want to rip his clothes off" thought?

I was not maternal. I didn't have the first inkling on how to be nurturing. I mean, I was coming around to the idea of being a step-mom, but she was already five! Past the tricky baby and toddler stage. She could talk, fed herself, understand basic logic, and pee in the toilet. Tara was practically self-sufficient! And she had a *real* mom for all the shit I couldn't begin to handle.

I'd never been more grateful for or sympathetic toward Trish.

I wanted to sit her down and ask her a litany of questions titled "What to do when Morgan gets you pregnant."

I laughed hysterically and then started crying again.

What was I going to tell my family? Getting pregnant out of wedlock just wasn't done in my family! They were of the firm Baptist belief that one should be married, financially secure, and have a ten-year plan before pro-creating.

Then I had a flashback to a visual aid my college roommates and I had stumbled across in college about dilation. Apparently at 10 centimeters, a woman's vagina was the size of a mayonnaise jar lid. A mayonnaise jar! How in the hell did a woman push *a human being* through an opening that small!? That was just faulty engineering if you asked me!

And I was going to have to do it! I mean, there was always the C-section option, but having my abdomen sliced open didn't sound appealing either. It's not like I'd given an abundance of thought to either my vagina or abdomen over the years, but suddenly I was feeling very attached to them.

Calm down, calm down. I told myself.

Epidural—that's all there is to it. That first contraction hits and you tell the nurse, "excuse me, drug me now, please." And then you channel surf until it's time to push. That's how it was done these days, right? No hours and hours of agony and the serious possibility of drawn out death?

Women didn't still die from childbirth, did they? I mean, statistic wise, it's very rare, right? I should google that. Maybe I shouldn't google that.

I'm not sure an orgasm was worth it for this, I thought next. How is that a fair ratio? Nine seconds of bliss for nine months of misery followed by nineteen hours of unimaginable pain? That math equation was seriously unbalanced.

I was going to kill him. That's all there was to it.

But what if he dumped me first? I mean, killing him was strictly theoretical. I had to have him alive. No way I could do this on my own. But what if he decided the co-parenting was the way to go this time around too?

I didn't want to be a co-parent. I didn't want to share custody and have drop off and pick up times. I didn't want to be a single mom. And I sure as hell didn't want him to end up with someone else later on.

Maybe that had worked for Morgan and Trish. After all, she'd ended up with Zack, the man she really loved. Morgan was just a stand in. But to me he was the real deal, the guy I had loved since I was thirteen, the man I wanted to love until I was ninety-two and our family shipped us off to a nursing home together. (Or separately, depending on how things go.)

But what if that's not what he wanted? What if it was just sex to him?

--

So how was I going to tell him?

The whole invite him on a coffee date and spill the beans over expresso had been done, so that was out. I'm not a copycat. Well, I mean. . . just shut up, OK? Do you think it's enjoyable to be a man's *second* baby momma? Holy Shit, the term "baby momma" now applies to me. Freaking fantastic.

Before I could come up with a plan, I found that I had driven to his house without consciously deciding to go there. A few minutes later, he walked out of the barn and found me, sitting in my car, glaring at the steering wheel. He opened my door and popped his head in.

"Hey, do you want to go out for dinner tonight? Trish is dropping Tara off in a couple hours, and I told her we'd get pizza."

I looked at him and blurted out, "I'm pregnant."

Dead silence while he started at me. "This can't be happening again," Morgan said.

Rage shot through my whole body; rage and disbelief. That is what he said to me? That was all he could come up with? Pointing out his sperm's track record?

On the list of unacceptable responses to a woman telling you she's pregnant, number two is "this can't be happening again." Number one is "is it mine?" At least he had the damn decency to skip number one.

A better woman would have recognized his shock and allowed him to have his reaction, given him grace and space.

I think we've established I am not a better woman, haven't we?

I allowed the anger to erupt from me. "Well it is happening again! To me this time! And maybe this is just a rerun to you, but it's brand new to me! How big of a moron do you have to be to say something like that? Do you think I like having it pointed out that you just go around getting women pregnant willy-nilly! Do you think I like having it thrown in my face that you practically run a sperm bank!"

That might have been just over the line unfair.

"Three! That's the number of women I've been with: my first serious, college girlfriend of two years, Trish, and you! And between you and Trish there was five years. Five years and nine months roughly. Hell, we'll call it six years. Of no sex. So maybe I'm not a saint, but you can stop painting me into a. . . a—" he scrambled to find a word.

I suggested one, "Man whore? Dick? Careless son of a—"

"That's enough!"

"Fine. I'll take that part back. You're not a willy-nilly sperm donor. I'm sorry."

"Well, you should be!"

"And you shouldn't have responded with 'this can't be happening again.' I mean, you have to be aware of how it works right? How we didn't use protection the first time? By the way, why didn't we even talk about it? A guy who has a child already should be OCD about birth control!"

"Oh, so this is all on me, huh? What about you? I thought most promiscuous women used the pill?"

"Promiscuous! You just called me promiscuous?"

"You called me a walking sperm bank!"

"I apologized! But I take it back now!"

"Yeah, well guess what, there are some things you can't take back once they're out there."

"You should know!"

"I can't deal with this right now. I just need a second to process it, OK?"

"You've got to be kidding me! You got Trish pregnant, a woman you claim you didn't ever love, and yet you decide, over a five second cup of coffee, that you'll just handle it and be a dad? But ME, the woman who thought she was in a relationship with you, for ME and OUR child, you need time to think about it? What the hell, Morgan?"

"I didn't---that's not what I mean. Of course, I'm going to do the right thing. It's just you blurt out that you're pregnant and don't even give me a second to take a deep breath before you come out fighting!"

"You know what, Morgan? Just forget it. The last thing I want is for you to 'do the right thing' for the sake of doing the right thing, OK?" And then, without waiting for his next brilliant rebuttal, I yanked my door shut and drove away.

--

Twenty-One
Willie

I ignored all of his calls for three days. I called in sick to the library and stayed in bed trying to figure out what I was going to do. Ignoring my child's father and skipping work didn't give me a sense of confidence that I could handle my life either.

I napped way more than is good for a person, even a pregnant one. Even Lolly, who spent most of her life napping, was awake more than me. I ate everything in my fridge; terrified myself by watching and reading about real life birth stories. I fed Lolly and played with her, trying to convince myself that keeping a cat alive was a prerequisite for raising a human. I also let myself go, forgetting to brush my teeth and shower. At some point, I was going to have to pull myself together. I knew that, but for now I took the easy way out.

On the fourth day, I was startled out of my four-pm nap by someone pounding on my door. I stumbled to the door and peeked out of the curtain.

"Crap," I said, as I let my Granny and Mom in. I'd forgotten that a week ago, I'd invited them over for dinner tonight. Besides Morgan, I hadn't told a single person about the baby. I had specifically been avoiding my mother and grandmother because I didn't feel like I could fool them.

They took one look at me and my house and raised their eyebrows in the exact same way. It was eerie.

"Hi, Mom. Hi, Granny. Umm, I kind of forgot about our dinner."

"Honey, are you not feeling well?" my mom

asked as she leaned down to hoist Lolly into her arm.

"Obviously not." Gran chimed in, without waiting for my response. "She smells like she hasn't showered in three days!"

"What is it? Your stomach? A cold?" Mom asked.

There was another knock on the door. I went to see who it was, leaving Granny and my mom standing there, trying to diagnosis my exact condition, wondering when they'd whittle it down to with-child.

"Great," I muttered to myself seeing who it was. Then, "Go away, Morgan!"

"Not a chance. Open the damn door, Wilma."

"I don't have anything to say to you."

"I have something to say to you. And either I come inside or yell it loud enough for all your neighbors to hear about how we're having a baby." In the pause between that and his next words, I glanced at my mom and grandmother, memorizing their mirrored looks of complete shock. Then, as if Morgan just realized there was another car in the drive that wasn't mine, he said, "ahh, shit!"

I wrenched open the door.

"What?" I growled as I pulled him in and shut the door.

"You look terrible." He gave a brief nod to my Granny and Mom but focused his attention on me. Out of the corner of my eye, I saw Gran and Mom edge over to the kitchen table and both sit down. Mom had her hand over her mouth; Granny looked like she was reviewing a do-it-yourself manual on castration. I could not deal with them right now. Later, I told them silently before lashing into Morgan.

"Honestly, Morgan, the stupid things you say

to me never cease to amaze me."

"I don't mean it like that. If I didn't find you attractive we wouldn't be in this situation, now would we?" he asked, giving me a look that let me know exactly what he was remembering. In spite of myself, I blushed. He reached out and hooked a greasy strand of hair behind my ear. "I just meant, are you feeling OK? Is the baby OK? I didn't even ask you."

And then I started crying. I've never been a good crier either. I tend to snivel and blubber and get snot and spit all over myself.

"Oh, baby. I'm so sorry," he whispered as he pulled me into his chest and hugged me.

For the first time in days, I relaxed. "I'm so afraid," I whispered. "Everyone's going to judge me."

"Don't worry; I've been through this before and have a few survival tips," he said, but this time there was humor in his voice, and I couldn't help it, I giggled. I'm pretty sure I heard a half-grunt, half chuckle come from the maternal cavalry sitting at my kitchen table too.

"You've really got to stop bringing that up," I said into his shirt. Then I took a deep breath and leaned back to look at him, "So. How are we going to do this? I can't promise I'll be as gracious at co-parenting as Trish. . ."

"Who the hell said anything about co-parenting?" he demanded.

"Well, I just assumed—"

"You just assumed what?"

"I don't know! It's not like we were a real couple! Or in love or anything?"

"Is that so?"

"Come on, Morgan! You've never even asked me out on a proper date!"

"I'm confused. What did you think we were doing? We've been together nearly every day for months! We've gone on a long road trip together!" (More sound effects from the maternal cavalry.) "I've let you get to know my daughter; let her get attached to you! And you honestly believed I'd do all that for some literal roll in the hay?" (My Mom choked on a drink of water, and Granny pounded on her back while she sputtered.) "Come on Willie, give me some credit!" Morgan said.

"We never talked about being boyfriend and girlfriend, let alone hinted at the future!"

"How's this for a hint?" He asked harshly, reaching into the pocket of his jeans and pulling out a ring, grabbing my hand, and shoving the ring onto my finger. "I'm in love with you, though God knows why! You're a complete pain in the ass, you've done nothing but make me crazy for months. But there's no way in hell I'm going to co-parent with you and be satisfied with that."

Then he grabbed me and kissed me with enough passion to start something right there.

Granny gave a loud throat-clearing and said, "Your mother is about to have a fainting spell, Wilma Louise."

"I am not! You don't have to act like I'm a prude, Mom. Willie knows she can come to me about sex stuff, don't you dear?" Mom asked.

"Ahhh," I hesitated.

"Fine. I apologize. Your mother has no qualms whatsoever about your pre-marital pregnancy, dear. She is, in fact, not freaking out about how to tell your father," Granny said.

"Oh, I'm freaking out about that. I'm one-hundred percent freaking out about that," Mom said.

"How far along are you, Wilma?" Granny asked.

"Ahh, six weeks?" It came out like a question.

"Are you asking me? How should I know? I wasn't there," Granny said to me, then turned to Mom. "We could try the whole pre-mature angle, if they get married immediately."

Mom shook her head. "No one will buy it. Wilma was a nine-pound baby and Morgan's not exactly a small man. You can't pass off a ten-pound preemie," Mom said.

"It's no use. Best just to face these things head on." Granny nodded. "Do you know, I've actually seen wedding photos where the bride has a baby bump and is literally holding a shotgun? Different world we live in, I tell you." She shook her head. "In my day, if you had a shotgun wedding, you didn't draw attention to it!"

I stared at Morgan, trying to apologize with my eyes. "Umm, Gran, Mom? Would you mind giving Morgan and I some time to work this out?"

"A bit late to be concerned about leaving you alone, isn't it?" Granny asked. Then seeing my look, she rose from her chair with a sigh, "Fine, dear, we'll go. Jesus and I have some talking to do. I specifically prayed against this. . . Come on, Cassandra. You need a glass of wine and a plan on how you're going to tell Ben."

Despite all their comments, they both pulled me into a hug at the door.

"It'll be OK, honey. I love you," Mom whispered in my ear before ducking out, trying to hide her tears from me.

"I'm so sorry you had to see that," I told

Morgan after they left.

"That? That was nothing. You have no idea how many sermons I still get five years after I told my family about Tara."

"Apparently, you didn't learn a thing."

He growled at me as he pulled me to him. "Are you going to marry me or not?"

"Guess I'm gonna' have to, to salvage your reputation if nothing else."

"Damn straight." And he kissed me.

--

We didn't announce my pregnancy from the courthouse rooftop, but we didn't hide it either. People's reactions still varied from awkward to down-right sucky, with a few delayed, but sincere congratulations thrown in. But it was, if not enjoyable, at least bearable.

Then there was Tara's reaction that made up for everyone else's. When we told her over a dinner of mac n cheese, carrot sticks, apple slices, and cupcakes that we wanted to be a family and she was going to have another sibling, she literally squealed. She jumped off her chair and did a happy dance.

My heart swelled with love for that girl; I teared up. It was the first moment I thought, I can do this. I can be a mom because I already have a daughter. Morgan caught my eye and winked at me.

Alright, I thought to myself. This is OK. We're OK. We're a family and forget anyone who judges that. After that, I took a deep breath, and stopped caring about whether or not people were gossiping about me.

We got married in a small church wedding on Saturday October 19th, 2013 with just our closest family and friends. Leanna was my maid of honor;

Morgan's brother Isaiah was his best man. And, of course, Tara was our flower girl. However, Tara told me, matter-of-factly, she was old enough to be my maid of honor if Leanna didn't work out. I was half worried she was going to knock Leanna off, the way Tara kept casting sidelong glares at Leanna at the rehearsal dinner.

I was about eleven weeks along the day we got married, almost to the second trimester. I wasn't showing much, just the slightest thickening at my belly. I wore a simple lacy wedding gown with full length lace sleeves, with my hair in long, loose curls beneath my veil. It was one of the few times in my life that I was so certain I was actually beautiful.

Morgan really was the most beautiful man in the world that day. I couldn't stop looking at him. He wore a black tux, and, in honor of my thirteen-year-old self's wishes, he'd picked out a navy-blue tie. (I'd told him all the embarrassing thoughts I'd had the first time I'd met him; he took it upon himself to bring it up as much as possible. I'd lost count of the number of chocolate milkshakes he'd bought to tease me. But joke or not, this pregnant girl wouldn't reject a milkshake.)

The day went by in a blur: I have snapshot images forever locked in my memory. Our reflection in the full length mirror as my mom fastened passed-down pearls around my neck; Morgan's grin as he saw me walking down the aisle; Tara fidgeting and dancing from foot to foot during the service because she forgot to pee before; the feeling of Gran pressing her cheek to mine in the receiving line, whispering, "I love you, my girl." I can see the mason jar centerpieces; the four-layer cake; the roof of the white tent strung with lights. I can hear the playlist; the toasts; the clinking of forks against glasses as our guests demanded to see a kiss. I can feel my dad's arms around me for our dance, the way my peep toe heels rubbed blisters onto my toes, the cake Morgan smashed into my face.

Most of all though, I remember looking at Morgan, over and over again, thinking, "I get to be with him. This is really happening. I'm his wife."
--

Twenty-Two
Willie

Morgan was kissing my belly, my slip rucked up around my breasts. I wove my fingers through his hair, twisting strands and messaging my husband's head. My husband. I had a husband.

I'd planned to jump him as soon as we slipped the "Do not disturb" sign on the door. But as he unlaced the back of my dress, I found myself actually dozing off. He kissed my shoulder, eased the dress the rest of the way off, leaving me in my push up bra, underwear, and slip. Then he carried me to bed.

I mumbled something about just needing a minute and fell asleep.

I woke up at two am and found him asleep next to me, his arm draped protectively across my belly. I slipped out of my underwear, but left everything else on, and climbed on top of him and kissed him awake. We made love in our dark hotel room, both half asleep and completely relaxed.

It was only afterward that we fully woke up. I was on my back, breathing hard and giggling, and he rolled onto his side to look at me.

"Did you really just take advantage of me while I was sleeping?" he asked.

"Yup. And you liked it."

"I did. You have my permission to wake me up that way any time you want."

"I'll make a note of that," I said.

And now, here we were, the bedside lamp turned on, him tracing shapes on my belly, while I played with his hair. I couldn't think of a single moment when I had been happier. I wanted to stay like that forever. Just us, completely in tune with each other, content to just be.

"I have a question for you," he asked after a while.

"Hmm?" I responded sleepily.

"Why did you change outfits at my grandma's funeral?"

I snapped fully awake. "You KNOW about that? You never said anything!"

"Everybody knew about the girl in the tiny black dress in below freezing temps. My cousins couldn't stop going outside to 'check on the line length,'" he made air quotes, "and my aunts had a running bet about how long you would last."

Even though it was years in the past, my cheeks still flamed with embarrassment. "What?" I groaned. "Do you think they all remember that? And know your wife was that girl?"

He chuckled. "Oh, John and Blake do for sure. Actually—yup everybody. That outfit in that setting—pretty hard to forget."

"So you really did remember me?" I asked, half accusing, half wondering.

"How could I forget these legs?" he asked, running his hand down first one leg and then the other. "Seriously though? What were you thinking? It was like 30 degrees that day!"

"Twenty-eight, actually. With snow flurries. It was to get your attention. And I always thought it failed."

"No, you got my attention all right."

"At your grandma's funeral! Shame on you!"

"Hey, I was grieving, not blind! And shame on you! Do you have any idea the kind of lecture my Grandma would have given you for coming dressed like that to *her* funeral?"

"Oh, trust me. I got the Grandma lecture." I shuddered at the memory.

"My aunt Nell wanted to ask you to leave," he said.

"Your aunt Nell. . . oh! The butcher's ex-wife! She wasn't at the wedding, though was she?"

"No, she's been not speaking to anyone for several years on account of us all liking Uncle Mitch more than her. She made an exception to come to Grandma's funeral and was miserable to everyone until she centered on the inappropriately dressed girl in the parking lot. Then she was bearable to the rest of us, so thanks for that. I actually saw her that night in the grocery store when I came to see you that one time—"

"HOLD UP! Angry deli lady is YOUR AUNT?"

He sighed. "Yes."

"And you didn't tell me?"

"I was trying to get you to go out with me! And you didn't exactly like me, remember? I couldn't imagine saying, 'hey, this angry lady chewing you out about lunch meat is my aunt' would help."

"Point taken. I thought you said she was divorced though? She told me something about her husband being picky about sliced lunch meat."

"She remarried. He's a piece of work though. An alcoholic. She left my uncle—the butcher—to have an affair with this guy and he turned out to be horrible. We think he might actually be abusive; we've tried to get her to leave him several times, but she always screams about how we've just never forgiven her for leaving Uncle Mitch. I don't know.

It's really sad, actually, when I can see past her whole angry, bitter shell. But she makes it hard. It's hard to help someone who cusses you out for asking how they're doing."

"Yeah, that sounds hard." I agreed.

"She used to be so much fun too. She never had any kids, so she pretty much adopted all her nieces and nephews as her own. She bought the coolest presents, surprised each of us with fun little adventures. One time, she checked me out of school, saying there was a family emergency. And then she took me to the zoo. My mom was so mad that she removed Aunt Nell's name from the list of people who could check me out from school." He chuckled. "I miss her, the real Aunt Nell."

"That is sad," I said, softening just slightly toward angry deli lady.

He shook his head, as if he were literally shaking the sad thoughts out of his head. "But let's not talk about sad things. I can't be sad tonight."

"Have you thought of any baby names?" I asked changing the subject for him.

"Not really. You?"

"Umm, what about Theodore for a boy?" I asked.

"Tara already has a Leo for a brother. I don't think we can give her a Theo."

"Oh, that's true."

"I've always liked Vivian for a girl." Morgan said.

"Tara and Vivian. I like it," I said.

--

Twenty-Three
Cheryl and Jane
An Adapted Excerpt from Cheryl's Personal
Journals
1962

Simon slid into bed with his sleeping wife, pulling her body against his own.

"Mmmm, you're home. Finally," she said, rousing from sleep.

"Sorry. I missed dinner time. And bedtime. Again. I didn't want to."

"Who needed you more this time?"

"The Franklin's. Tom passed tonight."

"Oh, Simon. I am sorry."

"Me too. He was a good man and a good friend. He will be missed."

"The arrangements?"

"They'll start making them tomorrow. I imagine it will be at the end of the week. I'll ask Reverend Nicolas to be on call if I'm needed elsewhere." He rubbed Cheryl's bulging belly, smiling at the nudge of their unborn child's foot.

"I think I love this one too," he whispered in Cheryl's ear.

"Lucky girl she is then, to have a papa like you." Cheryl smiled.

"Umm, girl?"

"Just a hunch."

"And do you have just a hunch on the name too, then?"

"How about Nell?"

"How about it."

--

Willie
End of 2013

For three more months, I was the happiest I'd
ever been. We found out the gender at twenty weeks.
We took Tara with us to the ultrasound and she sat on
Morgan's lap, as the technician moved the wand over
my gel-smeared belly, pointing out limbs and organs,
and then saying, "you're having a girl."

Vivian.

I was showing by then; had bought maternity
pants and tops. But my second trimester was bliss
compared to the first, and I was growing more used to
the idea of motherhood every day. Me, the girl who'd
had no interest in babies before, was approaching
strangers in the grocery store to coo over their infants.

By my baby's first for-sure kick, I was in
love. The kind of love mothers of all times have been
trying to describe, but never quite finding the right
words. That's why if you ask a woman to describe
what it is to feel a baby move inside her, she'll only
be able to offer the lamest clichés: the butterfly
flutters, or toads jumping, or sort of like indigestion
mixed with love.

--

Willie
January 2014

I was at the library when I first started having
sharp cramps. They'd come and go, growing in
intensity each time and winding me. But I told
myself not to freak out.

I'd been freaking out over every new ache and

189

pain, calling my doctor often to ask what was normal. And each time, he would patiently calm me down and assure me it was normal.

I was six months along now, just shy of my third trimester. That morning I'd woken up feeling different; it had taken me a while to figure out why. Then, midmorning, I realized my roommate was uncommonly still.

I tried all the tricks, drinking cold drinks, eating a sugary snack, bouncing around a bit, trying to get Vivian to move. She didn't.

I googled—always a bad idea for expecting mothers. After the sixth horror story, I was in tears.

"Just call your doctor, if you're that worried, honey," Morgan told me.

"I don't want to keep bugging him! I call him all the time! They probably recognize my number and roll their eyes, saying it's the hypochondriac again."

"It's their job! I doubt you're bugging them, but even if you are, so what? If it gives you peace of mind that's what matters."

Then Morgan just called for me and talked to my doctor, saying "Ok, yeah, here she is." Morgan handed me the phone.

"Hi Wilma."

"Hi."

"Your husband told me you're worried about lack of movement?"

"Yes."

"OK, when was the last time you remember her moving around regularly?"

"Last night was normal. But I haven't felt anything all morning."

"OK. What we're going to do is a kick count.

Over the next hour, I want you to write down every movement you feel, no matter how light. Then call me back. But Wilma, she is most likely fine. In the third trimester, it is normal for the baby's movements to be less as they run out of room to move."

I got off the phone and did as he instructed. And lo and behold, Vivian started moving. Not as much as usual, but enough to satisfy my doctor which reassured me.

I was scheduled for my regular appointment the next day anyway.

But then the cramps started.

They're just normal cramps, I told myself. Nothing to worry about.

After the library, I went to the bank. It was a Friday and extra busy, with a long line of people before and behind me. I stood in line, smelling everything very strongly. The man in front of me smelled vaguely of cat pee and after shave, the pastor behind me smelled of Tide laundry soap and old books.

I started feeling dizzy and light headed; the cramps were getting stronger and rolling right into each other, one cramp barely releasing my uterus before another grabbed and twisted.

By then, I knew I was feeling contractions; I knew something was wrong, really wrong, and yet, I was rooted to my spot in line, clutching my deposit slip. I couldn't get my brain to work. Couldn't think of what I should do, who I should call. I didn't want to draw attention to myself by calling out, didn't want to go into preterm labor in a small-town bank.

For the rest of my life, some images will be fixed in my mind: the 90's style wallpaper, the pens dangling on chains, the FDIC signs propped in every teller's window, the fresh perm of one of the tellers, the receding hairline and kind eyes of the pastor looking at me as he caught me when I began to fall.

I woke up in the ambulance.

"What's happening?" I asked the EMT, panic in my voice.

"It's going to be OK. We're getting you to the hospital. You're in labor."

"But it's too soon!"

"It'll be OK. Just try to stay calm. It's going to be OK."

--

Twenty-Four
Willie

It wasn't OK.

They told us, in the hospital room, that there was no heartbeat, said they were so very sorry. My doctor cried. The nurses too.

And then I had to give birth.

--

I can't take you there. Not really.

Words fail that kind of grief.

I remember everything and nothing: Morgan's wet cheeks and swollen eyes, the ripped hangnail on his right ring finger. I fixated on that hangnail as I gripped his hands through fruitless contractions.

For a long time, I couldn't look at my husband's hands without also seeing our stillborn daughter cradled in them, that hangnail finger tracing patterns softly across her cheeks.

--

Is it called postpartum depression if your baby is dead? Or is there a different label for that kind of depression?

In the weeks and months to come, after we buried Vivian, I was consumed by a grief so raw that I can't, even now, explain it with words. That kind of grief is just guttural. And I think that's what frightened me the most: the silence, the utter failure of language in the face of a small coffin.

For what do you say at a child's funeral when there are no stories of her to tell? No "remember that time she. . ." No photos except for ultrasound pictures and heartbreaking snapshots of her lifeless body out of the womb. We shared none of those photos.

Grief shared, they say, is bearable.

But how could I share this?

I, alone, really knew her. And all I knew were her kicks and flutters, the secret, whispered, one-sided conversations I had with her as I rubbed my belly. To everyone else, she was mostly theoretical, a bulging womb, a Babies R Us registry, a person-coming-soon.

We all speculated what she would look like, what her personality would be. One of the greatest joys of impeding birth is the not knowing, the endless possibilities, the promise of a lifetime of discovering who this tiny person will become.

That is why a miscarriage or stillbirth is not a lessened grief, but a doubled grief: because there are no stories to share! No memories to cling to! Almost no knowledge at all of who that child is!

And I'm angry! Even now—as my son runs through the house chasing his big sister Tara—even now, I'm angry with a rage that can take my breath away.
--

During that time, I thought again and again of Carolyn; of that day Morgan and I stood in that cemetery and stared at her child's gravestone.

I was now not an outsider to her grief. I was a fellow mother in mourning.

I became convinced that Carolyn had committed suicide after the death of her child. Hadn't Rob said she died years ago? Was that the real family shame? Not that she'd gotten pregnant, but that they'd abandoned her when she needed them most, and she'd killed herself.

Maybe it was far-fetched, this belief that she'd

killed herself. But my mind went to some dark places during that time.

If I wasn't suicidal, I at least struggled to find a reason to want to live. Had it not been for Morgan and Tara, I'm not sure what would have happened to me.

I don't believe that you should put your salvation on other people's shoulders. They couldn't pull me out; they were hurting so badly themselves.

That's what saved me. Their pain forced me to face my own. I chose life because I chose them.

--

Even after I decided to choose life, I struggled with the *how*. How to get out of bed. How to find joy. How to keep breathing, keep going.

Perhaps one day I'll be far enough out from this to be able to find meaning. I'm not there yet. Maybe one day I'll be able to walk with other newly grieving mothers, reteach them how to put toothpaste on their toothbrushes and go from there.

But I'm not really in that place yet.

So if you're waiting for me to write some *this is the meaning I found in my child's death* you'll have to keep waiting.

--

Twenty-Five
Cheryl and Jane
An Adapted Excerpt from Cheryl's Personal
Journals
1962

"I hate to be that friend who says I told you so, but: I told you so." Cheryl said to Jane, leaning over the bed to get a good look at Cassandra.

"You did," Jane whispered. She wasn't looking at Cheryl though. She couldn't tear her eyes away from her daughter's face. "You believed when I couldn't."

"That's not all either. I don't want to take direct credit for this beauty's conception. But I did give up my romantic get-away that led to her creation. So I'll take partial credit."

For this comment, Jane did look at her friend, pointedly and knowingly at her midsection.

"Umm, hmm. And it does appear that you made the best of that terrible weekend of sacrifice."

Cheryl laughed. "I did indeed. Tell me, why is it that having a child-free evening so often leads to another child with me and Simon?"

"Honey, if you need me to answer that question, I'm not sure you've been paying attention."

Cheryl laughed again. "Oh, I've been paying attention. At this exact moment, I'm very much paying attention to the fact that I'm going to have to do this all over again." She grimaced and placed her hand against her back, massaging against the cramp.

"I was secretly hoping we'd give birth on the same day and have birthday twins," Jane said.

"Umm, well. I supposed one day apart is close enough. Scoot on over in that hospital bed, will you?"

"Cheryl! Are you serious?"

"This is my third go 'round, Jane. I'm as serious as a broken condom."

"Nurse!" Jane called out, waving one over. "Honestly, Cheryl. The things you say. It's hard to believe you're a pastor's wife sometimes."

"Stick around. I don't labor well. Other things are going to be said."

--

Three hours later, Cheryl was watching Simon hold their third child.

"Hi, my little Nell. I'm your Daddy."

Cheryl watched the two of them closely, waiting for what Simon would say next. After the births of Patsy and Jack, Simon had held them and made prophecies over their lives. A sort of blessing and birthright, spoken from a man who communed continuously with God.

As he gazed at Nell's tiny face, his silence lengthened. When he placed his hand against his mouth, and began crying, Cheryl grew alarmed.

"What? What is it?"

"I don't want to tell you."

"Tell me Simon!"

"Oh Nell, my sweet girl," he whispered, caressing her soft cheek. "You'll know great sorrow, but even greater joy. And all that you give up, will be restored to you."

--

Willie
Early 2014

I have discovered that healing is offered from the strangest hands. The people I expected to have something to say, stuttered. Or said the worst thing. They wounded with good intentions.

It was the broken people who showed up and bandaged me. The people, who before I avoided out of fear that their grief was contagious, who taught me how to survive. The weary, worn out warriors, who sighed and crouched down on my bathroom floor with me. They're the ones who didn't try to make it better, didn't utter a single callous cliché. They just sat with me, and occasionally remind me to eat.
--

My weary, worn out warrior showed up in the doorway of Morgan's and my bedroom, three weeks after the birth and burial of Vivian.

I stared at her through swollen, blood shot eyes, trying to place her.

And then—my mind clicked. Angry deli-lady. Old biddy. Morgan's estranged aunt Nell who couldn't be bothered to come to our wedding. Here, in my bedroom, now, looking at me without blinking, confronting my grief, when everyone else shifted their gaze after a moment.

"What do you want?" I demanded.

"They say you're not getting out of bed."

"So? What's it to you?"

"Bedsores won't make the grief any easier."

"Who gives a shit? What does it matter? Just leave me alone!"

"I can't."

"You don't even like me."

"That's true," she said. "I don't. But I don't really like anyone."

I blinked at her, dumbfounded. She came over and sat down on the bed next to me, an intimacy that had me scooting away.

"You have to get up, Wilma. Like it or not, you're not dead."

"I want to be."

She shrugged. "Doesn't matter."

"You're a real bitch, you know."

She nodded. "I've been told."

And yet, I obeyed her. Let her help me up and lead me to the shower.

--

Aunt Nell kept showing up. She was exactly who I needed because we didn't like each other; didn't worry about offending or shocking the other with our anger. She was one step removed from me, distant enough that I didn't feel the need to spare her from my grief.

Morgan, my mom, my Granny—the people I was closest to, could only walk so far with me, could only stand so much of my pain because they had their own to carry.

Aunt Nell—she was the bitter aunt nobody knew how to like. She was the woman who couldn't be bothered to show up in times of celebration yet came without flinching in times of grief.

Nobody got her. Except me now. I knew, even before she told me. I knew, because broken mothers recognize each other like we're looking in a mirror. It turns out, you don't have to like each other, to get it.

--

Eventually, she told me, even though I already had it figured out.

Nell, the super fun aunt, married Mitch when they were both really young. He'd moved to Parke County from the south and met Nell at a church picnic. They were crazy, stupidly in love. In 1983, they were poor and just starting out, building their butchering business from nothing. And trying to start a family.

They got pregnant. Quickly, easily. Picked out names and crib sheets.

She miscarriage at two months.

They grieved; recovered; healed.

Got pregnant again.

Miscarried at six weeks.

Repeated this seven times in ten years. Seven miscarriages. Seven dead children. Each one, taking a little more of their parents with them to the grave.

After the seventh, the doctors told her to stop. She was literally killing herself. But what they didn't understand was that she wanted to die.

This aunt who had memorized all of her nieces' and nephews' birthdates, birth stats, favorite foods, movies, animals, and colors, who delighted in buying them gifts and taking them on adventures, couldn't have her own children. And it crushed her spirit.

This woman, who loved her husband so fiercely, couldn't bear both his grief and her own.

She tried to get him to leave her; he wouldn't.

She was angry, broken, physically depleted, spiritually, mentally and emotionally exhausted. She had an affair as a way to get out of her marriage.

It worked. In 1995, Mitch, betrayed and broken himself, gave in and divorced her.

She remarried the man she'd had an affair with, even though by then he was already verbally abusive. They'd been married one year when he began hitting her. She stayed.

That had been nearly twenty years ago. Morgan had been in elementary school, watching helplessly as his beloved, fun aunt became less and less of herself, leaving behind an angry, hurt, scared version of herself no one knew how to reach.

And the saying that hurting people hurt people is the only way to describe how she morphed into angry deli lady, estranged from her family, her own prison guard in a violent marriage to a man she didn't really even love.

--

Twenty-Six
Willie
2014

I'd given birth to our stillborn daughter at twenty-four weeks gestation on January 17th, 2014. She had died in my womb; never took a breath; never cried; never opened her eyes. She weighed one pound, one ounce. Her skin was almost translucent it was so thin. Her organs, especially her lungs, had not finished developing. She was smaller than any of Tara's baby dolls; she literally fit in the palm of one of Morgan's hands.

She was the most heartbreakingly beautiful person I'd ever seen. I held her, studying everything about her: her fingers and toes, the curve of her skull, her papery skin.

When they gently eased her out of my arms, I thought I would die. I wanted to die.

I remember Nell showing up a lot that winter; I remember being forced to eat; I remember the way six-year-old Tara grew too quiet, became this somber wraith of a child struggling to understand that the sister she'd planned for was dead.

For weeks, I couldn't look at Morgan without breaking down. He would try to hold me, and I just couldn't bear it. I felt guilty. I felt I had failed him. Failed our child. It didn't matter what my own Mom or Morgan or the doctors or Granny told me. Vivian had died on my watch, in my womb. Unreasonable or not, I wrestled with that.

I couldn't stop remembering how I'd wished her away in the beginning. How I'd felt when I first found out I was pregnant. How I had wished I wasn't because I didn't want to face it: the judgement, the whispers, the hardship of becoming a mother without first being a wife. Never mind that I'd soon come to love her more fiercely than I've ever loved anyone, those initial feelings haunted me.

I also believed that God was punishing me. I'd had premarital sex and not even been sorry about it. Wasn't that God's go-to punishment for women? Give them babies and then take them away? The Genesis story lies: childbirth isn't the curse; the physical pain isn't the curse. It's the possibility of losing your child to death that haunts women. And even if your child is living, that threat is always there, always hovering.

If God was punishing me, if this seemed *just* to Him, then I was holding my middle finger up to the sky. A giant screw you, God. I'm not forgiving this. I'm not forgetting this.

Spring still came in 2014, even though I didn't want it to. How dare things green up? How dare anything be fertile and bear life in the shadow of my empty womb and empty arms?

My Mom and Granny made me plant a garden with them. As if burying potato eyes and green bean seeds would remind me of the circle of life or something. As if I'd sit back on my hunches, my Crocs covered in mud, and say "Ahh, I get it now."

I didn't get it. There's no "getting it."

I planted the garden anyway. It helped them feel better. That's the only reason I did things: because doing things made other people feel better, made them feel like they were helping.

Things that did not help me feel better (all of which were suggested to me):

Gardening.
Being outside.
Reading the book of Job.
Going to church and having everyone pat
the back of my hand and look at me with
sad, puppy eyes.
Being alone.
Being around people.
Eating
Watching TV.
Reading novels.
Writing.
Seeing other people's babies. (This was a
big one.)
Trying to initiate sex with my husband
after my six week "healing" period.

The first several times we tried to resume our
sex life were pure agony. We'd begun seeing a
therapist for three different sessions: individual,
couple, and family. Our marriage, still so new, was
beginning to flounder. Morgan and I couldn't figure
out how to comfort each other.

Our therapist kept harping on about sexual
intimacy; how the longer we put it off, the harder it
would be to find our closeness again.

But I was just so damn screwed up and
confused about sex. I'd spent the first twenty-two
years of my life being lectured about sex and
abstinence before marriage which led to a whole lot
of deep-seated guilt and shame when I'd gotten "my
cart before the horse" to quote my Granny.

Then I conceived a child out of that forbidden
sex, went through telling everyone and facing their
opinions, speculations, judgments about my moral
character, and had just begun to work through all of

that when our child died.

So you know what? I associated sex with Morgan with the death of our child. How are those thoughts for foreplay?

I was terrified of losing Morgan and Tara too. I'd googled real life stories of stillbirths; a terrible idea. Over and over, I read of couples whose relationships were destroyed because they couldn't figure out how to grieve together.

That was what was happening to us. I also knew that Morgan needed our physical and sexual relationship to resume. I knew he needed me to reach out to him. But every time I tried, I broke down and cried.

In the beginning of April, Nell showed up at our house and demanded that I get dressed. She was taking me for a girls' day to the salon and mall. Everyone kept doing that too; pampering me with highlights and pedicures. Physically, I'd never been better groomed.

She took me to her salon in Terre Haute where they touched up my roots, trimmed my layers, and waxed my brows. Then we went to the mall to browse.

We were sharing a pretzel, making pointless small talk, when Nell bluntly said to me, out of nowhere, "Don't do what I did."

"What's that Nell?"

"Drive your husband away in an effort to save yourself. It won't work. I should know."

I was instantly angry; angry at a lot of people but I unleashed my anger on just one. "Well, no offense Nell, but I'm not running off, having sex with the nearest man I can fine to get my husband to divorce me!"

"I didn't tell you that so you could throw it back in my face," she said.

"Then why did you tell me?"

"Because," she said, drawing out her words slowly, "I want you to learn from my mistakes. I want you to choose joy; choose life. I want you to find a way to go on with your husband and not be looking back in twenty years like I am, realizing you cheated yourself out of the goodness of life because you were too scared."

"Bullshit. Bullshit to your crap, hallmark-channel speech. I'm not interested."

She shook her head. "It's not bullshit, Willie. Look at me. Look at what I let grief do to me. I'm married to a man who hits me on a regular basis, and I don't care enough to fight back. To get out. I've pushed away every single person who's tried to help me, tried to love me in twenty years. Do you know how many times Mitch asked me to come back? Five. He finally stopped asking ten years ago."

"If you know this, then leave him. Leave him. Go back to Mitch; don't go back to Mitch, but leave the asshole. My God, Nell, I don't get you! You know all this, sit here and say it like you're discussing the plotline of a novel you read, not your own damn life! Why don't you take what you're saying, what you *know* and apply it to your freaking life!"

She shrugged. She actually shrugged. "I've made my choices. I just want you to learn from me."

"No, don't you dare make this about me! I'm not you, you got that?"

"Tell me, Willie, what's the emotion you feel most often these days?"

I didn't answer her.

"It's anger, isn't it? No, not anger. Rage.

Rage so intense you actually know why people say the cliché my blood's boiling."

I said, "Yeah, I'm angry. Anger is a normal stage of grief."

"But you can't stay there. And I can see you settling in; gathering your anger around you, pushing everyone else away. It's exactly what I did; that's why I can see it."

"For the last time, I am not doing that! I AM NOT YOU!"

It wasn't until a brief silence fell over the food court that I realized I'd been screaming. It's hard to convince yourself you aren't an angry person when your outburst silences an entire mall food court for an awkward few seconds.

I mumbled an apology to Nell. She waved me off.

"I don't care if you bite my head off. I'm not that easily scared off anymore. All I'm saying is you're going to have to find a way to face your anger or it will steal your whole life. I love you and I love my nephew and Tara. It breaks my heart to think you guys wouldn't find a way through this."

"I'll try." It was the best I could offer. Nell accepted that and let it go.

--

Twenty-Seven
Cheryl and Jane
An Adapted Excerpt from Cheryl's Personal
Journals
2009

"Morgan, lunch is ready!" Cheryl hollered out the back door, watching for his wave before she shut the door.

Jane bounced an almost sleeping Tara against her shoulder, patting her back in that old familiar way that brought back a flood of memories. How many hours had she spent patting babies to sleep in her lifetime? She smiled as she remembered, watching Tara's eyelashes flutter against the curve of her cheek.

Jane loved that exact moment when a baby finally, finally drifted off, her body relaxing under the weight of sleep.

"Oh, good. She's out. Put her in this contraption. It rocks and plays music, you know. Practically changes the baby's diaper too," Cheryl said to Jane.

"In a minute. I'll hold her for a bit."

"With your arthritis?"

"I'm fine."

Cheryl shrugged.

Morgan walked in a few minutes later. "Is she asleep?" He whispered from the door where he was shucking off his boots.

"Yes, honey. Come have lunch," Cheryl said.

Morgan pulled his Grandma into a bear hug. "What would I do without you?" He asked.

"Let's not think of it," Cheryl teased. "Now, wash up."

Jane joined them at the table, rubbing her arms. "It's hard to believe I used to hold a baby for hours on end at one time," Jane said, reaching for the salad tongs.

"You still have the touch. I can't get her to stop screaming, and you pick her up and five minutes later, she's out," Morgan said. "How do you do it?"

"Grandma magic, dear," Jane said.

"And a dollup of whiskey for the gums," Cheryl piped in. "Puts them out like a light every time." She winked.

"A Baptist and a Quaker with whiskey? I'm not buying it. But who am I to question to old grannies?"

"Old?! I'm insulted. Cheryl, are you insulted?"

"I would be but it takes too much energy to get worked up these days," Cheryl replied.

"Well, you are five months older than me. Going downhill much quicker than me too."

"Well, then let me give you some advice. When you finally trip at the top of the hill, dear, tuck and roll. Just tuck and roll. Less broken bones if you don't fight it," Cheryl said.

For a while they all ate in silence, and then Cheryl said, in feigned casualness, "So Jane, how is Willie these days?"

"She's enjoying college. Although what she's going to do with a writing major, I have no idea."

"Oh, and is she dating anyone?"

"No, I don't believe that she is, Cheryl."

"It won't stay that way for long, I'm sure. She's grown up to be quite beautiful, Jane."

209

"Oh, yes. I hate to brag, of course, but I do have attractive grandchildren."

"Is there something you two would like to say, or should I continue acting like I don't know what you're hinting at?" Morgan asked.

"We aren't hinting at anything," Cheryl said.

"Not at all. We are just making grandma-small talk and fishing for compliments on each other's grandchildren," Jane said. "It's something women do in our old age."

"Whatever would we be hinting at?" Cheryl continued.

"Honestly, kids these days. You can't say anything around them without being accused of things," Jane said, shaking her head.

"I would never accuse you two of being sneaky about anything. You're far more likely to just beat someone about the head with it. Now if you don't mind, I have more work to do while Tara's still sleeping."

"Alright, dear. Put your dishes in the sink, though. If you insist on being alone, you'll have to learn to look after yourself," Cheryl said.

Morgan walked back, picked up his plate, and kissed his grandma on the top of the head on his way out of the dining room.

They heard water run in the sink, then shortly after, the front door open and close.

"What in the world was that about?" Jane demanded.

"Oh, honestly, Jane. Like you don't know."

"Willie's barely a freshman in college, and Morgan's a grown man with a one-year old daughter. I hardly know what you're thinking."

"Jane, do you know how I *know* things?"

"Oh, here we go again. The Lord speaks to you and all that. I thought I was the Quaker."

"Well, I do know things. I've watched for years for one of my kids to notice one of yours. When that didn't happen, I watched for our grandkids. And I'm telling you, it's Willie and Morgan."

"That might be, but you could be a little less obvious about it."

"Morgan is going to need a bit of a nudge. And by that, I mean a firm push. And perhaps a kick in the pants. Otherwise he'll be single and lonely the rest of his life, and I won't stand for that."

"Oh, he will not."

"I know my Morgan. The boy is one extreme or the other. Either too causal about his love life, hence that precious baby sleeping in there. Or so gun shy he won't try again."

"Did he really get his heart broken that badly with Trish?" Jane asked.

"Hardly. He is actually going to her wedding, did you know that?"

"Oh, now that is taking it too far."

"I agree. I'm glad they can get along so well for Tara's sake, but I hardly think he needs to go to the wedding of an old lover," Cheryl said.

"Do kids these days even use the word lover?"

"Probably not, but I'm not up on the lingo regarding causal sexual relationships."

"Oh, you aren't? I'm shocked," Jane said.

--

Willie
2014

When I got back home that day, after my trip to the mall with Nell, I was surprised to find Erin's car in our drive. I'd given her Carolyn's story, all that I'd discovered anyway, months ago. We'd briefly talked about it then, and I'd let it go, been consumed with my pregnancy and marriage.

And then the death and birth of my daughter.

I hadn't spared Erin or Carolyn a thought in months. Didn't have the emotional energy to go there. I cared for Tara, Morgan, and my cat, that was the extent of my mental and emotional capabilities. There was nothing left for the mystery of Carolyn.

Inside, Erin and Morgan were making small talk in the kitchen. I joined them, exchanged pleasantries with her, asked about her Dad and the new renters. She told me they'd moved out because they bought a house. The Judson house was currently empty.

Then, in a lull in the conversation, Erin said, "This isn't good enough Willie."

"I know. Look, you don't have to pay me," I told her.

"You need to finish this!"

"There's nowhere to go! No more hints! I'm done chasing Carolyn's sad story."

"Hey, I know you're going through a lot—" Erin started. I cut her off.

"Don't," I told her, my voice threatening. As in, don't you dare bring up Vivian to me.

She sighed. "I'm sorry. I'm just frustrated. The story can't end here—in a graveyard."

I stared at her. Who did she think she was talking to? She was *frustrated*; frustrated about a dead baby. And she excepted me, a mom with empty arms, to somehow find the courage to dive back into a story about another dead child?

How dare she ask that of me*?*

"Maybe we could track down Gerald's family?"

"And say what? Let it go Erin," Morgan told her.

"I can't!"

"Then take what I've given you and do it yourself! But I'm done!" I yelled.

She kept speaking, but at that point Morgan saw that I was on the verge of a breakdown, and gently, but firmly took Erin by the arm and escorted her to the door.

When she was safely on the outside, I slipped down against the kitchen cabinets and started crying. Morgan sat down next to me and gathered me into his arms, pressing his chin against the top of my head. I released into him and, for a long time, we stayed like that, crying together on our kitchen floor. Crying over Carolyn's dead child and our own.

--

A couple days later, I went to the cemetery to visit my daughter. I pulled my jacket tighter against my torso, absentmindedly placing my hand against the last place I'd held my daughter alive.

When I looked toward her grave, I noticed someone was already hunched against the wind, standing at her grave.

I looked for the car and smiled to see whose it was.

"What are you doing here, Granny?" I asked

as I approached her.

"Visiting my people. There are more and more to see every time," she said, reaching out to pull my hand into hers and give it a squeeze.

We stood there in silence for a while.

"I don't know why I come here," I said. "I never get the profound moment of closure I'm waiting for."

"Maybe you should come without expectations then."

"I think Morgan and I are drifting apart. I don't know how to fix us. I don't know how to survive this myself, let alone save our marriage."

I waited, expecting some grandmotherly wisdom to come out of her mouth. She shocked me instead.

"I nearly left your Grandpa when I was your age, did you know that? No, of course not. No one knows that. Besides Cheryl, and she never told a soul. Well, probably Simon; I imagine she told Simon."

"What? You left Grandpa?"

"No, I nearly left Grandpa. I had my suitcase packed, the note written. He was set to find it when he got home from work."

"Why?"

"A thousand good reasons and none at all. We'd tried for years to have kids and couldn't. I was lonely. Marriage wasn't what I had expected. We both worked all the time, had the same conversations over and over, and I eventually realized we weren't saying anything at all. Your Grandpa hadn't had a very nice childhood. It left a lot of scars. Well anyway, I couldn't fix him, and he couldn't fix me. And in the beginning, I thought children would surely be what fixed us both, but they didn't come."

"So, what changed?"

"Cheryl couldn't mind her own damn business. She never could. She showed up on the day I was planning on leaving, repacked my suitcase, ripped up my note, and told me to give it one more chance. She sent us away on a trip that was meant for her and Simon."

Granny paused and looked at me. "On that trip, your mother was conceived."

"And just like that, you were fixed?" I asked.

"No, of course not. Babies never fix broken marriages. That's a terrible burden to put on children to begin with. But Cassie gave us a reason to do the work for each other."

"What if you hadn't had Mom? Would you have stayed?"

Granny shrugged. "Who can say? I hope so. In the end, it was my choice, and I'm glad for it."

"I love Morgan," I whispered.

"I know you do, honey." She squeezed my hand again. "I've known that for a long time. Almost as long as Cheryl."

"I'm glad she wanted us to be together."

"Honey, if Cheryl got it in her head that two people should be together, by golly, they were going to be together! If nothing else, they'd eventually admit defeat and get married just to get her to stop setting them up. Which is why I know you and Morgan will be OK because Cheryl will be driving the Lord crazy with her meddling."

I smiled. "I like to think of her and Vivian up there together, watching over us."

"She always was a baby-hog. And she was fierce about her own. She always said, one day the two of us would share grandma-rights to a grandbaby. When she died, and then you and Morgan got together, I was sad that she didn't live to see it. That day I found out you were pregnant? I vowed to Cheryl that I would love your baby double, until she got to meet her one day. I didn't know it would go the other way 'round, and she'd be loving your baby double until I get there."

--

Twenty-Eight
Willie

That night, after I finished brushing my teeth, I stared at my reflection in the mirror and I knew it was time. I took my long t-shirt and pajama shorts off, took a deep breath, and walked into our bedroom in just my underwear.

Morgan looked up from our bed where he had a stack of students' history papers and his laptop on his lap, grading. He didn't say anything, just looked at me over the top of the glasses slipping down his nose. Then he moved the stack of papers and computer to the nightstand and held the covers open to me.

I walked over to our bed and climbed on top of him and began tenderly kissing his face: his forehead, cheeks, nose, closed eye lids, lips. After a few moments, he stared crying, tears slipping quietly down his cheeks.

It hit me then: how strong he'd been for me, for Tara. Everyone had been so focused on me, keeping me going. I realized Morgan had been neglected, his grief put on hold for weeks because mine took priority.

I cupped his face in my hands. "Look at me."

He did. I swallowed the lump in my throat and said, "Together. We mourn her together." He nodded.

We made love that night for the first time since the week before Vivian was born. It had been months. We were both grieving and broken and out of sync with each other, but somehow, we managed to find our way back.

Afterward, we stayed awake, holding hands, talking about Vivian. We really talked about her, each offering the other our speculations on who she would have been, what she would have liked.

It hurt like hell. But talking about her, wondering about her, kept her alive, just a bit. And that eased a small part of our grief.

I'll never get over losing a child. I'll always feel it. I'll never stop missing Vivian, stop wondering what-if.

That night was not some magic cure-all and we woke the next morning and put her behind us. But it was a turning point, the night we chose to face our pain and let it change us, not ruin us. We chose to honor Vivian's life, not let death steal any more from us.

Slowly life became bearable again.

--

Erin didn't let it go. A few weeks later she texted me, *I found Gerald.*

I thought of ignoring the text, but curiosity got the best of me.

Me: *What do you mean you found him? He'd be ancient by now.*

Erin: *88 to be exact*

Me: *Leave him alone Erin. What are you going to do, confront an 88 year old man about an affair he had decades ago? You could actually kill him.*

Erin: *I already did.*

Me: *You already tried to kill him?!*

Erin: *Calm down. No, of course not. Well, it crossed my mind. . . kidding. . . No, I tried to confront him about it.*

Me: *I don't even want to know.*

Erin: *Yes, you do.*

I didn't respond. She didn't care. *He's in a nursing home. He has Alzheimer's. The really advanced kind. He thinks he's ten years old.*

Me: *I TOLD YOU TO LET IT GO!*

Erin: *And I told you I can't! This is MY family's story. . . not yours. So, it's my call. . .not yours. But I'm not a monster. What do you think, that I interrogated an old man, who thinks he's ten, about an affair he had?*

Me: *Then what did you do?*

Erin: *I talked to him about fishing. And baseball. And then I met his wife.*

Me: *She stayed with him?*

Erin: *I knew you were curious. Yes. She visits him every other day.*

Me: *I don't know if that's sweet or heartbreaking. I wonder if she ever knew about Carolyn?*

Erin: *I'm going to ask her tomorrow.*

Me: *What?*

Erin: *I asked her if I could interview her about her husband's career in Parke County politics, and she agreed to meet me tomorrow at her house.*

Me: *Erin. Don't do this.*

Erin: *Come with me.*

Me: *No.*

Erin: *Willie, I'm going. You can come or not. I'm meeting her at ten am tomorrow.* Erin texted me the address.

I tossed and turned all night. The whole thing just seemed wrong to me. I couldn't let Erin blindside some elderly lady. It wasn't right, and it wasn't fair. If his wife didn't know, what was the point of learning it now? Now, when her husband's memory was so far gone, her anger and betrayal would have nowhere to go?

What if she did know? If she did, she'd stayed with him. That was her business, her choice. Erin had no right to dredge it up. What had happened to Carolyn was tragic and sad, but what good could come from punishing and humiliating the wife?

No, I could not let Erin do this. I had to stop her.

She wouldn't answer my calls or texts. I had no choice but to go to the woman's home.

I pulled into the drive right behind Erin and got out. She actually grinned at me.

"I knew you'd come!"

"I came to stop you!" I hissed, walking up to her. "You can't do this; it isn't right."

Erin shrugged. "It leaves a bad taste in my mouth too, Willie, but it has to be done." She rang the doorbell.

Before I could say anything, the door was being opened and, there, on the other side of the glass door, was a slightly stooped, but well-groomed, well-dressed woman in her eighties.

"Hello Erin, dear. Come on in, and who is this?"

We walked inside. I held out my hand, hating myself for being there; hating Erin more. "Hi, I'm Willie."

"She's a writer. She's come to help me interview you!" Erin's cheery voice made me want to stomp on her toes.

The woman smiled kindly at me. "Oh, that's lovely! I'm Gertrude. But everyone calls me Gerty."

Gerald and Gerty. It was too cutesy. Too married-for-sixty-years adorable. I wanted to cry.

Instead, I took the seat offered to me at Gerty's kitchen table. I drank hot tea from her porcelain, floral-print mug. I accepted a homemade banana nut muffin.

Erin pulled out a tape recorder, yellow legal pad and pen. She tried to slide them over to me. I shook my head at her. No way; if she did this, I wasn't being party to it.

Erin shrugged and took it back. She began making polite small talk and then gradually eased into questions about Gerty's and Gerald's life.

It was painful and embarrassing to watch. Erin was not a natural interviewer. She didn't understand how to let an interview ebb and flow naturally; didn't know when to refocus and redirect the person, when to be flexible and let her change and steer the conversation in a different direction. Erin didn't understand how to tease out more details; read body language.

Twenty minutes in, I was beginning to wonder if she even understood how to have a basic conversation with a real-life human being.

I also picked up on her nervousness at her own deceit; I cringed at the fake questions, knowing she really didn't give two shits about Gerty's childhood.

The writer and the granddaughter in me was boiling. I also began to notice that Gerty knew something was up. She kept flicking her gaze from Erin to me. Enough was enough.

"Erin, I'm sorry, but I have to stop you right there." I turned toward Gerty, and took her hands in mine, noticing the liver spots, the boniness, and sagging skin. "I'm sorry to do this, but Erin got herself invited here under false pretenses. She really wants to ask you about her great-aunt, a woman named Carolyn Calvert. Does that name mean anything to you? If it doesn't, we'll leave right now and apologize for wasting your time."

Gerty stared at me for a long moment, during which her unsure smile faltered and dropped off of her face. She seemed to struggle with a dozen different thoughts and emotions before gently pulling her hands out from mine and leaning back in her chair with a sigh.

"I always wondered when someone would come asking about her. Five decades is much longer than I'd imagined."

"So, you know her?" Erin asked.

Gerty turned to her sharply. "Of course, I knew her. Knew of her. Every scorned wife knows the name of her husband's mistress."

Erin looked at me helplessly. Nope, I told her with my eyes, you opened this wound, so face it.

After several long moments of painful silence, Gerty demanded, "Well? Aren't you going to ask me something? And none of that nonsense about whether or not Gerry always knew he wanted to be a politician."

"Do you know what happened to her?" Erin's voice came out small.

"No, I do not. Nor do I care," Gerty said.

Who could blame her?

"Her baby died," Erin continued.

At this, Gerty flinched, just a little. Then sighed again and said, "That, I did know."

"How?"

Gerty stared at Erin for a long time, before pushing herself up from the table and leaving the room.

222

Was she done with us? Kicking us out? I couldn't say that I would blame her. Erin and I waited for several minutes and were just about to leave, when Gerty came back in holding a yellowed envelope.

"Here." She handed it to Erin, who angled it so I could see too.

It was a large square envelope, postmarked 1961 with Grant Brothers' Funeral Home as a return address. Erin sucked in a breath and opened it.

She pulled out a black and white square photograph. It was like déjà vu; a scene I was too familiar with. It was a picture of the child's gravestone. Nothing more. No letter. No notes on the back.

"That picture nearly killed him. He wanted to find her," Gerty said. "I wouldn't let him. I told him that if he went after her, I'd make sure he lost his other children too."

I couldn't help myself; I had to ask. "Did you know—I mean before this picture, about the baby?"

"Of course, I knew. She came here and told me herself. Told me she would take him away from me; they would be a family. God, I nearly scratched her eyes out, right here in this exact kitchen. She was so sure of herself! So arrogant! What kind of woman stands in her lover's wife's kitchen like that? She had no shame; no remorse."

"What did you do?"

"I damn well nearly killed them. I wanted to. But I had my children to think about. I would be damned before I'd let some little tramp steal their father away. Good riddance to him as a husband. But my children would not suffer."

"So, you stayed with him?"

"Yes."

"You forgave him?"

She shook her head. "No, I never forgave him. At least, I didn't forget. Perhaps I could have if he had been sorry. But he missed her. That was unforgivable."

"No," I said, "Gerald hated her after she got pregnant. She wrote the whole thing out! How he tried to claim the child wasn't his, tried to force her into a creepy marriage with a man named Sanders."

Gerty shook her head. "He didn't hate her. He wanted her, even then. But he feared her too, and he feared me. These two women with the power to ruin him, ruin everything he'd spent his life building. And the truth is, Gerald never loved anyone as much as he loved himself, not me, not her, not his children."

"So, he stayed for his career?" I asked.

"He stayed because I threatened to expose him. I would have done it too; if he had left me and our children for her, I would have ruined them both, and not lost a night's sleep over it. Don't look at me like that!" She told Erin. "They made their choices! What do you think, that a betrayed wife should just bow out gracefully? Well, not me!"

Gerty paused to catch her breath before continuing, "So to save himself, he did what I told him. I did some snooping on her. It wasn't hard, just a matter of asking the right people. A lot of people didn't like her, you know. She was arrogant, so conceited about her looks and charms, sure she was better than the rest of us. I'm sorry, dearie, to speak of your relation so poorly, but the truth is the truth.

"It didn't take me long at all to find Sanders. He'd just been medically discharged from the army and come home a few months before. This poor boy she's led on again and again. I convinced him—easily, mind you—to claim the child was his. Gerald was harder to convince. He was appalled at me actually, refused for days, like he suddenly had morals. But in the end, he went along."

Gerty paused again to take a sip of now-cold tea, before saying, "Then she had the good sense to disappear. We didn't hear anything about her for weeks and weeks, and then this picture arrived. Gerald couldn't get out of bed for a week. I hated him for that. For being able to grieve that child, but not feel the slightest remorse for what he'd done to me and our children. And then we never heard anything from her again. Good riddance."

Gerty had worked herself up; she had to take several deep breaths to calm herself. But she also seemed strangely energized and excited, as if she was glad to finally have someone to share her side with. I couldn't imagine that she was the kind of person who talked openly about this over the years.

Erin and I left after that. I didn't say anything to Erin, just got in my car and left.

I couldn't say what I thought or felt. Part of me understood and sympathized with Gerty; part of me hated the anger, the bitterness that boiled out of her. She'd stayed with her husband out of duty, out of a desire to protect appearance, but she'd never really healed.

Mostly, I was sad. And tired.

What good had come of this? We hadn't really gained any information. Sure, we knew Gerty was the mastermind behind the forced marriage plan; we knew that in some sick, selfish way Gerald had sort of loved Carolyn. Had grieved the death of his third child.

Did that redeem him? Or make it worse? I couldn't decide. I wanted someone to be the monster; I didn't want to sympathize with any of them! Yet I did. I hated and loved all three of them. This triangle of adults ruined by an affair, and a dead, innocent baby in the middle.

The end was still the same. Their child died, and no one knew what had become of Carolyn. Now, on top of that tragedy there was a man in a nursing home with a withered mind, and his wife who remembered it all, who relived it every day in the kitchen she hadn't updated in fifty years.

Carolyn had spoken of winning, of taking him away from Gerty. But the truth is, they had all lost.

--

Twenty-Nine
Willie

After that, I was determined really and truly to let Carolyn go. And I did. Honestly.

I focused on Morgan and Tara. Got my job back at the library part-time. Toyed with the idea of braving a second pregnancy. And began writing a new novel.

Then, one Friday, Tara and I got home from picking her up from her mom's. It was Spring break, and the weekend fell on our time. Morgan and I had Tara until Tuesday, after which, Tara, Trish, Zack, and Leo were going on a mini spring break vacation.

Morgan was staying late at school to finish up some grading, so we could have a relaxing weekend, a rare time in the year before the hay started growing and Morgan would spend all of his free time baling.

I was digging through the freezer, trying to decide what to make for dinner. Tara was watching a movie while she colored. I felt my phone buzz in my back jean pocket and pulled it out to answer it. It was a number I didn't recognize.

"Hello?"

"Hello. Yes, is this Willie?" A gruff voice demanded. Instantly, I knew who he was.

"Yes. Is this Gibson?"

"Left an impression, did I?" He asked.

"Yes, sir you did. How can I help you?"

"I think it is how I can help you, missy. Do you still want to know about Carolyn Calvert?"

I sighed. "Yes."

"Can you meet me at the funeral home? In Asheville? This weekend?"

I thought for a moment. "Yes. If my husband and daughter can come too, yes. It's our spring break, and we're supposed to be having family time before Tara goes back to her mom's. I'm her step-mom, you see."

Gibson cut me off. "I'm sure that's all interesting, but could you give me a definite answer?"

"Yes. We'll leave tonight. Can I call you on this number?"

He sighed. "Yes. It's one of those dadgum cell phones. My niece's. She'll be with me. I'll see you in a couple days."

--

We were on our way to Asheville to meet Gibson. We'd only been in the car for ten minutes, hadn't even made it out of Rockville, when Morgan started making this weird, almost silent, screaming noise deep in his throat. We were stopped at the light at the intersection of 41 and 36.

I looked over at him. Tara stared at him too.

"Daddy, what's the matter with you!?" She yelled.

"Mouse. A Mouse. Oh my God, a mouse just crawled up my leg! Ohmygodohmygodohmygod."

"Daddy! You aren't supposed to say OH MY GOD! Jesus will be sad!"

"I think Daddy's praying, not cussing honey," I told Tara.

Now he was actually making a low keening sound. The light was still red. I thought his eyes were going to bulge out of his head.

"IT'S IN MY PANTS!" He yelled.

"In your pants?!? Oh shit! I thought you meant it crawled over the outside of your pants or something! Why do we have a mouse in the truck, anyway?"

"LOOK AROUND! IT'S LIKE A BUFFET SMORGASHBORGE IN HERE! OH GOD—I CAN'T DO THIS!" And with that, just as the light was turning green, Morgan put the truck in park, then threw his whole weight against the door as he opened it and jumped out.

Before I knew what was happening, or could stop him, my husband, in the middle of the busiest intersection of Rockville, was yanking his jeans down to let the mouse out.

I saw the tiny creature dart off just before I saw flashing blue and red lights pull up behind us.

"Oh, sweet Jesus," I mumbled as I buried my head in my hands.

"Willie!" Tara yelled.

"Still praying, sweetie! Still praying!"

"Hello officer," Morgan said as he buttoned his jeans.

The officer tilted his head and said, "Sir, I'm going to need you to get in and pull your truck into the CVS parking lot and wait for me."

"Sure thing." Morgan got in, fastened his seat belt, signaled to the seriously annoyed and shocked drivers around us, and pulled into the parking lot. Then he killed the engine and waited for the cop.

The three of us didn't speak.

The office tapped on our window, and seeing him, I chuckled.

Morgan rolled down the window.

"Hey, Nate," I said.

He glanced at me, then looked again and smiled. "Oh! Hey Willie! How are you?"

"Not bad. Married to a crazy man who takes his pants down in public, but you know, other than

229

that. . ."

Morgan was looking back and forth between us. Tara, not understanding my tone, mumbled from the back, "My Daddy's not crazy."

Nate, serious again, said, "Yes. About that. Explain."

"There was a mouse. In my pants," Morgan said simply and badly.

"So you stripped in public?"

"Have you ever had a mouse in your pants?" Morgan demanded, in a tone one probably shouldn't use toward law enforcement.

"Can't say that I have," Nate said.

"Talk to me when it happens to you."

"Is Daddy in trouble?" Tara chimed in.

Nate gave Morgan what I think was supposed to be a stern, don't-let-mice-in-your-pants-while-driving look, but then turned to me and Tara and smiled.

"Nah. I don't want to write this up on a ticket. I'd never hear the end of it. You all take care; supposed to have some bad storms rolling in. Nice to see you again, Willie." He walked away.

"How do you know Officer Nate?" Morgan asked.

"We were in the same class, and he dated my cousin Leanna. I mean, they were like, super serious for all of high school and everyone swore they'd get married. So basically, he's my cousin because he witnessed a lot of family drama over a lot to Thanksgiving dinners. My family went into mourning when Leanna dumped him. Especially Granny."

"Gran liked him that much?" Morgan asked in a tone that made me grin.

"Loves him. Still. What? Are you jealous?"

"No! It's just well, I thought I was her favorite."

"Well, I can tell you right now, you wouldn't be the favorite if your name was in the *Sentinel* for public indecency. You've never been on Granny's bad side, but let me tell you, she has strong opinions on being fully clothed in public."

"There was a mouse! IN MY PANTS!"

"Yes, because that explanation makes it less embarrassing."

"I'd rather have that than everyone in the county thinking I'm some kind of pervy lunatic!"

"Maybe nobody who knows you saw you."

"Yeah. OK. Right."

"So, write the whole thing up as a Facebook status and clear your name. It'll be fine. Can we go now?"

"No! We very well cannot go! I've got to check the whole truck to make sure there's not more mice!"

"Look, Daddy! Look, Willie! I found one!" Tara exclaimed.

Morgan and I both whipped our heads around and saw Tara cradling a tiny baby mouse in her hands.

"MOTHER OF GOD! SWEET BABY JESUS!" Morgan yelled.

Tara glared at him. "That was *not* a prayer, Daddy. Here, hold Mr. Mousey. I'll get the rest!"

"The rest!?" I squealed and jumped out of the truck.

--

Thirty
Carolyn
Excerpt from *Nymph of the Oak Tree: A Tale of Coming Home*
May 1st 1962

Carolyn, Gibson, Claudia, and George were sitting in the Grant's kitchen in their apartment over the funeral home. It was late, but they were still all awake, sipping hot tea and talking.

It had been a few weeks since they had placed the gravestone over an empty grave. March 21st. The death date of the child still safely cocooned in her womb. She rubbed her hand over the extended bulge of her belly. Any day now, really.

Carolyn worried constantly that she'd jinxed her child's life; that in faking her baby's death, she'd really foreshadowed it.

But what choice did she have? At first, when she slipped out of that hotel room in Chicago, leaving Colleen sleeping, she'd thought running away would be enough. She hadn't even known where she was going. Just away.

But sometime on the train, her mind had presented her with the image of that business card she'd been using as a bookmark. The Grant Brothers' Funeral Home. She didn't know them, but she knew of them. Their father and her father had served together in the war. They weren't close enough to stay in actual contact, but they exchanged the occasional letter and Christmas card. The father had owned a funeral home in Asheville; his sons had written sometime in her childhood—maybe a decade ago or so—to say that their parents had both died and that they had taken over the funeral home.

Carolyn was a packrat; she gathered and kept bits and pieces of things for years. That funeral home's business card had been the perfect sized bookmark for nearly a decade, and somehow, she'd never lost it. Carolyn was not the sort of person who lost things; her mind was an inventory of possessions and grievances. Nothing was too trivial to be forgotten.

On the train, it came to her all at once. The universe was telling her what to do; where to go. The brothers had a connection to her, yet were distant enough that no one would think of it. She could start over.

They'd been cautious of her at first. Of course, who wouldn't be? She hadn't lied either; told them the straight truth, who she was, what she'd done, how she was expecting the child of a married man. As if there was much missing that. The only thing she hadn't told them, was the thing she never spoke of to anyone. Only Colleen. And look where that had gotten her.

Claudia had been the first to come around. When Carolyn had explained how her lover and family had tried to force her into a marriage to a man who made her skin crawl, Claudia became visibly angry. Right then and there, Carolyn knew to make Claudia an ally.

Once Claudia was on her side, George didn't stand a chance. If his wife loved someone, he loved her too.

Gibson was much harder. For the first two weeks, he barely spoke to her directly, but she would find him watching her often. Watching her like he was taking the measurements of her character: weighing out words like "adulteress" and "expecting mother" against each other to see how they balanced. She knew, instinctively, that Gibson took his time deciding whether or not to love someone. He didn't seem like the kind of man to make casual acquaintances; he either invested in you a hundred percent or not at all.

And maybe it would have been "not at all" in regards to her if it hadn't been for the nightmares.

Carolyn had arrived at the Grants' that winter; they'd agreed to let her stay in the guest bedroom. By the end of January, Claudia had turned over all the funeral home receptionist's duties to Carolyn so that she could focus on her writing.

Carolyn had a job and a place to live. The baby was due in May; she was beginning to feel like she was getting her life together, like maybe she could support and raise a child on her own. By February, no one—not her parents, not Gerald, not Sanders—had come after her. She breathed a sigh of relief. Maybe she'd be left alone.

But then the nightmares started. She dreamed of being forced to marry Sandy while Gerald's wife sat in the front row, holding *her* newborn. She dreamed of Gerald finding her and taking *her* child. What could she do to stop him? He was a lawyer; he knew the laws and the loopholes. He had the perfect family image, the connections, the favor of everyone he knew.

Her own family didn't support her or believe her. What protection did she have for herself and her child?

The nightmares were so vivid that she would wake herself crying out as her child was lifted out of her arms. She'd slept with a married man; more than that, she'd had the arrogance to stand in his wife's kitchen and taunt her. Carolyn saw herself for who she was; no one could call her names she hadn't called herself. But *surely*, even she didn't deserve to have her child ripped from her arms?

Even if she did deserve that, she wouldn't allow it. This child was the first true blessing she'd been given; deserved or not, she was fighting to keep her.

But how could she protect her little family?

She had the nightmares every night, then couldn't sleep afterwards. She began wandering into the kitchen to make herself some hot tea. On the second night, she stumbled into the kitchen to find the light already on and Gibson sitting at the table.

"Oh, hello. I was just, ahh, getting a drink. I didn't mean to bother you. I'll leave."

"No, stay. Please," he said.

She hesitated, then turned back and sat down.

"There's still hot water in the kettle if you want some," Gibson told her.

"Thank you." She got up and got a mug, poured her water, and put a tea bag in to steep.

"Bad dreams?" he asked after a few moments.

"Umm, yes. How did you know?"

"I heard you cry out."

She blushed and stared into her mug.

"I'm sorry if I woke you," she said.

"You didn't," he said.

"Oh."

"I've never been able to sleep for longer than a few hours at a time. I usually get up around two a.m. and can't get back to sleep until three thirty or four, and then I'm up at six."

"Oh," she said again.

"So, would you like to tell me what your nightmares are about?" He asked.

"I thought if you spoke of a bad dream it made it come true," she said.

He arched an eyebrow. "Horse shit. Fear loses its power when you speak about it."

"Is that so? What other things do you know, oh wise one?"

He chuckled. "I know that if you steep that tea any longer, you might just as well chewed on the tea bag."

She fished the tea bag out, took a drink, and made a face.

"Told you," he said.

"I don't really like tea to begin with. It just seemed like the beverage of choice for late night trips to the kitchen."

"You could have a glass of warm milk."

"I never understood that. Why would anyone want their milk warm?" Carolyn said.

"It's supposed to be comforting."

"More like curdled," she said, making a face.

"Well, if you don't want hot tea or warm milk as a nightcap, I believe that leaves things in the alcoholic family. But then, that won't work either." Gibson flicked his gaze to her belly and she blushed again.

"How could you do it?" Gibson asked her. "I've been trying to figure you out, and it just doesn't add up. How you can be so compassionate with grieving families, yet were able to have sex with a married man? I'm afraid I'd like you to be one or the other: either completely despicable, a Jezebel if you will, or a saint like the Mother Mary. I find it incredibly frustrating that you're both; I find *you* incredibly frustrating."

"Well, I find you incredibly rude and insensitive! How dare you? This is none of your business! I am none of your business!"

Gibson just shrugged and took another sip of his tea, unfazed by her yelling. "Adultery is everyone's business. That's the point. It's a violation of a couple's deepest intimacy; there is no privacy because it affects everyone else. You can't sleep with another woman's husband and insist on your own privacy. It doesn't work like that. You betrayed a marriage, the fabric of society, and yourself."

"So, stone me," she snarled at him.

"I should hardly think I'm qualified for that." He shook his head and held out of his hands. "I've never had a very good aim anyway."

"Seems pretty spot on to me."

"I'm not judging you or condemning you. I'm just pointing out the facts."

"Well, thank you. Honestly, I wasn't sure what the facts were."

"Grace."

"Excuse me?"

"I said grace. Instead of stoning. Although, I imagine, being stoned would be less painful."

"What are you, some kind of priest or something?"

He laughed. "I'm not Catholic."

"What are you then?"

He stared at her for a long moment before answering, "I'm just a man in a wheelchair with a lot of time to think."

She rolled her eyes, got up, and left.

--

But after that, their middle of the night talks over tea became a regular thing. She boiled the water and took down the mugs, he doctored her tea with just the right amount of sugar and milk, so that she found she liked hot tea after all.

They talked for two hours straight every night and then each went back to bed.

Over the next month, her child continued to grow, stretching the skin of her belly so tautly that she was constantly itchy. The hot tea seemed to wake her child too; he or she would somersault and roll, throwing legs and elbows.

Carolyn began taking Gibson's hand and placing it on her belly, allowing him to feel her child move around. Gibson would get a small, half smile on his face and watch in fascination.

Perhaps it was that intimacy that made her open up about her nightmare. Before long, she'd told Gibson her greatest fear: that Gerald would be able to take her child from her.

In the end, it was Gibson's idea that they place a tombstone in the cemetery and send back word to Gerald and her family that the child had died. If they sent a picture of the tombstone, why would anyone question it? Demand to see a death certificate? It could work, Gibson told her.

It was Gibson who convinced Claudia and George to go along with it. If they were deceiving some people, they were doing it to protect an unborn child and her mother. Anyway, Gerald and her parents had made their choice; they had pushed Carolyn into a corner.

Was it right, what they did? Placing the

tombstone, taking a picture, and mailing that picture and nothing else, to both her parents and Gerald? Would they accept that without question or come looking for her? Perhaps they'd made a terrible mistake. Perhaps she'd heaped still more sins on her head.

It was May now; her child due anytime. And tonight, they were all sitting in the kitchen, laughing about that day's funeral mishaps. It had been the funeral of an elderly woman who had a lively cast of family members who squabbled through the service but gave each other tearful hugs at the grave side.

As they were sitting around the table, laughing, Carolyn found herself watching George and Claudia: the way they looked at each other, having silent conversations even in the midst of a larger group conversation.

Carolyn was hit with a wave of longing for what they had. But what right did she have to ask for that? When she'd taken that from another wife? In cheating another woman, she had cheated herself.

Then out of nowhere, Carolyn was hit with an image: of George and Claudia, holding a brand-new baby girl, their daughter. That knowing, that the three of them would be a family, felt like a stab to her heart.

--

Thirty-One
Adley Grant
Excerpt from *Claudia Grant: A Daughter's Perspective*

"I like to picture God as a homeless man, sitting on a bench in the middle of a busy park, feeding the birds from a crumpled, brown, paper bag.

Or I like to picture God as a jolly baker, round belly straining against his flour-coated apron, laughing at his latest creation.

Or I like to picture God (and I think this is the most scandalous) as a woman.

'But Jesus is a man!' the people say.

'Ya got me there.

But the mystery of the trinity, pre-incarnation, is tricky and gender-less, or gender-more. Because God is Spirit, both genders and neither. Male and Female were created in the image of God. So if masculine is divine, so is feminine. And maybe, just maybe it's time for the Church to calm down about women being spiritual equals of men. Stop telling us to serve in the scullery but be silent in the sanctuary.

If you think I'm talking nonsense, that of course women and men are spiritually equal then let me ask you this. How does it make you feel when I say, 'God has been so good to me; She is generous.'

If that makes you feel angry, but you're totally cool with God being referred to in the masculine pronoun, you need to repent. Yup, I said repent.

If both pronouns make you uncomfortable, because you recognize that it is inadequate to limit Yahweh to a human pronoun, then we're in *agreement. God is more and beyond; our language and humanity fails to capture 'Him.' But we do the best we can with our measly pronouns and names for The Big Guy In the Sky.*

'She' has her own name for 'Herself.' It is too lofty for us to imagine, let alone speak. Our simple minds would explode, our finite tongues would fester to speak the Infinite. There is a holy language, but we only faintly remember it. Our best writers and artists, our most brilliant theologians, even they only know the guttural, simplest one syllable words of this language.

So, to speak of the abstract, the Spirit, that which we do not, and cannot yet comprehend, we use the concrete, the simple, the human, the gender-specific pronouns. And God mercifully allows this.

And if God allows Himself to be spoken of as a man, She's just as willing to be referred to as a woman."

You should have read the comments and emails I got from some ultra-conservative Christians after the publication of the above in a devotional. I was called a liberal, a heretic, and a whore. I didn't think Christians were allowed to call women whores, but that's between them and Jesus. As for liberal: I've learned to embrace the title. As for heretic, well that chafes a bit. I'm uncomfortable with images of the burning stake.

But I am a divorced woman who used to be in leadership ministry; I dared to preach to men as well as women and children. I am used to being uncomfortable. I am, sadly, also used to being condemned.

Here is where many of you are warming up your Bible verses. I am familiar with Paul. I daresay

I've wrestled with his words far more than you have. I don't mean that disrespectfully; I simply wish to assure you that I have spent years, *years* of my life studying, questioning, praying about God's calling on my life. Me, a person with a vagina. It's really too bad I wasn't born with a penis instead; then I could know for sure that preaching the Gospel, from a pulpit, wasn't a sin.

Oh, well now I'm getting snippy again. And I probably made you uncomfortable saying "penis" and "vagina." Whoops.

Many people who were able to overcome my womanhood, and graciously concede that my mind and spirit just might have useful things to say about God, could not overcome my divorced-ness. I was asked to resign from the church where I had been pastoring for fifteen years. One man even helpfully commented that perhaps it was my arrogance to believe that I could preach that had cost me my marriage. To serve God's flock, I had undoubtedly forsaken and neglected my husband.

Now I just sound downright angry. That's because I am.

Churches put pastors on pedestals, but only to elevate them to the microscope. God help you if you're found fallible. And God Himself can't help you if you're found fallible and female.

Male pastors are allowed to have family and marriage troubles. People are sympathetic to him; they often remind his wife and children to be understanding of the church's demands on him. There are whole sections in Christians bookstores instructing a woman on how to be a good pastor's wife, how to provide him with the home stability he needs to go forth and lead.

Would you like to know how many books there are for *husbands* of pastors? Even that sentence feels wrong, doesn't it?

If a woman-pastor's marriage fails, she is blamed. She should have been a wife first; and the poor children, how will they ever survive having a mother who dared to lead?

Maybe that's not every church, every Christian's response. I hope it isn't. But that was the reaction of my church, of the people I carried to Jesus until I stumbled and they tumbled out of my arms.

From the dirt, where they laid sprawled and confused, with broken legs and twisted ankles and scuffed up elbows, they stared up at me in betrayal. My brokenness was offensive to them. In response, God's flock duct taped this shepherdess's mouth. They left my hands unbound though, so I picked up my pen.

--

Let me give you a quick timeline of my life: I was born in 1962 to George and Claudia Grant. I went to college in 1980-84. During '85-'89 I got married, went to seminary, and gave birth to twin boys. In 1990, I began pastoring a Methodist church. In 1995, when I was thirty-three, my boys nine, my marriage ten, and my ministry five, my parents got in a car accident and both died on impact.

That grief transformed me, as a wife, as a mother, as a pastor, as a woman. That's an understatement, but I can't go into that here. This is a quick, factual overview void (or mostly void) of emotion.

A decade later, in 2004, I was hit by another blow; my husband asked for a divorce. The boys had graduated high school that spring and left for colleges that fall. Their absence forced us to realize that we'd had a broken marriage for a long time; we had just been too busy to realize it. There was no infidelity; no abuse. No catastrophic, and therefore "acceptable" reason to get divorced. Just a lifetime of unresolved conflict, petty resentments, mismanagement of money, and too little sex. He just wasn't in love with me anymore. And while I was willing to stay married, he was not.

Again, I skip over the details for the sake of brevity and self-preservation.

By 2005, we were divorced; by that spring, I was asked to resign from the church.

I had shamelessly piggy-backed off of my mother's name as a writer and established a modest writing career for myself starting in the early '90s. In contrast to my mother's agnosticism, I wrote about faith: mostly short devotionals and short, modern-day fairy tales with spiritual themes.

In the two years prior to my parents' death, I had been working on a novel about a modern-day Nymph, inspired by my Aunt Lynn, the woman who I swore could talk to trees. I was fifty thousand words deep into *The Riddlemaker* when my parents collided into a tree at sixty miles per hour, killing them both instantly.

Six months after their burial, I tried to return to that story, but it was emotional agony. I put it away. (I've revisited it every few years, wondering if now will be the time when the Muse comes back, but it never is.)

I made a small, secondary income off of my writing. After the divorce and job loss, I needed that income to become primary and larger. Much larger. Even with alimony, I was struggling financially.

So. I visited their graves and asked for permission. Then I went to Gibson and asked for his blessing. When I felt that I had both, I submitted a book proposal about a biography on my mother. My agent jumped on the idea. My mother's novels were still printed; they were read in college lit courses, on airplanes, in bedrooms. Loved anew by each generation.

A few biographies had been written during her life, with her begrudging permission. But even with her interviews, the biographies were only a vague picture of the real Claudia Grant. And here was her child, her only child, offering her up.

I nearly gave myself ulcers over it. No one was more protective of my mother and father than I was. I felt cheap and dirty, as if I was selling them. I felt like a traitor.

The flip side was that I was the only person I trusted to tell their stories with dignity and grace. I could decide what went in and what stayed out.

Even telling myself this, I found it difficult to sleep.

It wasn't until Uncle Gib looked me in the eye and said, "Let me ask you something, sweet pea."

"What Gib?"

"Are you going to be able to put those boys of yours through school without selling your mama's story?"

"Well, no. Probably not."

"Then she'd want you to sell it," he said, nodding his head.

"You don't know that."

"Like hell I don't! Chris and Kyle were her whole world. She left you nearly all of the money she made from writing, and if it wasn't for your skunk of an ex-husband, it'd be that money putting them through college now."

That was true. In the midst of our divorce, it came out that my ex had gambled away nearly *all* of the small fortune we'd inherited from my parents. Brad had managed our finances for our entire marriage. I'd always hated numbers and justified my hands-off attitude by saying "I trust my husband completely. He'll always do what's best for us."

He hadn't. I had been foolish; refusing to see what I didn't want to see. As a result, all of the money we'd set aside for Chris and Kyle's tuition was gone. Just gone.

My parents had paid for my college, even seminary, though my mother didn't believe in God, and despised the church. Not being burdened with student debt was a great gift; it was something I wanted to give my sons.

Aunt Lynn sat down two plates of BLT's, one in front of Gibson and one in front of me, and then squeezed my shoulder. "Write it, Ad. Gibson's right; she'd write it herself for her grandsons. And you're the only person who can do her and George justice. Just do me a favor, will you?"

"What?"

"Don't use my maiden name when I come up," she said.

I gave her a puzzled look. I had to think hard to even remember Aunt Lynn's maiden name; I'd only heard it referenced a few times in my whole life. Calvert; that was it, wasn't it?

"OK," I said, not seeing why it mattered.

"Thanks."

"Now, if I were you, I'd leave out the time she got food poisoning and threw up during a book reading. She hated that story. Other than that, I think she'd be OK with the truth," Gibson told me.

"You mean, the whole her leaving Daddy part," I said.

"Yes, I mean that. She wasn't ashamed of that. And to understand your mother and daddy, you have to understand that season in their marriage. She never would have become a writer if she hadn't left him for those years."

I grabbed a scrap envelope out of their pile of mail strewn across the table and pulled a cap off of a pen with my teeth. "OK, tell me what you remember, Uncle Gib."

--

I didn't realize how much I didn't know about my parents until I started writing out their whole life story. My mother had told me that I could read her journals when she was good and dead, but not before then. After they died, I still only read bits and pieces. While her personal journals brought me comfort, they were also agony to read because they made me realize how much I still missed her. Even now. Always.

I'd skipped almost entirely over the journals she kept just prior to and during her estrangement from Daddy. Some things a child just doesn't want to know. I was afraid of what I'd find out about both of them. Afraid they'd crush me with their human-ness. Mom always told me to be careful when you go snooping. You never know who you're going to find.

But in the end, it wasn't those broken-marriage journals that shocked me. It was a couple of entries from the year 1962, the year I was born.

--

Thirty-Two
Willie
2014

We arrived at the funeral home the next afternoon, parked next to a minivan with a chair lift. I'd spoken with Gibson on the phone an hour earlier; he'd said they were already there and would wait in the cemetery.

We got out of the truck and walked across the lawn toward the plot. Tara was her regular chatty self, but after a few moments, she picked up on Morgan's and my silence and tension.

What had I been thinking coming here? To the grave of an infant, when my own had only been buried for a few months? I wanted to turn back and run. Yet I kept walking.

We spotted them right away. A bent, frail old man in a powerchair and a middle-aged woman standing next to him.

In that moment, I knew what he'd asked me here for; knew what he had to tell me; maybe I'd known it all along.

Maybe that's why I'd come.

Because my child was dead, but Carolyn's was very much alive.

--

I don't remember fainting, but I woke up inside the funeral home on a couch in the same office where I'd first spoken to Gibson over the phone. That had been nearly a year ago now. There he was, sitting in his powerchair, peering over the top of his

248

glasses at me. Tara was sitting in his lap, slowly powering his chair back and forth. No one paid her enough attention to tell her to stop.

"Well, that was a bit dramatic, my dear," he told me in that gravelly voice of his.

I eased up slowly, gave my worried husband a faint smile. "Why do I get the feeling you live for dramatic scenes?" I asked Gibson.

He chuckled. "I fear by the end of this day, your fainting will have been the least dramatic part. Child, if you do not stop pushing this chair back and forth you're going to make me seasick."

"Tara, stop," Morgan said, and then, for good measure, lifted her off of Gibson's lap and plopped her down next to me. I looked at her and she grinned, a jolly rancher slipping out of her mouth and onto her leg.

"Whoops," she said, picking it up and popping it right back into her mouth.

At that moment, Verona stuck her head in and asked, "Would anyone like some sweet tea? Sandwiches? I've a tray made up here." She bustled into the room and pretended to be busy arranging things, but I'm fairly certain she was looking for a reason to hover.

"I suppose we should do introductions, although I'm sure we've all figured out who's who." Gibson held out a gnarled hand, his skin so thin I could see every vein. "I'm Gibson. And this is my niece Adley Grant. And you are Wilma, Morgan, and Tara. There now that introductions are through, I can get to why I asked you to meet me."

I interrupted him. "That's obvious. To tell me that that grave out there is empty. Am I right?"

He nodded.

"So Carolyn's child has always been alive. And, I assume Carolyn is alive too?"

He nodded again.

"Do you know where she is?"

"Of course. You could say we've kept in touch."

"So it was an open adoption then?" I asked, glancing at Adley.

"Open adoption?" He asked, then catching my gaze, burst out laughing. "My dear, perhaps you don't know nearly as much as you think you do."

"Oh?"

"Adley is not Carolyn's child."

"Isn't she though? You helped Carolyn fake her child's death so Gerald couldn't come after her. Then Carolyn gave Adley up for adoption to your brother and his wife."

"What a lovely story! But no, the truth is both less and more complex than all that."

"What do you say you just tell us the truth then?" Morgan asked.

"I can't. It's not my story to tell. You'll have to ask my wife."

"You wife?" I asked, rubbing my temples.

"Yes. My wife. Carolyn Calvert, though she's been going by Lynn Grant for so long now, neither of us think of her as Carolyn Calvert anymore."

Lynn Grant. That name tickled in the back of my mind but I couldn't place where I'd heard it. I pushed it aside for the larger revelation.

"You married her!"

"Does this surprise you?" He looked at me.

"No. Ahh, it's just. Well! You haven't exactly made this very easy! The first time I asked you about Carolyn Calvert you nearly bit my head off insisting you didn't know her. And now you're saying she's your wife."

"I'm sorry for our first conversation. You said you were connected to the Calvert family. My wife has been nothing but hurt by them. It was eventually easier just to let them all go. I wasn't so sure digging up the past was a good idea. You can't make a new body out of old bones."

I wasn't entirely sure what that meant. "So why am I here now?" I asked.

He shrugged. "My wife has always suffered from nightmares. For as long as I've known her. They've usually been bearable though; just a few a month or so. But now she has nightmares nearly every night and can't sleep. I think, perhaps, it is time."

"Time for what?"

"Time for her to face it. Time for her to go back. Time for her to forgive herself."

"Does she know you asked me here?"

He got a guilty look on his face. "Uhh, no, she doesn't exactly know about you at all."

"You didn't tell her that she has a great niece who's looking for her?"

"Well, no."

"And you didn't tell her I've been snooping around in her past trying to figure out what happened to her so I could report back to her niece?"

"I did not."

"And now, we're just going to blindside her with all this?"

"That's the gist."

"Fantastic."

My gut told me that this was a bad idea. But

we left Morgan, Tara, and Adley and went anyway.

We met up with Lynn at the Biltmore Estate. Gibson had told me on the way (I was driving his mini-van despite my protests that I didn't feel comfortable driving his vehicle) that Lynn had worked for years on the gardening crew there. Her age had finally forced her to retire, but she still volunteered a couple days a week to pull weeds and give advice.

Gibson had told her something vague about me being a writer, and then asked, "How 'bout you give her the grand tour of the gardens, Honey?" So she did.

After the tour, the three of us sat down on a bench; well, Gibson sat next to the park bench, but you get the idea. I had been studying Carolyn— Lynn, I mean. Her hair was a mix of white and gray; long and wavy and tied back into a loose French braid. She wore square-rimmed glasses, no make-up besides a touch of lipstick, faded Levi's, a brown billowing tunic, and bright pink Toms.

She wore her crows feet and wrinkles around her mouth like she owned them. Her hands were a gardener's hands: her nails clipped and filed, but with dirt peeking through the coral polish. The only jewelry she wore was a plain gold wedding band, no diamond.

Everything about her appearance—besides her bright pink shoes—was simple, minimalistic, earthy.

It was unnerving to be in her presence after I had assumed she was dead. Even more so because I knew the nitty-gritty details of her past, but she didn't know that I knew.

"Lynn, Willie here wasn't actually interested in the garden tour," Gibson said. Lynn had been talking for several minutes about the various flowers and plants.

"That's not true!" I protested. "I was very much interested."

"Fine. She's a regular tree-hugging, new age hippie. But that's not the only reason she wanted to meet you."

He was making it sound like this was all on me. I glared at Gibson.

"Err, what I mean to say is—ahh, damn. Willie is from Parke County and she's been writing and researching about you."

The look she gave me made my soul shrivel a little. When I said Lynn was earthy what I meant was she was barely contained thunderstorm.

"Excuse me?" she demanded.

I gave Gibson a look that was meant to convey: "I'll knock those wheels out from under you if you don't fix this" but he was engrossed in his hands.

"Well, I ahh. I rented the house you grew up in, you see? Off of a man named Rob—he'd be your nephew, you sister Colleen's?"

"I am aware of my family tree," she said.

"Yes. Of course. Well no, that's just the point. Maybe you're aware, but your family, at least Rob and his daughter Erin, have no idea what happened to you. Rob straight up told me that you died before he was born. And Erin has spent her whole life wondering what happened to you. So she found your journals and asked me to read them and then try to figure out what became of you."

"You read my journals?"

"Umm, yes. But only because Erin paid me to."

"My great niece—whom I've never met—
paid you to snoop in my journals?"

"Ahhh. . ."

"Answer the question."

"Yes."

"You've made money off of my past?"

"Well, I never actually took the check. I felt
like I failed because I couldn't find out anything after
we found your child's grave—fake grave. . ."

"Who's we?"

"My husband."

"So there are more people you invited into
snooping about me?"

"Well, just him and Erin. And I might have
asked around about you, to you know, like the
librarian and some of the court house past employees,
and," my voice dropped very quietly, "umm,
Gertrude."

I don't want to belabor the storm metaphor,
and go on about her eyes shooting lightning bolts, but
that's really what it was like. She just sat there in
silence, staring at me, this inner rage visible in her
eyes.

"And how did you find me?" she finally
asked.

"Well, this Grant Brothers' Funeral Home
business card fell out of your journal, and Morgan,
that's my husband, told me we should visit. So, we
did, and that's how we met Verona, who had contact
information for Gibson. He blew me off at first, and
I'd seen your child's grave, so I kind of assumed the
worst. I went back home and tried to forget about
you, and ahh, some personal stuff happened. . ."

She interrupted me, "Oh, so you get to have
vague personal stuff, but we're folding my dirty

laundry on a park bench?"

"Alright. Fair enough. I got pregnant. Married Morgan. And had premature labor and my daughter was stillborn."

She didn't offer her condolences; she didn't soften even a little toward me; she continued to stare so unflinchingly that I felt like she could actually read my mind. Finally, she nodded, just slightly, as if to say, I still don't like you, or trust you, but I recognize you've suffered too.

"And then?" she asked.

"And then what?"

"How did you end up sitting here with me today?"

"Well, Erin refused to give up. She found out Gerald was still alive—" Lynn flinched just a bit. I questioned if I should tell her the next bit, but I was this far into it. "He has advanced Alzheimer's and is in the nursing home. Erin contacted Gerty, ahh, Gerald's wife."

"I know full well who she is," Lynn snapped.

By now, I'd decided the best way through this was just to charge straight ahead, get it out and over with, so I kept talking. "Erin told me she was going to interview Gerty and I went, more to stop her than anything. It went horribly. In the end, Gerty didn't tell us anything we didn't already know. Except that she tried to force you to marry Sanders."

"It was her idea?"

"Yes."

"Go on."

"And you ran away, and the next and last time they heard anything about you it was when you sent that picture of your child's gravestone." Again, I debated adding the next part, but went ahead. "She said he didn't get out of bed for days after that picture came."

"And that should make me feel guilty?" She demanded.

"I don't know. I'm not your judge. I'm just reporting to you."

"Reporting to me about my own damn life. You can sit there and pretend to be unbiased, pretend to be some objective journalist just following the story. But the truth is, you've meddled in my life! I've moved on. Made my peace as best I could; and here you are digging it all up!"

"You haven't made you peace with anything, Lynn." Gibson said. Finally, something from him.

"I was wondering when you'd pipe up, you old bastard," she snapped at him. "This is your doing, of course."

Gibson, for all of his earlier silence, didn't so much as blink at her "old bastard" comment (a comment I thought bordered on verbal abuse—but who's asking me). If anything, he sat up to his full height, straightening out his bent spine, and met his wife's glare directly.

"Yes, you're damn right it is my doing. I've spent decades letting you run from your past, thinking I was protecting you. And look where it's got us? We haven't seen our son in years; not since he called to tell you Colleen had cancer and asked you to come see her."

My mind was trying to keep up and read between the lines. Their son? He meant Carolyn and Gerald's child or did Gibson and Carolyn go on to have more children?

Gibson was still talking. "You refused to see her. She was your sister, Lynn! She deserved better than that; better than you ignoring her while she died."

"You think I don't know that? You think that doesn't haunt me, every single day?" Lynn yelled, then lowered her voice.

"Then why did you do it?" Gibson asked.

"Because I couldn't go back there! You know that!"

"Lynn, it was decades ago! You need to let this go."

"But it doesn't matter how many years have gone by; if I were to go back, I'd still be that eighteen-year-old girl. It won't matter who I've been since; what I've done with my life."

"But nobody really knows," I said. "I mean, most of the people I talked to had stories about you just up to you graduating high school. Gerald and Gerty stayed in a miserable marriage just to avoid the rumors. Your own family didn't even believe it when you told them the truth. I think Gibson is right; you seem to be your own prison guard in this."

"And *you* should butt out. What do you know about scandals and small towns? What do you know about your past haunting your whole life?" Lynn demanded.

"I know my fair share, thank you," I snapped back. "What, you think you're the only woman in the world who's been judged? Come on. I'm not saying what you did was OK. Not at all. Gerty told me she wanted to murder you, and I can't say that I blame her one bit. But you're still allowed to change, Carolyn. You're allowed to not be that girl anymore."

"Thank you for the motivational speech. Really, it was lovely. Passive-aggressively condescending, but lovely. But there's no point in going back. My parents are dead, and now Colleen. What would I even go back for?"

"But Erin wants to know you!" I protested.

"And our son wants you to make peace about this, so he can. I miss him, Lynn," Gibson said.

"You think I don't? But he knows he can call anytime. Can come home, to his real home, anytime. Quite frankly, I don't appreciate him trying to stonewall me into this. I won't be bullied. Not by any of you! Willie, I demand that you stop this project immediately. Under no circumstances, do I give you my permission to give my contact information to Erin. And Gibson, once and for all, you should stop trying to fix my past! *This* is my home! *This* is my life! Leave me alone about it!" She crossed her arms and glared at both of us.

"Willie," she continued, shifting toward me, "don't take this the wrong way, but I never want to see you again. You'll of course have to help get Gibson back to Adley. I've got to get back to work. Gibson, I'll see you at home, and I suggest we pretend this awful experience never happened." She stood up, appeared about to storm off, but stopped to give Gibson a mostly angry, but begrudgingly affectionate kiss on the lips. Then she glared at him; nodded curtly at me, and walked off, her shirt billowing out behind her.

Gibson and I sat in awkward silence for a while. Then I said dryly, "Well, we'd better get you back to Adley, you old bastard."

He burst out laughing and laughed until he gave himself a coughing fit. He wiped his eyes while he collected himself. "You can see why I love her then?"

"Oh, yes. She's a regular peach. I thoroughly

enjoyed our lovely chat."

He smiled at me. "Not many people can come through her anger unscathed. You're alright in my book, girl."

"I might look unscathed, but I'm fairly certain I'll be crying in a bathroom stall later."

"You and me both, my girl. You and me both."

"I do have one question for you Gibson."

"What's that?"

"Who is Adley, then?"

"Adley? But I told you, she's my niece. My brother George and Claudia's daughter."

"So she wasn't secretly Carolyn's and they adopted her?" I really didn't want to let this theory go.

Gibson chuckled. "No. That would have been a good twist to the story, but no. Claudia had Adley six months after our son was born. They were both only children and grew up more as siblings than cousins. Whew, they were a pair. Still are. She goes and visits him and reports back to us. And since she stayed close, and Claudia and George are both gone, she takes care of us like we're her parents. She was married once; has two grown sons, twins like me and George. Anyway, that's the family history for you."

"So you really haven't seen your son in years?"

Gibson shook his head. "Lynn and Bud had been on rocky ground for a good long while. She refused to understand why he wanted to connect with both her family and Gerald's."

"And that didn't bother you?"

Gibson shrugged. "He's my boy. My son. I wanted him from the first time Lynn pressed my hand against her belly, and I felt him squirm. Maybe I didn't like it, that he wanted to meet his biological father. But it was something he needed for himself. I could understand that."

"How have you stood it then? Not seeing him at all?"

"Oh, I talk to him every day. He calls; I call. Now we even do that—oh what's it called? With the computer?"

"Skype?"

"Yes. Skype. I'd go see him too, Lynn be damned. But I can't travel much with my health. Long trips take a toll on me. And he refuses, just refuses to come home. Like his mother, to a fault. And speaking of my health, I do think we should be getting back, my girl. This day has worn me out."

--

Thirty-Three
Willie

Two things happened that June of 2014. I found out that I was pregnant, and Nell called me to tell me she was getting a divorce. We cried together on the phone, and we weren't sure if they were tears of joy or relief or fear.

That summer Nell ripped her life away from an abusive husband and I grew a second human being. We were both terrified, sure that at any moment it was all going to end badly.

By the end of the summer, she was legally divorced with a restraining order. She moved to Terre Haute, got an apartment, and a new job as a receptionist. She saw a therapist and found a support group and attended both weekly. She started practicing yoga.

Morgan and I helped her move; well, I watched and carried throw pillows. Standing in her apartment, I couldn't help but think back on the first time I'd met Nell at the deli. She was a new woman; a woman who had finally fought for herself and come out on the other side. Now she got her lunch meat sliced however she damn well pleased.

--

I wasn't exactly surprised when Nell informed me, that fall, that she and Mitch had started talking again. She told me over a cinnamon roll in the mall (because apparently that's where we have all our major conversations).

She tried to say it casually and I had the good graces to play along.

"Oh?" I said. "And how's Mitch?"

"Good. Really good." I noticed the breathlessness in her voice, the small smile, but I didn't point them out.

Instead, I asked if she was ready to baby shop in bulk. I was trying to stock up on clothes for my little boy.

--

A week before Christmas, and about two months before my due date, I pulled into the parking lot of Nell's apartment building at nine am. We were supposed to get a jump on our last-minute Christmas shopping. We were early risers about procrastinating.

I penguin-waddled my pregnant self to the door, and when I knocked, Mitch answered.

"Oh, hey. Uhh, Nell and I are supposed to go shopping," I said.

"She told me. Come on in, Willie. She's in the shower."

He was in a T-shirt and shorts and had very clearly spent the night. His hair was also still wet. I felt a little awkward, but he was unfazed.

"Want some breakfast?" He asked. "I was just getting started on some bacon and eggs."

I was going to say no, but my stomach gave a loud grumble. "If you have extra, but I don't want to intrude," I said.

He waved me off as he walked toward the kitchen. "You can make the toast."

I fed slices of toast into the toaster while he cracked eggs into one skillet and fried bacon in another. "Nell microwaves the bacon," he said, shaking his head. "She insists it's just as good, but I think it's a waste."

"Morgan does the same thing. He has one of those infomercial bacon cookers. You know, the plastic
thing that you drape the bacon over?" I said.

"This thing?" Mitch pulled one out of a cabinet.

"Yup."

"I hate this thing. Nell always lets the grease set up and then, guess who gets to scrape it out later?"

"Stop harping about my bacon cooker," Nell said, walking into the kitchen as she tousled her hair with a towel. "It works perfectly! Cooks the bacon completely evenly and drains the grease! No painful splatters while you're frying. No messy skillet to clean."

"She auditions for infomercials in her free time," Mitch told me.

"I'm bound to get one sometime too! Just look at these model hands!" She picked up the butter dish and gestured around it, showing it off from every angle. It was then that I noticed the new diamond ring on her finger. I grabbed her hand and yanked her toward me.

"What is this?" I demanded, looking between the two of them.

Nell blushed and gave me a sheepish look while Mitch grinned at me. "I convinced her to marry me again."

"You're getting married?!?"

"Not getting married. We are married," he said.

"WHAT? And you didn't tell me?? Nell!"

"Don't be mad at me," she said quietly.

"You could have at least invited me," I pouted.

"Look Willie, we love you. But this needed to be between me and Nell, OK? When you've been through everything we've been through, you don't really want everyone and their opinions at your second wedding."

I nodded. "I get that." I smiled at Nell. "I'm happy for you. Really. You both deserve so much happiness."

She hugged me, then pulled back and said to Mitch, "You're burning that bacon, honey. Guess my bacon cooker isn't such a dumb thing after all, is it?"

--

Willie
February 2015

When I was in high school, I started writing at least a dozen different novels. I'd have this brilliant idea for a plot, or a strong female character; I write furiously for about twenty pages, then have terrible writer's block and let the story go. I have a whole binder somewhere of embarrassing starts to romance novels. As soon as I find it, it's going straight to the shredder and then the burn barrel.

The main reason I'd stop writing each story was lack of life experience. I'd try to write my characters through experiences I had no clue about. Like once, I tried to write about my main character giving birth. But I couldn't do it because I had no idea how to describe it. Can and should a writer describe pain she's never lived through? Is it credible? Is it a disservice to those who have really suffered that same pain?

I don't know. But in high school, I couldn't do it. Couldn't write about pregnancy or labor. I foolishly wished to have experienced contractions so that I could describe them. Now that I've experienced both pregnancy and labor, I still find it nearly impossible to describe.

I had severe anxiety throughout my entire pregnancy with my son. I kept waiting for him to die. I was afraid to hope, afraid to plan.

With Vivian, I'd gone through labor, but it was so shrouded with grief that I struggled to remember the physical feelings of contractions and pushing.

So even though this was my second pregnancy and second labor and second child, it was like it was the first time again. I had no concept of what was "normal."

With my son, I went full term and then some. Every part of my body was sore and swollen; my skin was stretched so tautly that it constantly itched. If I drank two ounces of water, I had to pee twenty minutes later. I got up no less than four times to waddle to the bathroom at night.   I was uncomfortable, tired, moody, and terrified. Then I would have random outburst of happiness and cry folding tiny baby boy clothes. I wanted Morgan to rub my feet, but not touch me while he was doing it. I wanted to eat all the time. But I didn't know what sounded good, and I didn't understand why Morgan couldn't just read my mind and figure it out.

My feet ached. My back ached. My pelvic floor ached. I'd never given a thought about my "pelvic floor" until it started aching. I was suddenly, constantly aware of every bone and muscle in my body because they all hurt. Even my fingers felt different, like fat little sausages bulging against their casings.

My hair had never looked better, and my boobs could put a lingerie model out of a job (well, until they saw the rest of me).

I was beyond annoyed with people asking me when my due date was, or how I felt, or if I was nervous about labor. I had a complete emotional breakdown in the grocery store with Tara when a stranger asked me how long my labor was with Tara because my second labor would probably be half the time. How could I explain, in the ice cream aisle, that this is my third child, but kind of still my first because I didn't get Tara till she was five, but I love her like she grew in my uterus anyway, and my second daughter actually died in my uterus, and thanks for asking, yes, sure, I'm mostly fine, and do you know if the *Prairie Farm's* ice cream is on sale or is just the *Ben and Jerry's*?

My water broke on February 12th at 5:03 p.m. in my car while I was in line at the drive through at Burger King. I was getting a pre-dinner chocolate milkshake and Tara chicken nuggets if she promised to keep her mouth shut to her Dad. *Technically*, Morgan and I had been eating clean and healthy for my entire pregnancy. I'd been willing to try (or avoid) anything to help my body carry and deliver this child safely.

But I was officially forty-one weeks pregnant, borderline hysterical, and out of will power. I looked at my bulging belly hourly and barked "GET OUT!" He wasn't listening, so I was eating my feelings.

So anyway, two cars from the window, I had this "Oh shit, I'm peeing myself. Well, this is a new low" moment, but then when I tried to, you know, clench to stop peeing, and I had no control over it. It just kept seeping out.

So then I sat there, wondering is my water breaking or am I peeing myself? When my water breaks, won't it be a dramatic gush? It's always a GUSH in the movies. This is a trickle. But it doesn't smell like pee. How am I going to be able to clean this out of my car seats? I should still get my milkshake, though, right?

"Ahhh, shit," I mumbled under my breath because whatever this liquid was, it just kept trickling out of me. I wiggled uncomfortably in my wet seat.

"Willie, you said a bad word," Tara, the cursing police, announced in her 'I'm telling Jesus' voice.

"Yup. I did. And I meant it. Hand me my cell phone, please, Tara."

"I'm watching something!"

"Phone, Tara. Now."

She leaned forward and placed it into my outstretched hand. I called Morgan.

He answered as I pulled up to the drive through window.

"Hey, honey," Morgan said.

The cashier announced my total at the same time.

"Where are you?" Morgan asked.

I handed the girl my debit card while I answered Morgan. "I'm at Burger King."

"What are you doing at Burger King?"

"Here's your card and your receipt," the cashier said.

"What do you think I'm doing at Burger King, Morgan?" I leaned out the window and took my card back. "I'm getting my pregnant self some effing ice cream. Is that OK with you?" The girl handed me Tara's chicken nuggets; she had a look on her face that indicated she'd heard me yelling at my husband.

She mumbled at me to have a great day and graciously let the window close before (I'm assuming) turning to her co-workers and talking about the crazy, preggo lady.

"Willie, are you OK?" Morgan asked.

I was not.

"Willie said a bad word, Daddy!" Tara yelled.

I ignored Tara and said, "I'm not sure, but I think my water broke." And then I slurped milkshake through my straw while I drove out of the parking lot.

"You think your water broke and you stopped to get ice cream?!?"

"No. It broke while I was getting ice cream."

"And, yet, you still got the ice cream."

"The ice cream is not the point, Morgan."

"The point is, if you are in labor, you shouldn't be eating anything."

"My doctor said light eating is fine."

"A milkshake is not light eating, Wilma."

"It's a small."

"Willie."

"Fine." I plopped my milkshake in my cup-holder and pouted.

"We need to get to the hospital then, right?"

"Yeah. I'll be home in ten."

"You're driving?! You shouldn't be driving!"

"Well, I am."

"Pull over! I will come and get you!"

"I'll be home quicker than the time it will take for you to get the truck warmed up. Just chill out. I'm like five miles away now," I said.

"Fine."

"I'll see you in a minute," I said.

"Don't drink that milkshake," Morgan repeated.

"I hate you."

"I know."

I got off the phone just as my first real contraction hit, and I said a word that had Tara lecturing me all over again.

--

Thirty-Four
Willie

I'd had morning sickness nearly every morning for the entire first trimester. And I told myself, during my daily puking time, that it was a sign of a healthy pregnancy, and to be grateful. But I was so glad when that stage was over though because it was miserable.

That was supposed to be the end of vomiting. Bad morning sickness during the beginning, terrible contraction pain at the end. I accepted that's how it would be. The two weren't supposed to mix.

But the contractions were so intense that I threw up three times while I was in labor. Three. Times. I will never, ever drink a chocolate milkshake again. (Yeah, yeah, that's a lie. Don't call a girl out on all the outrageous things she says while in labor.)

I knew by about the third contraction that I was not a light music and breathe through the pain kind of girl. I was an epidural girl. When I was five centimeters dilated and having contractions every four-to-five minutes, I got my epidural. To my dying day, I will always have warm feelings for the man who gave me my epidural. In the moment, I think I loved him more than Morgan.

After that, my mind wasn't so consumed by the pain that I felt much more "present" for the birth of my son. I could still vaguely feel, and see, my contractions but they were more of a tightening sensation and slight to moderate cramp rather than f-bomb dropping, toe curling, cat-scratching my uterus to shreds, agony.

I labored for fourteen hours; transitioned the last three centimeters in thirty minutes, pushed for twenty after that, tore slightly and then there he was, out of my womb and onto my chest at 7:44 am on Friday, February 13th 2015.

He was breathing. He was screaming, his tiny, perfect face screwed up in a thoroughly-pissed-off expression.

"He's really real," I whispered in amazement.

A nurse chuckled at my comment. "You'd be surprised how many moms say that."

There was so much activity going on around us. I was vaguely aware of delivering my placenta and then of my doctor stitching me up. But those were secondary memories, eclipsed by what was going on with my son. They let me hold him for as long as I wanted at first before starting all of his routines and tests. I knew I needed to let the nurse have him, but after he squalled for a few minutes, he settled into me, his skin against mine, and I never wanted to let him go. I knew, as soon as I did, time would start again, our lives would lurch forward and it would never be just him and me again. Other people, countless people, would want to hold him, snuggle him, know him. And I would have to share.

We named him Franklin Charles Lewis. Frankie.

After he passed his Apgar test, the nurses cleaned him up, diapered, and swaddled him. They went to pass him back to me, but I told them to let Morgan hold him. Morgan had been patiently waiting, hovering protectively over me and Frankie in turn, bouncing on the balls of his feet in anticipation. As much as I wanted to have Frankie all to myself forever and forever, I felt an equal desire to see him in Morgan's arms.

Morgan had none of that new Dad unease around our seven-pound, two-ounce son. He scooped Frankie out of the nurse's arms with a gentleness and protectiveness that made me tear up. Then he carefully made his way over to the "dad chair," sat down, and cradled our son, staring at him, mesmerized.

I snapped a dozen pictures on my iPhone of those first father-son moments. Over the next couple days, we took so many "firsts" pictures: Tara and Frankie meeting for the first time; Tara deemed him "just precious and squishable"; Frankie and all of his grandparents, aunts and uncles, cousins. Frankie and Granny; Frankie and Aunt Nell and Uncle Mitch.

And so many of Frankie and me, his momma.

Labor hadn't done much for my appearance. I looked and felt utterly exhausted. My hair was greasy in a messy bun; I had bags and dark circles under my eyes. My face and hands (and whole body really) was puffy. Excuse the expression, but I felt (and I imagine looked) like raw meat, run over by a semi truck "down there." It was several hours after his birth before I could get a shower. I had no desire or energy to apply make-up and do my hair. I had just labored and given birth, and I felt strangely proud of my exhausted, but triumphant appearance. I felt like I had earned it.

So I took countless selfies with Frankie and grinned big when I saw Morgan pointing his iPhone in my direction. No way was I letting vanity steal from those moments. I was a momma; I was a warrior; and I was celebrating.

There's a picture blown up and framed at home, of Morgan with Tara hooked on his hip, leaning over the hospital bed where I'm sitting and holding Frankie in my arms. It's our first family picture, a candid, raw shot capturing both joy and pain, because our family of four should have been a family of five.

We were happy, but not quite whole.

--

Thirty-Five
Willie
2015

Vivian.

Frankie's birth both lessened and compounded the staggering loss of his sister. Her death made way for his life. Something I will always be forever grateful for and forever grieved by. It's a paradox; a "both-and" emotional roller coaster.

I often wonder about it all. All of those not-answerable, what-if questions. If Vivian hadn't been born prematurely and died, would Frankie exist?

She was born at almost six months gestation; we lost her in January of 2014. Had she gone full term, she would have been born in May of 2014.

Frankie was conceived sometime in May 2014, about four months after Vivian's death. Physically and emotionally, I probably should have waited longer, but that's just how it happened.

Had Vivian gone full term she would have been born around the time, or just before the time, I conceived Frankie. So had she been born at full term, Frankie wouldn't have been conceived when he was.

Had Vivian lived as a preemie, there's no way I would have gotten pregnant again so quickly. She would have stayed in the hospital for months; Morgan and I both would have been so consumed with her; another child would have been the last thing on our radar. (I suppose it could have happened, but it seems very unlikely.)

So, if we had gotten to keep Vivian, would that mean we wouldn't have gotten Frankie? Or would his life just be on a different time table; would he just have been born a year or two later than his actual birthdate? And if so, would he really be "Frankie" or a slightly (or completely) different person? Because it would be a different ovulation cycle, a different egg, different sperm, different stage in my life, different pregnancy. There are so many factors. His genetics would be different: possibly his gender, his personality, eye color, the whole bit.

Then you get into the question of a person's soul. What makes Frankie, Frankie. Because the real Frankie is not just his gender, physical appearance, personality, and birth date. It's all of that, yet something more. Frankie is Frankie because of his God-given, God-breathed soul. His soul is beyond and outside of gender and genetics and time.

I like to think, I have to think, that even if Vivian had lived, God would have still given us Frankie. Maybe later, maybe in different packaging, but God would have looked at Frankie's soul, and said, "Oh yes. This one just has to be born. Give him to Morgan and Willie. They need this one too."

I'm not sure if that's how it works. Better minds than mine have wrestled out the questions of the soul and body and how they influence and relate to each other. I'm not a philosopher. I'm just a mother who has to believe that one day I'll get to have and hold *all* of my babies.

--

Frankie was a happy baby. Unless we tried to put him down. Then he was an angry baby, a very angry baby. He was OK with Morgan and Tara and his Grandmas and aunts holding him for small amounts of time, but who he really wanted, almost twenty-four seven, was me.

Which I loved. Most of the time.

I had those "I can hold my child forever" moments a lot. I tried to soak in and soak up every single snuggle; I tried (and mostly succeeded) in not being overwhelmed by his total clinginess.

But a girl's still got to eat. And shower. And go to the bathroom.

It was hard not to feel like a selfish monster for taking a shower when I could hear Frankie screaming in Morgan's arms the entire time. I only showered every three days or so; it just wasn't worth the emotional stress.

"You're just going to have to let him cry." The Helpful People were always telling me. Of course, these are people whose children were older or grown; people who hadn't lived with a screaming infant in recent history.

I'm making notes for my future self; notes of all the things I will not say to moms of newborns. The "just let him cry" crap-advice will be highlighted as particularly not-helpful. Because even when I did it, let him cry so I could shower or pee or whatever, it was literally emotional agony. Even if I was out of earshot of him, I still knew he was crying for me. And I literally could not turn off that "I need to get to my child now" part of myself.

After the first several weeks, things "sort of" got easier. Frankie started sleeping for three hour stretches. When he was awake, he would, occasionally and begrudgingly, allow me to put him down for ten minutes at a time. If I was careful, and planned it just right, I could manage to get small tasks done before he started wailing.

--

I continued to see my therapist. I think we were both monitoring me closely for post-partum depression, especially since the birth of Frankie came just a month after the one-year anniversary of Vivian's birth and death.

But by being careful and honest with myself, and keeping up with therapy, I managed to avoid a second round of crippling depression. I had the baby blues the first few weeks, and after that, the regular I'm-exhausted-and-emotional mom hormones. But I didn't descend back into the under-world.

I will forever be grateful for that. Grateful that I was able to be mentally and emotionally present for Frankie's first weeks and months. Grateful for the fact that, though I continued to grieve Vivian, I could celebrate and enjoy the newness of Frankie.

--

When Frankie was nine months old, in November of 2015, my little family was living a good season.

I had settled into motherhood; I wouldn't say that it had gotten "easy." But we were in a good routine. We'd survived Frankie's newborn and little baby days; he was eating more and more solids and finally beginning to sleep decently. Note: decently meant he only woke two or three times a night, instead of hourly. He could crawl, pull up and stand, and was eager to walk. He laughed this rumbly belly laugh and flashed his gummy-gap tooth smile which made us forgive all of his mischief and moodiness.

Tara was almost eight; in the second grade, and honestly, the best little helper I could ask for. Frankie's teeth were coming in, and hers were going out. She was a mix of farm-girl and girly-girl. She wore muddy muck-boots and sparkly bows and nail polish to cover up the dirt under her nails. She loved to read and write and I called her my step-but-soul daughter whenever people asked. Trish, Zack, Leo, and Debbie (Tara's new baby sister) lived in Crawfordsville now, which was only about twenty-five minutes from us. So even though Tara lived with Trish during the week, we saw her multiple evenings, and had her every other weekend. During school breaks, our time was more evenly split.

Morgan was teaching high school history; I was staying home, being a mediocre-at-best housewife, but devoted mama. I'd become a passable cook; kept the house, if not "clean" at least livable. The only thing I was writing were overly emotional mom journals. I recorded every illness, every tooth development, every rash, bath-time escapade, newest motor skill. I wrote in two tones, either a.) sappy, time is going too fast or b.) overwhelmed, I'VE BEEN A MOTHER FOR A THOUSAND YEARS! WHY ISN'T IT BEDTIME YET???

I tried writing a motherhood blog. But every blog post made me feel vaguely like I was exploiting my children's privacy and using them for material. I couldn't find the line between capturing their stories without capturing *them*, so I gave it up.

Motherhood had made me realize so many things, but one major revelation was that the world is creepy, and the internet makes it easier for creepers to be creepy. I didn't trust a single security measure or privacy control; my mantra before posting anything online was: am I OK with putting this out there and never being able to take it back? I was haunted by the words "digital shadow."

I regretted posting Frankie's full name and birth date when he was born; I refused to post diaper pictures, bath-time pictures, or (future) potty-training pictures. I was stingy with my kids' stories; careful about posting their favorite things; never updated where we were at with the creepy location app. If Morgan was working late, I resisted the urge to post a ranty wife-and-kids-alone-at-home status. I reviewed and cleaned out my friends list regularly. I never accepted friends if I didn't actually know them. And I requested that friends and family ask me or Morgan before posting or sharing a picture of our kids.

I probably seemed snobby or paranoid or both. (Ask me if I care.)

Mamas, to their core, are still cavewomen. The dangers are different; the primal urge to protect our young is the exact same. I would die to protect my kids. I'm fairly confident I would kill to protect them too. Otherwise, I am completely non-violent. Those are my settings: primal cavewoman or pacifist. No in between.

I'm getting off topic though. See, this is what motherhood does to a woman's brain: turns it to mush. I'm always thinking a thousand thoughts and not focused on any.

Actually, no, I had a point. My point: this isn't entirely a story about my kids. I've written about them because it is impossible not to; they fill up my whole life and spill out. What happened to me and Morgan, Vivian's death, Frankie's life, Tara's growing up is what shaped how I interpreted Carolyn's story. I can't separate the two. I suppose it is a story about me as well as Carolyn, yet I'm stingy. A lot happened in that nine months between Frankie's birth and November, but I've deliberately left it out because it was so every-day, so routine, and so precious to me, that I don't feel like giving it away. My marriage, my children, my personal life: you, dear reader, only get so much of that.

Which made me realize, for the first time, what I'd really done to Carolyn. I'd taken and told her story without permission.

That's the trouble with being a storyteller. A writer is influenced by every event, every experience, every person in her life. To write her own story, or the story she's been given, is to write a dozen other people's stories too. We don't even realize we're doing it sometimes: we just look back on our work and gasp and say, oh there's my Grandma, there's my sister, my mother and father, my cousin, my best friend, my hometown. I hope they don't hate me for this. I hope they know I wrote to honor. I wrote to find the truth; to find them. To find myself.

But the trouble with that is people are messy and complicated. And any story worth telling is worth telling honestly. Maybe not a one hundred percent tell-all, but too much polishing, too much glossing over leaves everyone rolling their eyes, and saying so-and-so wasn't really like that at all.

I developed a writer's rule for myself: (besides for my own therapeutic journaling) I would not write stories out of rage or revenge. If it didn't come from a place of peace and grace, I didn't write it. If I was angry, I didn't write it (again, personal journal non-withstanding). And if I was actually writing the biography of a real-life person, I did so only with permission. I would write to heal (and sometimes healing is brutal), but I would never write to wound.

Since Carolyn had told me not to write about her anymore, I stopped. It was hard, really hard, but I did it. I boxed up all of her journals, all of my research, and all of my writing on her and mailed it to her. That was pricey shipping.

Carolyn did not respond. After our first encounter, I didn't hear anything from her, Gibson, or Adley. I never actually learned who their son was or if they'd reunited with him.

For Thanksgiving on Morgan's Dad's side, we went to Mitch and Nell's house. It was Nell's first family holiday dinner, and their house was packed. Nell was one of Cheryl's five living kids. (Quick family tree: Cheryl and Simon had a daughter Patsy, a son Jack who is Morgan's dad, then Nell, then a baby boy named Steven who died at six weeks, then a daughter Linda, and a son William. All of them were married; all, but Nell and Mitch, had kids. Many of those "kids" were now married themselves with kids of their own, The Greats, ages ranging from ten years to two months. If I list everyone's names it would just be overwhelming and confusing, so I won't.)

Not everyone was there; it was almost impossible to get everyone together at the same time. But most of the family was there, each family group streaming in with casseroles and pies, diaper bags and crying babies, pre-teens and college students in tow.

Like most families, we had our roles memorized, our conversations practiced. We told each other only carefully selected, carefully crafted stories. We were our real selves with make-up on, and the kids lectured in the car before we went inside. Work was going great; the baby was finally sleeping; breast feeding was a breeze; and the dishwasher was just humming along at home, washing those pots and pans I used to whip up this wholesome, farmer's market, organic, 100 percent pure-love casserole.

That was the first hour anyway. Then we got our bellies and bladders full and we each had to use one of the two restrooms and hope the aerosol air freshener held out. After that, we loosened up and took the foil off of the pies.

We watched football; chased each other's toddlers away from light sockets and end tables; passed around the Black Friday ads; and gossiped about the family members who were not present. And in between, we told "remember when Grandma Cheryl. . ." stories that had us both tearing up and laughing.

It was one of my favorite Thanksgivings. My parents had gone south to spend the holiday with my sister and her family. My brothers had each gone to their girlfriends' houses. While I missed my family, it was nice not to have to run to a million family dinners. We stayed all afternoon and evening at Nell's, pulling the leftovers out and microwaving them for dinner. Tara was with us; we were dropping her off at Trish's on our way home.

Morgan's family slowly left, a family here, and family there, until it was just Nell, Mitch, and our little family. I wrestled a very tired and grumpy Frankie into his fleece, footy pajamas, and settled into the couch to nurse him. Tara came and snuggled up against me while Nell put on a movie for her.

Nell brought me a cup of hot, decaf tea and yet another piece of pumpkin pie and sat down on the other side of Tara. Mitch and Morgan were both dozing off on the couch and recliner. We stayed like that for another hour and a half, no one really talking, nothing really happening, just relaxing together, watching a movie.

At one point, I looked over at Nell, and she was snuggling Tara with this contented little smile on her face. I smiled seeing her smile. I think I'll always remember that: what it was like to see Nell at peace.

--

Thirty-Six
Willie

The day was December 29th 2015. It was a Tuesday; I remember because Frankie had an ear infection. We'd just been to the doctor and then went to the Rockville CVS to get his antibiotic filled and stock up on more baby Motrin.

It was raining hard, on top of what had already been a rainy winter. But it hadn't been cold enough to turn the rain to snow. It was starting to flood in places. I'd be driving down a back road and have to turn around because a creek had overflowed onto the road.

At CVS, I got Frankie out of his car-seat, bundled back into his hooded coat, and jogged while carrying him across the parking lot into the store. By then I was soaked; he was damp; we both were grumpy. I grabbed a cart, plopped my sodden and sullen ten-month-old into the seat and strapped him in.

I took a deep breath, gave myself a silent pep talk, and zoomed through the store with Frankie screaming the whole way. After paying, we went back into the rain, across the parking lot. I fumbled for my keys, wrestled Frankie out of his coat, back into his car-seat, threw the bags onto the floor, left my cart and dashed to my side to get in. Just as I'd put the key into the ignition my cellphone rang. I fished it out of my purse, and answered it, over Frankie's now, all-out hysteria.

It was Morgan. I launched right into my "we're having an awful" day speech, so it took me a moment to register that Morgan wasn't saying anything. And his silence felt wrong.

"Morgan?" I asked, interrupting myself. "What's wrong?"

"Mitch had a heart attack."

"What? Is he OK?"

"No. Nell called the ambulance and they rushed him to Union. Then she called me and I'm on my way down there now to sit with her."

"OK. OK," I said, thinking. Frankie was still screaming; I rubbed my temples. "What do you need me to do? Do you need me to come?"

"Frankie sounds miserable," Morgan said.

"He is. I just got his prescription and I'm giving him some more Motrin now." I said as I fished the CVS bag off of the backseat floorboard, then opened the box, twisted the seal off, and measured out medicine into the syringe all while keeping the phone pressed between my shoulder and ear.

"Why don't you take him home? I'll get to the hospital, and find out what's going on, and I'll call you back, OK? Oh, and honey, could you call the church and have them start the prayer chain?"

"Yeah, of course."

"OK, thanks. I'll call you probably in a couple of hours. I love you."

"Love you too. Be careful. And tell Nell— tell Nell, I love her too."

--

I got Frankie home, changed his diaper and put clean, dry clothes on him, gave him his first dose of antibiotic, and changed my own clothes. Then I settled us both on the couch and nursed him, the only thing that calmed him down when he was this upset. Pretty soon, he was dozing off, still latched on.

Lolly peeked her head out of our bedroom, where she'd been hiding from Frankie's shrieks. Satisfied that the monster was snoozing, she leaped onto the couch and nestled against me, meowing until I reached out a hand to pet her.

After a few moments, I shooed her away again. I needed a free hand to use my phone. Plus a baby on the boob and a cat on my lap was just a little too much needy for me in that moment. I started making phone calls. Called the pastor, who started the pray chain; called my Mom. She came right over with her Grandma-emergency bag and started folding my laundry and talking to me in a steady stream of small talk. We worked out a tentative plan that she would stay with Frankie, and I would go to the hospital as soon as I heard from Morgan.

I was torn between wanting to be with Morgan and Nell in the waiting room and not wanting to leave my sick baby boy. I knew my mom was more than capable of caring for her sick grandson; she'd raised four children and often babysat Frankie and Tara and my sister's kids. Besides that, she was a second-grade teacher: nurturing kids was her whole life.

I was his mom, though. It was my job to take care of him when he was miserable.

But when Morgan called me back, I heard fear in his voice and knew I had to go.

--

286

Hospital waiting rooms are just awful. The chairs are uncomfortable, as if even the furniture is telling you that you don't want to stay there long. They almost always have clocks that tick too loudly, coffee that smells stale and burnt, and outdated magazine with crinkled covers from far too many nervous hands holding them.

After a few "where are you" texts, I found Nell and Morgan sitting in an open concept waiting room, Morgan staring unblinking at the TV screen, Nell holding a magazine upside down, with a puzzled look on her face, like she couldn't figure out what was wrong with the words.

She saw me first, stood up, and was sobbing by the time I reached her and pulled her into a hug. What do you say to a woman who's lost everything she loved, got it back, and now faced losing it again? I didn't say anything, just hugged her and whispered that shhh-ing sound people make to comfort other people.

She finally let go of me, plopped back down in her chair, and started wiping her eyes. I sat down next to Morgan; he didn't say anything; just gripped my hand hard and didn't let go.

Eventually, they started talking and filled me in: Mitch was in surgery for an emergency bypass.

"I called his parents as soon we got here. They're coming. His cousin is bringing them up, but it'll be a few more hours," Nell said.

I realized as she said this that I really didn't know much about Mitch's family. In my mind, we were Mitch's family; it struck me that other people were on their way, other people's lives had just been turned upside down and I didn't even know their names.

Mitch came through the surgery. He was stable but had a long recovery and several life style changes ahead of him. About an hour after his surgery, they let Nell in to see him for about ten minutes. Then we moved to a new waiting room.

Later that evening, Morgan and I went home. We'd brought Nell dinner, visited with a groggy Mitch, and then left. Nell was spending the night with Mitch, and we told them we'd be back in the morning.

It was ten a.m. before we made it back down there. We got into the main entrance and realized that we didn't remember Mitch's new room number, so we went to the front desk.

At this same time, out of the corner of my eye, I saw a woman rush up on my left, coat open and billowing, gray-white hair streaming out wildly around her shoulders, and a look of terror on her face. And as I was turning my head to look at her fully, in came a frail old man on his powerchair.

She was saying, breathless, "Bud—I mean, Mitch—Mitchell Grant's room number please."

--

Thirty-Seven
Willie

It was pretty much self-explanatory, but we wrestled it out anyway as we waited.

Mitch—Aunt Nell's first and third husband, our uncle by marriage, the "extra" Grandpa to our kids—was Bud, Carolyn's son conceived by Gerald, named and raised by Gibson. Bud was his middle name that he'd gone by for the first nineteen years of his life.

When he wanted to move to Indiana, meet his biological families and find out if he wanted to know them, Carolyn raged against that idea. He'd done it anyway, moved to Parke County, started going by his first name. Met and fell in love with Nell; married her, started their business, tried to start a family. The miscarriages, the divorce, the whole bit.

Through all of this, Carolyn and Bud (she refused to call him Mitch) had a patched up, sometimes explosive, sometimes egg-shell calm relationship. He still went home for visits a few times a year and called his mom often, until his Aunt Colleen (one of the few people who actually knew who he really was) was diagnosed with cancer. When it got bad, Mitch begged his mom to come see her; come make peace with Colleen. She refused; he kept asking; she kept refusing.

When Colleen died, in 2005, Mitch severed all communication with his Mom, unable to forgive her for what he saw as a grudge and bitterness against her family and past. He stayed in contact with Gibson and Adley but stonewalled his mom out of his life.

She matched his silent treatment with one of her own, a silence thickened and deepened by years.

And now here we were. Quite the dysfunctional group of individuals linked by one man we all loved. Me and Morgan, Adley, Gibson and Carolyn, and Nell all circling our wagons, holding hands, passing each other vending machine snacks and magazines.

--

I feel stupid, even now, that I didn't put it together. So many things should have intersected sooner, but somehow didn't.

For instance, Nell and Mitch never knew about my writing project about Carolyn. When I first got to know Nell, I was in the throes of grief over Vivian. Carolyn's story was, quite honestly, nothing to me.

By the time I resumed Carolyn's story, it was because Erin made me. That day in Gerty's kitchen felt shameful to me; I hadn't wanted to share it with anyone. And besides Morgan, I hadn't.

Then when we made that second trip to Asheville, met Gibson, Adley, and Carolyn, she had directly told me to let her story go; that I had neither her permission nor blessing to keep writing about her. I respected that.

I came home and let it go. Found out I was pregnant. Nell got divorced; then remarried Mitch. Life went on. I was consumed with my little family, the never-ending tasks of motherhood. When I thought of Carolyn, it was a passing thought, and I reminded myself to let it go.

We saw Mitch and Nell often. They basically adopted Tara and Frankie as their grandkids; babysat them on a regular basis. We relied on them a lot; I grew very close to Nell. She'd seen me through the worst of my grief; had become my friend as well as another mother figure.

It seems ridiculous that these two segments of my life never crossed, that Mitch was there all along, watching Disney movies with Tara and tossing Frankie into the air to his delighted giggles, yet we never made the connection.

I can remember now a few references Nell made to her mother-in-law; I think she even called her Lynn once. But it was one of those passing comments that flinted and floated right out of my brain. And Mitch, for reasons we've already gone over, didn't talk about his mom.

The mystery was finally solved: that baby I'd grieved, in that cemetery in Asheville, was a grown man recovering from his life-long love affair with bacon.

But the story doesn't end there; you know it doesn't. Carolyn rushed to her son when she thought he was dying, but their first encounter in his hospital room registered level ten on "Family Awkwardness" scale.

If so many of my questions were finally answered, a dozen new ones had surfaced. If Mitch had built a relationship with his Aunt Colleen, why didn't Rob and Erin know about it? Mitch had been living in Parke County for most, if not all, of Erin's life, yet she had no idea he existed. Heck, they'd probably seen each other so many times; it was a small county where everybody knew everybody. Mitch had to know about Rob and Erin but had chosen not to tell them who he was. Why?

And what about Gerald and Gerty? Gerty insisted that the gravestone picture was the last they knew about Gerald and Carolyn's child. Was that the truth? Carolyn had told me in the waiting room that Mitch moved back with the intention of meeting his families, and then deciding if he wanted to introduce himself or not.

So, had Mitch met Gerald and Gerty? And maybe then decided he didn't want relationships with them? Or was Gerty lying? And didn't Mitch have half siblings? What about them?

I wanted to ask Mitch all of this, but it seemed inappropriate to spring it on him.

Oh, hey Uncle Mitch, I know you're recovering from a massive heart attack and everything, but it turns out that a while ago, I started writing about your mom's affair with a married man, which resulted in your birth, and I was wondering if I could ask you a few questions?

I loved that man; I didn't want to cause him another heart attack. I reminded myself to butt out.

As you can see from the remaining pages, that I am not so good at butting out.

--

Thirty-Eight
Willie

Mitch was released four days later; he had strict restrictions and a diet and exercise plan in place along with new medications. He was a complete bear about all of it.

He needed an around-the-clock nurse, but Nell had to return to work at least part of the time. I had my own literal baby boy to take care off; he was in the middle of a ten-day round of medicine, and while his ear infection seemed to be clearing up, he had a bad case of diarrhea and diaper rash from the antibiotic. This momma bear was booked solid.

That left Carolyn, Mitch's own momma bear.

Adley had to take Gibson back home to the assisted living center; he had his own health issues that required the training of skilled nurses. But they decided—Adley and Gibson, that is—that Carolyn would stay behind.

Carolyn, from years of taking care of her husband, was pretty skilled and knowledgeable in nursing, though she wasn't actually a nurse. That wasn't the issue. The issue was Mitch and Carolyn both balked at the idea of being alone together after years of estrangement.

Unfortunately for them, the rest of us were emotionally and physically exhausted and had to go back to our jobs and lives; we didn't have any time for their whining. "Suck it up and love each other or kill each other" was actually a phrase Morgan uttered more than once.

--

For the first week of Mitch's recovery, Carolyn lived in their spare bedroom.

It drove them all nuts.

At the end of the week, she called me, and said, without any opening small talk, "That house in Judson—did my nephew rent it out after you moved out?"

"Uhh, yeah, for a while. But it's vacant now."

She sighed. "Could you ask him if he would rent it to me for a short time?"

"Sure. Umm, should I tell him who you are?"

"Well, obviously, he's going to want to know his potential renter's name. Which is Lynn Grant," she said slowly.

"I know what you go by," I snapped. "I mean, are we telling him *who* you are?"

"*We* aren't telling him anything. When are you going to get that this is my life, and if I want to make any big announcements and upset people's whole lives, I'll do it on my own? You don't get to manage my life for me, Wilma."

"I'm not trying to manage your freakin' life, *Carolyn*. I just wanted to get that straight before I put my foot in my mouth."

"Oh, trying something new, are you?"

"Do you want me to call or not?"

"Yes," she said. Then, "Please."

Rob agreed to meet Lynn the following evening. That was a strange experience. She forced me to go with her; this hard, sharp-tongued woman, suddenly terrified of meeting her own nephew who didn't even know she still existed.

It was early January 2016; the complete opposite season and weather from the first time I'd shown up at this house, waiting to meet Rob, in the summer of 2013. Only a few years, but so much had changed. So much about me had changed.

Back then, I hadn't known anything about this house's history; the family who lived there; how their family had been severed by an eighteen-year old's affair and pregnancy. I didn't know how my life was on the brink of being tangled up with a whole cast of characters: Morgan and Tara, Mitch and Nell, Gibson and Adley and Carolyn, Rob and Erin, Gerty, and even Gerald, who I'd never actually met.

This house, not to sound dramatic, had changed the course of my life. I'd lived here for only a few short months, but I felt bonded to it, like it was an old, dear friend who knew all of my secrets. And in exchange, I knew some of its stories.

But if I was struggling emotionally with going back, it was nothing compared to Carolyn's struggle. Not that she actually said anything.

It wasn't like we were exactly chatty and chummy normally, but she was extra tight-lipped that day. Literally, her lips were pressed together so tightly it looked uncomfortable.

We waited in the car, the heat blasting, until Rob pulled up. Thank God, Erin wasn't with him. She'd never told him about our project; he had nothing to suspect. But I don't think I would have been able to fool her. Not that I was trying to fool Rob. Oh sheesh. It was like I couldn't win; this is not my story, I reminded myself. Not my business.

Poor Rob. He didn't have a clue. He was his regular, jolly, tell-you-anything self.

The eerie thing was they hit it off right away. Well, Rob could get along with anyone. But Carolyn—excuse me, Lynn—was equally drawn to him. She clearly liked him.

At first, on the porch, while he fished out the key and grunted about the door sticking, she just stared at his face intently. Then, something he said, the way he looked—I don't really know—*something* about him made her smile. A real smile that took over her whole face. I didn't even know she could do that. Be happy and like people, I mean.

Honestly, it was irritating. Carolyn made it very clear—on multiple occasions—that she couldn't stand me. I had assumed that she was just incapable of liking anyone which made it less insulting. But here she was, liking Rob, and it left me feeling, I don't know? Insulted? Insecure? Like maybe I should try harder for her affection? Maybe the problem was me?

Rob gave her the whole tour of the house, filling her in on his mom's life story, not knowing this was Colleen's sister; that she knew more about Colleen's childhood and this house than he did. It was painful to witness; I was relieved when they went upstairs and left me in the kitchen.

Out of habit or nerves, I grabbed a broom and started sweeping.

They came back downstairs, laughing about something. They seemed to have reached a deal on the rent.

I really just wanted to get out of there, but they lingered and kept talking.

"So—your accent. Where are you from, Lynn?"

She didn't so much as hesitate. "Asheville, North Carolina."

"I've been there! Took my mom to the Biltmore once! Just up out of nowhere—mid '90's I think it was—she wanted to go to Asheville. Just wouldn't let it go. Strangest thing though: she was so excited about taking that trip, but then when we got there, she just sort of deflated, came back depressed. I never knew what that was all about. The Biltmore though! Just amazing! So, what brings you here? Why do you need a temporary place to rent?"

This time Lynn did hesitate and go a little pale. I waited. "My son. He lives here and he had a heart attack. I'm helping take care of him."

Rob shook his head, murmuring his sympathy. "Mothers always do. I tell you, not a day goes by that I don't miss my own Mom and wish I could tell her how much I appreciate everything she did for me." He actually teared up. I'm not exaggerating.

"Who's your son, Lynn?" Rob asked.

"Mitch. Mitch Grant," she said.

"Mitch! You don't say! Mitch and I go waaay back! We were roommates; lived in this very house, did you know that? He suggested you stay here, I take it? We were real good buddies back in the day. Well, I guess not *that* good because I didn't know about his heart attack, but you know how life gets, you lose touch with people. . . dang, I'm sorry to hear that! How's he doing?"

"He's going to be alright, I think," Lynn said.

"Good, good. Well, you give him my best! Maybe I'll stop in and see him sometime. Did I hear that he got remarried to Nell? I always hoped they'd work it out."

Lynn nodded. Maybe it was just me, but she looked a little deflated herself.

--

"You're really going to live in that house again?" I asked Carolyn in the car as we left.

"Of course. It's just a house. Four walls and a roof," she told me.

I shrugged. "If you say so. It's haunted, you know."

She snorted. "Do I look like I'm scared of a couple ghosts?"

I shouldn't have, but I blurted, "If they're your parents and sister, then yeah."

That actually took her aback. But just for a moment, then her walls were back in place. "If my parents are haunting that house, they should fear me."

I couldn't think of a response to that, so I changed the subject. "Would you like to get some lunch with me? I could go through the drive thru in Rockville and get us a couple cheeseburgers."

"I don't do drive thrus. Or cheeseburgers," she said.

"Oh yeah, I've been meaning to ask you about that," I said. "How is it that you're a vegetarian and your son owns his own butchering business?"

She gave me a long look. "And what do you imagine gave him the inspiration to do that? Spite."

"Come on, he did not."

"Ask him sometime. I know you're in the throes of brand new motherhood and like to think the bond between mother and son can't be broken, but trust me, honey. It can."

"Don't you hear how terribly sad that is?"

She shrugged. "That's life. My life anyway. Bud and I haven't been close in decades. Even before he moved here, we had rough patches as often as we had good ones. Gibson is the parent who he adored. Gibson's the one who deserved him."

"You know what I think, Carolyn?" I said.

"Lynn," she corrected me. "And I suppose you're going to tell me either way."

"I think you're full of bullshit. I think you're one of those people who is only happy if you're miserable. And I think the only person interested in making you pay for your past still is YOU. And only you. The only reason Mitch is mad at you,"

She cut me off, in that tone I was all too familiar with. "Don't you dare tell me why my son is mad at me. Don't you dare pretend you have it all figured out.   You might have spent months snooping into my past, but you don't know me at all!"

I had a flashback of me yelling almost these exact words at Nell in the food court.

Lynn and I didn't get lunch together. I couldn't drop her off soon enough, and I think the feeling was mutual.

--

Thirty-Nine
Willie

I took Frankie with me to visit Uncle Mitch about a month after his heart attack. I honestly wasn't *planning* on interviewing him; no, seriously. It just sort of happened. I fixed Frankie a waffle with butter—no syrup—and plopped him down on the couch. Frankie was very close to walking, he could pull himself up and walk along furniture, and I had to watch him constantly because he was a danger to himself with his mobility. But he was still sleepy, so I figured with a waffle, milk, and cartoons, I might get a few more moments of calm.

Mothers everywhere laugh at me for having that thought.

Frankie refused to sit still. He flipped and flopped, slid down the couch and cried to be picked back up. We went through this routine a dozen times while I talked to Mitch about how he was feeling.

"You know, Frankie is just like Morgan," Mitch said.

"I didn't realize you knew Morgan when he was this age."

"I held him when he was just a day old."

"Oh. So you moved back here in what, the early eighties? Well, not 'back' since you never lived here, but you know what I mean."

"I moved here when I was nineteen, so 1981 I guess. Been here ever since."

"So how come you never told anyone who you are?" I asked Mitch.

"Who do you mean?"

"Who do I mean?" I mimicked. "Oh, Rob. Erin. Gerty. Gerald. Your half siblings. None of them know who you are, do they?"

"I know who they are. Rob and I go back since the early eighties. And my siblings—Jacob and Teresa and Jack—we're on first name basis. We run into each other and talk about our lives all the time. Jack, the youngest, was in Nell's class, so we see him once a month at the class dinners. And Teresa cleans my teeth at the dentist. Jacob's a lawyer and I've gone to him for legal advice a time or two."

"But how is that fair Mitch? Your sister cleans your teeth but doesn't even know you have the same father!"

"Well, what do you suggest? That I mumble it as she's flossing my teeth or wait until she's handing me my goodie bag? Hey, Teresa, by the way, you don't know this, but the birth order is really Jacob, you, ME, and then Jack. Yep, that's right, we have the same father. Thanks for the tooth brush, have a nice day!"

"Well, of course, not like that. Not out of nowhere. But I think you could come up with a way to ease into it."

"Oh, do you? There's no easing into that sort of thing, Willie. No preamble that makes that kind of announcement less horrible. My siblings grew up thinking their parents had a solid marriage; to this day, that's the thing they're the most proud of. You think I haven't wanted to tell them? To be part of their family? But I never could."

"They don't know? How do you know they don't know?"

"You mean, besides being invited to Gerald and Gerty's fiftieth anniversary party and listening to

Jack give a speech about his parents' lifelong commitment and faithfulness? Well, besides that, I know because Gerald told me that they don't know. And asked me not to tell them."

"He did? And wait! So Gerald knows who you are?"

"Yup."

"Care to elaborate?"

"Do I have a choice? By the way, Frankie's going for the DVD's again."

I waved that off. "I want to know why, when I asked Gerty about Carolyn's child, she insisted that you were dead. She was lying to me."

"It's not lying if that's what she believed was the truth."

"So Gerald knew, but didn't tell her?"

"That's the gist of it," Mitch said, a familiar phrase of Gibson's.

"Did you and Gerald have a close relationship?"

"I wouldn't say close."

"When did you tell him?"

Mitch sighed. Then at Frankie, he said, "Young man, don't you even think about stashing your waffle down that couch cushion." Frankie, who had pulled himself up against the couch, and was indeed, preparing to squirrel away his waffle for later, whipped his head around and gave Mitch a gummy, guilty grin. "I'm onto you," Mitch said, "If Auntie Nell finds butter stains on the cushions, she'll blame me. And it'll be double trouble for me, young man, because I'm not supposed to be eating butter."

I went and gathered Frankie into my arms, kissing his plump cheek. He tasted like butter. "Oh, yum, yum. I'm just going to gobble you up."

Frankie laughed. "Num, Num Mama!"

"Here, sit on Uncle Mitch's lap, honey bunch. And don't pull his beard." But Frankie already had his finger woven into Mitch's beard and was tugging despite his Uncle's protests. It was a game they played.

"Oh, ouch! Stop, stop! I can't take it! I'll tickle you!" Mitch tickled Frankie under his chin, mercilessly, until Frankie squealed and squirmed away. He slid down Mitch's legs and then crawled back to his waffle that was half sticking out of the couch cushions.

It struck me, as it often did, how amazing Mitch would have been as a father, a mix of strong and gentle, playful and stern. Frankie and Tara loved him. I think they secretly delighted in not having to share Mitch and Nell, like they had to share their grandparents with their cousins.

"So, when did you tell him?" I repeated.

"Were you this persistent when you interviewed Mom?" Mitch asked me.

"I umm, didn't actually get to interview her. And I'm not interviewing you; we're just talking."

"Are you this nosy with everyone you talk to?"

"No. Just family. And random people who leave behind their journals in houses I live in."

"I still can't believe you read my Mom's journals, then wrote about her, and she didn't actually murder you."

"She nearly did. If Gibson hadn't been on my side, I think she would have. Even with that, she called him an old bastard."

"Oh, that's a common pet name. Term of endearment, really."

"What does he call her?"

"When he wants to piss her off? Or when he's being sweet?"

"Both."

"He calls her Honey Cakes just to mess with her. She hates lovey-dovey pet names, but Honey Cakes literally sets her teeth on edge. But Gibson is who started calling Mom Lynn, instead of Carolyn. He is literally the only person who's allowed to call her LynnyLou. She's his LynnyLou and he's her old bastard."

"Seems fair."

"That's Mom. I can't really explain it or their relationship. She's kind of happiest when she's a little bit mad at him. I think she expresses affection through nit-picking. And it doesn't really faze him."

"You love them," I said.

He gave me a puzzled look. "Of course, I love them. They're my parents."

"But you went years without talking to your mom. And you can barely stand to be around her now."

"I didn't say they were likable. Well, Dad's likable. I always got along with him. But Mom and I have had a complicated relationship."

"Did it change when you found out about Gerald?"

"I didn't *find out* like you're implying. Like one day I believed Gibson was my biological father, and the next they sat me down after dinner and told me the truth. I always knew, even as a child, that Gibson wasn't biologically my father. They didn't ever try to pretend or hide it, but it was just a vague confession until I was older. When I was eighteen, Mom told me that if I wanted to know the whole story, she would tell me. I said I did, so she told me. And she didn't spare herself; in fact, I remember thinking that she was too hard on herself, too unforgiving."

"Were you mad at her?"

"For having an affair with a married man?"

"Yeah," I said.

"Disappointed more, I'd say. You like to think your mother is a saint. But I loved her, and I had a good life, so it didn't crush me like it would some other teenagers. I think a lot of that was Gibson. He wouldn't allow me to disrespect her; days later, I got mad at her about something else, and made a cruel comment about her being a slut, just to see if I'd get away with it, I guess. Gibson just about came out of that wheelchair! If he'd been physically able, I think he would have had me up against the wall by my throat, for calling Mom that. It was probably the only time he was really, honest to God, pissed at me. He taught me more about loving a woman in that one angry moment, than he did in the rest of my life. And then he came to me later, and told me, I didn't have to like how I was conceived. Damn it, he didn't like it either! He said I was allowed to be upset and confused, but if he ever heard me call my mother that awful name again, that I could just pack my bags. Because this was her home, and she would not be disrespected in her own home."

"So were you mad at her or not?"

"What's this 'either/or' with you Willie? I was both. But we'd already had a messy relationship, I guess because we were so much alike, so stubborn. We fought all the time; neither of us knew how to back down. But after she told me the truth, I decided I wanted to move to Indiana, meet my biological family and decide, for myself, if I wanted to know them. And she couldn't handle that. She screamed at me that I was ungrateful. That I was betraying her by moving here; spitting on all of her sacrifices to give me a good life. Gibson eventually talked her out of the worst of her hysteria. I came here, and for years we had a somewhat normal relationship until Aunt Colleen got sick and Mom refused to come see her."

"So your Aunt Colleen and you were close?"

He grinned. "Yeah. We were."

"Then how come Rob and Erin didn't know you existed? Still don't?"

He shrugged. "I don't have a good answer for that. Except that I think Colleen always blamed herself for Carolyn running away. Her family always idealized her; the perfect Christian woman who never wronged anyone. She didn't know how, or couldn't stand the idea of ruining that image."

"That's stupid."

"That's human nature. We all have our roles; a lifetime of people thinking about you a certain way. And the 'better' you are, the harder it is to fail. We like people to be either good or bad; we can't stand that we're all both."

"So she kept you a secret?"

"You make it sound like I was a child she kept in the attic. But yes, she kept me a secret. My identity, I mean. I've been good friends with Rob for years; we lived together in the Judson house for a while, did you know that? But he doesn't know we're cousins."

I shook my head. "I just don't get this secrecy."

"Join the club."

"How did you meet Colleen?"

"I met her on accident, really. I was trying to work up the nerve to meet my aunt, but I hadn't. Then I met Nell and got distracted from the whole reason I'd moved here. I kept driving by that house, the Judson house, every week though, going real slow. She saw me one too many times; she didn't live there, and by then my grandparents had passed away. But she was there often to keep the property and house tidy. Anyway, the last time I was cruising by the house, I was looking at it instead of the road. I had to slam on the brakes because she was standing in the middle of the street, hands on her hips. I nearly ran her over.

"She came right up to my window; I had to crank it down while trying to get my heart out of my throat, and she said sternly, 'if you're casing this place to rob it, I should warn you it's haunted and poor. I'd try the neighbors.' And then she got this real funny look on her face. Then she told me she knew who I was. She made me come inside, and we talked for two hours that first day."

"I don't get it," I said. "How did Colleen and Carolyn never cross paths after that? What about your wedding?"

"Mom didn't come to my wedding," he said.

"She didn't come to her only son's wedding?" I demanded.

He shook his head. "We had it here, so no. What part of this don't you get? Anything that had to do with her past, her family, this community, she shunned. No exceptions. Not for my first marriage to Nell; not for the miscarriages of her seven grandkids; not for her sister dying. And that is what was unforgivable to me. That she didn't show up to any of it.

Forty
Mitch
Excerpt from *Becoming Hoosier*
Summer 1981

He was going, that's all there was to it. He drove to the little country church, pulling in right at 10:28 am and forced himself out of the truck. He fell in line behind some other stragglers, a family of four, the mother carrying a china baking dish in her gloved hands.

He could count on one hand the number of times he'd been to church. Mom—for reasons he just now understood—would not enter a church. Dad found God in nature and in literature. He always said he found God in a good conversation with a good friend, over tea. Iced or hot.

Aunt Claudia also disdained church. One, most of the Christians she'd ever met were plain and simple hypocrites. Two, she didn't believe in God.

Uncle George had a secret faith on Wednesday evenings, Christmas Eve, and Easter. Aunt Claudia begrudgingly excused him from family dinners, for one hour, on the high holidays for corporate worship; she, however, did not know about his Wednesday worshipping.

Adley was the only one among them who was openly religious. If Mom and Aunt Claudia were adamantly atheists, Adley was equally stubborn in the opposite direction. She'd gotten saved, by accident, at age sixteen and been addicted to the Holy Spirit ever since.

She'd come home from her first semester of college and announced at Christmas dinner that she was a ministry major. Uncle George choked on a chicken leg bone; Aunt Claudia froze while scooping out sweet potatoes casserole, the orange glob suspended on the spoon, mid plop. Mom crossed her arms, and leaned back in her chair, eyeing Adley like she was really seeing her for the first time. Mitch looked around at his family, his plate extended under Aunt Claudia's posed spoon, waiting for the scoop of sweet potatoes to descend. Finally, he reached up and took the spoon from her and helped himself. Aunt Claudia sat down heavily on Uncle George's knee.

Dad was the only one unfazed. He met Adley's stubborn gaze for a long moment, gave her a nod and went back to eating. After that, the brief moment of shocked silence ended, and a heated, high pitched, female argument ensued.

That had been months ago. It had been Adley's stubbornness and bravery that had pushed Mitch into what he'd been wanting to do since his Mom told him the truth when he turned eighteen.

He'd dropped out of college after one semester and moved back home.

He wasn't sure why he called it *home*. It wasn't really home, of course. He'd never been here. Not once in his first eighteen and a half years. And perhaps it was that, the absence, the secrecy, that drew him here.

He'd disappointed his Mom terribly by moving here. He knew this because she told him. She'd tried every one of her tricks to stop him too; layered on the guilt so thickly that it stopped working. She'd yelled, lectured, pouted. Tried the whole "if you drop out of college, we're cutting your funds. We're not paying for you to travel all over and find yourself. That's a waste of time, Bud. You aren't lost."

In the end, it was Dad who saved him; it was always Dad. His Mom was hot-headed and stubborn; Dad was the calm one. Dad could talk Mom out of hysteria with just a few choice words and a look. If Mom was driven by emotions and passion, Dad coasted along on logic and the sincere belief that if you gave something enough time, it would right itself.

Dad understood human nature in an almost irritating extreme. He was one of those people who should have been a psychologist; he could rarely stay mad (or even get mad) at people because he knew where they were coming from, why they thought and acted the way they did.

He was a natural mediator, a person who listened beyond the words.

He was also the best damn father a boy could get. Mitch knew this. It was his love for his Dad, his *real* Dad, that gave him a twinge of guilt far more than Mom's guilt trips did. What was this need to meet his biological father when he'd been blessed with Dad? Was it ungrateful? A slap in the face?

But whereas Mom had only begrudgingly given her acceptance, Dad had given his blessing. "Go," he'd said, when Mitch had tried to explain. "You need to do this."

With Adley's courage and Dad's blessing tucked in his back pocket, he went. He'd been in Parke County for weeks now, trying to work up the courage to meet them all. His other families. First he'd meet them as a stranger, then he'd decide if he wanted to tell them the truth.

When Mom had finally told him the truth, when he turned eighteen, she'd told him, "You better ask everything you want to know now, because I'm not bringing it up again."

Mitch had kept Mom at the kitchen table for hours, grueling her with all the questions that had been brewing his whole life. He'd always known that Dad wasn't biologically his father; they'd never pretended. But before that night, they hadn't volunteered much information.

That night he learned it all: her affair with a married man named Gerald when she was eighteen. He knew where she was from, a tiny town in Parke County, Indiana. He knew—and wished he didn't— that she'd been raped in the church she grew up in, by a boy in her class. Knew that Gerald and her parents had tried to force her to marry this same boy. Knew that she'd fled south, to two brothers she didn't even know; knew that they'd faked his death to be left in peace; knew that when he was six months old, she'd married Dad and the three of them had become a family. A refuge from her past.

That night, a lot of things about his Mom clicked into place. He understood why she flinched when touched unexpectedly. He understood a lifetime of emotional outbursts, of unexplainable anxiety. He understood why, when they were house hunting, when he was ten, she'd refused to even consider their dream house after she learned it had a basement.

And yet, understanding his mother didn't make it any easier to live with her. He shouldn't admit that, but it was true.

Understanding why she'd done what she'd done, even being able to forgive her for the affair and the secrecy, didn't fulfill that void inside of him, that need to know where and who he came from.

So, half-hating himself for it, he went.

Now, here he was in Mom's hometown, standing on the first step of the church where her life had been devastated in such a way that it trickled down to his. He found himself unable to go inside.

He felt panicked. His heart was racing. He swiped his sweaty palms on his dress pants. His mouth was dry. He could hear the first hymn spilling out of the sanctuary, a chorus of pitchy voices, a smattering of hands clapping out of beat.

Just go inside, he told himself. But he had this overwhelming feeling that if he stepped foot in that church, he'd be betraying his mom.

There was only one person responsible for Mom being raped. It wasn't the fault of the people sitting in there. It wasn't like they were even guilty of covering it up because they hadn't known. Nobody had known, she'd told him. She'd wanted it that way. And it wasn't the physical church building's fault that evil had happened in its basement. It's not as if the evil act had seeped into the walls and stayed there.

Go inside, he told himself.

Yet still he stayed on the first step, unable to move.

"You know," a voice caught him off guard, "your face will freeze in that scowl if you hold it any longer."

He turned to see who was talking to him.

He could smell her hairspray. That was the first thing he noticed, and the most vivid thing he'd always remember. She darted past him, and stopped on the top step, hand posed to open the door. She looked back at him, and said, "Well, are you coming? You're lucky: we're not handling the snakes today." And then she laughed and went inside. He followed.

The service had already started. They were doing announcements and prayer requests, various people standing up, clearing their throats, and twisting their hands as they made brief speeches. The pastor was standing behind the pulpit, scribbling notes.

Mitch slipped into a pew in the back, trying to make himself invisible. A few people turned to look at him and smiled or nodded.

Hairspray girl had sat down in the second pew from the front on the right side. She'd slid into a pew packed with other teenagers, ignoring their complaints, and nudging the boy who wouldn't scoot over for her.

A middle-aged woman—her mother?—looked down the row and gave each teen a stern and pointed look before turning her attention back to the pastor. The pastor flinted his gaze to her, winked just slightly.

Ahh.

He didn't know much about church or church families, but it became pretty obvious that those front row people were the pastor's family. Hairspray girl was the pastor's daughter.

Mitch sat up straighter; resisted the urge to straighten his tie.

The sermon was something about sheep and goats. The pastor had one of those booming, effusive styles of preaching. He preached with his whole body, pacing, gesturing, sweating. He shouted; he sang when the mood struck him; he clapped unexpectedly; and Praised the Lord in a voice loud enough to make people squirm. But he also told jokes; he volunteered his own personal failures; he laughed at his own blunders.

It was obvious that he was loved by the people and that he loved them back.

It was unsettling to Mitch. Ever since his mom had told him what had happened to her here, Mitch had pictured a dark place, a place of people pretending to be holy but hiding terrible secrets.

But the light was streaming in through the stained-glass windows. These people were laughing at times, crying at others, smiling to each other. And afterward, there was an announcement reminding everyone to stay for the church picnic. Children darted out of pews; a group of teenagers formed a tight knot in a corner, laughing about something; mothers gathered up stray bulletins, purses, forgotten crayons, toys, and books their children had left in their race for the door. Men were making small talk, smacking each other heartily on the back, catching up on so-and-so's week.

There was joy here.

In the foyer, the pastor and his wife were shaking hands. Mitch had no choice but to go through the line and meet them.

The pastor grabbed his hand in a firm hand shake and grinned. "We've got a newcomer today! Welcome brother! What's your name?"

It was on the tip of his tongue to say Bud, his middle name that everybody called him back home. But instead he said, "Mitch. Mitch Grant."

"Nice to meet you Mitch! I'm Pastor Simon, and this is my wife Cheryl."

He went to shake Cheryl's hand, but she pulled him into a hug instead. "I'm a hugger. I hope you'll stay for the picnic," she said, releasing him.

"I didn't bring anything," Mitch told her.

She waved him off. "We've got plenty. Here,

let me introduce you to the kids your age. Come with me. Half of this group are mine, but the rest of them are OK," she told him with a wink.

It was a group of about a dozen teenagers, all right around Mitch's age. Right in the middle of the group was hairspray girl. She was watching him.

"Guys and gals, this is Mitch. He's new here, make him feel welcome. Mitch, this is my daughter Nell," Cheryl said, beginning to name off everyone.

"*Mom*, I think we can be trusted to make our own introductions," Nell told her.

"Alright, alright, I was just trying to get you started," Cheryl said.

After she left, everyone rattled off their names. Mitch struggled to keep up and forgot most of them.

He thought there was a Rob, and a William, but couldn't recall any of the other guy's names. He could only focus on one of the girls.

"Like my mom so helpfully said for me, I'm Nell," she was saying, "Just Nell. Don't call me Nellie."

"OK," he said. "Just Nell then." But he knew he would secretly always call her Hairspray Girl.
--

He was possibly being interrogated as he ate a plate of baked beans and potato salad while a wheelbarrow race took place in the yard behind him.

Maybe interrogated was the wrong word. Maybe Pastor Simon was just genuinely curious about everyone who visited his church. Especially the young men who laughed a little too loudly at his daughter's jokes.

It wasn't that the pastor was being rude. But Pastor Simon didn't make small talk either. He asked what he wanted to know, bluntly and directly.

"So where are you from, Mitch?"

Such a simple question, but Mitch paused. How much did he tell?

"Asheville, North Carolina, sir."

"What brought you up here? Just passing through, or are you going to stick around?"

Mitch shrugged. "I haven't decided. I just got a job at a gas station, so I guess I'll stick around for a while anyway."

"Where are you staying?"

"So far I've just been renting a motel room by the night. But I'm looking for a place to rent."

"Well, I am just the guy to help you out." Pastor Simon slapped his hands on the picnic table, grinning. "See that woman over there?"

He nodded to a woman in the food line. She was wearing a floral print, knee length dress with shoulder pads. She was holding a bulging paper plate of food and laughing at something the person in front of her was saying.

"Yeah."

"Her name's Colleen Beal. I believe you met her son. She's got her parents' old place here in Judson that she's looking to rent out. She doesn't like for it to sit empty."

That was her. His aunt. So Rob was his cousin.

His mom had told him that she had a sister. She'd told him that she hadn't seen or heard from Colleen since she left when she was pregnant with him.

"If you're going to meet her," Mom had said with bitterness in her voice, "you should know that she doesn't know you're alive."

"What the hell, Mom?" He had demanded.

She'd shrugged. "I did it to protect you! I didn't want Gerald to know you were alive; I didn't want him to be able to take you away from me. And to get him to believe it, I had to lie to them too. Don't look at me like that Bud! They deserved it! They made their choices, and I made mine."

"So, what? I'm just supposed to continue your lie?" He had asked.

She shrugged again and it irritated him to no end, her casualness with his origin. "You'll do what you have to do," Mom had said.

And now, the moment was here.

"How long have you been preaching here?" Mitch asked suddenly.

"Since oh, 1958. Twenty-two years. I can always remember because my first daughter was born shortly after I came here and she's twenty-two now. That's her, over there, Patsy, with her own firstborn."

Mitch followed his gaze and nodded to acknowledge what Pastor Simon had said, but his mind was elsewhere.

Mom had been baptized and raped on the same day, June 14th, 1959. And this man sitting next to him, this man who flirted with his wife, and teased his children, and took an extra portion of peach cobbler had been pastor here then. Had baptized his mother on the day her life and body were violated. Had pronounced her saved as she stood, unknowingly, at the brink of destruction.

Yet Pastor Simon didn't know. He didn't condone it. He didn't excuse it. I can't blame him because he didn't know, Mitch told himself. Who was to say how Pastor Simon would have handled it had he known about it? Perhaps things would have gone differently for Mom if she'd sought help, told people.

But she hadn't.

What right did he, Mitch, have to take that choice from her now?

So he said nothing. Didn't ask if Pastor Simon remembered a Carolyn Calvert. Didn't ask if he'd ever wondered what had become of her. Didn't ask if her parents and sister ever mentioned her. Didn't confess that he was her son.

He made an excuse to get out of meeting his aunt. He wasn't ready for that. He mumbled something about needing to leave, and did just that, sparing one backward glance for Nell, who was laughing with Rob, his cousin.

--

Forty-One
Mitch
Excerpt from *Becoming Hoosier*
Summer 1981

He hadn't thought this through. He'd been so naïve about moving here, about meeting his families. What had he thought? That he could just show up, just announce his presence to people who didn't even know he existed?

Damn, but that hurt, that they didn't know he existed. He was angry, but he didn't exactly know who he was the most angry with. His mom, for sure. For lying about his death, for deceiving his family. What right had she had to do that? It was one thing to cut herself off from them; he could even understand her reasoning, her anger. But it was another to pass that grudge on to him without his permission. It had altered his whole life, her one choice to alienate both of them from their family.

But what about them? Had they even been grieved at his "death"? Had they even tried to find their daughter and sister, tried to heal things? What kind of parents just accept the death of their grandchild without asking questions, without searching out their daughter to comfort her? He didn't care what she'd done! Mom hadn't deserved that! That abandonment! That rejection!

What kind of person was his Aunt Colleen? She alone had known what had happened to his mom. She alone had comforted and sustained his mom for two years after she'd been raped, only to reject her and condemn her for an affair and pregnancy? What kind of sister supports the idea of marriage to the man who'd raped her sister?

He didn't want to meet her. He thought if he met her, his rage would erupt. He would blurt it all out, who he was, who his mom was.

Yet, here he was, for at least the fifth time, driving slowly past the Judson house his mom had grown up in. His truck grumbled about idling. He'd had enough saved up to buy an old junker of a truck. The thing had more rust than paint, and it barely ran. But it got him back and forth.

It had even gotten him and Nell to the drive-in theatre in Terre Haute for their first date. He grinned at the memory. Even now, he could smell her hairspray lingering in his truck. He hoped it stayed until he could pick her up again for another date. For this one, they were going canoeing on Sugar Creek. Three days from now.

Nell. The unexpectedly good thing about his move here. She distracted him, made the rest of it easier. Not that she knew that; he hadn't told her any of it. Didn't know if he would.

He sighed and decided today wasn't the day either. He wouldn't stop at this house, wouldn't face the place his Mom had grown up in. He went to drive away, and his truck died, right there in the middle of the street.

He cursed, tried to restart it. It made that grinding sound the first couple times he turned the key, then begrudgingly sputtered to life. He put it into gear, released the clutch, and started driving again. He gave the house one last glance, then looked at the road, and slammed on his brakes when he realized there was a woman standing not three feet from his bumper!

It was his Aunt Colleen. And he'd almost run her over. He heart was thumping as he rolled down his window and she walked over. She was holding the rake she'd been using to clean the yard.

"If you're casing this place to rob it, I should warn you it's haunted and poor. I'd try the neighbor's."

"I'm not, I'm not casing the place," he stammered.

"Oh? Well, that's a relief. I wasn't looking forward to knocking your tail lights out."

"You were going to bust my taillights? Why?"

"Well, I figured I needed to report suspicious activity to the sheriff's office. And it would be helpful to tell them to watch out for a rusted pickup truck with busted taillights. Between that and your southern accent, you'd stand out like a sore thumb."

"What's wrong with my southern accent?"

"Nothing. It's just noticeable. People have been talking, that's all. I'm glad to hear you're not a thief though. Being an outsider is one thing, and being a local thief is one thing. But being an outsider thief, that's quite another."

"There's different standards for your local criminals and outsider criminals?"

"Well sure. It's easier to have mercy on a thief if you have to sit next to his Granny at church on Sunday."

"Is that so?"

"Unless you don't like his Granny to begin with. Then he'll probably rot."

"Thanks for the head's up. I'll try to avoid breaking any laws while I'm here."

"I'd advise that. Unless you have some kind

of relation, that's say, a lawyer, in your back pocket." She told him, giving him a look.

"I'm not related to anyone around here," he said.

"Hmmm. Not a thief, but definitely a liar."

"Excuse me?"

"I wasn't for sure until I heard you curse and saw you gesture when your truck died. You do both just like she did when she was angry. Tell me, how is my sister?"

--

He hadn't had much choice in the matter. He was sitting in the kitchen, drinking a glass of tap water, and having the truth pulled out of him.

He wanted to be angry at this woman, but he couldn't get past being bewildered by her. There were bits of his mom in her, phrases they both used, the way they both tucked hair behind their ears.

He even recognized some of himself in her; they had the same brown eyes, the same shape of ears, pointy at the tops. Adley had always teased him about his ears, told him he must have descended from elves. Told him he should get a job as Santa's helper at the mall during Christmas. He could play the part without needing to wear the fake ears.

For weeks, Mitch had been dodging anyone and everyone's questions about who he was, why he'd moved there. (And everyone asked. Everyone is this small county wanted to trace you out, pin you down to a common ancestor, or at least a common neighbor.)

But in twenty minutes, his aunt had gotten him to confess nearly everything that his mom had told him. He'd told her about the Grant Brothers; the fake grave; about his mom's marriage to his dad;

about growing up as a Grant in Asheville.

She mostly listened, her hand pressed against her mouth, occasionally prompting him with more questions, digging in a little deeper.

"Can I ask you something?" He finally asked.

She nodded.

"Why aren't you shocked? That I'm alive, I mean."

"Because I always knew," she told him.

"What? How?"

"I saw the picture, the one she mailed of that gravestone. But I knew in my gut that it was a lie, a way to try to protect you and protect herself. From Gerald. And Sanders. And," Colleen paused. "And from us. Me and Mom and Dad."

"So you had a gut feeling? And that was enough to go off of, your gut?"

"Well, yes, and no. When you were about five, your Dad contacted me."

"My Dad? Gerald?"

"No," she said, harshly. "Your Dad. Your real Dad. What would Gerald know about you anyway?"

"Nothing. So Dad contacted you? Why?"

"He said he couldn't live with the lie anymore. He said he had no trouble deceiving Gerald, but I kept him awake at night. He said Carolyn, he called her Lynn though, that she grieved me, missed me, though she'd never admit it. And he said her rage toward me let him know there was great love between us, because you can't be *that* hurt by someone you didn't love. He said for those reasons, I deserved to know the truth. That she, and you, were alive and well. And happy. He asked me not to do anything about it, though, not to try to contact her."

"Why?! And why didn't you? Why did you just let it go, let me go?"

"Tell me Mitch, how do you think your mom would have reacted to finding out Gibson had contacted me?"

He paused, then said, "she would have felt betrayed."

"Exactly. It would have been another betrayal to her. Another person failing her. And this time, it would have been her husband. I couldn't do that to her. So I left her alone. Hoped she'd eventually contact me."

"But she never did."

"No, she never did. She never came home. But you did."

"It doesn't matter."

"Doesn't it?"

"This isn't *my* home," Mitch said. "I'm not from here; I'm from Asheville."

She reached her hand across the table, slid it into his. "Honey, everyone is from every place their ancestors ever lived. This is your mom's home, and it trickled down to you, whether you like it or not."

--

Forty-Two
Mitch
Excerpt from *Becoming Hoosier*
1983

That first meeting had been almost two years ago, and he had formed a bond with his Aunt Colleen during that time. He ate at their house more often than he ate alone. Rob, who still lived at home and commuted to college, had become a good friend to Mitch. Rob just assumed Mitch was over so much because they were friends which was true. But Mitch also came to see his aunt Colleen.

Shortly after they met, Mitch had pressed Aunt Colleen to come clean to Rob. He knew how it felt to be the son who didn't know the whole truth, and Mitch didn't want to perpetuate that one someone else.

But Aunt Colleen couldn't stand the idea of telling Rob the whole story. Not after all these years. Not after she'd let Rob believe his aunt Carolyn had died long ago. Colleen balked at the idea, twisted her hands and bit her lip nervously when Mitch asked her.

"I'll think about it," she'd said at first.

But, days later, she pulled him aside and said, "Honey, I can't. I just can't. I'm sorry, but please don't ask me to."

So once again, Mitch was forced to keep someone else's secrets.

Shortly after that, Aunt Colleen told them over dinner one evening, "Boys, I've been thinking. Why don't the two of you live together in the Judson house? Rob, you know how I hate for your

Grandma's house to just sit empty. And two young boys like yourselves could keep it up. I'm getting too old to mess with it."

"You're not even close to fifty, yet." Mitch snapped. What was she up to? She wanted him to *live* with his cousin, but not let it slip out that they were cousins?

Rob gave him a puzzled look. "I think it's a great idea," he said.

"I think so too," Colleen said. "You just cover the utilities and basic up-keep and I won't charge you rent."

Fantastic. She was making it too cheap to say no. It's like she knew he was trying to save money to marry Nell. He'd left his job at the gas station months ago to go work in a factory. It paid more, but he still had to live frugally.

Nell wanted a Christmas wedding, six months from now. Six months of no rent could help him come up with the down payment for a small mortgage. Surely, he could hack living with Rob for six months without blurting the truth out.

--

He was explaining his new living situation to Nell, telling her about how much he'd be able to save.

"So how is Rob as a roommate?" Nell asked him, before turning her attention to her little niece. "Miranda, just one." They were at the corner grocery store in Marshall, babysitting Nell's (and soon his) two-year-old niece for the afternoon. They'd gone to the park, and then walked Miranda up to the corner store for an ice cream. Miranda was having trouble deciding what she wanted and getting her fingerprints all over the sliding glass door.

Finally, she settled on an ice cream sandwich. Mitch grabbed a couple drumsticks too and then fished crumbled dollar bills out of his jeans and paid the cashier. They went outside and sat on the curb to eat their ice cream, Nell keeping a grip on Miranda's petite shoulder, lest she run out into the street. But the toddler was too absorbed in her ice cream to dodge into traffic. Plus, Marshall didn't really have traffic.

"So, we were talking about Rob as a roommate," Nell said.

Mitch shrugged. "He's OK. Your typical guy roommate. Leaves his dirty dishes and socks everywhere. I'm looking forward to living with a girl."

Nell rolled her eyes. "If you think I'm going to be good as a maid, you've got another thing coming."

"I wasn't talking about housework," Mitch gave her a look. She blushed and nudged him with her shoulder.

Shortly after that, they finished their ice cream and got up to start walking back to Miranda's house. Mitch swung Miranda onto his shoulder where she rode, giggling the whole way. Patsy was home from her shift at the restaurant; they dropped Miranda off and left.

They decided to drive around the county and look for potential houses to buy. Nell was beyond excited, turning him down first one street and then another. But Mitch found himself distracted. Again.

The closer it got to their wedding, the more Mitch knew it was time to tell Nell the whole truth. How could he marry her, but not trust her with the truth? But he was afraid he'd waited too long, afraid she'd feel deceived.

He'd talked about his family, of course; his *Grant* family. His childhood in Asheville. She knew most of those stories. She was looking forward to meeting his family, for the first time, when they came for the wedding.

That was why he had to tell her. Because Mom wasn't coming to their wedding. She refused, point blank.

"Mitch, hey, where are you?" Nell asked, waving her palm in front of his face.

He sighed and pulled off to the side of a gravel road.

"There's something I have to tell you," he said, looking down at his hands.

"OK. This sounds serious."

"It is. I'm afraid you're going to be mad at me."

"I swear to God, Mitchell, if you are backing out on marrying me. . ."

"No, no! Of course not! I'd marry you right now if you didn't want this big fancy wedding."

"OK, good. And I do; want the big fancy wedding, that is. I've dreamed about it since I was little. A Christmas Eve wedding."

"My mom isn't coming," he blurted out.

"What?! Why?"

"That's what I have to tell you. And I'm afraid you'll be angry at me for not telling you sooner."

"I've been angry at you before, and we've got through it. Just tell me."

"My mom's maiden name is Carolyn Calvert. The Calverts from Judson. Rob is my cousin. He doesn't know it either. Colleen is my aunt, my mom's sister. My mom grew up in this county; she went to church where your dad still preaches. He baptized her and everything."

Nell was quiet for a few moments, watching him, with a slightly guilty look on her face. She dropped her gaze. "Now it's my turn to worry you'll be mad at me. I already knew all that."

"You did? How?"

"My Dad told me."

"How did he know? I didn't tell him."

"He said it wasn't hard to figure out. You look like your mom. And then Colleen came to him and confirmed it."

"And he told you."

She nodded. "You and I were already dating pretty seriously. He said he thought I should know, thought it would help. He sat me down in his study at home, he has all his serious talks in there, it's called the confessional armchair—and he told me, eventually, you were going to tell me. He was worried I'd feel angry and blindsided. He wanted to ease me into it, I think. Make sure that when you finally told me, I wouldn't make it about myself; wouldn't see it as a betrayal. He loves you, you know that, right?"

"What else did he tell you?" Mitch asked.

Nell shrugged and gave him a puzzled look, before saying,"Just that. Just that your mom grew up here and is Colleen's sister. Honestly, I'm confused on what the big deal is and why it's a secret anyway."

"So you don't know anything else?"

"No, and I'm not sure I want to, but you'd better tell me anyway." She reached over and took his hand.

He took a deep breath and began talking.

Mitch
Excerpt from *Becoming Hoosier*
Christmas Eve 1983

Their wedding day was the best day of his life, dimmed only by the absence of his own mother.

Dad had come. Uncle George, Aunt Claudia, and Adley had come too. They'd all fought Mom on this one, refused to buckle under. They were all outraged and heartbroken that she'd refused to come to her son's wedding.

"Her stubbornness be damned. She should be here for this," Aunt Claudia told him, placing both hands against his face and kissing his forehead. "She'll regret this forever."

His two aunts: one who'd known Carolyn best for the first half of her life, and the other who knew her best for her second half, had joined forces and tried to morph into a mother figure for him on his wedding day. He loved them for it, but they were trying too hard. (Plus, Aunt Colleen was clearly relived that Carolyn hadn't come, though she wouldn't ever say it. Her relief at avoiding an awkward scene annoyed Mitch. Her overcompensating by hovering over him annoyed him more.)

His mother's absence hurt like hell. It really did. But he couldn't dwell on it. He was sincerely happy on this day.

It was a beautiful Christmas Eve wedding. They got married at seven p.m. the church lit by a hundred candles and decorated in holly and poinsettias and mistletoe. Their bridal party wore red and black. Nell wore a ball gown style, satin wedding dress with a fur throw over her shoulders. Her hair was loose, teased curls under her veil. He could smell her hair spray.

And when they left the church, hand in hand, and walked through the church doors onto the steps, to the sound of the bells chiming, it was snowing.
--

Forty-Three
Willie
February 2016

I took Tara and Frankie over to Grandpa Simon's on Valentine's Day afternoon so he could give them their cards and candy baskets. Cheryl had always made the grandbabies treat baskets for every holiday; it was a tradition Simon continued. He handed Tara and Frankie their baskets, and they squealed in delight, then darted off quickly.

"Just a couple pieces of candy!" I admonished them as they dug in, knowing it was pointless. If grandparents were bad about spoiling, great-grandparents were even worse.

"Oh, now, a little candy never hurt anyone," Simon told me. I looked pointedly at the insulin shot he had resting on the kitchen table. He followed my gaze, and then shuffled across the kitchen. "Better put this up; wouldn't want Frankie grabbing it." He spent a few moments clearing the table of his medications.

"Want some help with that?" I asked.

"No, no, dear. I have a system. I hope you don't mind me giving the kids treats? I made sure not to put in anything Frankie could choke on."

"It's alright, Simon. Really. I'll just pop home and get them their overnight bags so they can stay with you." I teased him.

He chuckled. "I'm not sure if I'd be watching them or if they'd be watching me."

I laughed.

"Now, where did I put your present?" Simon asked himself as he looked around.

"You didn't have to get me anything. I'm going to confiscate that candy just as soon as we leave here and eat it myself."

"Well, it's not so much a present, as it is a loan."

"Oh?"

"Yes, here they are." Simon fished out a box he had tucked in the corner, and grunted as he hefted it up and lugged it to the table.

"I'm not sure you'll want to accept this gift because it's a bit of a job."

"Now I am curious." I leaned over and peered inside as he put the box on the table. My writer's heart did a jig when I realized what was in there.

"It's Cheryl's journals," Simon said, confirming what I'd suspected.

"Yes?" I prompted, trying to not appear overly eager and greedy.

"Would you like to take them and try to decipher them? Cheryl had terrible penmanship, and writing was not her strong suit. But she diligently recorded our life together. I'd be grateful if you could do something with them. Make them easier to read somehow, I guess. I'd like to give them out to all the kids."

"I think that's a fabulous idea, Simon! And I would love to."

He smiled and gestured for me to dig into the box. Then a momentary flicker of panic crossed his face, "I want her journals back, though," he told me.

"Of course. I know what they mean to you. I won't let anything happen to them."

The kids were parked in front in front of the

TV, more candy wrappers than I wanted to acknowledge scattered across the floor. I should go put a stop to that, I thought. But the damage was done, what was a few more minutes, especially when they were calm for once?

I gave in to my guilty pleasure, pulled out a kitchen chair, sat down, and lifted out the first journal.

--

Willie
Valentine's Day 2016

Lynn had a tendency to "forget" her cell phone and go wandering that winter. And we had a tendency to forget that she'd grown up here, was familiar with the whole county. Her age made us think words like "senility" and "broken hip."

But the one time Mitch suggested to his mother, that she *not* hike alone at Turkey Run State Park, after it snowed, she bit his head off. Mitch, unfazed, demanded she wait until the ice melted, at least.

The rest of us were less brave with Lynn and let her do as "she damned well pleased."

Which was why, on Valentine's Day, she was unaccounted for, for hours. Gibson and Adley had made a surprise trip up so Gibson could be "with his sweetheart." But they couldn't find her anywhere.

While I was still at Simon's with the kids, lost in Cheryl's journals, I got three increasingly concerned voicemails from Mitch. When I called him back and said I didn't know where she was, I could hear the worry in his voice.

"I'll be right there," I said. I loaded up the kids, and picked Morgan up. Then we all headed over to the Judson House.

By evening, we were getting frantic; there was talk of posting a "missing elderly woman" report on Facebook. Adley was scrolling through her phone to find a recent and decent picture of Lynn because we all knew there would be hell to pay later for posting a missing person's status, and double hell to pay if we chose an un-faltering photo.

We were all standing in the Judson house: Me, Morgan, and the kids, Rob, Mitch and Nell, Gibson and Adley. Rob was just as distraught as the rest of us, but he still thought he was just worrying over his tenant, a woman who faintly made him think of his own mother for some reason.

It started snowing heavily and the temperature dropped. We worried all the more.

Lynn had been borrowing Mitch's old truck, but it was still in the drive. Her cell phone rested on the counter, the battery dead. Her winter boots and long, white, fleece lined coat and hat and gloves were gone. Whenever she'd gone, she'd gone on foot.

It came to me as a snapshot image: not Carolyn as a young girl, standing in the creek in a white nightgown on a spring morning. But Lynn as an old woman, standing in the creek in a white coat on a winter night.

Winter night; frozen creek. Oh GOD.

"Come with me! I know where she's at!"

--

Forty-Four
Lynn
Excerpt from *Nymph of the Oak Tree: A Tale of Coming Home*
Valentine's Day 2016

She'd been gone too long, wandering the town and woods outside of Judson. They were going to have a conniption fit if she didn't get back already. It was spitting snow. Bud had lectured her about "wandering off" like she was the child, and he the parent.

"I'm just worried you'll get lost, Mom."

Ha! If her mind was slipping—and it wasn't—then weren't childhood memories the last to go? She would remember this land, this town, this creek forever. And hadn't she tried to forget?

Gib had been right, though she'd never tell him that. She'd been walking her past in her dreams for too long. He'd told her that she'd better walk her hometown streets for real one last time before she died.

"You don't want to go into the afterlife with unresolved issues on Earth." He'd been saying that—or some variation of that—for years. Since the '70s, at least.

She always told him, "You know I don't believe in the afterlife, so what does it matter if I show up to death with baggage?"

To which he either gave her a look or reached out and hooked an arm around her waist, pulling her onto his lap, and nuzzled her neck. For a man with limp spaghetti legs, he had strong arms.

How she loved that man. She wished, not for

the first time, that she was more demonstrative with her love. She wished she was one of those wives who could melt, so entirely, around her husband. But Lynn was always just a little bit restrained, a little bit hard.

With Gib. And with Mitch. The two people she loved the most, yet always felt like she couldn't love enough. Like she was failing them.

Her mind had been lost in regrets; she hadn't realized where she was going. Or maybe she had. She found herself standing on the creek bank, looking at the small pool where she'd been baptized all those years ago.

A fake baptism for a fake convert.

How foolish she'd been that day, thinking the worst thing was people caring about her soul, nagging her about salvation.

She had stood, that day, on the brink of one of the worst things.

She'd heard a Christian say once, callously, self-righteously, that God only protected those who were His. You can't claim God's protection or God's blessing if you aren't saved. He only answered the prayers of His sheep.

And she'd wondered, deep down, if she'd gotten saved for real that day, would God had prevented her getting raped? Did He really look down from Heaven, as her body and soul were being plundered and exploited, and say "Ahh, if only you were mine, I would supernaturally stop this evil happening to you."

If so, that was bullshit, and she wanted no part of God.

She could not resign herself to a conditional-love God; a God who turned a deaf ear to people who didn't check the right denomination box.

She was overcome by the insane urge to descend into the creek water again, to submerge and come up unsaved. To undo her baptism. The anti-baptism. The rejection of the religious ritual that ushered in the damnedest chapter of her life.

Perhaps the baptism and rape were separate events, total moral opposites that just happened to coincide on the same day. Perhaps some pastors and counselors and Christian lay people would tell her to disassociate the two events: they would say, You were baptized, and you were raped. You were not raped because you were baptized.

But she could not separate the two events! To remember one was to be haunted by the other. She associated the pretended-salvation of her soul with the violation of her body. And she had spent the rest of her life rejecting, suppressing, and ignoring the soul aspect of herself in order to preserve her body.

She could see it now, looking back. Her obsession with nature, science, and body. She'd spent her whole life carefully monitoring what happened to her body: what she ate, how she exercised, how she expressed her sexuality. Every choice she'd made had been a desperate attempt to maintain control over her physical body.

But what she'd ignored was how out of control she felt about her soul. Ever since she had allowed herself to be submerged in a baptism she didn't choose, she'd felt like she'd had her soul wrested from her, her soul smooshed into a tiny, religious box.

Perhaps that's why she could not disassociate the two events: because both felt like thievery to her. Sanders had taken her body with evil intentions. Her family and community, with good, well-meaning intentions, had taken her soul, tried to make it conform to what they believed was Truth.

But she hadn't believed. She'd been forced into something at the wrong time before she'd wrestled it out for herself.

Isn't that what the church in every damn generation has failed to grasp? That you can't force conversion, not with a sword, not with guilt, not with fire and brimstone screaming.

She'd spent her whole life in the practice of reclaiming her body. And Dammit, now she wanted her soul back too!

It was beyond stupid, what she was doing. She knew that with the rational part of her brain, but she wasn't operating with the rational part of her brain. She was on a different plain, outside of time and space and nature's laws.

The creek was iced over; it looked thick enough.

I'm just going to step out there, just for a moment. I'm going to stand on the spot where they baptized me, and I'm going to reclaim my soul. This is personal. There's no audience. No religious agenda. No expectations. No one to please.

Just me, and my Maker, whoever she is.

I'm going to start over.

She cautiously glided across the ice until she was standing in the middle of the pool. The ice was creaking, but it was holding. She closed her eyes, took a deep breath through her nose, opening up her lungs.

My Soul belongs to me. I worship the God of Mystery not religion. Only She is allowed to claim me; show me who you are.

It was the first real prayer Lynn had ever prayed. And it was answered with the sickening CRACK of the ice giving way under her weight.
--

"Hello?" She demanded. Her heart was racing, the hairs on her arms standing on end. And she knew who was in the basement with her.

"Let me out, Sanders."

"In a minute." He told her; she heard, rather than saw, him undo his belt. Her stomach gave a lurch. Oh, hell no, she thought. You aren't raping *me*.

She burst forward, ramming into him, trying to make a break for the door. She got there, but her hands were sweaty and slipped on the doorknob. She was trembling. That mistake gave him time to recover and grab her.

He slammed her back against the concrete block wall. Her head smacked against the concrete, dazing her. One of his hands gripped her throat; the other pawed at her, yanking her dress up, her underwear and nylons down.

Then his fingers were inside of her, *inside of her*. Uninvited; unwanted. She felt rage rip through her, but it was rage layered under disbelief and confusion. Her head was swimming; her body pinned by his force. She couldn't understand what was happening, how it was happening, why it was happening. She tried to struggled; tried to scream, but he was choking her.

She could barely breathe; her lungs were on fire. All of her fight was used up on just trying to stay alive.

She couldn't stop him. She would tell herself that for years afterward when she was reliving it, condemning herself for not fighting harder. For allowing herself to become a victim.

It took less than ten minutes from the time he closed the door until when he climbed off of her, leaving his sperm oozing down her upper thigh. She was on the floor, her dress rucked up, her nylons and underwear tossed aside.

He fixed himself. As he was fastening his pants and putting on his belt, he looked down at her and said, "You're a goddamn cold bitch, you know that? You could have tried a little participation. Keep that in mind for next time." And then he left.

Time had no measure. She might have laid there for five minutes or a hundred years. She finally found the courage to get up; she forced herself to stumble to the bathroom, to turn on the light and to look in the mirror. There were his fingertip marks on her neck where he'd choked her. How could she hide those? For she knew she wanted to hide this. No one could know. She would tell no one, and then she would forget.

There was a knock on the bathroom door. Carolyn flinched.

"Car, is that you?" It was Colleen. "It's time to go. Everyone else has left. We're supposed to lock up. What are you doing in there? You've been in for ages!"

"Go away, Colleen. I'll meet you at home!"
"No, I have to use the bathroom. Let me in!"
"Use it at home!"
"I've had to go all night!"
"Five more minutes won't kill you!"
"Carolyn!"
"Fine!" Carolyn swung the door open with too much force and Colleen, who'd been leaning on

it, tripped inside. Colleen hustled to the toilet, too distracted by her bladder to notice her sister turning her body away.

"Ahh. That's better," Colleen said as she flushed the toilet. It was only when she was washing her hands that she noticed her sister refusing to look at her, practically hiding herself in the corner. "Why are you acting so odd?"

"I'm not. Are you finished?"

"Carolyn, look at me." She approached her sister. She grabbed Carolyn's shoulder; Carolyn flinched and pulled away. "Look at me! What happened?"

"Nothing."

"Nothing? Oh my God! Carolyn! Your neck! Who did this to you?"

"It doesn't matter."

"Doesn't matter? Carolyn, there is blood on your legs! I said, who did this to you?" Carolyn had never heard her soft-spoken sister yell like this. She answered her.

"Sanders."

"I'll kill him."

"Will you? You? Little Miss Christian?"

"Well—we have to tell Dad. And the police."

"No."

"Carolyn, you've been raped,"

"I said NO, goddamn it! NO! I don't want anyone to know. I didn't want *you* to know! But you barged in here anyway! Damn it, Colleen! Why can't you ever just leave me be?"

"Carolyn. Look at me!" Colleen demanded, but her voice was quieter, gentle again. She took her sister's hands, refusing to let her pull away. "This is not your fault. You have to fight for yourself."

Carolyn looked away, then forced herself to look back. "I know that. I do. But it is my life. I don't want everyone to know; I don't want to be the topic of conversation. Please. Please, don't tell."

"What about justice!? What about stopping him!?"

"I don't want to live through *justice*. Do you think I want to sit in court and talk about this? Would you want to talk about it?"

"But what if he comes after you again?"

"I'll be smarter. Faster. He won't get me again."

"Carolyn, please," Colleen begged.

"Colleen, don't tell. Don't tell anyone. That's what I want. That's how you can help me."

Colleen hesitated, a fierce internal battle played out across her face. Carolyn had always been able to read her sister's thoughts; Carolyn stared her down, pulling herself up to her eldest sister height. In the end, Colleen always bent to Carolyn's stubbornness. Birth order was a powerful force. They had their roles.

Finally, Colleen nodded. Then in silence, she helped clean her sister up, tenderly washing blood and sperm away, pulling her own powder and lipstick from her purse. She steered Carolyn to the toilet seat and combed out her hair, applied makeup. Carolyn allowed her eyes to close, allowed herself the small comfort of her sister grooming her, trying to put her back together again. Then Colleen went and retrieved Carolyn's nylons and underwear; Carolyn forced herself to put them back on, the image of the snags and runs in the nylons searing into her memory.

What she wanted was to get out of this basement bathroom, get out and never come back.

But before she left, she had to have herself and her appearance under control.

"My powder covers it enough to get you home tonight. No one will see in the dark and you'll just have to go straight to bed without seeing Mother and Dad. But tomorrow you'll have to have a heavier concealer. I have some in my room you can have, but we'll need to buy more. I imagine these marks will take a while to fade."

And deep inside, Carolyn thought it'll take my whole life. I'll have to wear concealer my whole damned life.

--

Where was she? She had a vague, terrifying memory of her descent into icy, black water. That's where she was: in the creek, drowning.

An image came to mind, as vividly as if she were actually living it again: It was 1995.

Colleen was standing on her doorstep. Asking for forgiveness. Asking her to come home.

Carolyn slammed the door in her face. Stared out the curtain for a long time, watching Colleen hover on the door step. Watching Colleen finally walk away.

Back in real time: A fight to break the surface, a scramble to grab the oak branch stretched above her. Something was the matter with her ankle. The water was deep enough to submerge her if she let go. She didn't have the strength to pull herself out.

How long had she been here?

Had she screamed? Had anyone heard?

It was dark now. Snowing was falling hard.

She was cold. No, not cold. She couldn't think of the word to describe this temperature.

She couldn't think in words. Images were coming to her instead.
--
It was the day after Colleen came and left. Lynn was sitting at Claudia's kitchen table, telling her.

"So you turned her away?" Claudia asked, handing her a glass of sweet tea, staring at Lynn over the top of her glasses.

"You think I made a mistake." Lynn said.

"No. Mistake implies ignorance; a wrong choice made from good intentions. You didn't make a mistake. You made a deliberate, selfish choice to slam the door in her face."

"That's hurtful. You don't know what I've been through. You don't know what she told me to do."

"Yes. I do. You told me. Years ago. Remember?"

"Maybe I shouldn't have."

Claudia shrugged. "If I was writing your story, you'd go home, you'd forgive your sister. You'd be there for your son. That's all I'm saying."

"I don't need to go back there to be there for Bud."

"Seven babies. Seven babies, Lynn. He's lost seven children. And now he's losing his wife, and you can't show up for him? You expect him to come to you?"

"I can't fix this for him."

"No, you can't. But you can be there. You should be there. The only rule to motherhood is showing up."
--

And then, another image. Claudia, her body hunched in a car, her neck and head snapped at an unnatural angle. George, next to her, in the driver's seat, dead too.

Lynn had driven by the accident on her way to the store, recognized their car twisted around the tree. She veered off, put her car in park, and darted out toward them as sirens pierced the air, coming closer. No, no, no, not them, she kept saying. Not Claudia and George.

Bud came home for the funeral—without Nell. He was graying at the temples. His eyes were aged.

He stood next to Adley the entire viewing and funeral, literally wrapping his arm around her shoulders and holding her up as she buried her parents.

Lynn watched those two: her son and her niece. Cousins, but pretty much siblings. They'd grown up in the same house for a good portion of their childhoods. They'd tormented and teased each other, fought over anything and everything.

Now, as adults, they were friends, supporting each other. Bud, a father carrying around seven tiny ghosts in his aching arms, was in the midst of a divorce. Adley, an adult orphan, was in the midst of motherhood and marriage and ministry. They were both consumed by grief, trying to be strong for each other.

Lynn watched them, as she clutched Gib's hand. He seemed far away, eyes glazed over. He didn't seem to hear anyone talking; people had to repeat themselves multiple times to get his attention. He just kept staring at the two coffins, as if trying to figure out how George got to die without him. Trying to figure out how they were born together, but Claudia's and not his, was the coffin next to George's.

In the aftermath, Lynn told herself that she stayed in Asheville for Gibson, Adley, and the boys. They needed her. Gibson needed her especially. This was her home. She'd done her best to comfort Bud while he was home; what could she do for him, really, back in Indiana?

But she was haunted by Bud and Adley showing up for each other, as siblings should. She was haunted by Gibson's crippling grief for his brother. She was haunted by these images of what sibling love should look like: being so present in your brother's life that his death felt like your own.

For as ravished by grief as Gibson was, she knew he'd made the better choice. She knew his pain was evidence that he'd loved his brother and sister-in-law well.

She should have gone home then; then, when there was still the chance to love her sister well. Colleen hadn't died until 2005; they could have had a decade.

Yet Lynn had slammed that door shut, and never opened it.

And now, she was at her end, treading water in a lifetime of regrets.

--

Forty-Five
Willie
February 2016

Rob, Mitch, Morgan and I paused just long enough to throw on coats and boots and then we piled into Rob's truck.

"Go to the creek!" I yelled.

"The creek?" Rob said. "Which direction?"

I pointed, unable to think of whether it would be north or south, east or west. I'd never been good with directions.

Rob took off, tires crunching on the snow, down the block, out of town, around the curve.

"Stop!" I yelled. "Here! She's here."

Rob threw it into park and went to kill the engine. "Leave it running," I told him. "We'll need it warm."

No one questioned how I knew this. I didn't even know myself. How I could sense what was happening to this woman I could barely stand to be around?

We all pulled out our cell phones, modern day flash lights, and used their beams to pick our way to the creek.

I can't explain the calm that descended on me, like the snow falling silently on my hair and shoulders. I knew it was bad before we saw her, yet it was like my mind hovered over my body, instructing me, calmly, telling me which part of the creek to walk to.

She was where the creek curved and widened out, forming a six feet deep pool. It had frozen over that winter, but only a couple inches thick, not enough to sustain the weight of a woman.

She had fallen through but had managed to hold onto an oak branch that stretched out over the creek. She hadn't had enough upper body strength to haul herself out of the water. To this day, I can't figure out how she managed to hold on.

I heard Rob, Mitch, and Morgan all emit the same guttural scream of her name. "MOM!" for Mitch; "Lynn" for Morgan and Rob. But I was silent, operating still in this strange peace, as if I'd lived through this before and knew it was going to be OK.

It's hard for me to describe the following minutes; they were both slow motion and lightning speed. Time didn't really exist, and yet, time was all that mattered.

We slipped and slid our way to the creek bank; Morgan and Rob threw themselves down on their bellies and each grabbed an arm, hoisting Lynn out of the frigid water and pulling her onto the bank. She was delirious and barely conscious.

--

Lynn

Voices. She couldn't place them.

Arms. Someone was reaching down, hooking arms under hers and hauling her up.

She was looking into her sister's eyes. "Colleen," she whispered, or thought she did.

"What'd she say?" A voice asked.

"Who cares? She's still alive! Get her to the truck."

--

Willie

Somehow, they managed to carry her without falling; they slid her into the backseat and we all piled back in. Rob took off for the house; Morgan was already calling an ambulance, saying words like "fell through the ice" and "hypothermia."

The rest really is a blur. Multiple hands stripping Lynn's wet clothes off, wrapping her in every blanket we could find, rubbing heat back into her skin with our palms, chanting over and over, "come on, Lynn; stay with us."

I remember the sounds: the wail of an ambulance piercing the silence of the night; the whimpers from my children from the living room couch; Mitch's chants of "Oh, God, Please. Not my Mom."

--

Lynn

She was in and out. Your physical body: that's what's subject to nature's laws, to space, and time. The mind: it wanders. The soul: it leads.

Lynn, in the first forty-eight hours in the hospital, dreamed over and over of drowning, of descending into the water, and being unable to break the surface. Faces loomed above her, watery, blurred images, people arguing about whether or not to save her, what they should save her *for*.

But then, the oak tree on the bank morphed into a female figure, an ancient, gnarled tree fairy. She swung out her branch-arms, swiping the people out of the way, and reaching down through the broken ice.

She scooped Lynn out of the depths, set her on her feet, and morphed back into a tree.

When Lynn looked up, she saw Willie, Claudia, and Adley sitting under the tree, scribbling furiously on the tree's leaves, which became parchment as they wrote, and then binding them together into a sort of book.

Then, Lynn noticed Colleen, standing on the bank, a towel open in her outstretched arms, beckoning Lynn to come and get dried off. Without thinking, Lynn walked out of the water toward her sister.

As Colleen wrapped the towel around her, Willie walked toward them. Willie held out the leaf booklet as an offering. "This is your story; finish it."

Only when Lynn reached out and accepted it, did she wake.

--

Forty-Six
Willie and Lynn

Willie was there, sitting in the chair by her hospital bed. She was texting; that child was always texting.

"Oh, you're awake! I'll go get someone." Willie made a move to rise. Lynn lifted her hand to stop her.

"Not yet."

"OK, but. . . it's just everyone's so worried. I should tell them. . ."

"I said not yet!"

"OK." Willie sat back down.

"You don't know everything."

"What?"

"About me. You don't know everything about me."

"Lynn, I'm sorry. I shouldn't have read your journals."

"That's what I'm telling you. I didn't write it all down. I read what you wrote about me when you sent me all my journals and your biography on me. And all I could think is, this woman—this version of me—doesn't make sense. And it's because you don't know everything."

"OK." Willie paused. "Do you want to tell me? You don't have to."

"When I was sixteen, on the day I was baptized, I was also raped. In my church. By a boy in my class. And Colleen is the only one who knew about it then."

"Oh, Lynn."

"Carolyn. My name's Carolyn."

Willie nodded. "I don't know what to say."

"I didn't tell you so that you'd say anything. I told you so you'd know me. I want to be known."

Willie's phone buzzed, and she glanced at the screen.

"Aren't you supposed to turn your cell phone off in a hospital room?" Carolyn asked.

"I don't know."

"What do you mean you don't know? I'm hooked up to all these machines, and you don't know if your cell phone might mess them up?"

Willie shrugged. "I've been here off and on for two days, texting people updates, and you haven't died."

"Are you sure you aren't trying to make my machines go haywire and stop my heart?"

"I really don't think it works like that. Anyway, as far as I know, nothing is hooked up to your heart. But I'm not a doctor."

"Your lackadaisical attitude is not reassuring."

"Would you like me to go get a nurse?"

"You'd better. Is Bud here?"

"Of course. Do you want him too?"

Carolyn nodded.

--

Willie

Lynn lived. But she nearly lost a foot to frost bite; she came down with pneumonia. Her age prolonged the healing process, and she was in the hospital for a month.

It was during her stay at the hospital that Rob finally found out.

For some reason, I had a tendency to always be present when these major revelations happened. Gift or Curse, I really don't know.

On one visit, Gibson had brought Lynn the old photo albums that I had mailed to her when I stopped my writing project.

He powered his chair right up to her bed, and said, "Honey, you need to look at these."

She turned her head away and looked out the window, refusing to answer him. Gibson left the album on her bedside table.

A week later, Rob came to visit her, unannounced, and walked in on her crying over pictures of his own mother.

"Hey!" He said. "That's my mom! Why have I never seen these before? And why do you have them?"

"This girl standing next to her?" Lynn began, pointing.

"Yeah? My aunt Carolyn. She died before I was born."

Lynn shook her head. "No. She didn't. She's alive. She goes by Lynn now."

Rob stared at her, just stared, for several long moments.

"Who are you?" He finally demanded in a strangled voice.

"Your aunt. Carolyn. Your mom's sister."

"Then Mitch?"

"Your cousin."

"Does he know?"

"Yes."

"Did Mom know who he was?"

"Yes."

"And no one could ever be bothered to tell me? Why?"

"I don't have the answer to that, honey," Lynn said softly, reaching out for his hand. He snatched it away.

"Don't call me 'honey', like I'm your nephew; like you've been there my whole life. And don't touch me!" He spun on his heel and left.

--

Rob's anger, unsettling to everyone, was the kind that kept on feeding itself. The story kept tumbling out too: revelation and betrayal one on top of the other.

First, his own mother not telling him. Then Mitch; then Lynn. Decades of lies.

Then it came out that Erin and I had started all of this with our snooping and writing.

By the end of the week, Rob wasn't speaking to any of us, not even his own daughter.

I would have felt bad, if pouting hadn't looked so ridiculous on him. I *did* feel bad, it's just I was also tired of the whole thing. Honestly, it wasn't even that complex of a plot line. Just a damn lack of communication between two sisters and a grudge that should have been resolved five decades ago.

It's called family therapy, people. Try it.

--

"Rob," I was saying, as he tacked a piece of computer paper to the Judson House front door. "You cannot evict an old woman who's coming home from the hospital. It's just not done."

"I don't care. She lied to me. And she's not welcome in my mother's house."

"This is more of Lynn's house than it is yours," I told him. "She grew up here just as much as your mother did."

"Don't you speak of my mother! Don't you dare!"

Rob had decided to gloss over his mom not telling him about Carolyn and laid the full blame in the land of the living. He'd also mostly forgiven Erin because she was expecting his first grandchild. So that left me and Lynn: Lynn the troubled sister who broke his mother's heart, and me, the snoopy writer who'd dared to suggest Colleen wasn't completely innocent in all of this either.

"Why are you even here?" He asked.

"Well, if you really are going to evict her, I need to at least collect her things. Can I go in, please?"

"It's not like she's going to be homeless. She has a home. In Asheville. And she can go back to it. And no, you very well cannot go inside and get her things. I'll do it."

"Now you listen here, Rob. You have a right to be angry and hurt. I won't deny that. But Lynn asked me to pack up her things, and no matter how mad you are, you don't have a right to pack up her underwear if she doesn't want you to! No matter how much you don't like her, she still has a right to privacy!"

He gave me a look. Point taken. But still, I wasn't backing down.

Finally, he sighed, opened the door, and let me in. "Make it quick," he told me.

--

Nell and I took Lynn back to Asheville. Lynn was sleeping in the front passenger seat. Nell and I were having a quiet conversation about all kinds of things while the radio played softly as background noise. We were treating Lynn as I treated Frankie, I realized. Afraid to wake her; leaving the radio set to the station it was on when she fell asleep.

"You know, there's one thing I still can't figure out," I was telling Nell.

"What?"

"How in the world did Lynn manage to hold onto that tree branch for so long?"

Before Nell could respond, Lynn mumbled, without opening her eyes, "I didn't. It held onto me."

--

Forty-Seven
Willie
Easter 2016

The week before Easter, Lynn, Gibson, and Adley came to spend it with Mitch and Nell.

It seemed like everything had, after decades, been resolved. Everyone knew who everyone was. We'd survived all the major revelations. Rob had begun to come around, even agreed to come to Easter dinner. He even allowed Gibson, Adley, and Lynn to stay in the Judson house. "But no snooping in the attic." As if a wheelchair-bound man and a woman recovering from her past and pneumonia were going to brave those stairs.

We were all ready for some peace.

And then Gerald died.

He was the character I never explored in all of this; the man-child in a nursing home. There's only so many characters you can redeem in one story. And the truth is, Gerald and Gerty deserve the space for their story to be told fully, or not at all.

Mitch, of course, went to the funeral. He asked his Mom if she wanted to come, but we all knew it was a courtesy question; an offer Lynn would decline. Some things just aren't done.

"Let her bury him in peace," she said, and that was it.

--

Lynn asked if she could cook Easter dinner at her house. That's how she said it, "my house." I didn't point that out. But I filed it away in my brain: Lynn's use of the possessive.

We all showed up at the Judson house and walked inside to the smells of glazed ham and yeast rolls, and the sight of Gibson cat napping and Adley washing dishes, but no Lynn.

"She's back down at the creek," Adley said.

"Damn it, Adley, why didn't you stop her?" Mitch yelled.

Adley turned and gave him a look. "You know damn well why, Mitchell Bud. And don't you talk to me like that."

He let out an exasperated sigh. "I'll go get her," Mitch said, turning back toward the door.

"No," Adley said forcefully. "Willie will go."

"I will?" I asked. I sort of had my hands full with a squirming Frankie and a hot casserole.

"It's supposed to be you," Adley told me matter of fact. Then she and Nell took Frankie and the casserole out of my arms.

I decided to walk to the creek; it wasn't that far. A few yards down the road, I got tired of my high heels sinking down, and I took them off and walked barefoot, wincing slightly against the gravel.

I found her in the same spot.

"Everyone's looking for you," I said to her. She was leaning against the oak tree, the hem of her dress soaked, her feet bare, hair a loose, tangled mess with a few leaves and twigs caught in her tangles.

She didn't acknowledge my comment. Instead she said, "I got baptized in this creek, you know. This exact spot. Colleen did too. It was the same day. Her idea really; I just hitched a ride on her salvation. Figured I should get it out of the way, you know. Colleen believed. I'm not sure I ever really did."

I was struggling to come up with an

appropriate comment, but she didn't need or wait for my response.

"Colleen was always their favorite. You said you thought we looked like a tight knit family before, before I was raped, before my affair with Gerald. But I always knew that they favored Colleen, and I resented that. But I couldn't really blame them either. I was head strong and harsh. I held grudges. I was beautiful and I knew it. Haughty. That's the word. Colleen was just—sweet. Genuinely good. She forgave people easily; got along with everyone. She was easier to love." This last sentence came out as a whisper, and her voice broke. I looked up to see that she was crying.

"Oh, Lynn," I said. "Did you always think that? That you aren't easy to love?"

She nodded, wiping her eyes. "Look at me. An old woman blubbering like an idiot. I don't cry." She gave me a look, daring me to contradict her.

"I believe you, trust me."

She shook her head. "I should be over this by now. I let my resentment ruin my whole life, really. Ruin my relationship with my sister. Ruin my relationship with Mitch. Gibson is all I have, and hell, we both know he's living on sheer stubbornness and medication. And Adley. I have Adley and her boys. But I'll probably ruin that too. I ruin things Willie, that's what I'm good at."

"Don't forget your skill at being a complete hard ass on yourself. You've got that down too," I said.

She chuckled. She was silent for a while, then said quietly, "I should have come home."

I didn't have to ask when. "Why didn't you?"

She was quiet again for so long that I didn't

think she was going to answer; this would be the part of the story I didn't get: what had happened between her and Colleen.

"She believed me. About Gerald, I mean. My parents said all sorts of awful things to me. I'll not get into it. But Colleen accepted what I said. She believed that Gerald was the father. That made it worse though because Colleen was so—so—churchy. And not the fake kind. She honest to Christ, was a moral young woman. And she loved me, but she was so disappointed in me. My God, she prayed for my eternal soul when I told her the truth." Carolyn paused, looking out across the creek.

"A girl can only take so much of that. It's hard to watch somebody be so devastated about your bad choices. Anyway, I told her on our trip in Chicago.

"She told me I needed to accept consequences for my bad choices, face the responsibility. She told me to marry Sanders. I was angry; enraged far more than I'd been at our parents. Because she was my sister. She was this woman who loved and forgave everyone, who harped on and on about grace and second chances. But for me—her sister—she wanted to assign me to a lifetime of hell for my sins. She knew Sanders had raped me. She implied that maybe I hadn't been raped. Maybe I'd given Sanders some sort of green light; an invitation. And then changed my mind. If I was capable of having an affair with a married man, maybe I'd not been the innocent victim with Sanders. She told me this was God's will! She broke my heart that night. I left after she fell asleep."

"And you never saw her again?" I asked.

"In the nineties, she showed up on my doorstep in Asheville. I opened it, saw her, and slammed the door shut. That was the last time."

"Oh, Carolyn," I said weakly.

"I told you. I hold grudges. She came to make it right, and I refused to forgive her. And now, she is dead." She paused then looked me right in the eyes. "So, tell me something, Willie. If a woman has the worst thing happen to her *after* her baptism, and if she *does* the worst things *after* her baptism instead of before, if she's her worst self after religion, does that mean grace isn't for her?"

"I'm not very religious. I don't think I can answer that."

"Are you human? Then you're allowed to have opinions about spiritual matters; I didn't ask for a sermon. I just want your opinion."

"I think—I think that grace is either for everyone or it's for no one."

She nodded, closed her eyes, and then looked at the creek. "Good. Then baptize me."

"Excuse me?"

"Baptize me. Right now. Right here."

"Ahh, I don't think I'm comfortable with this."

"Why?"

"Why!? Because I'm not a pastor or a priest or even very faithful about going to church. Don't you have to be trained to baptize people? Like ordained or something?"

"I think you just have to be physically able to pull them up out of the water."

"How much do you weigh?"

"Haha. You're strong enough."

"Don't you think we should go get a pastor to do this?"

"You'll do."

"I don't even know the words."

"How about: Dear Jesus, please forgive this asshole."

"That seems wrong. I think there's less cussing in creeds."

"You'll think of the words. I need you to do this for me Willie. You heard my confessions, you *wrote* my story, so you're practically my priest already." And with that she waded into the water.

What choice did I have? I followed her, stood at her right side so that our bodies intersected. "Umm, close your eyes and don't swallow the creek water," I told her. And then using every bit of strength I had, I eased her body backwards toward the water, nearly going down with her. "In the name of the Father and the Son and the Holy Ghost, I hope this works." Then I whooshed her under and back up.

She came up out of the creek, sputtering and forgiven, I think. She pointed at a white towel hanging off the oak branch. When I handed it to her so she could wipe her eyes, and towel dry her hair, I thought I caught a glimpse of a figure sitting underneath the oak tree, but when I glanced back, she was gone.

I smiled though, sure of what I'd seen: Colleen, even now, even after death, piggy-backing her sister to Christ.

--

Forty-Eight
Willie
Spring 2016

Carolyn stayed on after Easter, though Gibson had to go back. She was back in full form, recovered from her fall and near-drowning. And her unorthodox creek baptism had lightened her spirit. She had a tendency to just show up unannounced with elaborate plans for me.

"Hi, Carolyn." I said, stepping onto the porch and drawing my sweater tighter around my torso. "What's up?"

"Come on, then, let's go," she said and walked back toward the driveway. Turning back toward me, she added, "You can drive."

"Forget your way around these back roads, did you?" I called out, not budging.

"No, my memory serves me fine. I just don't like to drive. Never have. Come along then."

"Where? What—I just can't leave, Lynn. The kids are inside."

"Where's your husband?"

"Inside."

"So, what's the problem?"

"Well, I—I mean. I can't just take off like that, without planning. It's lunch time. He'll need help. And then Frankie will need to be put down for a nap."

"And your husband is capable of creating children, but not feeding them?"

"Of course he's capable. We just have a routine."

"Not today, you don't. They'll survive without you. I'll give you two minutes to get in the car."

"This is ridiculous. You are ridiculous. You can't just show up and make demands like this. It's rude."

"It's also rude to read a woman's most intimate journals. But here we are anyway."

I trudged back into the house, leaving her on the porch.

It was full pandemonium. Tara was running around in just her underwear, scream-singing and dancing like she was possessed by fairies. Or sugar. I noticed two crumpled packets of fruit gummies in her hands.

Frankie was strapped into his high chair, one sock missing, blueberry slush smeared from nose to belly. He was also screaming, fat tears making rivulets through his blueberry smudges. His sippy cup, bowl, and spoon were thrown onto the floor.

Morgan was staring into the open fridge with a look of pure puzzlement on his face. "What the hell am I supposed to feed these kids? And where did you go?" He asked in a voice laced in betrayal. I'd stepped out for five minutes and come back to a full-scale riot.

"Carolyn's here. And you feed them this," I said, reaching around him to pull out yogurt, "And this," I grabbed carrots, "And this." I grabbed the bag of frozen chicken nuggets out of the freezer. For good measure, I slapped his backside and kissed his neck.

"Umm. Right. I was just about to grab that.

What did Lynn want?" Morgan rubbed his temples; Frankie was not letting up. Morgan walked over and pulled him out of the highchair. Frankie pointed frantically toward me, his little body jerking with hysteria.

I took Frankie into my arms, nestled him against me and started patting his back. He tangled his fingers into a loose tendril of my hair. I pushed the button to pre-heat the oven.

"She wants me to go with her somewhere. She's still out there."

"Now?" Morgan asked incredulously.

Tara let out a screech at the same moment we heard a crash from her bedroom.

"What the—" Morgan yelled, rushing off to her room. Frankie and I followed.

Tara was crumbled on the floor, holding her leg. Her bookshelf was turned over, books spilt everywhere.

"How many times have I told you not to stand on that, Tara?" Morgan demanded as he scooped Tara off of the floor into his arms. "Huh, how many times?!"

"I dunno. Lots," Tara mumbled into his chest.

"And will you listen, now?"

She nodded.

Morgan let out a frustrated sigh-growl.

"Are you hurt?"

"My knee!"

He pulled her leg out to look at it; sure enough, a big carpet burn and a bruise were already visible. "Alright. Let's go clean this up and get a band-aid."

Off they trudged to the bathroom.

Just then the smoke alarm started screaming,

which set Frankie back into full hysteria. Not to be outdone, Tara joined him. Apparently, the oven I'd been meaning to clean for weeks had caught fire to the crumbs and grease. Smoke billowed out when Morgan opened the oven door.

"Oh, for the love of—!"

This seemed like a great time to leave.

--

"I gave you two minutes! It's been at least fifteen!" Carolyn said by the time I slide into the driver's seat.

"Oh, hush. My husband's probably going to divorce me for leaving him alone in there, so I don't want to hear about it."

"That bad, huh?"

"Worse. The noise. So much noise. Why is there so much noise?"

"Couldn't tell you. That's why I didn't invite myself in. I remember toddler-land and shudder. I used to wear earplugs. I thought it would get better once Bud wasn't a toddler or little boy. But then he was a teenager, specifically a teenager with zero rhythm, thinking he could start a rock band. So you just trade one kind of noise for another."

"Mitch was in a rock band?" I asked, trying to imagine it.

"Umm, yes. For six whole months. Longest six months of my life. Sometimes mothers are secretly glad when their kids fail at things and give them up."

"Surely not." I joked.

"Just wait. Now drive like a bat out of hell or we won't make it."

"Where exactly are we going?"

"Yoga."

"Nuu-uhh," I said. "I tried that once. She kept telling me to follow my breath and clear my thoughts. And then I literally forgot how to breathe, and started freaking out that I am the most uncoordinated person on the planet because I couldn't figure out if I should inhale or exhale on cat position. So, by the end of it, I was borderline hyperventilating."

"Are you coordinated enough to talk and drive?"

"I said, I'm not going."

"Listen, the only, and I mean the only, good thing this county has gained in all the years I've been gone, is that yoga studio. You realize I dislike ninety percent of the people I see, right? Well, yoga keeps me from hating the solid one hundred percent. Drive. Now. Nell is meeting us there."

"Nell's coming? Well, Mitch really shouldn't be left alone. I'll go sit with him."

"He's taking a nap. He'll be fine. Just like your husband will be fine. It's good for men to be reminded they can do things without us. Now, I really, really hate being late."

"I'm not dressed for yoga."

Carolyn slowly gave me the once-over: taking in my stained *yoga* pants, baggey tee, and sweater. "Half of your outfit is designed for working out and the other half is a cry for help."

"Wow, thanks."

"Dear, I'm going to put this bluntly because we are down to seven minutes to get there on time. Motherhood is looking a bit rough on you."

I started to protests, exclamations of how much I love my children on my lips, but she cut me off.

"It's not an insult. You're doing well. You give those kids every bit of yourself. And that's the trouble; you're running out. Now, you can go back into that house right now, to the wailing toddler and the piles of laundry and the overwhelming paradox that mothering a child might last an eternity or it might end tomorrow. And you don't know which is more terrifying. Of course, all of these thoughts will be subconscious because your conscious brain power is used up on spills and diapers changes and Dr. Seuss. So, when you end up crying in the bathroom, staring down at those oatmeal stained yoga pants, you won't be quite sure what you're crying about. And then six months from now, you have a nervous breakdown and get diagnosed with postpartum depression, even though your child is almost two at that point."

I stared at her.

"Or," she said, with a shoulder shrug. "You could start the car and take a damn hour for yourself."

"Ok then," I said, putting the key into the ignition.

"Very good. Six minutes. Petal to the floorboard."

--

I was mostly fine doing yoga. And by fine I mean terrible and dying. They made me stretch muscles I didn't know existed. I was also having flashbacks to the sixth grade when I'd tried cheerleading: I was consistently a half step behind everyone in the movements.

And seriously, no joke, I couldn't figure out how to breathe correctly.

As we were doing cat and cow, arching our backs and then dropping our bellies, I kept getting mixed up on when I should exhale and inhale.

Child's pose: I even managed to do that one wrong.

Meanwhile, in front of me was Carolyn, and next to me was Nell, and they were irritating in their agility and flexibility. For goodness sake, Carolyn was old enough to be my grandmother, and had just recently nearly killed herself, and been in the hospital as a result. Nell was old enough to be my mom. Yet I was huffing and puffing, and muttering curse words instead of affirmations, while they were moving gracefully through warrior one and warrior two.

I kept trying to glance at the time, but the only clock was behind me and I thought that would be too obvious.

"Clear your mind and follow your breath. In and Out. Feel it through your heart center. Let it all go. This is your time; it's OK to take time for yourself."

I tried to stop thinking: stop imagining Frankie crying for Mama to come back. But the one time I successfully cleared my mind, and focused on oxygen filling my lungs, I farted. Loud. And smelly. Like rotten eggs smelly. Yeah.

Nell shot me the side eye, not breaking out of her perfect cobra position. Carolyn's body in front of me was vibrating either with suppressed laughter or the strain of tired muscles. I prefer to think it was the strain of muscles.

Everyone else had the good grace to politely ignore the sound and the smell. And that was no easy feat considering I was gagging myself. "Please God, let this be over. Please, please God, let this be over."

And then it was.

"See, that wasn't so bad," Carolyn said to me

back in the car.

"Where you in the same room as me?" I demanded.

"Oh, everyone passes gas doing yoga. Just… well, perhaps not quite as off-smelling as you. What did that baby do to your digestive system anyway?"

"Apparently bad things. Thanks. I didn't realize I was quite so off-smelling. That's a real encouragement. I look forward to showing my face in public."

"Oh, calm down. It's not like you know any of those people."

"Excuse me? I know *all* of them. The wife of my high school ex-boyfriend was in there, as was the restaurant manager from my first job. And my eye doctor."

"I doubt they'll even remember. We always magnify our own embarrassment and think everyone else goes around reliving it too. When truthfully we're all too self-focused to waste time remembering other people's embarrassing moments."

"Is that so, oh wise one?"

"Umm. Of course, the quickest way to get over it would be to come back. Perhaps farting while stretching was your body's way of asking for more exercise, more control."

"When do you return to Asheville?"

"Whenever I start missing Gibson too much. Until then, you're my project."

--

So that's how I ended up doing yoga regularly. And like an uncontrollable fungus, it grew on me until I actually looked forward to going.

I started thinking of myself as a whole, instead of fragmenting myself into categories: body, mind, spirit. I was all One, a holy trinity of myself.

At the end of a candle-light session on a Sunday evening, we were working on balancing.

"And now you're a tree. Plant your feet. Feel your strength rise up through your trunk; branches in the air. Good. Now, don't forget to breathe. Imagine a puppeteer is pulling a string out of the top of your head, pulling you up straight and strong.

"OK, now: plant your right foot into your mat; spread your toes wide for balance. Slowly lift your left leg, rest it against your right calf or thigh. Not your knee; that's dangerous to your knee.

"Balance. Inhale; exhale. Arms out to the side or wave them overhead, whatever helps you most. Or fold them into prayer position at your heart center. See how that gives your added strength, with your palms pressing against each other? Oops, try again. If you knock into each other, it's good luck.

"Focus your eyes on something that isn't moving, the wall, the candle in front of you. Don't look at me! I might fall, and then you'll wobble too. That's the secret to balance. It's only so much about your muscles and skill level. The battle is really won and lost by what you fix your eyes on.

"Breathe in; breathe out. Feel the joy of simply being in your own body. It's your body, given to you."

Carolyn was standing tall, a slightly swaying pillar of peace. Our instructor was right though; I couldn't look at her and keep my own balance. I stared instead at a spot on the wall in front of me. For reasons I couldn't explain, I was silently crying as I stretched and balanced my body, tall and steady like an oak.

Epilogue
Willie
Summer 2016

Rob began talking about renting the Judson house out again; I think he said it just to rile Carolyn. It worked. By that summer, in an effort to prevent other people from moving in, Carolyn began visiting more frequently and staying longer. Sometimes Gibson and Adley would come; sometimes just Carolyn. The Judson house transformed a bit with each visit; a picture here, handicap shower installed there.

It seemed as if she was trying to make up for all her lost time, both with her home and her son. Carolyn kept on insisting on celebrating even minor events with get-togethers and parties.

Which is how we ended up having a 54th belated, surprise birthday party for Mitch that summer at the Turkey Run Inn in the Strauss Room. Carolyn invited anyone and everyone even remotely connected with Mitch.

Frankie was having a bad day, so I was having a bad day. He hadn't slept well that night; we were out of his chocolate milk; he missed his nap; then he fell on the steps walking up to the Inn.

I carried him across the lobby as he was doing that limp-body, flailing-arms toddler routine. It looked like either his arms were going to pop out of socket, or I was going to drop him. He was also screaming that high-pitch wail that puts banshees to shame. Tara and Morgan walked behind us, but I noticed it was from a distance.

We got into the Strauss Room and I sort of eased him, sort of dropped him into a chair at the nearest table. I was two seconds away from throwing my own fit, but I smiled prettily at all the people witnessing my son's meltdown.

"Oh, he's just tired. Shhh, sweetie; it's OK." I cooed in my best (fake) mothering tone. What I really wanted to say was, "Here, sweetie, gag yourself with this napkin and stop screaming." (But I didn't.)

Frankie saw his Uncle Mitch, and promptly began screaming, across the room, "Itch, Itch! 'Ome here, Itch, 'ight NOW!" (That's: Mitch, Mitch, Come here, Mitch, right now.)

Mitch came over, scooped Frankie up into a big bear hug, and toted him across the room to Nell. Tara ventured off to play with a group of kids at another table. I plopped down in a seat and sighed. But my peace was short lived because people kept wanting to speak to Mitch (like it was his party or something) and Frankie did NOT want to share his 'Itch.

It was one meltdown after another.

Then he saw the cake. Why, why is there always cake at social gatherings? At least, let's eat the cake at one designated time and then put that shit out of sight. But no, we had to stare at the uncut cake for a solid forty-five minutes while Frankie's eyes bulged out of his head from the strain of waiting.

I spent that entire forty-five minutes chasing Frankie away from the cake table; gently scolding him for sticking his fingers in the icing; then pulling him off the floor from where he'd melted into a hysterical puddle of sugar-denied toddler.

Then I'd take him out of the room, crouch down in a corner, ignoring the strangers milling around us, and lecture him about not throwing fits. (Mostly I was trying to pretend I was effectively discipling my son.)

I'd calm him down (sort of). So we'd go back in and start again. Isn't that the definition of insanity: exposing your toddler to the same cake triggers and expecting different results?

Finally, it was cake time. I allowed him one small piece which he scarfed down. Before I'd even taken two bites of my own cake, he was demanding more. So the whole bit continued. For two hours.

I am horrible at faking it when it comes to motherhood; my facial expression gives me away. If I'm feeling a *bit* frazzled, I look like I just grabbed hold of the electric fence of motherhood and then someone turned up the voltage. People were giving me and Frankie either sympathetic or judgmental looks. *Everyone* was giving us a wide berth. Meanwhile, in male LaaLaa Land, Morgan was chatting up people we didn't even know, oblivious to how my body was jerking from the electrical shocks.

Morgan would take Frankie for a while, but two minutes later, Frankie would dart off back to me where he would continue to be his grumpiest self. He was in a mood where he was miserable and angry NO MATTER WHAT and IT WAS MY FAULT. Frankie wanted to be sure he was miserable in my presence so that I would KNOW how miserable he was.

When I was finally at my crap-I'm-going-to-make-a-scene-in-public breaking point, Morgan must have felt my vision drilling into his skull because he made eye contact with me and got this "Oh, shit, that's not good" look on his face.

He bee-lined his way toward me, took Frankie

out of my arms, and said, "How about I take the kids to the restaurant for a late lunch, and you visit and relax?"

"Sounds good," I said through clenched teeth. Like, Thanks honey, for finally knocking me loose from the electric fence. That was real good of you. But unfortunately for you, I think the crazed look in my eyes is permanent now. I also might have an unexplainable twitch.

Half an hour later, the party was winding down; only a handful of people left at a few tables. I had sequestered myself at a table in the corner and was nursing a cup of punch, wishing it was spiked.

"I have a gift for you," Carolyn told me.

I straightened up in my chair. "Oh? Why?"

"Why does everything have to have an explanation before you can accept it? Here, just open it."

She handed me a gift-wrapped box. When I took it, I was surprised by its weight and nearly dropped it.

I gave her a curious look, trying to gauge what was in there, but she gave nothing away. Pulling back a corner of silver wrapping, I continued to watch her.

"Oh, get on with it then!" She grabbed a large swath of paper and ripped it off.

Inside the box was a large, hard-cover journal, the print done in colorful garden gnomes.

"Garden gnomes? Really?" I asked her.

"Well the drugstore doesn't have the widest selection. I tried the Christian bookstore, but all the Christian clichés emblazoned across leather bound journals gave me indigestion."

I rolled my eyes. "You really are a terrible

convert."

"Thank you. My goal is to show up in Heaven and have a lot of people say, What the hell are you doing here?"

I choked on a sip of punch and spent the next several moments hacking. When I could breathe again, I pulled the gnome journal out of the tissue paper, placed it on the table, and opened the front cover.

Lynn's loopy cursive, in black ink, greeted me:

To Willie—

Because you really can't mind your own damn business, can you?

Then under that flattering dedication, she'd written the title:

Nymph of the Oak Tree: A Tale of Coming Home

By Carolyn Calvert Grant

I couldn't help it, I was crying. "You're giving me your story?"

"Well, for cripes' sake, I know it's been driving you crazy not to finish it. I figured I'd better write the damn thing myself instead of having someone else snoop around and mis-quote me. I should hate to be misquoted, you know."

I leafed through some pages, marveling at my gift.

"I also have an idea for you," Carolyn said, drawing me back to the present. "The OAK Foundation."

"The what?"

"My nonprofit foundation for the preservation of two seemingly unrelated things: personal narratives and forests."

"OK???" I said slowly, not getting it.

"Every day people die without their stories being recorded. Likewise, every day trees are cut down without their knowledge being passed down. Both are a terrible loss. Both grow, or are meant to grow, in communities, you know. And when a tree or person is cut down too soon, before all their wisdom is recorded, well, the whole community suffers. And we're going to fix that."

"We are?"

"Yes."

"How?"

"You know how you always bellyache about your useless writing degree?"

"I do not bellyache!"

"You do so! You've mentioned to me at least ten times how it's never made you a dime."

"I don't think I talk about it nearly that much," I protested. At her raised eye brows, I conceded. "Fine. Maybe I do. But I'll have you know, I was set to make three thousand off of it and then my subject matter had to get her panties in a bunch."

"That's because you didn't ask her for permission to write about her."

"I thought she was dead. It's much easier to write about the dead. They don't protest much."

"Joke's on you then, I'd say," Carolyn teased.

"Umm, you've no idea. I've never had such conflict in my life as I have since I opened your journal."

"Anyway, we were talking about your useless writing degree," Carolyn said.

"And how it's finally going to make me money?" I prompted.

"Hmm. No promises there. But I am going to put you to work."

"Oh, goodie. I love working for free."

"Are you going to let me tell you about my idea, or not?"

"Tell me about your idea."

"Well, I don't have the details worked out. But the basic theory is this: we offer your services as a ghost writer to people who want to record their memoirs, but don't have much writing talent themselves. They pay a set fee, but we use that money to support forest preservation. What do you think?"

"It sounds wonderful, but I'm not sure you realize how much work it is to write someone's memoir. I can't just crank someone's life story out in a month or two. It takes hours and hours of interviews and digging through documents and journals. I just don't see how I could take on more than one, maybe two, in a year. That's hardly going to generate much money to donate."

"I've thought of that, of course. I don't expect you to do it alone. That one's next on my list." Carolyn jabbed her finger toward the front of the room where Adley was helping Nell clear tables. "I just wanted to get you in my corner first."

"OK, so two writers and one crazy old forest fairy—I mean, you. To start a whole foundation? I feel very understaffed and overworked already."

"We start out small. One story, one tree at a time, and grow from there."

I stared at her for a moment, thinking about what she was asking. The logistics of it seemed daunting and overwhelming. I didn't know anything about forest preservation; my experience with writing someone's memoir was either a complete failure or total success, depending on how I looked at it.

For one thing, I was holding Carolyn's memoir in my hands right now.

For another, I hadn't written it. It was her voice, not mine.

It hit me then, and I dropped my eyes back to her journal. "You taught me something, you know," I said. "You taught me that telling other people's stories is second-best. The first choice should always be to let her tell her own."

She smiled at me. "Took you a while to get there, but you made it. But the truth is, Willie, you're going to read that and realize I'm not a writer. Yes, we should all tell our own stories, but some of us need help piecing it together. That's what I want you to do for me, take my words, my stories, and make them flow in a way that's enjoyable to read for Mitch and Adley when I'm gone."

"I don't want to tamper with your story any more, Carolyn."

"Since when is editing the same thing as tampering? I'm asking you to do this for me, and if you enjoy it, consider starting OAK and writing for other people too."

"I'll think about it, OK?"

"Well, don't think too long. I am getting old, you know," she winked at me as she got up. Her knees creaked and popped when she stood. "See? I'm rusting as we speak," she joked, then she walked over to help Nell and Adley.

I sat for a few more moments, pretending to think seriously about what she'd asked. But the truth is I already knew I'd do it. To do it, I'd probably have to put Frankie in part time daycare; that thought both relieved and grieved me. I loved him so much, how could I want a break from him so often?

Oh, wait! I was on a break from him right now, I remembered. I got up, only slightly reluctantly, to go find my kids and husband.

I walked into the main lobby, and there was Morgan, Tara, and Frankie, walking out of the restaurant. They passed the office where Cheryl and Granny worked together all those years ago. I smiled at the flashback, profoundly relieved that adolescence was behind me.

As they got closer, I noticed that Tara and Frankie had chocolate ice cream smudged around their mouths. Morgan had one arm crooked behind his back; the other hand was latched onto Frankie's collar in an attempt to keep him from running off. As I approached them, Morgan withdrew his arm and held a Styrofoam cup out to me, the mountain of whipped cream bulging against the lid.

"You looked like you could use a milkshake, Willie," Morgan said to me as I took a sip.

--

Author's Note

I might have written a novel just so I could write the author's note talking about *how I wrote a novel.* So, if you're not into shameless bragging, and somehow made it to the end of my novel with a good opinion of my writing, maybe skip this part. **Let's not ruin a good thing.** If you insist on reading this part, you should know that I will be using second person in this note, which according to every teacher and professor I've ever had, is really, really wrong. **You should not write in second person.** I do not condone writing in second person; it is intrusive and irritating if done incorrectly (see remaining paragraphs for an example).

I'm using second person here because I literally AM talking to YOU. I would address you each by name, but as I have no idea who will actually read this, that would be impossible. And possibly awkwardly brief. (Hi, Mom.) So, you'll just have to insert your own name.

Still reading? OK, then, sit back and imagine us having a cup of coffee together while I tell you the story of this story.

This novel was born out of a season of writer's block. For a year (2016), I hadn't written anything but personal journals, Facebook posts, and a couple blog posts. The year prior to that, 2015, the year I was pregnant and gave birth to my second child, Graham, I had written a novella, my longest and "best" fiction yet. When that character's story was told, and she flinted away to live in fictional peace, I descended into a funk.

I couldn't come up with a single idea for a

character or plot. The rare hours I carved out writing time, I stared at my blank computer screen. So, 2016 was a year without words, but I hardly noticed as I was chasing two small children.

What I did do was pay attention.

We live in Parke County, Indiana which is the land of three things: Covered Bridge Fest, farming, and Turkey Run State Park. Slow traffic is caused by Amish buggies, not rush hour. It is the perfect place if you need to drive aimlessly. Which I did. A lot.

Looking back on the spring and summer of 2016—when this story was just images and emotions swirling around under layers of mom-thoughts—I survived by driving around aimlessly. Just to get my children to nap. It was also our second season of custom hay farming (on top of Jeff's day job at Kessco). So, the only time the kids and I saw him was when we tracked him down to various hay fields in Parke County. I'd give him a soggy lunch meat sandwich, served with a side of guilt, while our kids either napped or screamed in the truck.

Nearly every afternoon of that summer, I drove through small ghost towns on back country roads, praying the jarring pot holes wouldn't wake my babies. The area I drove through most frequently was this little town of Judson; the town where my Grandma Loretta had grown up.

She'd lived in a little white house on main street with her parents and seven sisters. The house is still there. I've never been inside of the house, yet every time I pass it, it feels a bit like home. (Obviously, you've realized this real-life house served as the inspiration for the Judson House.)

So, during the summer when I might or might not have had post-partum depression, when I was so sleep-deprived that I was hysterical, when the only relief to the chaos of two small children was to load them up and strap them down and drive, I felt pulled toward this house.

I had this thought that I couldn't quite articulate then: I'm from this place, even though I'm not. I'm from every place my parents, grandparents, and great-grandparents grew up, going back and back and back. All of my ancestors' 'from-ness' layer upon each other to create my story.

I was also haunted by the fact that both of my grandmas had recently died within a year of each other. My Grandma Phyllis died when I was six months pregnant with my first child, Isabelle; my Grandma Loretta died when Izzy was six months old. I was realizing that I'd never asked them the womanhood and motherhood questions that matter.

All of those times when Grandma Loretta asked me, "Know any news, honey?" I should have said, "Grandma, screw small talk. Motherhood is knocking the shit out of me before nine am every day. Is this normal? What was it really, really like for you, raising four boys, each two years apart? Because dear God, this is hard."

And when I realized my Grandma Phyllis wasn't going to make it to see the birth of my first child, I should have asked her to tell her truest stories.

I was close to both my grandmothers, and I would say I knew them both really well. But becoming a mother myself made me miss them in a new way because I suddenly had list of questions I wanted to ask them.

So, for months I drove through these small towns, looking for my Grandmas in their youth and early motherhood. I cranked up the radio, stuffed

Oreos in my mouth, and cried and ranted aloud while my babies finally slept.

I drove by creeks and would vaguely think, there's something there, something to write. But I couldn't figure it out. The same thing would happen with trees, old houses, and quiet churches. For months, I was stock-piling images without realizing it. I wrote this story in images before it came to me in words.

That summer, I enrolled my kids in part-time daycare and went to work part-time at Kessco. (This is important because down-time at work would become my writing time.)

In December of 2016, we were going to Hilton Head, SC to meet my parents (who had been living and working in China) for Christmas. My siblings, their spouses, and their kids and my Grandpa Hobbs were going too. (That was a total of seven kids under seven in one big, beach house.) In the weeks leading up to this trip, I had an ongoing Facebook conversation with my mom about having writer's block. "Don't worry," she wrote me, "you'll get inspired at the beach."

I did not get inspired at the beach. I got tired. I blame my two toddlers who missed the memo that vacation = rest.

We drove back on Christmas Eve, and arrived at Jeff's mom's and sister's house at 5:00 Christmas morning. It was cold and snowy, and I've never loved frozen Indiana dirt more. Dirt is my home, people. Life starts in the dirt, you know.

The beach and palm trees didn't give me a story because I didn't need them too. Indiana dirt and oak trees had already been whispering a story to me for months. I just had to turn up the volume.

So, I started listening to the Muse of the oak tree and county creeks (calm down, I'm not going to go all weird on you here. I worship Jesus, OK?)

On a February Sunday in 2017, Jeff and I went to the Crawfordsville Kessco office to work on getting farming documents ready for taxes. While Jeff organized a year's worth of documents, I heard this little nagging voice say, "why don't you use this time to write?"

"Hard pass," I said. Then I decided I'd go get my hair cut. Unfortunately, I couldn't get a walk-in appointment.

Little nagging voice chimed in again, "Hey there, that's too bad. Why don't you use this time to write?"

"I could really use some new clothes," I responded, and took myself and my little nagging voice shopping.

Fortunately, or unfortunately (depending on how you look at it), I had two kids in diapers and was on a tight budget. My clothes-allowance of $27.35 was quickly spent on some discounted shirts.

"Well, that was quick," little nagging voice piped up, "why don't you use this time to write?"

"Shut up, little nagging voice; I don't pursue that lifestyle anymore," I said.

But I went back to the office, listened to Jeff mumbling about invoices and 2017 crop projections, and decided I really didn't want to help him with *that*. I left him alone to his slight mental breakdown, sat down at the computer, opened a Word doc, and stared at the screen.

"I've got nothing," I said to little nagging voice.

"Steal from your life," little nagging voice,

who apparently doesn't have scruples, retorted.

"Uhh, that sounds like a good way to end up in therapy or banned from family reunions," I said.

"One less to go to wouldn't be such a bad thing, would it?"

"Well. . ."

"Listen, I don't mean steal so much as pluck a little nugget of inspiration from your life, and go from there," little nagging voice said.

"Oh, I see. Yes, that sounds slightly less shady."

Then little nagging voice walked over to the light switch in my imagination, blew the cobwebs off, and flipped it on. The little bulb flickered briefly before burning out.

"Uhh, that's not a promising start," I said.

"Where do we keep the extra light bulbs in here?" Little nagging voice asked.

"We don't keep extra light bulbs! That one was the last one!"

"Oh, well, here then," little nagging voice said, fishing a half-burnt down birthday candle out of its pocket. "Write by this light."

"Wow, that's literally almost nothing to see by."

"All you need to get started is one little light, one little sentence," little nagging voice said.

"Fine. If I write one little sentence, will you leave me alone?"

"We'll see."

So, I lit that damn little birthday candle and used its light to wander through my imagination. Before long I bumped my shin into something: half memory, half fiction, this phantom of a character stepped out from the shadows.

"Hi Willie," I said, "who are you?"

All she told me, at first, was the story of how she met her future husband. It was a story based very loosely on the fact that Jeff's Grandma Joyce and my Grandma Phyllis worked together at the Turkey Run Inn. That's not how Jeff and I met, but I'd always wondered about how things could have gone if our paths had crossed then.

So, birthday candle sputtering, but somehow not burning out, I wrote. For two hours. By the time we left the office that day, I had an entire scene to read to Jeff on the drive home.

That scene is the first scene of this novel. By the end of writing that scene, Willie was no longer a phantom and the plot was no longer a stolen scene from my life. They were a part of me, yet separate; their *own* spoken into being by me and the Master Storyteller.

"That'll do," little nagging voice said, nodding in approval, and then left me be, making no more demands.

It didn't need to; the sputtering birthday candle had lit a bonfire.

About the Author
(in case the rambling Author's Note didn't give you enough of a clue)

Olivia Kessinger grew up in Parke County, Indiana, and loved it so much she moved back after college. She married a man she met at a gas station. It's working out well, although he needs to stop buying tractors. They have two curly haired children.

She's a 2013 graduate of Indiana Wesleyan University with a degree in English and Writing. She avoided every single math, accounting, and business class beyond the basic requirements of Gen. Ed, insisting she would never need such practical nonsense. She now spends her days doing all that math stuff for the business she owns with Jeff. (Which is Kessco Water, in case you're in the market for a Kinetico water softener.)

Because one business and two kids don't keep them busy enough, they also farm "on the side." Which amounts to Jeff cursing at broken-down tractors, and Olivia developing an eye twitch. From the months of April to October, you may find them having panic attacks in various hay fields across Parke County.

When she is not writing an awkward author bio of herself in third person, she crafts fiction that is hopefully worth reading. Why don't you buy this novel and find out?

Check out her blog at oliviakessinger.wordpress.com